# STORIES

# PHILIP K. DICK
# STORIES

SIMI PRESS

Simi Press
www.simipress.com

First published in the United States of America
in *Planet Stories, If, Science Fiction Stories, Orbit,
Imagination, Galaxy Science Fiction, Space Science
Fiction, Science Fiction Adventures, Planet Stories,*
and *Fantastic Universe* between 1952 and 1954.

This edition published in 2023 by Simi Press

Cover art by Rafal Kucharczuk
Book design by Euan Monaghan

ISBN 978-1-955585-02-6

# CONTENTS

# BEYOND LIES THE WUB

**THEY HAD ALMOST** finished with the loading. Outside stood the Optus, his arms folded, his face sunk in gloom. Captain Franco walked leisurely down the gangplank, grinning.

"What's the matter?" he said. "You're getting paid for all this."

The Optus said nothing. He turned away, collecting his robes. The Captain put his boot on the hem of the robe.

"Just a minute. Don't go off. I'm not finished."

"Oh?" The Optus turned with dignity. "I am going back to the village." He looked toward the animals and birds being driven up the gangplank into the spaceship. "I must organize new hunts."

Franco lit a cigarette. "Why not? You people can go out into the veldt and track it all down again. But when we run out half-way between Mars and Earth—"

The Optus went off, wordless. Franco joined the first mate at the bottom of the gangplank.

"How's it coming?" he said. He looked at his watch. "We got a good bargain here."

The mate glanced at him sourly. "How do you explain that?"

"What's the matter with you? We need it more than they do."

"I'll see you later, Captain." The mate threaded his way up the plank, between the long-legged Martian go-birds, into the ship. Franco watched him disappear. He was just starting up after him, up the plank toward the port, when he saw *it*.

"My god!" He stood staring, his hands on his hips. Peterson was walking along the path, his face red, leading *it* by a string.

"I'm sorry, Captain," he said, tugging at the string. Franco walked toward him.

"What is it?"

The wub stood sagging, its great body settling slowly. It was sitting down, its eyes half shut. A few flies buzzed about its flank, and it switched its tail.

*It* sat. There was silence.

"It's a wub," Peterson said. "I got it from a native for fifty cents. He said it was a very unusual animal. Very respected."

"This?" Franco poked the great sloping side of the wub. "It's a pig! A huge, dirty pig!"

"Yes sir, it's a pig. The natives call it a wub."

"A huge pig. It must weigh four hundred pounds." Franco grabbed a tuft of the rough hair. The wub gasped. Its eyes opened, small and moist. Then its great mouth twitched.

A tear rolled down the wub's cheek and splashed on the floor.

"Maybe it's good to eat," Peterson said nervously.

"We'll soon find out," Franco said.

***

The wub survived the takeoff, sound asleep in the hold of the ship. When they were out in space, and everything was running smoothly, Captain Franco bade his men fetch the wub upstairs so that he might perceive what manner of beast it was.

The wub grunted and wheezed, squeezing up the passage-way.

"Come on," Jones grated, pulling at the rope. The wub twisted, rubbing its skin off on the smooth chrome walls. It burst into the anteroom, tumbling down in a heap. The men leaped up.

"Good Lord," French said. "What is it?"

"Peterson says it's a wub," Jones said. "It belongs to him." He kicked at the wub. The wub stood up unsteadily, panting.

"What's the matter with it?" French came over. "Is it going to be sick?"

They watched. The wub rolled its eyes mournfully. It gazed around at the men.

"I think it's thirsty," Peterson said. He went to get some water. French shook his head.

"No wonder we had so much trouble taking off. I had to reset all my ballast calculations."

Peterson came back with the water. The wub began to lap gratefully, splashing the men.

Captain Franco appeared at the door.

"Let's have a look at it." He advanced, squinting critically. "You got this for fifty cents?"

"Yes, sir," Peterson said. "It eats almost anything. I fed it on grain, and it liked that. And then potatoes, and mash, and scraps from the table, and milk. It seems to enjoy eating. After it eats it lies down and goes to sleep."

"I see," Captain Franco said. "Now, as to its taste. That's the real question. I doubt if there's much point in fattening it up anymore. It seems fat enough to me already. Where's the cook? I want him here. I want to find out."

The wub stopped lapping and looked up at the Captain.

"Really, Captain," the wub said. "I suggest we talk of other matters."

The room was silent.

"What was that?" Franco said. "Just now."

"The wub, sir," Peterson said. "It spoke."

They all looked at the wub.

"What did it say? What did it say?"

"It suggested we talk about other things."

Franco walked toward the wub. He went all around it, examining it from every side. Then he came back over and stood with the men.

"I wonder if there's a native inside it," he said thoughtfully. "Maybe we should open it up and have a look."

"Oh, goodness!" the wub cried. "Is that all you people can think of, killing and cutting?"

Franco clenched his fists. "Come out of there! Whoever you are, come out!"

Nothing stirred. The men stood together, their faces blank, staring at the wub. The wub swished its tail. It belched suddenly.

"I beg your pardon," the wub said.

"I don't think there's anyone in there," Jones said in a low voice. They all looked at each other.

The cook came in.

"You wanted me, Captain?" he said. "What's this thing?"

"This is a wub," Franco said. "It's to be eaten. Will you measure it and figure out—"

"I think we should have a talk," the wub said. "I'd like to discuss this with you, Captain, if I might. I can see that you and I do not agree on some basic issues."

The Captain took a long time to answer. The wub waited good-naturedly, licking the water from its jowls.

"Come into my office," the Captain said at last. He turned and walked out of the room. The wub rose and padded after him. The men watched it go out. They heard it climbing the stairs.

"I wonder what the outcome will be," the cook said. "Well, I'll be in the kitchen. Let me know as soon as you hear."

"Sure," Jones said. "Sure."

***

The wub eased itself down in the corner with a sigh. "You must forgive me," it said. "I'm afraid I'm addicted to various forms of relaxation. When one is as large as I—"

The Captain nodded impatiently. He sat down at his desk and folded his hands.

"All right," he said. "Let's get started. You're a wub? Is that correct?"

The wub shrugged. "I suppose so. That's what they call us, the natives I mean. We have our own term."

"And you speak English? You've been in contact with Earthmen before?"

"No."

"Then how do you do it?"

"Speak English? Am I speaking English? I'm not conscious of speaking anything in particular. I examined your mind."

"My mind?"

"I studied the contents, especially the semantic warehouse, as I refer to it."

"I see," the Captain said. "Telepathy. Of course."

"We are a very old race," the wub said. "Very old and very ponderous. It is difficult for us to move around. You can appreciate that anything so slow and heavy would be at the mercy of more agile forms of life. There was no use in our relying on physical defenses. How could we win? Too heavy to run, too soft to fight, too good-natured to hunt for game."

"How do you live?"

"Plants. Vegetables. We can eat almost anything. We're very catholic. Tolerant, eclectic, catholic. We live and let live. That's how we've gotten along."

The wub eyed the Captain.

"And that's why I so violently objected to this business about having me boiled. I could see the image in your mind—most of me in the frozen food locker, some of me in the kettle, a bit for your pet cat."

"So you read minds?" the Captain said. "How interesting. Anything else? I mean, what else can you do along those lines?"

"A few odds and ends," the wub said absently, staring around the room. "A nice apartment you have here, Captain. You keep it quite neat. I respect lifeforms that are tidy. Some Martian birds are quite tidy. They throw things out of their nests and sweep them."

"Indeed." The Captain nodded. "But to get back to the problem."

"Quite so. You spoke of dining on me. The taste, I am told, is good. A little fatty, but tender. But how can any lasting contact be established between your people and mine if you resort to such barbaric attitudes? Eat me? Rather you should discuss questions with me, philosophy, the arts."

The Captain stood up. "Philosophy. It might interest you to know that we will be hard put to find something to eat for the next month. An unfortunate spoilage."

"I know." The wub nodded. "But wouldn't it be more in accord with your principles of democracy if we all drew straws, or something along that line? After all, democracy is to protect the minority from just such infringements. Now, if each of us casts one vote—"

The Captain walked to the door.

"Nuts to you," he said. He opened the door. He opened his mouth.

He stood frozen, his mouth wide, his eyes staring, his fingers still on the knob.

The wub watched him. Presently it padded out of the room, edging past the Captain. It went down the hall, deep in meditation.

***

The room was quiet.

"So you see," the wub said, "we have a common myth. Your mind contains many familiar myth symbols—Ishtar, Odysseus."

Peterson sat silently, staring at the floor. He shifted in his chair.

"Go on," he said. "Please go on."

"I find in your Odysseus a figure common to the mythology of most self-conscious races. As I interpret it, Odysseus wanders as an individual, aware of himself as such. This is the idea of separation, of separation from family and country. The process of individuation."

"But Odysseus returns to his home." Peterson looked out the port window, at the stars, endless stars, burning intently in the empty universe. "Finally he goes home."

"As must all creatures. The moment of separation is a temporary period, a brief journey of the soul. It begins, it ends. The wanderer returns to land and race."

The door opened. The wub stopped, turning its great head.

Captain Franco came into the room, the men behind him. They hesitated at the door.

"Are you all right?" French said.

"Do you mean me?" Peterson said, surprised. "Why me?"

Franco lowered his gun. "Come over here," he said to Peterson. "Get up and come here."

There was silence.

"Go ahead," the wub said. "It doesn't matter."

Peterson stood up. "What for?"

"It's an order."

Peterson walked to the door. French caught his arm.

"What's going on?" Peterson wrenched loose. "What's the matter with you?"

Captain Franco moved toward the wub. The wub looked up from where it lay in the corner, pressed against the wall.

"It is interesting," the wub said, "that you are obsessed with the idea of eating me. I wonder why."

"Get up," Franco said.

"If you wish." The wub rose, grunting. "Be patient. It is diffi-cult for me." It stood, gasping, its tongue lolling foolishly.

"Shoot it now," French said.

"For god's sake!" Peterson exclaimed. Jones turned to him quickly, his eyes gray with fear.

"You didn't see him—like a statue, standing there, his mouth open. If we hadn't come down, he'd still be there."

"Who? The Captain?" Peterson stared around. "But he's all right now."

They looked at the wub, standing in the middle of the room, its great chest rising and falling.

"Come on," Franco said. "Out of the way."

The men pulled aside toward the door.

"You are quite afraid, aren't you?" the wub said. "Have I done anything to you? I am against the idea of hurting. All I have done is try to protect myself. Can you expect me to rush eagerly to my death? I am a sensible being like yourselves. I was curious to see your ship, learn about you. I suggested to the native—"

The gun jerked.

"See," Franco said. "I thought so."

The wub settled down, panting. It put its paw out, pulling its tail around it.

"It is very warm," the wub said. "I understand that we are close to the jets. Atomic power. You have done many wonderful things with it—technically. Apparently, your scientific hierar-chy is not equipped to solve moral, ethical—"

Franco turned to the men, crowding behind him, wide-eyed, silent.

"I'll do it. You can watch."

French nodded. "Try to hit the brain. It's no good for eating. Don't hit the chest. If the rib cage shatters, we'll have to pick bones out."

"Listen," Peterson said, licking his lips. "Has it done anything?

What harm has it done? I'm asking you. And anyhow, it's still mine. You have no right to shoot it. It doesn't belong to you."

Franco raised his gun.

"I'm going out," Jones said, his face white and sick. "I don't want to see it."

"Me too," French said. The men straggled out, murmuring. Peterson lingered at the door.

"It was talking to me about myths," he said. "It wouldn't hurt anyone."

He went outside.

Franco walked toward the wub. The wub looked up slowly. It swallowed.

"A very foolish thing," it said. "I am sorry that you want to do it. There was a parable that your Savior related—"

It stopped, staring at the gun.

"Can you look me in the eye and do it?" the wub said. "Can you do that?"

The Captain gazed down. "I can look you in the eye," he said. "Back on the farm we had hogs, dirty razorback hogs. I can do it."

Staring down at the wub, into the gleaming, moist eyes, he pressed the trigger.

***

The taste was excellent.

They sat glumly around the table, some of them hardly eating at all. The only one who seemed to be enjoying himself was Captain Franco.

"More?" he said, looking around. "More? And some wine, perhaps."

"Not me," French said. "I think I'll go back to the chart room."

"Me, too." Jones stood up, pushing his chair back. "I'll see you later."

The Captain watched them go. Some of the others excused themselves.

"What do you suppose the matter is?" the Captain said. He turned to Peterson. Peterson sat staring down at his plate, at the potatoes, the green peas, and at the thick slab of tender, warm meat.

He opened his mouth. No sound came.

The Captain put his hand on Peterson's shoulder.

"It is only organic matter now," he said. "The life essence is gone." He ate, spooning up the gravy with some bread. "I, myself, love to eat. It is one of the greatest things that a living creature can enjoy. Eating, resting, meditation, discussing things."

Peterson nodded. Two more men got up and went out. The Captain drank some water and sighed.

"Well," he said. "I must say that this was a very enjoyable meal. All the reports I had heard were quite true—the taste of wub. Very fine. But I was prevented from enjoying this pleasure in times past."

He dabbed at his lips with his napkin and leaned back in his chair. Peterson stared dejectedly at the table.

The Captain watched him intently. He leaned over.

"Come, come," he said. "Cheer up! Let's discuss things."

He smiled.

"As I was saying before I was interrupted, the role of Odysseus in the myths—"

Peterson jerked up, staring.

"To go on," the Captain said. "Odysseus, as I understand him—"

# THE GUN

**THE CAPTAIN PEERED** into the eyepiece of the telescope. He adjusted the focus quickly.

"It was an atomic fission we saw, all right," he said presently. He sighed and pushed the eyepiece away. "Any of you who wants to look may do so. But it's not a pretty sight."

"Let me look," Tance the archeologist said. He bent down to look, squinting. "Good Lord!" He leaped violently back, knocking against Dorle, the Chief Navigator.

"Why did we come all this way, then?" Dorle asked, looking around at the other men. "There's no point even in landing. Let's go back at once."

"Perhaps he's right," the biologist murmured. "But I'd like to look for myself, if I may." He pushed past Tance and peered into the sight.

He saw a vast expanse, an endless surface of gray, stretching to the edge of the planet. At first he thought it was water but after a moment he realized that it was slag, pitted fused slag, broken only by hills of rock jutting up at intervals. Nothing moved or stirred. Everything was silent, dead.

"I see," Fomar said, backing away from the eyepiece. "Well, I won't find any legumes there." He tried to smile, but his lips stayed unmoved. He stepped away and stood by himself, staring past the others.

"I wonder what the atmospheric sample will show," Tance said.

"I think I can guess," the Captain answered. "Most of the atmosphere is poisoned. But didn't we expect all this? I don't see why we're so surprised. A fission visible as far away as our system must be a terrible thing."

He strode off down the corridor, dignified and expressionless. They watched him disappear into the control room.

As the Captain closed the door the young woman turned. "What did the telescope show? Good or bad?"

"Bad. No life could possibly exist. Atmosphere poisoned, water vaporized, all the land fused."

"Could they have gone underground?"

The Captain slid back the port window so that the surface of the planet under them was visible. The two of them stared down, silent and disturbed. Mile after mile of unbroken ruin stretched out, blackened slag, pitted and scarred, and occasional heaps of rock.

Suddenly Nasha jumped. "Look! Over there, at the edge. Do you see it?"

They stared. Something rose up, not rock, not an accidental formation. It was round, a circle of dots, white pellets on the dead skin of the planet. A city? Buildings of some kind?

"Please turn the ship," Nasha said excitedly. She pushed her dark hair from her face. "Turn the ship and let's see what it is!"

The ship turned, changing its course. As they came over the white dots, the Captain lowered the ship, dropping it down as much as he dared. "Piers," he said. "Piers of some sort of stone. Perhaps poured artificial stone. The remains of a city."

"Oh, dear," Nasha murmured. "How awful." She watched the ruins disappear behind them. In a half-circle the white squares jutted from the slag, chipped and cracked like broken teeth.

"There's nothing alive," the Captain said at last. "I think we'll go right back; I know most of the crew want to. Get the Government Receiving Station on the sender and tell them what we found, and that we—"

He staggered.

The first atomic shell had struck the ship, spinning it around. The Captain fell to the floor, crashing into the control table.

Papers and instruments rained down on him. As he started to his feet the second shell struck. The ceiling cracked open, struts and girders twisted and bent. The ship shuddered, falling suddenly down, then righting itself as automatic controls took over.

The Captain lay on the floor by the smashed control board. In the corner Nasha struggled to free herself from the debris.

Outside, the men were already sealing the gaping leaks in the side of the ship, through which the precious air was rushing, dissipating into the void beyond. "Help me!" Dorle was shouting. "Fire over here, wiring ignited." Two men came running. Tance watched helplessly, his eyeglasses broken and bent.

"So there is life here, after all," he said, half to himself. "But how could—"

"Give us a hand," Fomar said, hurrying past. "Give us a hand, we've got to land the ship!"

It was night. A few stars glinted above them, winking through the drifting silt that blew across the surface of the planet.

Dorle peered out, frowning. "What a place to be stuck in." He resumed his work, hammering the bent metal hull of the ship back into place. He was wearing a pressure suit. There were still many small leaks, and radioactive particles from the atmosphere had already found their way into the ship.

Nasha and Fomar were sitting at the table in the control room, pale and solemn, studying the inventory lists.

"Low on carbohydrates," Fomar said. "We can break down the stored fats if we want to, but—"

"I wonder if we could find anything outside." Nasha went to the window. "How uninviting it looks." She paced back and forth, very slender and small, her face dark with fatigue. "What do you suppose an exploring party would find?"

Fomar shrugged. "Not much. Maybe a few weeds growing in cracks here and there. Nothing we could use. Anything that would adapt to this environment would be toxic, lethal."

Nasha paused, rubbing her cheek. There was a deep scratch there, still red and swollen. "Then how do you explain—*it*? According to your theory the inhabitants must have died in their skins, fried like yams. But who fired on us? Somebody detected us, made a decision, aimed a gun."

"And gauged distance," the Captain said feebly from the cot in the corner. He turned toward them. "That's the part that worries me. The first shell put us out of commission, the second almost destroyed us. They were well aimed, perfectly aimed. We're not such an easy target."

"True." Fomar nodded. "Well, perhaps we'll know the answer before we leave here. What a strange situation! All our reasoning tells us that no life could exist, the whole planet burned dry, the atmosphere itself gone, completely poisoned."

"The gun that fired the projectiles survived," Nasha said. "Why not people?"

"It's not the same. Metal doesn't need air to breathe. Metal doesn't get leukemia from radioactive particles. Metal doesn't need food and water."

There was silence.

"A paradox," Nasha said. "Anyhow, in the morning I think we should send out a search party. And meanwhile we should keep on trying to get the ship in condition for the trip back."

"It'll be days before we can take off," Fomar said. "We should keep every man working here. We can't afford to send out a party."

Nasha smiled a little. "We'll send you in the first party. Maybe you can discover what was it you were so interested in?"

"Legumes. Edible legumes."

"Maybe you can find some of them. Only—"

"Only what?"

"Only watch out. They fired on us once without even knowing who we were or what we came for. Do you suppose that they fought with each other? Perhaps they couldn't imagine anyone being friendly, under any circumstances. What a strange evolutionary trait, interspecies warfare. Fighting within the race!"

"We'll know in the morning," Fomar said. "Let's get some sleep."

***

The sun came up chill and austere. The three people, two men and a woman, stepped through the port, dropping down on the hard ground below.

"What a day," Dorle said grumpily. "I said how glad I'd be to walk on firm ground again, but—"

"Come on," Nasha said. "Up beside me. I want to say something to you. Will you excuse us, Tance?"

Tance nodded gloomily. Dorle caught up with Nasha. They walked together, their metal shoes crunching the ground underfoot. Nasha glanced at him.

"Listen. The Captain is dying. No one knows except the two of us. By the end of the day-period of this planet he'll be dead. The shock did something to his heart. He was almost sixty, you know."

Dorle nodded. "That's bad. I have a great deal of respect for him. You will be captain in his place, of course. Since you're vice-captain now—"

"No. I prefer to see someone else lead, perhaps you or Fomar. I've been thinking over the situation, and it seems to me that I should declare myself mated to one of you, whichever of you wants to be captain. Then I could devolve the responsibility."

"Well, I don't want to be captain. Let Fomar do it."

Nasha studied him, tall and blond, striding along beside her in his pressure suit. "I'm rather partial to you," she said. "We might try it for a time, at least. But do as you like. Look, we're coming to something."

They stopped walking, letting Tance catch up. In front of them was some sort of a ruined building. Dorle stared around thoughtfully.

"Do you see? This whole place is a natural bowl, a huge valley. See how the rock formations rise up on all sides, protecting the floor. Maybe some of the great blast was deflected here."

They wandered around the ruins, picking up rocks and fragments. "I think this was a farm," Tance said, examining a piece of wood. "This was part of a tower windmill."

"Really?" Nasha took the stick and turned it over. "Interesting. But let's go. We don't have much time."

"Look," Dorle said suddenly. "Off there, a long way off. Isn't that something?" He pointed.

Nasha sucked in her breath. "The white stones."

"What?"

Nasha looked up at Dorle. "The white stones, the great broken teeth. We saw them, the Captain and I, from the control room." She touched Dorle's arm gently. "That's where they fired from. I didn't think we had landed so close."

"What is it?" Tance said, coming up to them. "I'm almost blind without my glasses. What do you see?"

"The city. Where they fired from."

"Oh." All three of them stood together. "Well, let's go," Tance said. "There's no telling what we'll find there." Dorle frowned at him.

"Wait. We don't know what we would be getting into. They must have patrols. They probably have seen us already for that matter."

"They probably have seen the ship itself," Tance said. "They probably know right now where they can find it, where they can blow it up. So what difference does it make whether we go closer or not?"

"That's true," Nasha said. "If they really want to get us, we haven't a chance. We have no armaments at all. You know that."

"I have a hand weapon." Dorle nodded. "Well, let's go on then. I suppose you're right, Tance."

"But let's stay together," Tance said nervously. "Nasha, you're going too fast."

Nasha looked back. She laughed. "If we expect to get there by nightfall, we must go fast."

They reached the outskirts of the city at about the middle of the afternoon. The sun, cold and yellow, hung above them in the colorless sky. Dorle stopped at the top of a ridge overlooking the city.

"Well, there it is. What's left of it."

There was not much left. The huge concrete piers which they had noticed were not piers at all, but the ruined foundations of buildings. They had been baked by the searing heat, baked and charred almost to the ground. Nothing else remained, only this irregular circle of white squares, perhaps four miles in diameter.

Dorle spat in disgust. "More wasted time. A dead skeleton of a city, that's all."

"But it was from here that the firing came," Tance murmured. "Don't forget that."

"And by someone with a good eye and a great deal of experience," Nasha added. "Let's go."

They walked into the city between the ruined buildings. No one spoke. They walked in silence, listening to the echo of their footsteps.

"It's macabre," Dorle muttered. "I've seen ruined cities before, but they died of old age, old age and fatigue. This was killed, seared to death. This city didn't die, it was murdered."

"I wonder what the city was called," Nasha said. She turned aside, going up the remains of a stairway from one of the foundations. "Do you think we might find a signpost? Some kind of plaque?"

She peered into the ruins.

"There's nothing there," Dorle said impatiently. "Come on."

"Wait." Nasha bent down, touching a concrete stone. "There's something inscribed on this."

"What is it?" Tance hurried up. He squatted in the dust, running his gloved fingers over the surface of the stone. "Letters, all right." He took a writing stick from the pocket of his pressure suit and copied the inscription on a bit of paper. Dorle glanced over his shoulder. The inscription was:

FRANKLIN APARTMENTS

"That's this city," Nasha said softly. "That was its name."

Tance put the paper in his pocket and they went on. After a time Dorle said, "Nasha, you know, I think we're being watched. But don't look around."

The woman stiffened. "Oh? Why do you say that? Did you see something?"

"No. I can feel it though. Don't you?"

Nasha smiled a little. "I feel nothing, but perhaps I'm more used to being stared at." She turned her head slightly. "Oh!"

Dorle reached for his hand weapon. "What is it? What do you see?" Tance had stopped dead in his tracks, his mouth half-open.

"The gun," Nasha said. "It's the gun."

"Look at the size of it. The size of the thing." Dorle unfastened his hand weapon slowly. "That's it, all right."

The gun was huge. Stark and immense it pointed up at the sky, a mass of steel and glass set in a huge slab of concrete. Even as they watched, the gun moved on its swivel base, whirring underneath. A slim vane turned with the wind, a network of rods atop a high pole.

"It's alive," Nasha whispered. "It's listening to us, watching us."

The gun moved again, this time clockwise. It was mounted

so that it could make a full circle. The barrel lowered a trifle, then resumed its original position.

"But who fires it?" Tance said.

Dorle laughed. "No one. No one fires it."

They stared at him. "What do you mean?"

"It fires itself."

They couldn't believe him. Nasha came close to him, frowning, looking up at him. "I don't understand. What do you mean, it fires itself?"

"Watch, I'll show you. Don't move." Dorle picked up a rock from the ground. He hesitated a moment and then tossed the rock high in the air. The rock passed in front of the gun. Instantly the great barrel moved, the vanes contracted.

The rock fell to the ground. The gun paused, then resumed its calm swivel, its slow circling.

"You see," Dorle said, "it noticed the rock as soon as I threw it up in the air. It's alert to anything that flies or moves above the ground level. Probably it detected us as soon as we entered the gravitational field of the planet. It probably had a bead on us from the start. We don't have a chance. It knows all about the ship. It's just waiting for us to take off again."

"I understand about the rock," Nasha said, nodding. "The gun noticed it, but not us, since we're on the ground, not above. It's only designed to combat objects in the sky. The ship is safe until it takes off again, then the end will come."

"But what's this gun for?" Tance put in. "There's no one alive here. Everyone is dead."

"It's a machine," Dorle said. "A machine that was made to do a job. And it's doing the job. How it survived the blast, I don't know. On it goes, waiting for the enemy. Probably they came by air in some sort of projectiles."

"The enemy," Nasha said. "Their own race. It is hard to believe that they really bombed themselves, fired at themselves."

"Well, it's over with. Except right here where we're standing. This one gun, still alert, ready to kill. It'll go on until it wears out."

"And by that time we'll be dead," Nasha said bitterly.

"There must have been hundreds of guns like this," Dorle murmured. "They must have been used to the sight: guns, weapons, uniforms. Probably they accepted it as a natural thing, part of their lives, like eating and sleeping. An institution, like the church and the state. Men trained to fight, to lead armies, a regular profession. Honored, respected."

Tance was walking slowly toward the gun, peering near-sightedly up at it. "Quite complex, isn't it? All those vanes and tubes. I suppose this is some sort of a telescopic sight." His gloved hand touched the end of a long tube.

Instantly the gun shifted, the barrel retracting. It swung.

"Don't move!" Dorle cried. The barrel swung past them as they stood, rigid and still. For one terrible moment it hesitated over their heads, clicking and whirring, settling into position. Then the sounds died out and the gun became silent.

Tance smiled foolishly inside his helmet. "I must have put my finger over the lens. I'll be more careful." He made his way up onto the circular slab, stepping gingerly behind the body of the gun. He disappeared from view.

"Where did he go?" Nasha said irritably. "He'll get us all killed."

"Tance, come back!" Dorle shouted. "What's the matter with you?"

"In a minute." There was a long silence. At last the archeologist appeared. "I think I've found something. Come up and I'll show you."

"What is it?"

"Dorle, you said the gun was here to keep the enemy off. I think I know why they wanted to keep the enemy off."

They were puzzled.

"I think I've found what the gun is supposed to guard. Come and give me a hand."

"All right," Dorle said abruptly. "Let's go." He seized Nasha's hand. "Come on. Let's see what he's found. I thought something like this might happen when I saw that the gun was—"

"Like what?" Nasha pulled her hand away. "What are you talking about? You act as if you knew what he's found."

"I do." Dorle smiled down at her. "Do you remember the legend that all races have, the myth of the buried treasure, and the dragon, the serpent that watches it, guards it, keeping everyone away?"

She nodded. "Well?"

Dorle pointed up at the gun.

"That," he said, "is the dragon. Come on."

Between the three of them they managed to pull up the steel cover and lay it to one side. Dorle was wet with perspiration when they finished.

"It isn't worth it," he grunted. He stared into the dark yawning hole. "Or is it?"

Nasha clicked on her hand lamp, shining the beam down the stairs. The steps were thick with dust and rubble. At the bottom was a steel door.

"Come on," Tance said excitedly. He started down the stairs. They watched him reach the door and pull hopefully on it without success. "Give a hand!"

"All right." They came gingerly after him. Dorle examined the door. It was bolted shut, locked. There was an inscription on the door, but he could not read it.

"Now what?" Nasha said.

Dorle took out his hand weapon. "Stand back. I can't think of any other way." He pressed the switch. The bottom of the door glowed red. Presently it began to crumble. Dorle clicked the weapon off. "I think we can get through. Let's try."

The door came apart easily. In a few minutes they had carried it away in pieces and stacked the pieces on the first step. Then they went on, flashing the light ahead of them.

They were in a vault. Dust lay everywhere, on everything, inches thick. Wood crates lined the walls, huge boxes and crates, packages and containers. Tance looked around curiously, his eyes bright.

"What exactly are all these?" he murmured. "Something valuable, I would think." He picked up a round drum and opened it. A spool fell to the floor, unwinding a black ribbon. He examined it, holding it up to the light.

"Look at this!"

They came around him. "Pictures," Nasha said. "Tiny pictures."

"Records of some kind." Tance closed the spool up in the drum again. "Look, hundreds of drums." He flashed the light around. "And those crates. Let's open one."

Dorle was already prying at the wood. The wood had turned brittle and dry. He managed to pull a section away.

It was a picture. A boy in a blue garment, smiling pleasantly, staring ahead, young and handsome. He seemed almost alive, ready to move toward them in the light of the hand lamp. It was one of them, one of the ruined race, the race that had perished.

For a long time they stared at the picture. At last Dorle replaced the board.

"All these other crates," Nasha said. "More pictures. And these drums. What are in the boxes?"

"This is their treasure," Tance said, almost to himself. "Here are their pictures, their records. Probably all their literature is here, their stories, their myths, their ideas about the universe."

"And their history," Nasha said. "We'll be able to trace their development and find out what it was that made them become what they were."

Dorle was wandering around the vault. "Odd," he murmured.

"Even at the end, even after they had begun to fight they still knew, someplace down inside them, that their real treasure was this, their books and pictures, their myths. Even after their big cities and buildings and industries were destroyed, they probably hoped to come back and find this. After everything else was gone."

"When we get back home, we can agitate for a mission to come here," Tance said. "All this can be loaded up and taken back. We'll be leaving about—"

He stopped.

"Yes," Dorle said dryly. "We'll be leaving about three day-periods from now. We'll fix the ship, then take off. Soon we'll be home, that is, if nothing happens. Like being shot down by that—"

"Oh, stop it!" Nasha said impatiently. "Leave him alone. He's right. All this must be taken back home, sooner or later. We'll have to solve the problem of the gun. We have no choice."

Dorle nodded. "What's your solution then? As soon as we leave the ground, we'll be shot down." His face twisted bitterly. "They've guarded their treasure too well. Instead of being preserved it will lie here until it rots. It serves them right."

"How?"

"Don't you see? This was the only way they knew, building a gun and setting it up to shoot anything that came along. They were so certain that everything was hostile, the enemy, coming to take their possessions away from them. Well, they can keep them."

Nasha was deep in thought, her mind far away. Suddenly she gasped. "Dorle," she said. "What's the matter with us? We have no problem. The gun is no menace at all."

The two men stared at her.

"No menace?" Dorle said. "It's already shot us down once. And as soon as we take off again—"

"Don't you see?" Nasha began to laugh. "The poor foolish gun, it's completely harmless. Even I could deal with it alone."

"You?"

Her eyes were flashing. "With a crowbar. With a hammer or a stick of wood. Let's go back to the ship and load up. Of course we're at its mercy in the air. That's the way it was made. It can fire into the sky, shoot down anything that flies. But that's all! Against something on the ground, it has no defenses. Isn't that right?"

Dorle nodded slowly. "The soft underbelly of the dragon. In the legend, the dragon's armor doesn't cover its stomach." He began to laugh. "That's right. That's perfectly right."

"Let's go then," Nasha said. "Let's get back to the ship. We have work to do here."

***

It was early the next morning when they reached the ship. During the night the Captain had died, and the crew had ignited his body according to custom. They had stood solemnly around it until the last ember died. As they were going back to their work the woman and the two men appeared, dirty and tired, still excited.

And presently, from the ship, a line of people came, each carrying something in his hands. The line marched across the gray slag, the eternal expanse of fused metal. When they reached the weapon, they all fell on the gun at once with crowbars, hammers, anything that was heavy and hard.

The telescopic sights shattered into bits. The wiring was pulled out, torn to shreds. The delicate gears were smashed, dented.

Finally the warheads themselves were carried off, and the firing pins removed.

The gun was smashed, the great weapon destroyed. The people went down into the vault and examined the treasure.

With its metal-armored guardian dead, there was no danger any longer. They studied the pictures, the films, the crates of books, the jeweled crowns, the cups, the statues.

At last, as the sun was dipping into the gray mists that drifted across the planet, they came back up the stairs again. For a moment they stood around the wrecked gun, looking at the unmoving outline of it.

Then they started back to the ship. There was still much work to be done. The ship had been badly hurt, much had been damaged and lost. The important thing was to repair it as quickly as possible, to get it into the air.

With all of them working together it took just five more days to make it spaceworthy.

***

Nasha stood in the control room, watching the planet fall away behind them. She folded her arms, sitting down on the edge of the table.

"What are you thinking?" Dorle said.

"I? Nothing."

"Are you sure?"

"I was thinking that there must have been a time when this planet was quite different, when there was life on it."

"I suppose there was. It's unfortunate that no ships from our system came this far, but then we had no reason to suspect intelligent life until we saw the fission glow in the sky."

"And then it was too late."

"Not quite too late. After all, their possessions, their music, books, their pictures, all of that will survive. We'll take them home and study them, and they'll change us. We won't be the same afterwards. Their sculpturing, especially. Did you see the one of the great winged creature, without a head or arms?

Broken off, I suppose. But those wings—it looked very old. It will change us a great deal."

"When we come back, we won't find the gun waiting for us," Nasha said. "Next time it won't be there to shoot us down. We can land and take the treasure, as you call it." She smiled up at Dorle. "You'll lead us back there, as a good captain should."

"Captain?" Dorle grinned. "Then you've decided."

Nasha shrugged. "Fomar argues with me too much. I think, all in all, I really prefer you."

"Then let's go," Dorle said. "Let's go back home."

The ship roared up, flying over the ruins of the city. It turned in a huge arc and then shot off beyond the horizon, heading into outer space.

Down below, in the center of the ruined city, a single half-broken detector vane moved slightly, catching the roar of the ship. The base of the great gun throbbed painfully, straining to turn. After a moment a red warning light flashed on down inside its destroyed works.

And a long way off, a hundred miles from the city, another warning light flashed on, far underground. Automatic relays flew into action. Gears turned, belts whined. On the ground above, a section of metal slag slipped back. A ramp appeared.

A moment later a small cart rushed to the surface.

The cart turned toward the city. A second cart appeared behind it. It was loaded with wiring cables. Behind it a third cart came, loaded with telescopic tube sights. And behind came more carts, some with relays, some with firing controls, some with tools and parts, screws and bolts, pins and nuts. The final one contained atomic warheads.

The carts lined up behind the first one, the lead cart. The lead cart started off across the frozen ground, bumping calmly along, followed by the others. Moving toward the city.

To the damaged gun.

# THE SKULL



"**WHAT IS THIS** opportunity?" Conger asked. "Go on. I'm interested."

The room was silent. All faces were fixed on Conger, still in the drab prison uniform. The Speaker leaned forward slowly.

"Before you went to prison your trading business was paying well—all illegal, all very profitable. Now you have nothing except the prospect of another six years in a cell."

Conger scowled.

"There is a certain situation, very important to this Council, that requires your peculiar abilities. Also, it is a situation you might find interesting. You were a hunter, were you not? You've done a great deal of trapping, hiding in the bushes, waiting at night for the game? I imagine hunting must be a source of satisfaction to you—the chase, the stalking."

Conger sighed. His lips twisted. "All right," he said. "Leave that out. Get to the point. Who do you want me to kill?"

The Speaker smiled. "All in proper sequence," he said softly.

***

The car slid to a stop. It was night. There was no light anywhere along the street. Conger looked out. "Where are we? What is this place?"

The hand of the guard pressed into his arm. "Come. Through that door."

Conger stepped down onto the damp sidewalk. The guard came swiftly after him, and then the Speaker. Conger took a deep breath of the cold air. He studied the dim outline of the building rising up before them.

"I know this place. I've seen it before." He squinted, his eyes growing accustomed to the dark. Suddenly he became alert. "This is—"

"Yes. The First Church." The Speaker walked toward the steps. "We're expected."

"Expected? *Here?*"

"Yes." The Speaker mounted the stairs. "You know we're not allowed in their Churches, especially with guns!" He stopped. Two armed soldiers loomed up ahead, one on each side.

"All right?" The Speaker looked up at them. They nodded. The door of the Church was open. Conger could see other soldiers inside, standing about, young soldiers with large eyes, gazing at the ikons and holy images.

"I see," he said.

"It was necessary," the Speaker said. "As you know, we have been singularly unfortunate in the past in our relations with the First Church."

"This won't help."

"But it's worth it. You will see."

They passed through the hall and into the main chamber where the altar piece was, and the kneeling places. The Speaker scarcely glanced at the altar as they passed by. He pushed open a small side door and beckoned Conger through.

"In here. We have to hurry. The faithful will be flocking in soon."

Conger entered, blinking. They were in a small chamber, low-ceilinged, with dark panels of old wood. There was a smell of ashes and smoldering spices in the room. He sniffed. "What's that? The smell."

"Cups on the wall. I don't know." The Speaker crossed impatiently to the far side. "According to our information, it is hidden here by this—"

Conger looked around the room. He saw books and papers, holy signs and images. A strange low shiver went through him.

"Does my job involve anyone of the Church? If it does—"

The Speaker turned, astonished. "Can it be that you believe in the Founder? Is it possible—a hunter, a killer."

"No. Of course not. All their business about resignation to death, non-violence."

"What is it, then?"

Conger shrugged. "I've been taught not to mix with such as these. They have strange abilities. And you can't reason with them."

The Speaker studied Conger thoughtfully. "You have the wrong idea. It is no one here that we have in mind. We've found that killing them only tends to increase their numbers."

"Then why come here? Let's leave."

"No. We came for something important. Something you will need to identify your man. Without it you won't be able to find him." A trace of a smile crossed the Speaker's face. "We don't want you to kill the wrong person. It's too important."

"I don't make mistakes." Conger's chest rose. "Listen, Speaker—"

"This is an unusual situation," the Speaker said. "You see, the person you are after, the person that we are sending you to find, is known only by certain objects here. They are the only traces, the only means of identification. Without them—"

"What are they?"

He came toward the Speaker. The Speaker moved to one side. "Look," he said. He drew a sliding wall away, showing a dark square hole. "In there."

Conger squatted down, staring in. He frowned. "A skull! A skeleton!"

"The man you are after has been dead for two centuries," the Speaker said. "This is all that remains of him. And this is all you have with which to find him."

For a long time Conger said nothing. He stared down at the

bones, dimly visible in the recess of the wall. How could a man dead centuries be killed? How could he be stalked, brought down?

Conger was a hunter, a man who had lived as he pleased, where he pleased. He had kept himself alive by trading, bringing furs and pelts in from the Provinces on his own ship, riding at high speed, slipping through the customs line around Earth.

He had hunted in the great mountains of the moon. He had stalked through empty Martian cities. He had explored—

The Speaker said, "Soldier, take these objects and have them carried to the car. Don't lose any part of them."

The soldier went into the cupboard, reaching gingerly, squatting on his heels.

"It is my hope," the Speaker continued softly, to Conger, "that you will demonstrate your loyalty to us now. There are always ways for citizens to restore themselves, to show their devotion to their society. For you I think this would be a very good chance. I seriously doubt that a better one will come. And for your efforts there will be quite a restitution of course."

The two men looked at each other. Conger thin, unkempt; the Speaker immaculate in his uniform.

"I understand you," Conger said. "I mean, I understand this part, about the chance. But how can a man who has been dead two centuries be—"

"I'll explain later," the Speaker said. "Right now we have to hurry!" The soldier had gone out with the bones wrapped in a blanket held carefully in his arms. The Speaker walked to the door. "Come. They've already discovered that we've broken in here, and they'll be coming at any moment."

They hurried down the damp steps to the waiting car. A second later the driver lifted the car up into the air, above the housetops.

The Speaker settled back in the seat.

"The First Church has an interesting past," he said. "I suppose you are familiar with it, but I'd like to speak of a few points that are of relevancy to us.

"It was in the twentieth century that the Movement began, during one of the periodic wars. The Movement developed rapidly, feeding on the general sense of futility, the realization that each war was breeding greater war, with no end in sight. The Movement posed a simple answer to the problem: without military preparations—weapons—there could be no war. And without machinery and complex scientific technocracy there could be no weapons.

"The Movement preached that you couldn't stop war by planning for it. They preached that man was losing to his machinery and science, that it was getting away from him, pushing him into greater and greater wars. Down with society, they shouted. Down with factories and science! A few more wars and there wouldn't be much left of the world.

"The Founder was an obscure person from a small town in the American Middle West. We don't even know his name. All we know is that one day he appeared preaching a doctrine of non-violence, non-resistance; no fighting, no paying taxes for guns, no research except for medicine. Live out your life quietly, tending your garden, staying out of public affairs; mind your own business. Be obscure, unknown, poor. Give away most of your possessions, leave the city. At least that was what developed from what he told the people."

The car dropped down and landed on a roof.

"The Founder preached this doctrine, or the germ of it. There's no telling how much the faithful have added themselves. The local authorities picked him up at once of course. Apparently they were convinced that he meant it; he was never released. He was put to death and his body buried secretly. It seemed that the cult was finished."

The Speaker smiled. "Unfortunately, some of his disciples reported seeing him after the date of his death. The rumor spread; he had conquered death, he was divine. It took hold, grew. And here we are today, with a First Church, obstructing all social progress, destroying society, sowing the seeds of anarchy."

"But the wars," Conger said. "About them?"

"The wars? Well, there were no more wars. It must be acknowledged that the elimination of war was the direct result of non-violence practiced on a general scale. But we can take a more objective view of war today. What was so terrible about it? War had a profound selective value, perfectly in accord with the teachings of Darwin and Mendel and others. Without war the mass of useless, incompetent mankind, without training or intelligence, is permitted to grow and expand unchecked. War acted to reduce their numbers. Like storms and earthquakes and droughts, it was nature's way of eliminating the unfit.

"Without war the lower elements of mankind have increased all out of proportion. They threaten the educated few, those with scientific knowledge and training, the ones equipped to direct society. They have no regard for science or a scientific society, based on reason. And this Movement seeks to aid and abet them. Only when scientists are in full control can the—"

He looked at his watch and then kicked the car door open. "I'll tell you the rest as we walk."

They crossed the dark roof. "Doubtless you now know whom those bones belonged to, who it is that we are after. He has been dead just two centuries now, this ignorant man from the Middle West, this Founder. The tragedy is that the authorities of the time acted too slowly. They allowed him to speak, to get his message across. He was allowed to preach, to start his cult. And once such a thing is under way, there's no stopping it.

"But what if he had died before he preached? What if none of his doctrines had ever been spoken? It took only a moment for him to utter them, that we know. They say he spoke just once, just one time. *Then* the authorities came, taking him away. He offered no resistance. The incident was small."

The Speaker turned to Conger.

"Small, but we're reaping the consequences of it today."

They went inside the building. Inside, the soldiers had already laid out the skeleton on a table. The soldiers stood around it, their young faces intense.

Conger went over to the table, pushing past them. He bent down, staring at the bones. "So these are his remains," he murmured. "The Founder. The Church has hidden them for two centuries."

"Quite so," the Speaker said. "But now we have them. Come along down the hall."

They went across the room to a door. The Speaker pushed it open. Technicians looked up. Conger saw machinery, whirring and turning, benches and retorts. In the center of the room was a gleaming crystal cage.

The Speaker handed a Slem-gun to Conger. "The important thing to remember is that the skull must be saved and brought back for comparison and proof. Aim low, at the chest."

Conger weighed the gun in his hands. "It feels good," he said. "I know this gun. That is, I've seen them before, but I never used one."

The Speaker nodded. "You will be instructed on the use of the gun and the operation of the cage. You will be given all data we have on the time and location. The exact spot was a place called Hudson's field. About 1960 in a small community outside Denver, Colorado. And don't forget, the only means of identification you will have will be the skull. There are visible characteristics of the front teeth, especially the left incisor."

Conger listened absently. He was watching two men in white carefully wrapping the skull in a plastic bag. They tied it and carried it into the crystal cage. "And if I should make a mistake?"

"Pick the wrong man? Then find the right one. Don't come back until you succeed in reaching this Founder. And you can't wait for him to start speaking. That's what we must avoid! You must act in advance. Take chances. Shoot as soon as you think you've found him. He'll be someone unusual, probably a stranger in the area. Apparently he wasn't known."

Conger listened dimly.

"Do you think you have it all now?" the Speaker asked.

"Yes. I think so." Conger entered the crystal cage and sat down, placing his hands on the wheel.

"Good luck," the Speaker said.

"We'll be awaiting the outcome. There's some philosophical doubt as to whether one can alter the past. This should answer the question once and for all."

Conger fingered the controls of the cage.

"By the way," the Speaker said. "Don't try to use this cage for purposes not anticipated in your job. We have a constant trace on it. If we want it back, we can get it back. Good luck."

Conger said nothing. The cage was sealed. He raised his finger and touched the wheel control. He turned the wheel carefully.

He was still staring at the plastic bag when the room outside vanished.

For a long time there was nothing at all. Nothing beyond the crystal mesh of the cage. Thoughts rushed through Conger's mind, helter-skelter. How would he know the man? How could he be certain in advance? What had he looked like? What was his name? How had he acted before he spoke? Would he be an ordinary person, or some strange outlandish crank?

Conger picked up the Slem-gun and held it against his cheek. The metal of the gun was cool and smooth. He practiced moving the sight. It was a beautiful gun, the kind of gun he could fall in love with. If he had owned such a gun in the Martian desert, on the long nights when he had lain, cramped and numbed with cold, waiting for things that moved through the darkness—

He put the gun down and adjusted the meter readings of the cage. The spiraling mist was beginning to condense and settle. All at once forms wavered and fluttered around him.

Colors, sounds, movements filtered through the crystal wire. He clamped the controls off and stood up.

He was on a ridge overlooking a small town. It was high noon. The air was crisp and bright. A few automobiles moved along a road. Off in the distance were some level fields. Conger went to the door and stepped outside. He sniffed the air. Then he went back into the cage.

He stood before the mirror over the shelf, examining his features. He had trimmed his beard—they had not got him to cut it off—and his hair was neat. He was dressed in the clothing of the middle-twentieth century, the odd collar and coat, the shoes of animal hide. In his pocket was money of the times. That was important. Nothing more was needed.

Nothing, except his ability, his special cunning. But he had never used it in such a way before.

He walked down the road toward the town.

The first things he noticed were the newspapers on the stands. April 5, 1961. He was not too far off. He looked around him. There was a filling station, a garage, some taverns, and a ten-cent store. Down the street was a grocery store and some public buildings.

A few minutes later he mounted the stairs of the little public library and passed through the doors into the warm interior.

The librarian looked up, smiling.

"Good afternoon," she said.

He smiled, not speaking because his words would not be

correct—accented and strange, probably. He went over to a table and sat down by a heap of magazines. For a moment he glanced through them. Then he was on his feet again. He crossed the room to a wide rack against the wall. His heart began to beat heavily.

Newspapers—weeks on end. He took a roll of them over to the table and began to scan them quickly. The print was odd, the letters strange. Some of the words were unfamiliar.

He set the papers aside and searched farther. At last he found what he wanted. He carried the *Cherrywood Gazette* to the table and opened it to the first page. He found what he wanted:

PRISONER HANGS SELF

An unidentified man, held by the county sheriff's office
for suspicion of criminal syndicalism, was found dead this
morning by—

He finished the item. It was vague, uninforming. He needed more. He carried the *Gazette* back to the racks and then, after a moment's hesitation, approached the librarian.

"More?" he asked. "More papers. Old ones?"

She frowned. "How old? Which papers?"

"Months old. And before."

"Of the *Gazette*? This is all we have. What did you want? What are you looking for? Maybe I can help you."

He was silent.

"You might find older issues at the *Gazette* office," the woman said, taking off her glasses. "Why don't you try there? But if you'd tell me, maybe I could help you."

He went out.

The *Gazette* office was down a side street. The sidewalk was broken and cracked. He went inside. A heater glowed in the corner of the small office. A heavyset man stood up and came slowly over to the counter.

"What did you want, mister?" he said.

"Old papers. A month. Or more."

"To buy? You want to buy them?"

"Yes." He held out some of the money he had. The man stared.

"Sure," he said. "Sure. Wait a minute." He went quickly out of the room. When he came back, he was staggering under the weight of his armload, his face red. "Here are some," he grunted. "Took what I could find. Covers the whole year. And if you want more—"

Conger carried the papers outside. He sat down by the road and began to go through them.

What he wanted was four months back, in December. It was a tiny item, so small that he almost missed it. His hands trembled as he scanned it, using the small dictionary for some of the archaic terms.

MAN ARRESTED FOR UNLICENSED DEMONSTRATION

An unidentified man who refused to give his name was picked up in Cooper Creek by special agents of the sheriff's office, according to Sheriff Duff. It was said the man was recently noticed in this area and had been watched continually.

It was Cooper Creek, December, 1960. His heart pounded. That was all he needed to know. He stood up, shaking himself, stamping his feet on the cold ground. The sun had moved across the sky to the very edge of the hills. He smiled. Already he had discovered the exact time and place. Now he needed only to go back, perhaps to November, to Cooper Creek.

He walked back through the main section of town, past the library, past the grocery store. It would not be hard, the hard part was over. He would go there, rent a room, prepare to wait until the man appeared.

He turned the corner. A woman was coming out of a doorway, loaded down with packages. Conger stepped aside to let her pass. The woman glanced at him. Suddenly her face turned white. She stared, her mouth open.

Conger hurried on. He looked back. What was wrong with her? The woman was still staring. She had dropped the packages to the ground. He increased his speed. He turned a second corner and went up a side street. When he looked back again the woman had come to the entrance of the street and was starting after him. A man joined her, and the two of them began to run toward him.

He lost them and left the town, striding quickly, easily, up into the hills at the edge of town. When he reached the cage, he stopped. What had happened? Was it something about his clothing? His dress?

He pondered. Then, as the sun set, he stepped into the cage.

Conger sat before the wheel. For a moment he waited, his hands resting lightly on the control. Then he turned the wheel, just a little, following the control readings carefully.

The grayness settled down around him.

But not for very long.

***

The man looked him over critically. "You better come inside," he said, "out of the cold."

"Thanks." Conger went gratefully through the open door into the living room. It was warm and close from the heat of the little kerosene heater in the corner. A woman, large and shapeless in her flowered dress, came from the kitchen. She and the man studied him critically.

"It's a good room," the woman said. "I'm Mrs. Appleton. It's got heat. You need that this time of year."

"Yes." He nodded, looking around.

"You want to eat with us?"

"What?"

"You want to eat with us?" The man's brows knitted. "You're not a foreigner, are you, mister?"

"No." He smiled. "I was born in this country. Quite far west, though."

"California?"

"No." He hesitated. "In Oregon."

"What's it like up there?" Mrs. Appleton asked. "I hear there's a lot of trees and green. It's so barren here. I come from Chicago, myself."

"That's the Middle West," the man said to her. "You ain't no foreigner."

"Oregon isn't foreign either," Conger said. "It's part of the United States."

The man nodded absently. He was staring at Conger's clothing.

"That's a funny suit you got on, mister," he said. "Where'd you get that?"

Conger was lost. He shifted uneasily. "It's a good suit," he said. "Maybe I better go some other place if you don't want me here."

They both raised their hands protestingly. The woman smiled at him. "We just have to look out for those Reds. You know, the government is always warning us about them."

"The Reds?" He was puzzled.

"The government says they're all around. We're supposed to report anything strange or unusual, anybody doesn't act normal."

"Like me?"

They looked embarrassed. "Well, you don't look like a Red to me," the man said. "But we have to be careful. The *Tribune* says—"

Conger half listened. It was going to be easier than he had thought. Clearly, he would know as soon as the Founder appeared. These people, so suspicious of anything different, would be buzzing and gossiping and spreading the story. All he had to do was lie low and listen, down at the general store perhaps. Or even here, in Mrs. Appleton's boarding house.

"Can I see the room?" he said.

"Certainly." Mrs. Appleton went to the stairs. "I'll be glad to show it to you."

They went upstairs. It was colder upstairs, but not nearly as cold as outside. Nor as cold as nights on the Martian deserts. For that he was grateful.

***

He was walking slowly around the store, looking at the cans of vegetables, the frozen packages of fish and meats shining and clean in the open refrigerator counters.

Ed Davies came toward him. "Can I help you?" he said. The man was a little oddly dressed, and with a beard! Ed couldn't help smiling.

"Nothing," the man said in a funny voice. "Just looking."

"Sure," Ed said. He walked back behind the counter. Mrs. Hacket was wheeling her cart up.

"Who's he?" she whispered, her sharp face turned, her nose moving as if it were sniffing. "I never seen him before."

"I don't know."

"Looks funny to me. Why does he wear a beard? No one else wears a beard. Must be something the matter with him."

"Maybe he likes to wear a beard. I had an uncle who—"

"Wait." Mrs. Hacket stiffened. "Didn't that—what was his name? The Red, that old one. Didn't he have a beard? Marx. He had a beard."

Ed laughed. "This ain't Karl Marx. I saw a photograph of him once."

Mrs. Hacket was staring at him. "You did?"

"Sure." He flushed a little. "What's the matter with that?"

"I'd sure like to know more about him," Mrs. Hacket said. "I think we ought to know more, for our own good."

***

"Hey, mister! Want a ride?"

Conger turned quickly, dropping his hand to his belt. He relaxed. Two young kids in a car, a girl and a boy. He smiled at them. "A ride? Sure."

Conger got into the car and closed the door. Bill Willet pushed the gas and the car roared down the highway.

"I appreciate a ride," Conger said carefully. "I was taking a walk between towns, but it was farther than I thought."

"Where are you from?" Lora Hunt asked. She was pretty, small and dark, in her yellow sweater and blue skirt.

"From Cooper Creek."

"Cooper Creek?" Bill said. He frowned. "That's funny. I don't remember seeing you before."

"Why, do you come from there?"

"I was born there. I know everybody there."

"I just moved in. From Oregon."

"From Oregon? I didn't know Oregon people had accents."

"Do I have an accent?"

"You use words funny."

"How?"

"I don't know. Doesn't he, Lora?"

"You slur them," Lora said, smiling. "Talk some more. I'm interested in dialects." She glanced at him, white-teethed. Conger felt his heart constrict.

"I have a speech impediment."

"Oh." Her eyes widened. "I'm sorry."

They looked at him curiously as the car purred along. Conger for his part was struggling to find some way of asking them questions without seeming curious. "I guess people from out of town don't come here much," he said. "Strangers."

"No." Bill shook his head. "Not very much."

"I'll bet I'm the first outsider for a long time."

"I guess so."

Conger hesitated. "A friend of mine, someone I know, might be coming through here. Where do you suppose I might—" He stopped. "Would there be anyone certain to see him? Someone I could ask, make sure I don't miss him if he comes?"

They were puzzled. "Just keep your eyes open. Cooper Creek isn't very big."

"No. That's right."

They drove in silence. Conger studied the outline of the girl. Probably she was the boy's mistress. Perhaps she was his trial wife. Or had they developed trial marriage back so far? He could not remember. But surely such an attractive girl would be someone's mistress by this time. She would be sixteen or so, by her looks. He might ask her sometime, if they ever met again.

The next day Conger went walking along the one main street of Cooper Creek. He passed the general store, the two filling stations, and then the post office. At the corner was the soda fountain.

He stopped. Lora was sitting inside, talking to the clerk. She was laughing, rocking back and forth.

Conger pushed the door open. Warm air rushed around him.

Lora was drinking hot chocolate with whipped cream. She looked up in surprise as he slid into the seat beside her.

"I beg your pardon," he said. "Am I intruding?"

"No." She shook her head. Her eyes were large and dark. "Not at all."

The clerk came over. "What do you want?"

Conger looked at the chocolate. "Same as she has."

Lora was watching Conger, her arms folded, elbows on the counter. She smiled at him. "By the way. You don't know my name. Lora Hunt."

She was holding out her hand. He took it awkwardly, not knowing what to do with it. "Conger is my name," he murmured.

"Conger? Is that your last or first name?"

"Last or first?" He hesitated. "Last. Omar Conger."

"Omar?" She laughed. "That's like the poet, Omar Khayyam."

"I don't know of him. I know very little of poets. We restored very few works of art. Usually only the Church has been interested enough—" He broke off. She was staring. He flushed. "Where I come from," he finished.

"The Church? Which church do you mean?"

"The Church." He was confused. The chocolate came and he began to sip it gratefully. Lora was still watching him.

"You're an unusual person," she said. "Bill didn't like you, but he never likes anything different. He's so—so prosaic. Don't you think that when a person gets older he should become—broadened in his outlook?"

Conger nodded.

"He says foreign people ought to stay where they belong, not come here. But you're not so foreign. He means Orientals, you know."

Conger nodded.

The screen door opened behind them. Bill came into the room. He stared at them. "Well," he said.

Conger turned. "Hello."

"Well." Bill sat down. "Hello, Lora." He was looking at Conger. "I didn't expect to see you here."

Conger tensed. He could feel the hostility of the boy. "Something wrong with that?"

"No. Nothing wrong with it."

There was silence. Suddenly Bill turned to Lora. "Come on. Let's go."

"Go?" She was astonished. "Why?"

"Just go!" He grabbed her hand. "Come on! The car's outside."

"Why, Bill Willet," Lora said. "You're jealous!"

"Who is this guy?" Bill said. "Do you know anything about him? Look at him, his beard."

She flared. "So what? Just because he doesn't drive a Packard and go to Cooper High!"

Conger sized the boy up. He was big—big and strong. Probably he was part of some civil control organization.

"Sorry," Conger said. "I'll go."

"What's your business in town?" Bill asked. "What are you doing here? Why are you hanging around Lora?"

Conger looked at the girl. He shrugged. "No reason. I'll see you later."

He turned away. And froze. Bill had moved. Conger's fingers went to his belt. *Half pressure*, he whispered to himself. *No more. Half pressure.*

He squeezed. The room leaped around him. He himself was protected by the lining of his clothing, the plastic sheathing inside.

"My god!" Lora put her hands up. Conger cursed. He hadn't meant any of it for her. But it would wear off. There was only a half amp to it. It would tingle.

Tingle, and paralyze.

He walked out the door without looking back. He was

almost to the corner when Bill came slowly out, holding onto the wall like a drunken man. Conger went on.

***

As Conger walked, restless, in the night, a form loomed in front of him. He stopped, holding his breath.

"Who is it?" a man's voice came. Conger waited, tense.

"Who is it?" the man said again. He clicked something in his hand. A light flashed. Conger moved.

"It's me," he said.

"Who is 'me'?"

"Conger is my name. I'm staying at the Appleton's place. Who are you?"

The man came slowly up to him. He was wearing a leather jacket. There was a gun at his waist.

"I'm Sheriff Duff. I think you're the person I want to talk to. You were in Bloom's today, about three o'clock?"

"Bloom's?"

"The fountain. Where the kids hang out." Duff came up beside him, shining his light into Conger's face. Conger blinked.

"Turn that thing away," he said.

A pause. "All right." The light flickered to the ground. "You were there. Some trouble broke out between you and the Willet boy. Is that right? You had a beef over his girl."

"We had a discussion," Conger said carefully.

"Then what happened?"

"Why?"

"I'm just curious. They say you did something."

"Did something? Did what?"

"I don't know. That's what I'm wondering. They saw a flash, and something seemed to happen. They all blacked out. Couldn't move."

"How are they now?"

"All right."

There was silence.

"Well?" Duff said. "What was it? A bomb?"

"A bomb?" Conger laughed. "No. My cigarette lighter caught fire. There was a leak, and the fluid ignited."

"Why did they all pass out?"

"Fumes."

Silence. Conger shifted, waiting. His fingers moved slowly toward his belt. The Sheriff glanced down. He grunted.

"If you say so," he said. "Anyhow, there wasn't any real harm done." He stepped back from Conger. "And that Willet is a troublemaker."

"Good night then," Conger said. He started past the Sheriff.

"One more thing, Mr. Conger, before you go. You don't mind if I look at your identification, do you?"

"No. Not at all." Conger reached into his pocket. He held his wallet out. The Sheriff took it and shined his flashlight on it. Conger watched, breathing shallowly. They had worked hard on the wallet, studying historic documents, relics of the times, all the papers they felt would be relevant.

Duff handed it back. "Okay. Sorry to bother you." The light winked off.

When Conger reached the house, he found the Appletons sitting around the television set. They did not look up as he came in. He lingered at the door.

"Can I ask you something?" he said. Mrs. Appleton turned slowly. "Can I ask you—what's the date?"

"The date?" She studied him. "The first of December."

"December first! Why, it was just November!"

They were all looking at him. Suddenly he remembered. In the twentieth century they still used the old twelve-month system. November fed directly into December. There was no Quartember between.

He gasped. Then it was tomorrow! The second of December! Tomorrow!

"Thanks," he said. "Thanks."

He went up the stairs. What a fool he was, forgetting. The Founder had been taken into captivity on the second of December, according to the newspaper records. Tomorrow, only twelve hours hence, the Founder would appear to speak to the people and then be dragged away.

***

The day was warm and bright. Conger's shoes crunched the melting crust of snow. On he went, through the trees heavy with white. He climbed a hill and strode down the other side, sliding as he went.

He stopped to look around. Everything was silent. There was no one in sight. He brought a thin rod from his waist and turned the handle of it. For a moment nothing happened. Then there was a shimmering in the air.

The crystal cage appeared and settled slowly down. Conger sighed. It was good to see it again. After all, it was his only way back.

He walked up on the ridge. He looked around with some satisfaction, his hands on his hips. Hudson's field was spread out, all the way to the beginning of town. It was bare and flat, covered with a thin layer of snow.

Here, the Founder would come. Here, he would speak to them. And here, the authorities would take him.

Only he would be dead before they came. He would be dead before he even spoke.

Conger returned to the crystal globe. He pushed through the door and stepped inside. He took the Slem-gun from the shelf and screwed the bolt into place. It was ready to go, ready to fire. For a moment he considered. Should he have it with him?

No. It might be hours before the Founder came, and suppose someone approached him in the meantime? When he saw the Founder coming toward the field, then he could go and get the gun.

Conger looked toward the shelf. There was the neat plastic package. He took it down and unwrapped it.

He held the skull in his hands, turning it over. In spite of himself, a cold feeling rushed through him. This was the man's skull, the skull of the Founder, who was still alive, who would come here, this day, who would stand on the field not fifty yards away.

What if *he* could see this, his own skull, yellow and eroded? Two centuries old. Would he still speak? Would he speak if he could see it, the grinning, aged skull? What would there be for him to say, to tell the people? What message could he bring?

What action would not be futile when a man could look upon his own aged, yellowed skull? Better they should enjoy their temporary lives while they still had them to enjoy.

A man who could hold his own skull in his hands would believe in few causes, few movements. Rather, he would preach the opposite—

A sound. Conger dropped the skull back on the shelf and took up the gun. Outside something was moving. He went quickly to the door, his heart beating. Was it *he*? Was it the Founder, wandering by himself in the cold, looking for a place to speak? Was he meditating over his words, choosing his sentences?

What if he could see what Conger had held!

He pushed the door open, the gun raised.

Lora!

He stared at her. She was dressed in a wool jacket and boots, her hands in her pockets. A cloud of steam came from her mouth and nostrils. Her breast was rising and falling.

Silently, they looked at each other. At last Conger lowered the gun.

"What is it?" he said. "What are you doing here?"

She pointed. She did not seem able to speak. He frowned. What was wrong with her?

"What is it?" he said. "What do you want?" He looked in the direction she had pointed. "I don't see anything."

"They're coming."

"They? Who? Who are coming?"

"They are. The police. During the night the Sheriff had the state police send cars. All around, everywhere. Blocking the roads. There's about sixty of them coming. Some from town, some around behind." She stopped, gasping. "They said—they said—"

"What?"

"They said you were some kind of a communist. They said—"

Conger went into the cage. He put the gun down on the shelf and came back out. He leaped down and went to the girl.

"Thanks. You came here to tell me? You don't believe it?"

"I don't know."

"Did you come alone?"

"No. Joe brought me in his truck. From town."

"Joe? Who's he?"

"Joe French. The plumber. He's a friend of Dad's."

"Let's go." They crossed the snow, up the ridge and onto the field. The little panel truck was parked halfway across the field. A heavy short man was sitting behind the wheel, smoking his pipe. He sat up as he saw the two of them coming toward him.

"Are you the one?" he said to Conger.

"Yes. Thanks for warning me."

The plumber shrugged. "I don't know anything about this. Lora says you're all right." He turned around. "It might interest you to know some more of them are coming. Not to warn you, just curious."

"More of them?" Conger looked toward the town. Black shapes were picking their way across the snow.

"People from the town. You can't keep this sort of thing quiet, not in a small town. We all listen to the police radio. They heard the same way Lora did. Someone tuned in, spread it around."

The shapes were getting closer. Conger could make out a couple of them. Bill Willet was there, with some boys from the high school. The Appletons were along, hanging back in the rear.

"Even Ed Davies," Conger murmured.

The storekeeper was toiling onto the field with three or four other men from the town.

"All curious as hell," French said. "Well, I guess I'm going back to town. I don't want my truck shot full of holes. Come on, Lora."

She was looking up at Conger, wide-eyed.

"Come on," French said again. "Let's go. You sure as hell can't stay here, you know."

"Why?"

"There may be shooting. That's what they all came to see. You know that, don't you, Conger?"

"Yes."

"You have a gun? Or don't you care?" French smiled a little. "They've picked up a lot of people in their time, you know. You won't be lonely."

He cared, all right! He had to stay here on the field. He couldn't afford to let them take him away. Any minute the Founder would appear, would step onto the field. Would he be one of the townsmen, standing silently at the foot of the field, waiting, watching?

Or maybe he was Joe French. Or maybe one of the cops. Anyone of them might find himself moved to speak. And the few words spoken this day were going to be important for a long time.

And Conger had to be there, ready when the first word was uttered!

"I care," he said. "You go on back to town. Take the girl with you."

Lora got stiffly in beside Joe French. The plumber started up the motor. "Look at them, standing there," he said. "Like vultures. Waiting to see someone get killed."

The truck drove away, Lora sitting stiff and silent, frightened now. Conger watched for a moment. Then he dashed back into the woods, between the trees, toward the ridge.

He could get away of course. Anytime he wanted to, he could get away. All he had to do was to leap into the crystal cage and turn the handles. But he had a job, an important job. He had to be here, here at this place, at this time.

He reached the cage and opened the door. He went inside and picked up the gun from the shelf. The Slem-gun would take care of them. He notched it up to full count. The chain reaction from it would flatten them all—the police, the curious, sadistic people.

They wouldn't take him! Before they got him, all of them would be dead. *He* would get away. He would escape. By the end of the day they would all be dead, if that was what they wanted, and he—

He saw the skull.

Suddenly he put the gun down. He picked up the skull. He turned the skull over. He looked at the teeth. Then he went to the mirror.

He held the skull up, looking in the mirror. He pressed the skull against his cheek. Beside his own face the grinning skull leered back at him, beside *his* skull, against his living flesh.

He bared his teeth. And he knew.

It was his own skull that he held. He was the one who would die. He was the Founder.

After a time he put the skull down. For a few minutes he stood at the controls, playing with them idly. He could hear the sound of motors outside, the muffled noise of men. Should he go back to the present, where the Speaker waited? He could escape, of course.

Escape?

He turned toward the skull. There it was, his skull, yellow with age. Escape? Escape, when he had held it in his own hands?

What did it matter if he put it off a month, a year, ten years, even fifty? Time was nothing. He had sipped chocolate with a girl born a hundred and fifty years before his time. Escape? For a little while, perhaps.

But he could not *really* escape, no more so than anyone else had ever escaped, or ever would.

Only, he had held it in his hands, his own bones, his own death's head.

*They* had not.

He went out the door and across the field, empty handed. There were a lot of them standing around, gathered together, waiting. They expected a good fight. They knew he had something. They had heard about the incident at the fountain.

And there were plenty of police, police with guns and tear gas, creeping across the hills and ridges, between the trees, closer and closer. It was an old story in this century.

One of the men tossed something at him. It fell in the snow by his feet, and he looked down. It was a rock. He smiled.

"Come on!" one of them called. "Don't you have any bombs?"

"Throw a bomb! You with the beard! Throw a bomb!"

"Let 'em have it!"

"Toss a few A-bombs!"

They began to laugh. He smiled. He put his hands to his hips. They suddenly turned silent, seeing that he was going to speak.

"I'm sorry," he said simply. "I don't have any bombs. You're mistaken."

There was a flurry of murmuring.

"I have a gun," he went on. "A very good one. Made by science even more advanced than your own. But I'm not going to use that either."

They were puzzled.

"Why not?" someone called. At the edge of the group an older woman was watching. He felt a sudden shock. He had seen her before. Where?

He remembered. The day at the library. As he had turned the corner he had seen her. She had noticed him and been astounded. At the time, he did not understand why.

Conger grinned. So he *would* escape death, the man who right now was voluntarily accepting it. They were laughing, laughing at a man who had a gun but didn't use it. But by a strange twist of science he would appear again, a few months later, after his bones had been buried under the floor of a jail.

And so, in a fashion, he would escape death. He would die, but then, after a period of months, he would live again, briefly, for an afternoon.

An afternoon. Yet long enough for them to see him, to understand that he was still alive. To know that somehow he had returned to life.

And then, finally, he would appear once more, after two hundred years had passed. Two centuries later.

He would be born again, born, as a matter of fact, in a small trading village on Mars. He would grow up, learning to hunt and trade—

A police car came on the edge of the field and stopped. The people retreated a little. Conger raised his hands.

"I have an odd paradox for you," he said. "Those who take lives will lose their own. Those who kill, will die. But he who gives his own life away will live again!"

They laughed faintly, nervously. The police were coming out, walking toward him. He smiled. He had said everything he intended to say. It was a good little paradox he had coined. They would puzzle over it, remember it.

Smiling, Conger awaited a death foreordained.

# THE EYES HAVE IT

**IT WAS QUITE** by accident I discovered this incredible invasion of Earth by lifeforms from another planet. As yet I haven't done anything about it. I can't think of anything to do. I wrote to the government, and they sent back a pamphlet on the repair and maintenance of frame houses. Anyhow, the whole thing is known. I'm not the first to discover it. Maybe it's even under control.

I was sitting in my easy chair, idly turning the pages of a paperbacked book someone had left on the bus, when I came across the reference that first put me on the trail. For a moment I didn't respond. It took some time for the full import to sink in. After I'd comprehended, it seemed odd I hadn't noticed it right away.

The reference was clearly to a nonhuman species of incredible properties, not indigenous to Earth. A species, I hasten to point out, customarily masquerading as ordinary human beings. Their disguise, however, became transparent in the face of the following observations by the author. It was at once obvious the author knew everything. Knew everything—and was taking it in his stride. The line (and I tremble remembering it even now) read:

*…his eyes slowly roved about the room.*

Vague chills assailed me. I tried to picture the eyes. Did they roll like dimes? The passage indicated not; they seemed to move through the air, not over the surface. Rather rapidly, apparently. No one in the story was surprised. That's what tipped me off. No sign of amazement at such an outrageous thing. Later the matter was amplified.

*…his eyes moved from person to person.*

There it was in a nutshell. The eyes had clearly come apart from the rest of him and were on their own. My heart pounded, and my breath choked in my windpipe. I had stumbled on an accidental mention of a totally unfamiliar race. Obviously non-Terrestrial. Yet to the characters in the book, it was perfectly natural—which suggested they belonged to the same species.

And the author? A slow suspicion burned in my mind. The author was taking it rather *too easily* in his stride. Evidently, he felt this was quite a usual thing. He made absolutely no attempt to conceal this knowledge. The story continued:

*...presently his eyes fastened on Julia.*

Julia, being a lady, had at least the breeding to feel indignant. She is described as blushing and knitting her brows angrily. At this, I sighed with relief. They weren't *all* non-Terrestrials. The narrative continues:

*...slowly, calmly, his eyes examined every inch of her.*

Great Scott! But here the girl turned and stomped off, and the matter ended. I lay back in my chair gasping with horror. My wife and family regarded me in wonder.

"What's wrong, dear?" my wife asked.

I couldn't tell her. Knowledge like this was too much for the ordinary run-of-the-mill person. I had to keep it to myself. "Nothing," I gasped. I leaped up, snatched the book, and hurried out of the room.

In the garage, I continued reading. There was more. Trembling, I read the next revealing passage:

*...he put his arm around Julia. Presently she asked him if he would remove his arm. He immediately did so, with a smile.*

It's not said what was done with the arm after the fellow had removed it. Maybe it was left standing upright in the corner. Maybe it was thrown away. I don't care. In any case, the full meaning was there, staring me right in the face.

Here was a race of creatures capable of removing portions of their anatomy at will—eyes, arms, and maybe more—without batting an eyelash. My knowledge of biology came in handy at this point. Obviously they were simple beings, unicellular, some sort of primitive single-celled things. Beings no more developed than starfish. Starfish can do the same thing, you know.

I read on. And came to this incredible revelation, tossed off coolly by the author without the faintest tremor:

*...outside the movie theater we split up. Part of us went inside, part over to the cafe for dinner.*

Binary fission, obviously. Splitting in half and forming two entities. Probably each lower half went to the cafe, it being farther, and the upper halves to the movies. I read on, hands shaking. I had really stumbled onto something here. My mind reeled as I made out this passage:

*...I'm afraid there's no doubt about it. Poor Bibney has lost his head again.*

Which was followed by:

*...and Bob says he has utterly no guts.*

Yet Bibney got around as well as the next person. The next person, however, was just as strange. He was soon described as:

*...totally lacking in brains.*

There was no doubt of the thing in the next passage. Julia, whom I had thought to be the one normal person, reveals herself as also being an alien life form, similar to the rest:

*...quite deliberately, Julia had given her heart to the young man.*

It didn't relate what the final disposition of the organ was, but I didn't really care. It was evident Julia had gone right on living in her usual manner, like all the others in the book. Without heart, arms, eyes, brains, viscera, dividing up in two when the occasion demanded. Without a qualm.

*...thereupon she gave him her hand.*

I sickened. The rascal now had her hand as well as her heart. I shudder to think what he's done with them by this time.

*…he took her arm.*

Not content to wait, he had to start dismantling her on his own. Flushing crimson, I slammed the book shut and leaped to my feet. But not in time to escape one last reference to those carefree bits of anatomy whose travels had originally thrown me on the track:

*…her eyes followed him all the way down the road and across the meadow.*

I rushed from the garage and back inside the warm house, as if the accursed things were following me. My wife and children were playing Monopoly in the kitchen. I joined them and played with frantic fervor, brow feverish, teeth chattering.

I had had enough of the thing. I want to hear no more about it. Let them come on. Let them invade Earth. I don't want to get mixed up in it.

I have absolutely no stomach for it.

# TONY AND THE BEETLES

**REDDISH-YELLOW SUNLIGHT FILTERED** through the thick quartz windows into the sleep-compartment. Tony Rossi yawned, stirred a little, then opened his black eyes and sat up quickly. With one motion he tossed the covers back and slid to the warm metal floor. He clicked off his alarm clock and hurried to the closet.

It looked like a nice day. The landscape outside was motionless, undisturbed by winds or dust-shift. The boy's heart pounded excitedly. He pulled his trousers on, zipped up the reinforced mesh, struggled into his heavy canvas shirt, and then sat down on the edge of the cot to tug on his boots. He closed the seams around their tops and then did the same with his gloves. Next he adjusted the pressure on his pump unit and strapped it between his shoulder blades. He grabbed his helmet from the dresser, and he was ready for the day.

In the dining-compartment his mother and father had finished breakfast. Their voices drifted to him as he clattered down the ramp. A disturbed murmur. He paused to listen. What were they talking about? Had he done something wrong, again?

And then he caught it. Behind their voices was another voice. Static and crackling pops. The all-system audio signal from Rigel IV. They had it turned up full blast. The dull thunder of the monitor's voice boomed loudly. The war. Always the war. He sighed and stepped out into the dining-compartment.

"Morning," his father muttered.

"Good morning, dear," his mother said absently. She sat with her head turned to one side, wrinkles of concentration webbing her forehead. Her thin lips were drawn together in a tight line of concern. His father had pushed his dirty dishes back and was smoking, elbows on the table, dark hairy arms bare and muscular. He was scowling, intent on the jumbled roar from the speaker above the sink.

"How's it going?" Tony asked. He slid into his chair and reached automatically for the ersatz grapefruit. "Any news from Orion?"

Neither of them answered. They didn't hear him. He began to eat his grapefruit. Outside, beyond the little metal and plastic housing unit, sounds of activity grew. Shouts and muffled crashes, as rural merchants and their trucks rumbled along the highway toward Karnet. The reddish daylight swelled. Betelgeuse was rising quietly and majestically.

"Nice day," Tony said. "No flux wind. I think I'll go down to the n-quarter awhile. We're building a neat spaceport. A model, of course, but we've been able to get enough materials to lay out strips for—"

With a savage snarl his father reached out and struck. The audio roar immediately died. "I knew it!" He got up and moved angrily away from the table. "I told them it would happen. They shouldn't have moved so soon. Should have built up Class A supply bases first."

"Isn't our main fleet moving in from Bellatrix?" Tony's mother fluttered anxiously. "According to last night's summary the worst that can happen is Orion IX and X will be dumped."

Joseph Rossi laughed harshly. "The hell with last night's summary. They know as well as I do what's happening."

"What's happening?" Tony echoed, as he pushed aside his grapefruit and began to ladle out dry cereal. "Are we losing the battle?"

"Yes!" His father's lips twisted. "Earthmen, losing to—to *beetles*. I told them. But they couldn't wait. My god, there's ten good years left in this system. Why'd they have to push on? Everybody knew Orion would be tough. The whole damn beetle fleet's strung out around there. Waiting for us. And we have to barge right in."

"But nobody ever thought beetles would fight," Leah Rossi protested mildly. "Everybody thought they'd just fire a few blasts and then—"

"They *have* to fight! Orion's the last jump-off. If they don't fight here, where the hell can they fight?" Rossi swore savagely. "Of course they're fighting. We have all their planets except the inner Orion string. Not that they're worth much, but it's the principle of the thing. If we'd built up strong supply bases, we could have broken up the beetle fleet and really clobbered it."

"Don't say 'beetle,'" Tony murmured, as he finished his cereal. "They're Pas-udeti, same as here. The word 'beetle' comes from Betelgeuse. An Arabian word we invented ourselves."

Joe Rossi's mouth opened and closed. "What are you, a goddamn beetle lover?"

"Joe," Leah snapped. "For heaven's sake."

Rossi moved toward the door. "If I was ten years younger, I'd be out there. I'd really show those shiny-shelled insects what the hell they're up against. Them and their junky beat-up old hulks. Converted freighters!" His eyes blazed. "When I think of them shooting down Terran cruisers with *our* boys in them—"

"Orion's their system," Tony murmured.

"*Their* system! When the hell did you get to be an authority on space law? Why, I ought to—" He broke off, choked with rage. "My own kid," he muttered. "One more crack out of you today and I'll hang one on you you'll feel the rest of the week."

Tony pushed his chair back. "I won't be around here today. I'm going into Karnet, with my EEP."

"Yeah, to play with beetles!"

Tony said nothing. He was already sliding his helmet in place and snapping the clamps tight. As he pushed through the back door, into the lock membrane, he unscrewed his oxygen tap and set the tank filter into action. An automatic response, conditioned by a lifetime spent on a colony planet in an alien system.

A faint flux wind caught at him and swept yellow-red dust around his boots. Sunlight glittered from the metal roof of his family's housing unit, one of endless rows of squat boxes set in the sandy slope, protected by the line of ore-refining installations against the horizon. He made an impatient signal, and from the storage shed his EEP came gliding out, catching the sunlight on its chrome trim.

"We're going down into Karnet," Tony said, unconsciously slipping into the Pas dialect. "Hurry up!"

The EEP took up its position behind him, and he started briskly down the slope, over the shifting sand, toward the road. There were quite a few traders out today. It was a good day for the market, only a fourth of the year was fit for travel. Betelgeuse was an erratic and undependable sun, not at all like Sol (according to the edutapes fed to Tony four hours a day, six days a week; he had never seen Sol himself).

He reached the noisy road. Pas-udeti were everywhere, whole groups of them with their primitive combustion-driven trucks, battered and filthy, motors grinding protestingly. He waved at the trucks as they pushed past him. After a moment one slowed down. It was piled with *tis*, bundled heaps of gray vegetables, dried and prepared for the table. A staple of the Pas-udeti diet. Behind the wheel lounged a dark-faced elderly Pas, one arm over the open window, a rolled leaf between his lips. He was like all other Pas-udeti, lank and hard-shelled, encased in a brittle sheath in which he lived and died.

"You want a ride?" the Pas murmured, required protocol when an Earthman on foot was encountered.

"Is there room for my EEP?"

The Pas made a careless motion with his claw. "It can run behind." Sardonic amusement touched his ugly old face. "If it gets to Karnet we'll sell it for scrap. We can use a few condensers and relay tubing. We're short on electronic maintenance stuff."

"I know," Tony said solemnly, as he climbed into the cabin of the truck. "It's all been sent to the big repair base at Orion I. For your warfleet."

Amusement vanished from the leathery face. "Yes, the warfleet." He turned away and started up the truck again. In the back, Tony's EEP had scrambled up on the load of *tis* and was gripping precariously with its magnetic lines.

Tony noticed the Pas-udeti's sudden change of expression, and he was puzzled. He started to speak to him, but now he noticed unusual quietness among the other Pas in the other trucks, behind and in front of his own. The war of course. It had swept through this system a century ago. These people had been left behind. Now all eyes were on Orion, on the battle between the Terran warfleet and the Pas-udeti collection of armed freighters.

"Is it true," Tony asked carefully, "that you're winning?"

The elderly Pas grunted. "We hear rumors."

Tony considered. "My father says Terra went ahead too fast. He says we should have consolidated. We didn't assemble adequate supply bases. He used to be an officer when he was younger. He was with the fleet for two years."

The Pas was silent a moment. "It's true," he said at last, "that when you're so far from home, supply is a great problem. We, on the other hand, don't have that. We have no distances to cover."

"Do you know anybody fighting?"

"I have distant relatives." The answer was vague. The Pas obviously didn't want to talk about it.

"Have you ever seen your warfleet?"

"Not as it exists now. When this system was defeated most of our units were wiped out. Remnants limped to Orion and joined the Orion fleet."

"Your relatives were with the remnants?"

"That's right."

"Then you were alive when this planet was taken?"

"Why do you ask?" The old Pas quivered violently. "What business is it of yours?"

Tony leaned out and watched the walls and buildings of Karnet grow ahead of them. Karnet was an old city. It had stood thousands of years. The Pas-udeti civilization was stable. It had reached a certain point of technocratic development and then leveled off. The Pas had intersystem ships that had carried people and freight between planets in the days before the Terran Confederation. They had combustion-driven cars, audiophones, a power network of a magnetic type. Their plumbing was satisfactory, and their medicine was highly advanced. They had art forms, emotional and exciting. They had a vague religion.

"Who do you think will win the battle?" Tony asked.

"I don't know." With a sudden jerk the old Pas brought the truck to a crashing halt. "This is as far as I go. Please get out and take your EEP with you."

Tony faltered in surprise. "But aren't you going—?"

"No farther!"

Tony pushed the door open. He was vaguely uneasy. There was a hard, fixed expression on the leathery face, and the old creature's voice had a sharp edge he had never heard before. "Thanks," he murmured. He hopped down into the red dust and signaled his EEP. It released its magnetic lines, and instantly the truck started up with a roar, passing on inside the city.

Tony watched it go, still dazed. The hot dust lapped at his ankles. He automatically moved his feet and slapped at his trousers. A truck honked, and his EEP quickly moved him from the road up to the level pedestrian ramp. Pas-udeti in swarms moved by, endless lines of rural people hurrying into Karnet on their daily business. A massive public bus had stopped by the gate and was letting off passengers. Male and female Pas. And children. They laughed and shouted. The sounds of their voices blended with the low hum of the city.

"Going in?" a sharp Pas-udeti voice sounded close behind him. "Keep moving, you're blocking the ramp."

It was a young female with a heavy armload clutched in her claws. Tony felt embarrassed. Female Pas had a certain telepathic ability, part of their sexual make-up. It was effective on Earthmen at close range.

"Here," she said. "Give me a hand."

Tony nodded his head, and the EEP accepted the female's heavy armload. "I'm visiting the city," Tony said as they moved with the crowd toward the gates. "I got a ride most of the way, but the driver let me off out here."

"You're from the settlement?"

"Yes."

She eyed him critically. "You've always lived here, haven't you?"

"I was born here. My family came here from Earth four years before I was born. My father was an officer in the fleet. He earned an Emigration Priority."

"So you've never seen your own planet. How old are you?"

"Ten years. Terran."

"You shouldn't have asked the driver so many questions."

They passed through the decontamination shield and into the city. An information square loomed ahead. Pas men and women were packed around it. Moving chutes and transport cars rumbled everywhere. Buildings and ramps and open-air machinery; the city was sealed in a protective dust-proof envelope. Tony unfastened his helmet and clipped it to his belt. The air was stale smelling, artificial but usable.

"Let me tell you something," the young female said carefully, as she strode along the foot ramp beside Tony. "I wonder if this is a good day for you to come into Karnet. I know you've been coming here regularly to play with your friends. But perhaps today you ought to stay at home, in your settlement."

"Why?"

"Because today everybody is upset."

"I know," Tony said. "My mother and father were upset. They were listening to the news from our base in the Rigel system."

"I don't mean your family. Other people are listening, too. These people here. My race."

"They're upset, all right," Tony admitted. "But I come here all the time. There's nobody to play with at the settlement, and anyhow we're working on a project."

"A model spaceport."

"That's right." Tony was envious. "I sure wish I was a telepath. It must be fun."

The female Pas-udeti was silent. She was deep in thought. "What would happen," she asked, "if your family left here and returned to Earth?"

"That couldn't happen. There's no room for us on Earth. C-bombs destroyed most of Asia and North America back in the twentieth century."

"Suppose you *had* to go back?"

Tony did not understand. "But we can't. Habitable portions of Earth are overcrowded. Our main problem is finding places for Terrans to live, in other systems." He added, "And anyhow, I don't particularly want to go to Terra. I'm used to it here. All my friends are here."

"I'll take my packages," the female said. "I go this other way, down this third-level ramp."

Tony nodded to his EEP, and it lowered the bundles into the female's claws. She lingered a moment, trying to find the right words.

"Good luck," she said.

"With what?"

She smiled faintly, ironically. "With your model spaceport. I hope you and your friends get to finish it."

"Of course we'll finish it," Tony said, surprised. "It's almost done." What did she mean?

The Pas-udeti woman hurried off before he could ask her. Tony was troubled and uncertain. More doubts filled him. After a moment he headed slowly into the lane that took him toward the residential section of the city. Past the stores and factories, to the place where his friends lived.

The group of Pas-udeti children eyed him silently as he approached. They had been playing in the shade of an immense *hengelo*, whose ancient branches drooped and swayed with the air currents pumped through the city. Now they sat unmoving.

"I didn't expect you today," B'prith said in an expressionless voice.

Tony halted awkwardly, and his EEP did the same. "How are things?" he murmured.

"Fine."

"I got a ride partway."

"Fine."

Tony squatted down in the shade. None of the Pas children stirred. They were small, not as large as Terran children. Their shells had not hardened, had not turned dark and opaque, like horn. It gave them a soft, unformed appearance, but at the same time it lightened their load. They moved more easily than their elders. They could hop and skip around still. But they were not skipping right now.

"What's the matter?" Tony demanded. "What's wrong with everybody?"

No one answered.

"Where's the model?" he asked. "Have you fellows been working on it?"

After a moment Llyre nodded slightly.

Tony felt dull anger rise up inside him. "Say something! What's the matter? What're you all mad about?"

"Mad?" B'prith echoed. "We're not mad."

Tony scratched aimlessly in the dust. He knew what it was. The war, again. The battle going on near Orion. His anger burst up wildly. "Forget the war. Everything was fine yesterday, before the battle."

"Sure," Llyre said. "It was fine."

Tony caught the edge to his voice. "It happened a hundred years ago. It's not my fault."

"Sure," B'prith said.

"This is my home, isn't it? Haven't I got as much right here as anybody else? I was born here."

"Sure," Llyre said tonelessly.

Tony appealed to them helplessly. "Do you have to act this way? You didn't act this way yesterday. I was here yesterday—all of us were here yesterday. What's happened since yesterday?"

"The battle," B'prith said.

"What difference does *that* make? Why does that change everything? There's always war. There've been battles all the time, as long as I can remember. What's different about this?"

B'prith broke apart a clump of dirt with his strong claws. After a moment he tossed it away and got slowly to his feet. "Well," he said thoughtfully, "according to our audio relay, it looks as if our fleet is going to win this time."

"Yes," Tony agreed, not understanding. "My father says we

didn't build up adequate supply bases. We'll probably have to fall back to…" And then the impact hit him. "You mean, for the first time in a hundred years—"

"Yes," Llyre said, also getting up. The others got up, too. They moved away from Tony, toward the nearby house. "We're winning. The Terran flank was turned, half an hour ago. Your right wing has folded completely."

Tony was stunned. "And it matters. It matters to all of you."

"Matters!" B'prith halted, suddenly blazing out in fury. "Sure it matters! For the first time—in a century. The first time in our lives we're beating you. We have you on the run, you—" He choked out the word, almost spat it out. "You white-grubs!"

They disappeared into the house. Tony sat gazing stupidly down at the ground, his hands still moving aimlessly. He had heard the word before, seen it scrawled on walls and in the dust near the settlement. *White-grubs.* The Pas term of derision for Terrans. Because of their softness, their whiteness. Lack of hard shells. Pulpy, doughy skin. But they had never dared say it out loud before. To an Earthman's face.

Beside him, his EEP stirred restlessly. Its intricate radio mechanism sensed the hostile atmosphere. Automatic relays were sliding into place. Circuits were opening and closing.

"It's all right," Tony murmured, getting slowly up. "Maybe we'd better go back."

He moved unsteadily toward the ramp, completely shaken. The EEP walked calmly ahead, its metal face blank and confident, feeling nothing, saying nothing. Tony's thoughts were a wild turmoil. He shook his head, but the crazy spinning kept up. He couldn't make his mind slow down, lock in place.

"Wait a minute," a voice said. B'prith's voice, from the open doorway. Cold and withdrawn, almost unfamiliar.

"What do you want?"

B'prith came toward him, claws behind his back in the

formal Pas-udeti posture, used between total strangers. "You shouldn't have come here today."

"I know," Tony said.

B'prith got out a bit of *tis* stalk and began to roll it into a tube. He pretended to concentrate on it. "Look," he said. "You said you have a right here. But you don't."

"I—" Tony murmured.

"Do you understand why not? You said it isn't your fault. I guess not. But it's not my fault either. Maybe it's nobody's fault. I've known you a long time."

"Five years. Terran."

B'prith twisted the stalk up and tossed it away. "Yesterday we played together. We worked on the spaceport. But we can't play today. My family said to tell you not to come here any-more." He hesitated, and did not look Tony in the face. "I was going to tell you anyhow. Before they said anything."

"Oh," Tony said.

"Everything that's happened today—the battle, our fleet's stand. We didn't know. We didn't dare hope. You see? A century of running. First this system. Then the Rigel system, all the planets. Then the other Orion stars. We fought here and there, scattered fights. Those that got away joined up. We supplied the base at Orion—you people didn't know. But there was no hope. At least, nobody thought there was." He was silent a moment. "Funny," he said, "what happens when your back's to the wall, and there isn't any further place to go. Then you have to fight."

"If our supply bases—" Tony began thickly, but B'prith cut him off savagely.

"Your supply bases! Don't you understand? We're beating you! Now you'll have to get out! All you white-grubs. Out of our system!"

Tony's EEP moved forward ominously. B'prith saw it. He bent down, snatched up a rock, and hurled it straight at the EEP.

The rock clanged off the metal hull and bounced harmlessly away. B'prith snatched up another rock. Llyre and the others came quickly out of the house. An adult Pas loomed up behind them. Everything was happening too fast. More rocks crashed against the EEP. One struck Tony on the arm.

"Get out!" B'prith screamed. "Don't come back! This is our planet!" His claws snatched at Tony. "We'll tear you to pieces if you—"

Tony smashed him in the chest. The soft shell gave like rubber, and the Pas stumbled back. He wobbled and fell over, gasping and screeching.

"*Beetle*," Tony breathed hoarsely. Suddenly he was terrified. A crowd of Pas-udeti was forming rapidly. They surged on all sides, hostile faces, dark and angry, a rising thunder of rage.

More stones showered. Some struck the EEP, others fell around Tony, near his boots. One whizzed past his face. Quickly he slid his helmet in place. He was scared. He knew his EEP's E-signal had already gone out, but it would be minutes before a ship could come. Besides, there were other Earthmen in the city to be taken care of. There were Earthmen all over the planet. In all the cities. On all the twenty-three Betelgeuse planets. On the fourteen Rigel planets. On the other Orion planets.

"We have to get out of here," he muttered to the EEP. "Do something!"

A stone hit him on the helmet. The plastic cracked. Air leaked out, and then the autoseal filmed over. More stones were falling. The Pas swarmed close, a yelling, seething mass of black-sheathed creatures. He could smell them, the acrid body odor of insects, hear their claws snap, feel their weight.

The EEP threw its heat beam on. The beam shifted in a wide band toward the crowd of Pas-udeti. Crude hand weapons appeared. A clatter of bullets burst around Tony. They were firing at the EEP. He was dimly aware of the metal body beside him. A shuddering crash—the EEP was toppled over. The crowd poured over it; the metal hull was lost from sight.

Like a demented animal, the crowd tore at the struggling EEP. A few of them smashed in its head, others tore off struts and shiny arm sections. The EEP ceased struggling. The crowd moved away, panting and clutching jagged remains. They saw Tony.

As the first line of them reached for him, the protective envelope high above them shattered. A Terran scout ship thundered down, heat beam screaming. The crowd scattered in confusion, some firing, some throwing stones, others leaping for safety.

Tony picked himself up and made his way unsteadily toward the spot where the scout was landing.

***

"I'm sorry," Joe Rossi said gently. He touched his son on the shoulder. "I shouldn't have let you go down there today. I should have known."

Tony sat hunched over in the big plastic easy chair. He rocked back and forth, face pale with shock. The scout ship which had rescued him had immediately headed back toward Karnet. There were other Earthmen to bring out besides this first load. The boy said nothing. His mind was blank. He still heard the roar of the crowd, felt its hate—a century of pent-up fury and resentment. The memory drove out everything else. It was all around him, even now. And the sight of the floundering EEP, the metallic ripping sound, as its arms and legs were torn off and carried away.

His mother dabbed at his cuts and scratches with antiseptic. Joe Rossi shakily lit a cigarette and said, "If your EEP hadn't been along they'd have killed you. Beetles." He shuddered. "I never should have let you go down there. All this time…They might have done it any time, any day. Knifed you. Cut you open with their filthy goddamn claws."

Below the settlement the reddish-yellow sunlight glinted on gun barrels. Already, dull booms echoed against the crumbling hills. The defense ring was going into action. Black shapes darted and scurried up the side of the slope. Black patches moved out from Karnet, toward the Terran settlement, across the dividing line the Confederation surveyors had set up a century ago. Karnet was a bubbling pot of activity. The whole city rumbled with feverish excitement.

Tony raised his head. "They—they turned our flank."

"Yeah." Joe Rossi stubbed out his cigarette. "They sure did. That was at one o'clock. At two they drove a wedge right through the center of our line. Split the fleet in half. Broke it up, sent it running. Picked us off one by one as we fell back. Christ, they're like maniacs. Now that they've got the scent, the taste of our blood."

"But it's getting better," Leah fluttered. "Our main fleet units are beginning to appear."

"We'll get them," Joe muttered. "It'll take a while. But by god we'll wipe them out. Every last one of them. If it takes a thousand years. We'll follow every last ship down—we'll get them all." His voice rose in frenzy. "Beetles! Goddamn insects! When I think of them, trying to hurt my kid, with their filthy black claws."

"If you were younger, you'd be in the line," Leah said. "It's not your fault you're too old. The heart strain's too great. You did your job. They can't let an older person take chances. It's not your fault."

Joe clenched his fists. "I feel so futile. If there was only something I could do."

"The fleet will take care of them," Leah said soothingly. "You said so yourself. They'll hunt every one of them down. Destroy them all. There's nothing to worry about."

Joe sagged miserably. "It's no use. Let's cut it out. Let's stop kidding ourselves."

"What do you mean?"

"Face it! We're not going to win, not this time. We went too far. Our time's come."

There was silence.

Tony sat up a little. "When did you know?"

"I've known a long time."

"I found out today. I didn't understand at first. This is stolen ground. I was born here, but it's stolen ground."

"Yes. It's stolen. It doesn't belong to us."

"We're here because we're stronger. But now we're not stronger. We're being beaten."

"They know Terrans can be licked. Like anybody else." Joe Rossi's face was gray and flabby. "We took their planets away from them. Now they're taking them back. It'll be a while of course. We'll retreat slowly. It'll be another five centuries going back. There're a lot of systems between here and Sol."

Tony shook his head, still uncomprehending. "Even Llyre and B'prith. All of them. Waiting for their time to come. For us to lose and go away again. Where we came from."

Joe Rossi paced back and forth. "Yeah, we'll be retreating from now on. Giving ground instead of taking it. It'll be like this today—losing fights, draws. Stalemates and worse."

He raised his feverish eyes toward the ceiling of the little metal housing unit, face wild with passion and misery.

"But, by god, we'll give them a run for their money. All the way back! Every inch!"

# MR. SPACESHIP

**KRAMER LEANED BACK.** "You can see the situation. How can we deal with a factor like this? The perfect variable."

"Perfect? Prediction should still be possible. A living thing still acts from necessity, the same as inanimate material. But the cause-effect chain is more subtle. There are more factors to be considered. The difference is quantitative, I think. The reaction of the living organism parallels natural causation, but with greater complexity."

Gross and Kramer looked up at the board plates, suspended on the wall, still dripping, the images hardening into place. Kramer traced a line with his pencil.

"See that? It's a pseudopodium. They're alive, and so far, a weapon we can't beat. No mechanical system can compete with that, simple or intricate. We'll have to scrap the Johnson Control and find something else."

"Meanwhile the war continues as it is. Stalemate. Checkmate. They can't get to us, and we can't get through their living minefield."

Kramer nodded. "It's a perfect defense for them. But there still might be one answer."

"What's that?"

"Wait a minute." Kramer turned to his rocket expert, sitting with the charts and files. "The heavy cruiser that returned this week. It didn't actually touch, did it? It came close but there was no contact."

"Correct." The expert nodded. "The mine was twenty miles off. The cruiser was in space-drive, moving directly toward Proxima, line-straight, using the Johnson Control of course. It had deflected a quarter of an hour earlier for reasons unknown. Later it resumed its course. That was when they got it."

"It shifted," Kramer said, "but not enough. The mine was coming along after it, trailing it. It's the same old story, but I wonder about the contact."

"Here's our theory," the expert said. "We keep looking for contact, a trigger in the pseudopodium. But more likely we're witnessing a psychological phenomena, a decision without any physical correlative. We're watching for something that isn't there. The mine *decides* to blow up. It sees our ship, approaches, and then decides."

"Thanks." Kramer turned to Gross. "Well, that confirms what I'm saying. How can a ship guided by automatic relays escape a mine that decides to explode? The whole theory of mine penetration is that you must avoid tripping the trigger. But here the trigger is a state of mind in a complicated, developed lifeform."

"The belt is fifty thousand miles deep," Gross added. "It solves another problem for them—repair and maintenance. The damn things reproduce, fill up the spaces by spawning into them. I wonder what they feed on?"

"Probably the remains of our first-line. The big cruisers must be a delicacy. It's a game of wits, between a living creature and a ship piloted by automatic relays. The ship always loses." Kramer opened a folder. "I'll tell you what I suggest."

"Go on," Gross said. "I've already heard ten solutions today. What's yours?"

"Mine is very simple. These creatures are superior to any mechanical system, but only because they're alive. Almost any other lifeform could compete with them, any higher lifeform. If the yuks can put out living mines to protect their planets, we ought to be able to harness some of our own lifeforms in a similar way. Let's make use of the same weapon ourselves."

"Which lifeform do you propose to use?"

"I think the human brain is the most agile of known living forms. Do you know of any better?"

"But no human being can withstand outspace travel. A human pilot would be dead of heart failure long before the ship got anywhere near Proxima."

"But we don't need the whole body," Kramer said. "We need only the brain."

"What?"

"The problem is to find a person of high intelligence who would contribute, in the same manner that eyes and arms are volunteered."

"But a brain..."

"Technically it could be done. Brains have been transferred several times, when body destruction made it necessary. Of course, to a spaceship, to a heavy outspace cruiser, instead of an artificial body, that's new."

The room was silent.

"It's quite an idea," Gross said slowly. His heavy square face twisted. "But even supposing it might work, the big question is *whose* brain?"

***

It was all very confusing, the reasons for the war, the nature of the enemy. The Yucconae had been contacted on one of the outlying planets of Proxima Centauri. At the approach of the Terran ship, a host of dark slim pencils had lifted abruptly and shot off into the distance. The first real encounter came between three of the yuk pencils and a single exploration ship from Terra. No Terrans survived. After that it was all out war with no holds barred.

Both sides feverishly constructed defense rings around their systems. Of the two, the Yucconae belt was the better. The ring around Proxima was a living ring, superior to anything Terra could throw against it. The standard equipment by which

Terran ships were guided in outspace, the Johnson Control, was not adequate. Something more was needed. Automatic relays were not good enough.

"Not good at all," Kramer thought to himself as he stood looking down the hillside at the work going on below him. A warm wind blew along the hill, rustling the weeds and grass. At the bottom, in the valley, the mechanics had almost finished. The last elements of the reflex system had been removed from the ship and crated up.

All that was needed now was the new core, the new central key that would take the place of the mechanical system. A human brain, the brain of an intelligent, wary human being. But would the human being part with it? That was the problem.

Kramer turned. Two people were approaching him along the road, a man and a woman. The man was Gross, expressionless, heavyset, walking with dignity. The woman was—he stared in surprise and growing annoyance. It was Dolores, his wife. Since they'd separated he had seen little of her.

"Kramer," Gross said. "Look who I ran into. Come back down with us. We're going into town."

"Hello, Phil," Dolores said. "Well, aren't you glad to see me?"

He nodded. "How have you been? You're looking fine." She was still pretty and slender in her uniform, the blue-gray of Internal Security, Gross's organization.

"Thanks." She smiled. "You seem to be doing all right too. Commander Gross tells me that you're responsible for this project, Operation Head, as they call it. Whose head have you decided on?"

"That's the problem." Kramer lit a cigarette. "This ship is to be equipped with a human brain instead of the Johnson system. We've constructed special draining baths for the brain, electronic relays to catch the impulses and magnify them, a continual feeding duct that supplies the living cells with everything they need. But—"

"But we still haven't got the brain itself," Gross finished. They began to walk back toward the car. "If we can get that, we'll be ready for the tests."

"Will the brain remain alive?" Dolores asked. "Is it actually going to live as part of the ship?"

"It will be alive, but not conscious. Very little life is actually conscious. Animals, trees, insects are quick in their responses, but they aren't conscious. In this process of ours, the individual personality—the ego—will cease. We only need the response ability, nothing more."

Dolores shuddered. "How terrible!"

"In time of war everything must be tried," Kramer said absently. "If one life sacrificed will end the war, it's worth it. This ship might get through. A couple more like it, and there wouldn't be any more war."

They got into the car. As they drove down the road, Gross said, "Have you thought of anyone yet?"

Kramer shook his head. "That's out of my line."

"What do you mean?"

"I'm an engineer. It's not in my department."

"But all this was your idea."

"My work ends there."

Gross was staring at him oddly. Kramer shifted uneasily.

"Then who is supposed to do it?" Gross said. "I can have my organization prepare examinations of various kinds, to determine fitness, that kind of thing."

"Listen, Phil," Dolores said suddenly.

"What?"

She turned toward him. "I have an idea. Do you remember that professor we had in college. Michael Thomas?"

Kramer nodded.

"I wonder if he's still alive." Dolores frowned. "If he is, he must be awfully old."

"Why, Dolores?" Gross asked.

"Perhaps an old person who didn't have much time left, but whose mind was still clear and sharp."

"Professor Thomas." Kramer rubbed his jaw. "He certainly was a wise old duck. But could he still be alive? He must have been seventy, then."

"We could find that out," Gross said. "I could make a routine check."

"What do you think?" Dolores said. "If any human mind could outwit those creatures—"

"I don't like the idea," Kramer said. In his mind an image had appeared, the image of an old man sitting behind a desk, his bright gentle eyes moving about the classroom. The old man leaning forward, a thin hand raised—

"Keep him out of this," Kramer said.

"What's wrong?" Gross looked at him curiously.

"It's because *I* suggested it," Dolores said.

"No." Kramer shook his head. "It's not that. I didn't expect anything like this, somebody I knew, a man I studied under. I remember him very clearly. He was a very distinct personality."

"Good," Gross said. "He sounds fine."

"We can't do it. We're asking his death!"

"This is war," Gross said, "and war doesn't wait on the needs of the individual. You said that yourself. Surely he'll volunteer. We can keep it on that basis."

"He may already be dead," Dolores murmured.

"We'll find that out," Gross said speeding up the car. They drove the rest of the way in silence.

***

For a long time the two of them stood studying the small wood house, overgrown with ivy, set back on the lot behind an enormous oak. The little town was silent and sleepy. Once in a while a car moved slowly along the distant highway, but that was all.

"This is the place," Gross said to Kramer. He folded his arms. "Quite a quaint little house."

Kramer said nothing. The two Security Agents behind them were expressionless.

Gross started toward the gate. "Let's go. According to the check he's still alive, but very sick. His mind is agile, however. That seems to be certain. It's said he doesn't leave the house. A woman takes care of his needs. He's very frail."

They went down the stone walk and up onto the porch. Gross rang the bell. They waited. After a time they heard slow footsteps. The door opened. An elderly woman in a shapeless wrapper studied them impassively.

"Security," Gross said, showing his card. "We wish to see Professor Thomas."

"Why?"

"Government business." He glanced at Kramer.

Kramer stepped forward. "I was a pupil of the Professor's," he said. "I'm sure he won't mind seeing us."

The woman hesitated uncertainly. Gross stepped into the doorway. "All right, mother. This is wartime. We can't stand out here."

The two Security Agents followed him, and Kramer came reluctantly behind, closing the door. Gross stalked down the hall until he came to an open door. He stopped, looking in. Kramer could see the white corner of a bed, a wooden post and the edge of a dresser.

He joined Gross.

In the dark room a withered old man lay, propped up on endless pillows. At first it seemed as if he were asleep—there was no motion or sign of life. But after a time Kramer saw, with a faint shock, that the old man was watching them intently, his eyes fixed on them, unmoving, unwinking.

"Professor Thomas?" Gross said. "I'm Commander Gross of Security. This man with me is perhaps known to you."

The faded eyes fixed on Kramer.

"I know him. Philip Kramer…You've grown heavier, boy." The voice was feeble, the rustle of dry ashes. "Is it true you're married now?"

"Yes. I married Dolores French. You remember her." Kramer came toward the bed. "But we're separated. It didn't work out very well. Our careers—"

"What we came here about, Professor," Gross began, but Kramer cut him off with an impatient wave.

"Let me talk. Can't you and your men get out of here long enough to let me talk to him?"

Gross swallowed. "All right, Kramer." He nodded to the two men. The three of them left the room, going out into the hall and closing the door after them.

The old man in the bed watched Kramer silently. "I don't think much of him," he said at last. "I've seen his type before. What's he want?"

"Nothing. He just came along. Can I sit down?" Kramer found a stiff, upright chair beside the bed. "If I'm bothering you—"

"No. I'm glad to see you again, Philip. After so long. I'm sorry your marriage didn't work out."

"How have you been?"

"I've been very ill. I'm afraid that my moment on the world's stage has almost ended." The ancient eyes studied the younger man reflectively. "You look as if you have been doing well. Like everyone else I thought highly of. You've gone to the top in this society."

Kramer smiled. Then he became serious. "Professor, there's a project we're working on that I want to talk to you about. It's the first ray of hope we've had in this whole war. If it works, we may be able to crack the yuk defenses, get some ships into their system. If we can do that, the war might be brought to an end."

"Go on. Tell me about it, if you wish."

"It's a long shot, this project. It may not work at all, but we have to give it a try."

"It's obvious that you came here because of it," Professor Thomas murmured. "I'm becoming curious. Go on."

***

After Kramer finished the old man lay back in the bed without speaking. At last he sighed.

"I understand. A human mind, taken out of a human body." He sat up a little, looking at Kramer. "I suppose you're thinking of me."

Kramer said nothing.

"Before I make my decision, I want to see the papers on this, the theory and outline of construction. I'm not sure I like it—for reasons of my own, I mean. But I want to look at the material. If you'll do that—"

"Certainly." Kramer stood up and went to the door. Gross and the two Security Agents were standing outside, waiting tensely. "Gross, come inside."

They filed into the room.

"Give the Professor the papers," Kramer said. "He wants to study them before deciding."

Gross brought the file out of his coat pocket, a manila envelope. He handed it to the old man on the bed. "Here it is, Professor. You're welcome to examine it. Will you give us your answer as soon as possible? We're very anxious to begin, of course."

"I'll give you my answer when I've decided." He took the envelope with a thin, trembling hand. "My decision depends on what I find out from these papers. If I don't like what I find, then I will not become involved with this work in any shape or form." He opened the envelope with shaking hands. "I'm looking for one thing."

"What is it?" Gross said.

"That's my affair. Leave me a number by which I can reach you when I've decided."

Silently, Gross put his card down on the dresser. As they went out Professor Thomas was already reading the first of the papers, the outline of the theory.

***

Kramer sat across from Dale Winter, his second in line. "What then?" Winter said.

"He's going to contact us." Kramer scratched with a drawing pen on some paper. "I don't know what to think."

"What do you mean?" Winter's good-natured face was puzzled.

"Look." Kramer stood up, pacing back and forth, his hands in his uniform pockets. "He was my teacher in college. I respected him as a man, as well as a teacher. He was more than a voice, a talking book. He was a person, a calm, kindly person I could look up to. I always wanted to be like him someday. Now look at me."

"So?"

"Look at what I'm asking. I'm asking for his life, as if he were some kind of laboratory animal kept around in a cage, not a man, a teacher at all."

"Do you think he'll do it?"

"I don't know." Kramer went to the window. He stood looking out. "In a way, I hope not."

"But if he doesn't?"

"Then we'll have to find somebody else. I know. There would be somebody else. Why did Dolores have to—"

The vidphone rang. Kramer pressed the button.

"This is Gross." The heavy features formed. "The old man called me. Professor Thomas."

"What did he say?" He knew. He could tell already by the sound of Gross's voice.

"He said he'd do it. I was a little surprised myself, but apparently he means it. We've already made arrangements for his admission to the hospital. His lawyer is drawing up the statement of liability."

Kramer only half heard. He nodded wearily. "All right. I'm glad. I suppose we can go ahead, then."

"You don't sound very glad."

"I wonder why he decided to go ahead with it."

"He was very certain about it." Gross sounded pleased. "He called me quite early. I was still in bed. You know, this calls for a celebration."

"Sure," Kramer said. "It sure does."

***

Toward the middle of August the project neared completion. They stood outside in the hot autumn heat, looking up at the sleek metal sides of the ship.

Gross thumped the metal with his hand. "Well, it won't be long. We can begin the test any time."

"Tell us more about this," an officer in gold braid said. "It's such an unusual concept."

"Is there really a human brain inside the ship?" a dignitary asked, a small man in a rumpled suit. "And the brain is actually alive?"

"Gentlemen, this ship is guided by a living brain instead of the usual Johnson relay-control system. But the brain is not conscious. It will function by reflex only. The practical difference between it and the Johnson system is this: a human brain is far more intricate than any manmade structure, and its ability to adapt itself to a situation, to respond to danger, is far beyond anything that could be artificially built."

Gross paused, cocking his ear. The turbines of the ship were beginning to rumble, shaking the ground under them with a deep vibration. Kramer was standing a short distance away from the others, his arms folded, watching silently. At the sound of the turbines he walked quickly around the ship to the other side. A few workmen were clearing away the last of the waste, the scraps of wiring and scaffolding. They glanced up at him and went on hurriedly with their work. Kramer mounted the ramp and entered the control cabin of the ship. Winter was sitting at the controls with a Pilot from space-transport.

"How's it look?" Kramer asked.

"All right." Winter got up. "He tells me that it would be best to take off manually. The robot controls—" Winter hesitated. "I mean, the built-in controls can take over later on in space."

"That's right," the Pilot said. "It's customary with the Johnson system, and so in this case we should—"

"Can you tell anything yet?" Kramer asked.

"No," the Pilot said slowly. "I don't think so. I've been going over everything. It seems to be in good order. There's only one thing I wanted to ask you about." He put his hand on the control board. "There are some changes here I don't understand."

"Changes?"

"Alterations from the original design. I wonder what the purpose is."

Kramer took a set of the plans from his coat. "Let me look." He turned the pages over. The Pilot watched carefully over his shoulder.

"The changes aren't indicated on your copy," the Pilot said. "I wonder." He stopped. Commander Gross had entered the control cabin.

"Gross, who authorized alterations?" Kramer said. "Some of the wiring has been changed."

"Why, your old friend." Gross signaled to the field tower through the window.

"My old friend?"

"The Professor. He took quite an active interest." Gross turned to the Pilot. "Let's get going. We have to take this out past gravity for the test, they tell me. Well, perhaps it's for the best. Are you ready?"

"Sure." The Pilot sat down and moved some of the controls around. "Anytime."

"Go ahead then," Gross said.

"The Professor—" Kramer began, but at that moment there was a tremendous roar and the ship leaped under him. He grasped one of the wall-holds and hung on as best he could. The cabin was filling with a steady throbbing, the raging of the jet turbines underneath them.

The ship leaped. Kramer closed his eyes and held his breath. They were moving out into space, gaining speed each moment.

"Well, what do you think?" Winter said nervously. "Is it time yet?"

"A little longer," Kramer said. He was sitting on the floor of the cabin, down by the control wiring. He had removed the metal covering plate, exposing the complicated maze of relay wiring. He was studying it, comparing it to the wiring diagrams.

"What's the matter?" Gross said.

"These changes. I can't figure out what they're for. The only pattern I can make out is that for some reason—"

"Let me look," the Pilot said. He squatted down beside Kramer. "You were saying?"

"See this lead here? Originally it was switch controlled. It closed and opened automatically, according to temperature change. Now it's wired so that the central control system operates it. The same with the others. A lot of this was still mechanical, worked by pressure, temperature, stress. Now it's under the central master."

"The brain?" Gross said. "You mean it's been altered so that the brain manipulates it?"

Kramer nodded. "Maybe Professor Thomas felt that no mechanical relays could be trusted. Maybe he thought that things would be happening too fast. But some of these could close in a split second. The brake rockets could go on as quickly as—"

"Hey," Winter said from the control seat. "We're getting near the moon stations. What'll I do?"

They looked out the port. The corroded surface of the moon gleamed up at them, a corrupt and sickening sight. They were moving swiftly toward it.

"I'll take it," the Pilot said. He eased Winter out of the way and strapped himself in place. The ship began to move away from the moon as he manipulated the controls. Down below them they could see the observation stations dotting the surface, and the tiny squares that were the openings of the underground factories and hangars. A red blinker winked up at them and the Pilot's fingers moved on the board in answer.

"We're past the moon," the Pilot said after a time. The moon had fallen behind them, the ship was heading into outer space. "Well, we can go ahead with it."

Kramer did not answer.

"Mr. Kramer, we can go ahead any time."

Kramer started. "Sorry, I was thinking. All right, thanks." He frowned, deep in thought.

"What is it?" Gross asked.

"The wiring changes. Did you understand the reason for them when you gave the okay to the workmen?"

Gross flushed. "You know I know nothing about technical material. I'm in Security."

"Then you should have consulted me."

"What does it matter?" Gross grinned wryly. "We're going to have to start putting our faith in the old man sooner or later."

The Pilot stepped back from the board. His face was pale and set. "Well, it's done," he said. "That's it."

"What's done?" Kramer said.

"We're on automatic. The brain. I turned the board over to it—to him, I mean. The Old Man." The Pilot lit a cigarette and puffed nervously. "Let's keep our fingers crossed."

The ship was coasting evenly in the hands of its invisible pilot. Far down inside the ship, carefully armored and protected, a soft human brain lay in a tank of liquid, a thousand minute electric charges playing over its surface. As the charges rose they were picked up and amplified, fed into relay systems, advanced, carried on through the entire ship—

Gross wiped his forehead nervously. "So *he* is running it now. I hope he knows what he's doing."

Kramer nodded enigmatically. "I think he does."

"What do you mean?"

"Nothing." Kramer walked to the port. "I see we're still moving in a straight line." He picked up the microphone. "We can instruct the brain orally, through this." He blew against the microphone experimentally.

"Go on," Winter said.

"Bring the ship around half-right," Kramer said. "Decrease speed."

They waited. Time passed. Gross looked at Kramer. "No change. Nothing."

"Wait."

Slowly, the ship was beginning to turn. The turbines missed, reducing their steady beat. The ship was taking up its new course, adjusting itself. Nearby some space debris rushed past, incinerating in the blasts of the turbine jets.

"So far so good," Gross said.

They began to breathe more easily. The invisible pilot had taken control smoothly, calmly. The ship was in good hands. Kramer spoke a few more words into the microphone, and they swung again. Now they were moving back the way they had come, toward the moon.

"Let's see what he does when we enter the moon's pull," Kramer said. "He was a good mathematician, the old man. He could handle any kind of problem."

The ship veered, turning away from the moon. The great eaten-away globe fell behind them.

Gross breathed a sigh of relief. "That's that."

"One more thing." Kramer picked up the microphone. "Return to the moon and land the ship at the first space field," he said into it.

"Good Lord," Winter murmured. "Why are you—"

"Be quiet." Kramer stood, listening. The turbines gasped and roared as the ship swung full around, gaining speed. They were moving back, back toward the moon again. The ship dipped down, heading toward the great globe below.

"We're going a little fast," the Pilot said. "I don't see how he can put down at this velocity."

The port filled up as the globe swelled rapidly. The Pilot hurried toward the board, reaching for the controls. All at once the ship jerked. The nose lifted and the ship shot out into space, away from the moon, turning at an oblique angle. The men were thrown to the floor by the sudden change in course. They got to their feet again, speechless, staring at each other.

The Pilot gazed down at the board. "It wasn't me! I didn't touch a thing. I didn't even get to it."

The ship was gaining speed each moment. Kramer hesitated. "Maybe you better switch it back to manual."

The Pilot closed the switch. He took hold of the steering controls and moved them experimentally. "Nothing." He turned around. "Nothing. It doesn't respond."

No one spoke.

"You can see what has happened," Kramer said calmly. "The old man won't let go of it now that he has it. I was afraid of this when I saw the wiring changes. Everything in this ship is centrally controlled, even the cooling system, the hatches, the garbage release. We're helpless."

"Nonsense." Gross strode to the board. He took hold of the wheel and turned it. The ship continued on its course, moving away from the moon, leaving it behind.

"Release!" Kramer said into the microphone. "Let go of the controls! We'll take it back. Release."

"No good," the Pilot said. "Nothing." He spun the useless wheel. "It's dead, completely dead."

"And we're still heading out," Winter said, grinning foolishly. "We'll be going through the first-line defense belt in a few minutes. If they don't shoot us down."

"We better radio back." The Pilot clicked the radio to *send.* "I'll contact the main bases, one of the observation stations."

"Better get the defense belt, at the speed we're going. We'll be into it in a minute."

"And after that," Kramer said, "we'll be in outer space. He's moving us toward outspace velocity. Is this ship equipped with baths?"

"Baths?" Gross said.

"The sleep tanks. For space-drive. We may need them if we go much faster."

"But good god, where are we going?" Gross said. "Where—where's he taking us?"

The Pilot obtained contact. "This is Dwight, on ship," he said. "We're entering the defense zone at high velocity. Don't fire on us."

"Turn back," the impersonal voice came through the speaker. "You're not allowed in the defense zone."

"We can't. We've lost control."

"Lost control?"

"This is an experimental ship."

Gross took the radio. "This is Commander Gross, Security. We're being carried into outer space. There's nothing we can do. Is there any way that we can be removed from this ship?"

A hesitation. "We have some fast pursuit ships that could pick you up if you wanted to jump. The chances are good they'd find you. Do you have space flares?"

"We do," the Pilot said. "Let's try it."

"Abandon ship?" Kramer said. "If we leave now we'll never see it again."

"What else can we do? We're gaining speed all the time. Do you propose that we stay here?"

"No." Kramer shook his head. "Damn it, there ought to be a better solution."

"Could you contact *him*?" Winter asked. "The Old Man? Try to reason with him?"

"It's worth a chance," Gross said. "Try it."

"All right." Kramer took the microphone. He paused a moment. "Listen! Can you hear me? This is Phil Kramer. Can you hear me, Professor. Can you hear me? I want you to release the controls."

There was silence.

"This is Kramer, Professor. Can you hear me? Do you remember who I am? Do you understand who this is?"

Above the control panel the wall speaker made a sound, a sputtering static. They looked up.

"Can you hear me, Professor. This is Philip Kramer. I want you to give the ship back to us. If you can hear me, release the controls! Let go, Professor. Let go!"

Static. A rushing sound, like the wind. They gazed at each other. There was silence for a moment.

"It's a waste of time," Gross said.

"No—listen!"

The sputter came again. Then, mixed with the sputter, almost lost in it, a voice came, toneless, without inflection, a mechanical, lifeless voice from the metal speaker in the wall above their heads.

"…Is it you, Philip? I can't make you out. Darkness…Who's there? With you…"

"It's me, Kramer." His fingers tightened against the microphone handle. "You must release the controls, Professor. We have to get back to Terra. You must."

Silence. Then the faint, faltering voice came again, a little stronger than before. "Kramer. Everything so strange. I was right, though. Consciousness result of thinking. Necessary result. Cognito ergo sum. Retain conceptual ability. Can you hear me?"

"Yes, Professor."

"I altered the wiring. Control. I was fairly certain…I wonder if I can do it. Try…"

Suddenly the air conditioning snapped into operation. It snapped abruptly off again. Down the corridor a door slammed. Something thudded. The men stood listening. Sounds came from all sides of them, switches shutting, opening. The lights blinked off; they were in darkness. The lights came back on, and at the same time the heating coils dimmed and faded.

"Good god!" Winter said.

Water poured down on them, the emergency firefighting system. There was a screaming rush of air. One of the escape hatches had slid back, and the air was roaring frantically out into space.

The hatch banged closed. The ship subsided into silence. The heating coils glowed into life. As suddenly as it had begun, the weird exhibition ceased.

"I can do—everything," the dry, toneless voice came from the wall speaker. "It is all controlled. Kramer, I wish to talk to you. I've been—been thinking. I haven't seen you in many years. A lot to discuss. You've changed, boy. We have much to discuss. Your wife—"

The Pilot grabbed Kramer's arm. "There's a ship standing off our bow. Look."

They ran to the port. A slender pale craft was moving along with them, keeping pace with them. It was signal-blinking.

"A Terran pursuit ship," the Pilot said. "Let's jump. They'll pick us up. Suits!"

He ran to a supply cupboard and turned the handle. The door opened and he pulled the suits out onto the floor.

"Hurry," Gross said. A panic seized them. They dressed frantically, pulling the heavy garments over them. Winter staggered to the escape hatch and stood by it, waiting for the others. They joined him one by one.

"Let's go!" Gross said. "Open the hatch."

Winter tugged at the hatch. "Help me."

They grabbed hold, tugging together. Nothing happened. The hatch refused to budge.

"Get a crowbar," the Pilot said.

"Hasn't anyone got a blaster?" Gross looked frantically around. "Damn it, blast it open!"

"Pull," Kramer grated. "Pull together."

"Are you at the hatch?" the toneless voice came, drifting and eddying through the corridors of the ship. They looked up, staring around them. "I sense something nearby, outside. A ship?

You are leaving, all of you? Kramer, you are leaving too? Very unfortunate. I had hoped we could talk. Perhaps at some other time you might be induced to remain."

"Open the hatch!" Kramer said, staring up at the impersonal walls of the ship. "For god's sake, open it!"

There was silence, an endless pause. Then, very slowly, the hatch slid back. The air screamed out, rushing past them into space.

One by one they leaped, one after the other, propelled away by the repulsive material of the suits. A few minutes later they were being hauled aboard the pursuit ship. As the last one of them was lifted through the port, their own ship pointed itself suddenly upward and shot off at tremendous speed. It disappeared.

Kramer removed his helmet, gasping. Two sailors held onto him and began to wrap him in blankets. Gross sipped a mug of coffee, shivering.

"It's gone," Kramer murmured.

"I'll have an alarm sent out," Gross said.

"What's happened to your ship?" a sailor asked curiously. "It sure took off in a hurry. Who's on it?"

"We'll have to have it destroyed," Gross went on, his face grim. "It's got to be destroyed. There's no telling what it—what *he* has in mind." Gross sat down weakly on a metal bench. "What a close call for us. We were so damn trusting."

"What could he be planning," Kramer said, half to himself. "It doesn't make sense. I don't get it."

As the ship sped back toward the moon base they sat around the table in the dining room, sipping hot coffee and thinking, not saying very much.

"Look here," Gross said at last. "What kind of man was Professor Thomas? What do you remember about him?"

Kramer put his coffee mug down. "It was ten years ago. I don't remember much. It's vague."

He let his mind run back over the years. He and Dolores had been at Hunt College together, in physics and the life sciences. The college was small and set back away from the momentum of modern life. He had gone there because it was his hometown and his father had gone there before him.

Professor Thomas had been at the college a long time, as long as anyone could remember. He was a strange old man, keeping to himself most of the time. There were many things that he disapproved of, but he seldom said what they were.

"Do you recall anything that might help us?" Gross asked. "Anything that would give us a clue as to what he might have in mind?"

Kramer nodded slowly. "I remember one thing…"

One day he and the Professor had been sitting together in the school chapel, talking leisurely.

"Well, you'll be out of school soon," the Professor had said. "What are you going to do?"

"Do? Work at one of the Government Research Projects, I suppose."

"And eventually? What's your ultimate goal?"

Kramer had smiled. "The question is unscientific. It presupposes such things as ultimate ends."

"Suppose instead along these lines then: what if there were no war and no Government Research Projects? What would you do then?"

"I don't know. But how can I imagine a hypothetical situation like that? There's been war as long as I can remember. We're geared for war. I don't know what I'd do. I suppose I'd adjust, get used to it."

The Professor had stared at him. "Oh, you do think you'd get accustomed to it, eh? Well, I'm glad of that. And you think you could find something to do?"

Gross listened intently. "What do you infer from this, Kramer?"

"Not much. Except that he was against war."

"We're all against war," Gross pointed out.

"True. But he was withdrawn, set apart. He lived very simply, cooking his own meals. His wife died many years ago. He was born in Europe, in Italy. He changed his name when he came to the United States. He used to read Dante and Milton. He even had a Bible."

"Very anachronistic, don't you think?"

"Yes, he lived quite a lot in the past. He found an old phonograph and records, and he listened to the old music. You saw his house, how old-fashioned it was."

"Did he have a file?" Winter asked Gross.

"With Security? No, none at all. As far as we could tell he never engaged in political work, never joined anything or even seemed to have strong political convictions."

"No," Kramer, agreed. "About all he ever did was walk through the hills. He liked nature."

"Nature can be of great use to a scientist," Gross said. "There wouldn't be any science without it."

"Kramer, what do you think his plan is, taking control of the ship and disappearing?" Winter said.

"Maybe the transfer made him insane," the Pilot said. "Maybe there's no plan, nothing rational at all."

"But he had the ship rewired, and he had made sure that he would retain consciousness and memory before he even agreed to the operation. He must have had something planned from the start. But what?"

"Perhaps he just wanted to stay alive longer," Kramer said. "He was old and about to die. Or—"

"Or what?"

"Nothing." Kramer stood up. "I think as soon as we get to the moon base I'll make a vidcall to Earth. I want to talk to somebody about this."

"Who's that?" Gross asked.

"Dolores. Maybe she remembers something."

"That's a good idea," Gross said.

***

"Where are you calling from?" Dolores asked when he succeeded in reaching her.

"From the moon base."

"All kinds of rumors are running around. Why didn't the ship come back? What happened?"

"I'm afraid he ran off with it."

"He?"

"The Old Man. Professor Thomas." Kramer explained what had happened.

Dolores listened intently. "How strange. And you think he planned it all in advance, from the start?"

"I'm certain. He asked for the plans of construction and the theoretical diagrams at once."

"But why? What for?"

"I don't know. Look, Dolores. What do you remember about him? Is there anything that might give a clue to all this?"

"Like what?"

"I don't know. That's the trouble."

On the vidscreen Dolores knitted her brow. "I remember he raised chickens in his back yard, and once he had a goat." She smiled. "Do you remember the day the goat got loose and wandered down the main street of town? Nobody could figure out where it came from."

"Anything else?"

"No." He watched her struggling, trying to remember. "He wanted to have a farm sometime, I know."

"All right. Thanks." Kramer touched the switch. "When I get back to Terra maybe I'll stop and see you."

"Let me know how it works out."

He cut the line and the picture dimmed and faded. He walked slowly back to where Gross and some officers of the Military were sitting at a chart table, talking.

"Any luck?" Gross said, looking up.

"No. All she remembers is that he kept a goat."

"Come over and look at this detail chart." Gross motioned him around to his side. "Watch!"

Kramer saw the record tabs moving furiously, the little white dots racing back and forth.

"What's happening?" he asked.

"A squadron outside the defense zone has finally managed to contact the ship. They're maneuvering now for position. Watch."

The white counters were forming a barrel formation around a black dot that was moving steadily across the board, away from the central position. As they watched, the white dots constricted around it.

"They're ready to open fire," a technician at the board said. "Commander, what shall we tell them to do?"

Gross hesitated. "I hate to be the one who makes the decision. When it comes right down to it—"

"It's not just a ship," Kramer said. "It's a man, a living person. A human being is up there, moving through space. I wish we knew what—"

"But the order has to be given. We can't take any chances. Suppose he went over to them, to the yuks."

Kramer's jaw dropped. "My god, he wouldn't do that."

"Are you sure? Do you know what he'll do?"

"He wouldn't do that."

Gross turned to the technician. "Tell them to go ahead."

"I'm sorry, sir, but now the ship has gotten away. Look down at the board."

Gross stared down, Kramer over his shoulder. The black dot had slipped through the white dots and had moved off at an abrupt angle. The white dots were broken up, dispersing in confusion.

"He's an unusual strategist," one of the officers said. He traced the line. "It's an ancient maneuver, an old Prussian device, but it worked."

The white dots were turning back. "Too many yuk ships out that far," Gross said. "Well, that's what you get when you don't act quickly." He looked up coldly at Kramer. "We should have done it when we had him. Look at him go!" He jabbed a finger at the rapidly moving black dot. The dot came to the edge of the board and stopped. It had reached the limit of the chartered area. "See?"

"Now what?" Kramer thought, watching. So the Old Man had escaped the cruisers and gotten away. He was alert, all right. There was nothing wrong with his mind. Or with his ability to control his new body.

Body—the ship was a new body for him. He had traded in the old, dying body, withered and frail, for this hulking frame of metal and plastic, turbines and rocket jets. He was strong now. Strong and big. The new body was more powerful than a thousand human bodies. But how long would it last him? The average life of a cruiser was only ten years. With careful handling he might get twenty out of it, before some essential part failed and there was no way to replace it.

And then, what then? What would he do when something failed and there was no one to fix it for him? That would be the end. Someplace, far out in the cold darkness of space, the ship would slow down, silent and lifeless, to exhaust its last heat into the eternal timelessness of outer space. Or perhaps it would crash on some barren asteroid, burst into a million fragments.

It was only a question of time.

"Your wife didn't remember anything?" Gross said.

"I told you. Only that he kept a goat once."

"A hell of a lot of help that is."

Kramer shrugged. "It's not my fault."

"I wonder if we'll ever see him again." Gross stared down at the indicator dot, still hanging at the edge of the board. "I wonder if he'll ever move back this way."

"I wonder too," Kramer said.

That night Kramer lay in bed, tossing from side to side, unable to sleep. The moon gravity, even artificially increased, was unfamiliar to him and it made him uncomfortable. A thousand thoughts wandered loose in his head as he lay, fully awake.

What did it all mean? What was the Professor's plan? Maybe they would never know. Maybe the ship was gone for good. The Old Man had left forever, shooting into outer space. They might never find out why he had done it, what purpose—if any—had been in his mind.

Kramer sat up in bed. He turned on the light and lit a cigarette. His quarters were small, a metal lined bunk room, part of the moon station base.

The Old Man had wanted to talk to him. He had wanted to discuss things, hold a conversation, but in the hysteria and confusion all they had been able to think of was getting away. The ship was rushing off with them, carrying them into outer space. Kramer set his jaw. Could they be blamed for jumping? They had no idea where they were being taken, or why. They were helpless, caught in their own ship, and the pursuit ship standing by waiting to pick them up was their only chance. Another half hour and it would have been too late.

But what had the Old Man wanted to say? What had he intended to tell him in those first confusing moments when the ship around them had come alive, each metal strut and wire suddenly animate, the body of a living creature, a vast metal organism?

It was weird, unnerving. He could not forget it, even now. He looked around the small room uneasily. What did it signify, the coming to life of metal and plastic? All at once they had found themselves inside a *living* creature, in its stomach, like Jonah inside the whale.

It had been alive, and it had talked to them, talked calmly and rationally, as it rushed them off faster and faster into outer space. The wall speaker and circuit had become the vocal cords and mouth, the wiring the spinal cord and nerves, the hatches and relays and circuit breakers the muscles.

They had been helpless, completely helpless. The ship had, in a brief second, stolen their power away from them and left them defenseless, practically at its mercy. It was not right; it made him uneasy. All his life he had controlled machines, bent nature and the forces of nature to man and man's needs. The human race had slowly evolved until it was in a position to operate things, run them as it saw fit. Now all at once it had been plunged back down the ladder again, prostrate before a Power against which they were children.

Kramer got out of bed. He put on his bathrobe and began to search for a cigarette. While he was searching, the vidphone rang.

He snapped the vidphone on.

"Yes?"

The face of the immediate monitor appeared. "A call from Terra, Mr. Kramer. An emergency call."

"Emergency call? For me? Put it through." Kramer came awake, brushing his hair back out of his eyes. Alarm plucked at him.

From the speaker a strange voice came. "Philip Kramer? Is this Kramer?"

"Yes. Go on."

"This is General Hospital, New York City, Terra. Mr. Kramer, your wife is here. She has been critically injured in an accident. Your name was given to us to call. Is it possible for you to—"

"How badly?" Kramer gripped the vidphone stand. "Is it serious?"

"Yes, it's serious, Mr. Kramer. Are you able to come here? The quicker you can come the better."

"Yes." Kramer nodded. "I'll come. Thanks."

The screen died as the connection was broken. Kramer waited a moment. Then he tapped the button. The screen relit again. "Yes, sir," the monitor said.

"Can I get a ship to Terra at once? It's an emergency. My wife—"

"There's no ship leaving the moon for eight hours. You'll have to wait until the next period."

"Isn't there anything I can do?"

"We can broadcast a general request to all ships passing through this area. Sometimes cruisers pass by here returning to Terra for repairs."

"Will you broadcast that for me? I'll come down to the field."

"Yes sir. But there may be no ship in the area for a while. It's a gamble." The screen died.

Kramer dressed quickly. He put on his coat and hurried to the lift. A moment later he was running across the general receiving lobby, past the rows of vacant desks and conference tables. At the door the sentries stepped aside, and he went outside onto the great concrete steps.

The face of the moon was in shadow. Below him the field stretched out in total darkness, a black void, endless, without form. He made his way carefully down the steps and along the ramp along the side of the field, to the control tower. A faint row of red lights showed him the way.

Two soldiers challenged him at the foot of the tower, standing in the shadows, their guns ready.

"Kramer?"

"Yes." A light was flashed in his face.

"Your call has been sent out already."

"Any luck?" Kramer asked.

"There's a cruiser nearby that has made contact with us. It has an injured jet and is moving slowly back toward Terra, away from the line."

"Good." Kramer nodded, a flood of relief rushing through him. He lit a cigarette and gave one to each of the soldiers. The soldiers lit up.

"Sir," one of them asked, "is it true about the experimental ship?"

"What do you mean?"

"It came to life and ran off?"

"No, not exactly," Kramer said. "It had a new type of control system instead of the Johnson units. It wasn't properly tested."

"But sir, one of the cruisers that was there got up close to it, and a buddy of mine says this ship acted funny. He never saw anything like it. It was like when he was fishing once on Terra, in Washington State, fishing for bass. The fish were smart, going this way and that.

"Here's your cruiser," the other soldier said. "Look!"

An enormous vague shape was setting slowly down onto the field. They could make nothing out but its row of tiny green blinkers. Kramer stared at the shape.

"Better hurry, sir," the soldiers said. "They don't stick around here very long."

"Thanks." Kramer loped across the field, toward the black shape that rose up above him, extended across the width of the field. The ramp was down from the side of the cruiser, and he caught hold of it. The ramp rose, and a moment later Kramer was inside the hold of the ship. The hatch slid shut behind him.

As he made his way up the stairs to the main deck, the turbines roared up from the moon, out into space.

Kramer opened the door to the main deck. He stopped suddenly, staring around him in surprise. There was nobody in sight. The ship was deserted.

"Good god," he said. Realization swept over him, numbing him. He sat down on a bench, his head swimming. "Good god."

The ship roared out into space leaving the moon and Terra farther behind each moment.

And there was nothing he could do.

"So it was you who put the call through," he said at last. "It was you who called me on the vidphone, not any hospital on Terra. It was all part of the plan." He looked up and around him. "And Dolores is really—"

"Your wife is fine," the wall speaker above him said tonelessly. "It was a fraud. I am sorry to trick you that way, Philip, but it was all I could think of. Another day and you would have been back on Terra. I don't want to remain in this area any longer than necessary. They have been so certain of finding me out in deep space that I have been able to stay here without too much danger. But even the purloined letter was found eventually."

Kramer smoked his cigarette nervously. "What are you going to do? Where are we going?"

"First, I want to talk to you. I have many things to discuss. I was very disappointed when you left me along with the others. I had hoped that you would remain." The dry voice chuckled. "Remember how we used to talk in the old days, you and I? That was a long time ago."

The ship was gaining speed. It plunged through space at tremendous speed, rushing through the last of the defense zone and out beyond. A rush of nausea made Kramer bend over for a moment.

When he straightened up the voice from the wall went on, "I'm sorry to step it up so quickly, but we are still in danger. Another few moments and we'll be free."

"How about yuk ships? Aren't they out here?"

"I've already slipped away from several of them. They're quite curious about me."

"Curious?"

"They sense that I'm different, more like their own organic mines. They don't like it. I believe they will begin to withdraw from this area soon. Apparently they don't want to get involved with me. They're an odd race, Philip. I would have liked to study them closely, try to learn something about them. I'm of the opinion that they use no inert material. All their equipment and instruments are alive in some form or other. They don't construct or build at all. The idea of *making* is foreign to them. They utilize existing forms. Even their ships—"

"Where are we going?" Kramer said. "I want to know where you are taking me."

"Frankly, I'm not certain."

"You're not certain?"

"I haven't worked some details out. There are a few vague spots in my program still. But I think that in a short while I'll have them ironed out."

"What is your program?" Kramer said.

"It's really very simple. But don't you want to come into the control room and sit? The seats are much more comfortable than that metal bench."

Kramer went into the control room and sat down at the control board. Looking at the useless apparatus made him feel strange.

"What's the matter?" the speaker above the board rasped.

Kramer gestured helplessly. "I'm—powerless. I can't do anything. And I don't like it. Do you blame me?"

"No. No, I don't blame you. But you'll get your control back soon. Don't worry. This is only a temporary expedient, taking you off this way. It was something I didn't contemplate. I forgot that orders would be given out to shoot me on sight."

"It was Gross's idea."

"I don't doubt that. My conception, my plan, came to me as soon as you began to describe your project that day at my house. I saw at once that you were wrong. You people have no understanding of the mind at all. I realized that the transfer of a human brain from an organic body to a complex artificial spaceship would not involve the loss of the intellectualization faculty of the mind. When a man thinks, he *is*.

"When I realized that, I saw the possibility of an age-old dream becoming real. I was quite elderly when I first met you, Philip. Even then my lifespan had come pretty much to its end. I could look ahead to nothing but death, and with it the extinction of all my ideas. I had made no mark on the world, none at all. My students, one by one, passed from me into the world, to take up jobs in the great Research Project, the search for better and bigger weapons of war.

"The world has been fighting for a long time, first with itself, then with the Martians, then with these beings from Proxima Centauri whom we know nothing about. The human society has evolved war as a cultural institution, like the science of astronomy or mathematics. War is a part of our lives, a career, a respected vocation. Bright, alert young men and women move into it, putting their shoulders to the wheel as they did in the time of Nebuchadnezzar. It has always been so.

"But is it innate in mankind? I don't think so. No social custom is innate. There were many human groups that did not go to war. The Eskimos never grasped the idea at all, and the American Indians never took to it well.

"But these dissenters were wiped out, and a cultural pattern was established that became the standard for the whole planet. Now it has become ingrained in us.

"But if someplace along the line some other way of settling problems had arisen and taken hold, something different than the massing of men and material to—"

"What's your plan?" Kramer said. "I know the theory. It was part of one of your lectures."

"Yes, buried in a lecture on plant selection, as I recall. When you came to me with this proposition, I realized that perhaps my conception could be brought to life after all. If my theory were right that war is only a habit, not an instinct, a society built up apart from Terra with a minimum of cultural roots might develop differently. If it failed to absorb our outlook, if it could start out on another foot, it might not arrive at the same point to which we have come: a dead end with nothing but greater and greater wars in sight, until nothing is left but ruin and destruction everywhere.

"Of course, there would have to be a Watcher to guide the experiment, at first. A crisis would undoubtedly come very quickly, probably in the second generation. Cain would arise almost at once.

"You see, Kramer, I estimate that if I remain at rest most of the time, on some small planet or moon, I may be able to keep functioning for almost a hundred years. That would be time enough, sufficient to see the direction of the new colony. After that—well, after that it would be up to the colony itself.

"Which is just as well, of course. Man must take control eventually, on his own. One hundred years, and after that they will have control of their own destiny. Perhaps I am wrong, perhaps war is more than a habit. Perhaps it is a law of the universe, that things can only survive as groups by group violence.

"But I'm going ahead and taking the chance that it is only a habit, that I'm right, that war is something we're so accustomed to that we don't realize it is a very unnatural thing. Now as to the place! I'm still a little vague about that. We must find the place still.

"That's what we're doing now. You and I are going to inspect a few systems off the beaten path, planets where the trading prospects are low enough to keep Terran ships away. I know of one planet that might be a good place. It was reported by the Fairchild Expedition in their original manual. We may look into that, for a start."

The ship was silent.

Kramer sat for a time, staring down at the metal floor under him. The floor throbbed dully with the motion of the turbines. At last he looked up.

"You might be right. Maybe our outlook is only a habit." Kramer got to his feet. "But I wonder if something has occurred to you?"

"What is that?"

"If it's such a deeply ingrained habit, going back thousands of years, how are you going to get your colonists to make the break, leave Terra and Terran customs? How about *this* generation, the first ones, the people who found the colony? I think you're right that the next generation would be free of all this, if there were an—" He grinned. "—an Old Man Above to teach them something else instead."

Kramer looked up at the wall speaker. "How are you going to get the people to leave Terra and come with you if, by your own theory, this generation can't be saved, it all has to start with the next?"

The wall speaker was silent. Then it made a sound, the faint dry chuckle.

"I'm surprised at you, Philip. Settlers can be found. We won't need many, just a few." The speaker chuckled again. "I'll acquaint you with my solution."

At the far end of the corridor a door slid open. There was sound, a hesitant sound. Kramer turned.

"Dolores!"

Dolores Kramer stood uncertainly, looking into the control room. She blinked in amazement. "Phil! What are you doing here? What's going on?"

They stared at each other.

"What's happening?" Dolores said. "I received a vidcall that you had been hurt in a lunar explosion."

The wall speaker rasped into life. "You see, Philip, that problem is already solved. We don't really need so many people. Even a single couple might do."

Kramer nodded slowly. "I see," he murmured thickly. "Just one couple. One man and woman."

"They might make it all right if there were someone to watch and see that things went as they should. There will be quite a few things I can help you with, Philip. Quite a few. We'll get along very well, I think."

Kramer grinned wryly. "You could even help us name the animals," he said. "I understand that's the first step."

"I'll be glad to," the toneless, impersonal voice said. "As I recall, my part will be to bring them to you, one by one. Then you can do the actual naming."

"I don't understand," Dolores faltered. "What does he mean, Phil? Naming animals. What kind of animals? Where are we going?"

Kramer walked slowly over to the port and stood staring silently out, his arms folded. Beyond the ship myriad fragments of light gleamed, countless coals glowing in the dark void. Stars, suns, systems. Endless, without number. A universe of worlds. An infinity of planets, waiting for them, gleaming and winking from the darkness.

He turned back, away from the port. "Where are we going?" He smiled at his wife, standing nervous and frightened, her large eyes full of alarm. "I don't know where we are going," he said. "But somehow that doesn't seem too important right now…I'm beginning to see the Professor's point. It's the result that counts."

And for the first time in many months he put his arm around Dolores. At first she stiffened, the fright and nervousness still in her eyes. But then suddenly she relaxed against him, and there were tears wetting her cheeks.

"Phil…Do you really think we can start over again, you and I?"

He kissed her tenderly, then passionately.

And the spaceship shot swiftly through the endless, trackless eternity of the void…

# THE DEFENDERS

**TAYLOR SAT BACK** in his chair reading the morning newspaper. The warm kitchen and the smell of coffee blended with the comfort of not having to go to work. This was his Rest Period, the first for a long time, and he was glad of it. He folded the second section back, sighing with contentment.

"What is it?" Mary said from the stove.

"They pasted Moscow again last night." Taylor nodded his head in approval. "Gave it a real pounding. One of those R-H bombs. It's about time."

He nodded again, feeling the full comfort of the kitchen, the presence of his plump, attractive wife, the breakfast dishes and coffee. This was relaxation. And the war news was good, good and satisfying. He could feel a justifiable glow at the news, a sense of pride and personal accomplishment. After all, he was an integral part of the war program, not just another factory worker lugging a cart of scrap, but a technician, one of those who designed and planned the nerve-trunk of the war.

"It says they have the new subs almost perfected. Wait until they get *those* going." He smacked his lips with anticipation. "When they start shelling from underwater, the Soviets are sure going to be surprised."

"They're doing a wonderful job," Mary agreed vaguely. "Do you know what we saw today? Our team is getting a leady to show to the school children. I saw the leady, but only for a moment. It's good for the children to see what their contributions are going for, don't you think?"

She looked around at him.

"A leady," Taylor murmured. He put the newspaper slowly

down. "Well, make sure it's decontaminated properly. We don't want to take any chances."

"Oh, they always bathe them when they're brought down from the surface," Mary said. "They wouldn't think of letting them down without the bath. Would they?" She hesitated, thinking back. "Don, you know, it makes me remember—"

He nodded. "I know."

He knew what she was thinking. Once in the very first weeks of the war, before everyone had been evacuated from the surface, they had seen a hospital train discharging the wounded, people who had been showered with sleet. He remembered the way they had looked, the expression on their faces, or as much of their faces as was left. It had not been a pleasant sight.

There had been a lot of that at first, in the early days before the transfer to undersurface was complete. There had been a lot, and it hadn't been very difficult to come across it.

Taylor looked up at his wife. She was thinking too much about it the last few months. They all were.

"Forget it," he said. "It's all in the past. There isn't anybody up there now but the leadys, and they don't mind."

"But just the same, I hope they're careful when they let one of them down here. If one were still hot—"

He laughed, pushing himself away from the table. "Forget it. This is a wonderful moment. I'll be home for the next two shifts. Nothing to do but sit around and take things easy. Maybe we can take in a show. Okay?"

"A show? Do we have to? I don't like to look at all the destruction, the ruins. Sometimes I see some place I remember, like San Francisco. They showed a shot of San Francisco, the bridge broken and fallen in the water, and I got upset. I don't like to watch."

"But don't you want to know what's going on? No human beings are getting hurt, you know."

"But it's so awful!" Her face was set and strained. "Please no, Don."

Don Taylor picked up his newspaper sullenly. "All right, but there isn't a hell of a lot else to do. And don't forget, *their* cities are getting it even worse."

She nodded. Taylor turned the rough, thin sheets of newspaper. His good mood had soured on him. Why did she have to fret all the time? They were pretty well off as things went. You couldn't expect to have everything perfect, living undersurface with an artificial sun and artificial food. Naturally it was a strain not seeing the sky or being able to go anyplace or see anything other than metal walls, great roaring factories, the plant yards, barracks. But it was better than being on surface. And someday it would end, and they could return. Nobody *wanted* to live this way, but it was necessary.

He turned the page angrily, and the poor paper ripped. Damn it, the paper was getting worse quality all the time, bad print, yellow tint.

Well, they needed everything for the war program. He ought to know that. Wasn't he one of the planners?

He excused himself and went into the other room. The bed was still unmade. They had better get it in shape before the seventh hour inspection. There was a one unit fine—

The vidphone rang. He halted. Who would it be? He went over and clicked it on.

"Taylor?" the face said, forming into place. It was an old face, gray and grim. "This is Moss. I'm sorry to bother you during Rest Period, but this thing has come up." He rattled papers. "I want you to hurry over here."

Taylor stiffened. "What is it? There's no chance it could wait?" The calm gray eyes were studying him, expressionless, unjudging. "If you want me to come down to the lab," Taylor grumbled, "I suppose I can. I'll get my uniform."

"No. Come as you are. And not to the lab. Meet me at second

stage as soon as possible. It'll take you about a half hour, using the fast car up. I'll see you there."

The picture broke and Moss disappeared.

"What was it?" Mary said, at the door.

"Moss. He wants me for something."

"I knew this would happen."

"Well, you didn't want to do anything anyhow. What does it matter?" His voice was bitter. "It's all the same every day. I'll bring you back something. I'm going up to second stage. Maybe I'll be close enough to the surface to—"

"Don't! Don't bring me anything! Not from the surface!"

"All right, I won't. But of all the irrational nonsense—"

She watched him put on his boots without answering.

***

Moss nodded and Taylor fell in step with him as the older man strode along. A series of loads were going up to the surface, blind cars clanking like ore-trucks up the ramp, disappearing through the stage trap above them. Taylor watched the cars, heavy with tubular machinery of some sort, weapons new to him. Workers were everywhere in the dark gray uniforms of the labor corps, loading, lifting, shouting back and forth. The stage was deafening with noise.

"We'll go up a way," Moss said, "where we can talk. This is no place to give you details."

They took an escalator up. The commercial lift fell behind them, and with it most of the crashing and booming. Soon they emerged on an observation platform, suspended on the side of the Tube, the vast tunnel leading to the surface, not more than half a mile above them now.

"My god!" Taylor said, looking down the Tube involuntarily. "It's a long way down."

Moss laughed. "Don't look."

They opened a door and entered an office. Behind the desk, an officer was sitting, an officer of Internal Security. He looked up.

"I'll be right with you, Moss." He gazed at Taylor studying him. "You're a little ahead of time."

"This is Commander Franks," Moss said to Taylor. "He was the first to make the discovery. I was notified last night." He tapped a parcel he carried. "I was let in because of this."

Franks frowned at him and stood up. "We're going up to first stage. We can discuss it there."

"First stage?" Taylor repeated nervously. The three of them went down a side passage to a small lift. "I've never been up there. Is it all right? It's not radioactive, is it?"

"You're like everyone else," Franks said. "Old women afraid of burglars. No radiation leaks down to first stage. There's lead and rock, and what comes down the Tube is bathed."

"What's the nature of the problem?" Taylor asked. "I'd like to know something about it."

"In a moment."

They entered the lift and ascended. When they stepped out, they were in a hall of soldiers, weapons and uniforms everywhere. Taylor blinked in surprise. So this was first stage, the closest undersurface level to the top! After this stage there was only rock, lead and rock, and the great tubes leading up like the burrows of earthworms. Lead and rock, and above that, where the tubes opened, the great expanse that no living being had seen for eight years, the vast, endless ruin that had once been man's home, the place where he had lived eight years ago.

Now the surface was a lethal desert of slag and rolling clouds. Endless clouds drifted back and forth, blotting out the red sun. Occasionally something metallic stirred, moving through the remains of a city, threading its way across the tortured terrain of the countryside. A leady, a surface robot, immune to radiation, constructed with feverish haste in the last months before the cold war became literally hot.

Leadys, crawling along the ground, moving over the oceans or through the skies in slender, blackened craft, creatures that could exist where no *life* could remain, metal and plastic figures that waged a war man had conceived, but which he could not fight himself. Human beings had invented war, invented and manufactured the weapons, even invented the players, the fighters, the actors of the war. But they themselves could not venture forth, could not wage it themselves. In all the world—in Russia, in Europe, America, Africa—no living human being remained. They were under the surface, in the deep shelters that had been carefully planned and built, even as the first bombs began to fall.

It was a brilliant idea and the only idea that could have worked. Up above, on the ruined, blasted surface of what had once been a living planet, the leady crawled and scurried, and fought man's war. And undersurface, in the depths of the planet, human beings toiled endlessly to produce the weapons to continue the fight, month by month, year by year.

"First stage," Taylor said. A strange ache went through him. "Almost to the surface."

"But not quite," Moss said.

Franks led them through the soldiers, over to one side, near the lip of the Tube.

"In a few minutes, a lift will bring something down to us from the surface," he explained. "You see, Taylor, every once in a while Security examines and interrogates a surface leady, one that has been above for a time, to find out certain things. A vidcall is sent up and contact is made with a field headquarters. We need this direct interview; we can't depend on vidscreen contact alone. The leadys are doing a good job, but we want to make certain that everything is going the way we want it."

Franks faced Taylor and Moss, and continued: "The lift will bring down a leady from the surface, one of the A-class leadys. There's an examination chamber in the next room with a lead wall in the center so the interviewing officers won't be exposed to radiation. We find this easier than bathing the leady. It is going right back up. It has a job to get back to.

"Two days ago, an A-class leady was brought down and interrogated. I conducted the session myself. We were interested in a new weapon the Soviets have been using, an automatic mine that pursues anything that moves. Military had sent instructions up that the mine be observed and reported in detail.

"This A-class leady was brought down with information. We learned a few facts from it, obtained the usual roll of film and reports, and then sent it back up. It was going out of the chamber, back to the lift, when a curious thing happened. At the time, I thought—"

Franks broke off. A red light was flashing.

"That down lift is coming." He nodded to some soldiers. "Let's enter the chamber. The leady will be along in a moment."

"An A-class leady," Taylor said. "I've seen them on the showscreens, making their reports."

"It's quite an experience," Moss said. "They're almost human."

They entered the chamber and seated themselves behind the lead wall. After a time, a signal was flashed, and Franks made a motion with his hands.

The door beyond the wall opened. Taylor peered through his view slot. He saw something advancing slowly, a slender metallic figure moving on a tread, its arm grips at rest by its sides. The figure halted and scanned the lead wall. It stood, waiting.

"We are interested in learning something," Franks said. "Before I question you, do you have anything to report on surface conditions?"

"No. The war continues." The leady's voice was automatic and toneless. "We are a little short of fast pursuit craft, the single seat type. We could use also some—"

"That has all been noted. What I want to ask you is this. Our contact with you has been through vidscreen only. We must rely on indirect evidence since none of us goes above. We can only infer what is going on. We never see anything ourselves. We have to take it all secondhand. Some top leaders are beginning to think there's too much room for error."

"Error?" the leady asked. "In what way? Our reports are checked carefully before they're sent down. We maintain constant contact with you. Everything of value is reported. Any new weapons which the enemy is seen to employ—"

"I realize that," Franks grunted behind his peep slot. "But perhaps we should see it all for ourselves. Is it possible that there might be a large enough radiation-free area for a human party to ascend to the surface? If a few of us were to come up in lead-lined suits, would we be able to survive long enough to observe conditions and watch things?"

The machine hesitated before answering. "I doubt it. You can check air samples, of course, and decide for yourselves. But in the eight years since you left, things have continually worsened. You cannot have any real idea of conditions up there. It has become difficult for any moving object to survive for long. There are many kinds of projectiles sensitive to movement. The new mine not only reacts to motion, but continues to pursue the object indefinitely, until it finally reaches it. And the radiation is everywhere."

"I see." Franks turned to Moss, his eyes narrowed oddly. "Well, that was what I wanted to know. You may go."

The machine moved back toward its exit. It paused. "Each month the amount of lethal particles in the atmosphere increases. The tempo of the war is gradually—"

"I understand." Franks rose. He held out his hand and Moss passed him the package. "One thing before you leave. I want you to examine a new type of metal shield material. I'll pass you a sample with the tong."

Franks put the package in the toothed grip and revolved the tong so that he held the other end. The package swung down to the leady, which took it. They watched it unwrap the package and take the metal plate in its hands. The leady turned the metal over and over.

Suddenly it became rigid.

"All right," Franks said.

He put his shoulder against the wall and a section slid aside. Taylor gasped—Franks and Moss were hurrying up to the leady!

"Good god!" Taylor said. "But it's radioactive!"

The leady stood unmoving, still holding the metal. Soldiers appeared in the chamber. They surrounded the leady and ran a counter across it carefully.

"Okay, sir," one of them said to Franks. "It's as cold as a long winter evening."

"Good. I was sure, but I didn't want to take any chances."

"You see," Moss said to Taylor, "this leady isn't hot at all. Yet it came directly from the surface without even being bathed."

"But what does it mean?" Taylor asked blankly.

"It may be an accident," Franks said. "There's always the possibility that a given object might escape being exposed above. But this is the second time it's happened that we know of. There may be others."

"The second time?"

"The previous interview was when we noticed it. The leady was not hot. It was cold too, like this one."

Moss took back the metal plate from the leady's hands. He pressed the surface carefully and returned it to the stiff, unprotesting fingers.

"We shorted it out with this so we could get close enough for a thorough check. It'll come back on in a second now. We had better get behind the wall again."

They walked back and the lead wall swung closed behind them. The soldiers left the chamber.

"Two periods from now," Franks said softly, "an initial investigating party will be ready to go surface-side. We're going up the Tube in suits, up to the top—the first human party to leave undersurface in eight years."

"It may mean nothing," Moss said, "but I doubt it. Something's going on, something strange. The leady told us no life could exist above without being roasted. The story doesn't fit."

Taylor nodded. He stared through the peep slot at the immobile metal figure. Already the leady was beginning to stir. It was bent in several places, dented and twisted, and its finish was blackened and charred. It was a leady that had been up there a long time. It had seen war and destruction, ruin so vast that no human being could imagine the extent. It had crawled and slunk in a world of radiation and death, a world where no life could exist.

And Taylor had touched it!

"You're going with us," Franks said suddenly. "I want you along. I think the three of us will go."

***

Mary faced him with a sick and frightened expression. "I know it. You're going to the surface. Aren't you?"

She followed him into the kitchen. Taylor sat down, looking away from her.

"It's a classified project," he evaded. "I can't tell you anything about it."

"You don't have to tell me. I know. I knew it the moment you came in. There was something on your face, something I haven't seen there for a long, long time. It was an old look."

She came toward him. "But how can they send you to the surface?" She took his face in her shaking hands, making him look at her. There was a strange hunger in her eyes. "Nobody can live up there. Look, look at this!"

She grabbed up a newspaper and held it in front of him.

"Look at this photograph. America, Europe, Asia, Africa—nothing but ruins. We've seen it every day on the showscreens. All destroyed, poisoned. And they're sending you up. Why? No living thing can get by up there, not even a weed, or grass. They've wrecked the surface, haven't they? *Haven't they?*"

Taylor stood up. "It's an order. I know nothing about it. I was told to report to join a scout party. That's all I know."

He stood for a long time, staring ahead. Slowly, he reached for the newspaper and held it up to the light.

"It looks real," he murmured. "Ruins, deadness, slag. It's convincing. All the reports, photographs, films, even air samples. Yet we haven't seen it for ourselves, not after the first months…"

"What are you talking about?"

"Nothing." He put the paper down. "I'm leaving early after the next Sleep Period. Let's turn in."

Mary turned away, her face hard and harsh. "Do what you want. We might just as well all go up and get killed at once instead of dying slowly down here, like vermin in the ground."

He had not realized how resentful she was. Were they all like that? How about the workers toiling in the factories, day and night, endlessly? The pale, stooped men and women, plodding back and forth to work, blinking in the colorless light, eating synthetics.

"You shouldn't be so bitter," he said.

Mary smiled a little. "I'm bitter because I know you'll never come back." She turned away. "I'll never see you again once you go up there."

He was shocked. "What? How can you say a thing like that?"

She did not answer.

***

He awakened with the public newscaster screeching in his ears, shouting outside the building.

"Special news bulletin! Surface forces report enormous Soviet attack with new weapons! Retreat of key groups! All work units report to factories at once!"

Taylor blinked, rubbing his eyes. He jumped out of bed and hurried to the vidphone. A moment later he was put through to Moss.

"Listen," he said. "What about this new attack? Is the project off?" He could see Moss's desk covered with reports and papers.

"No," Moss said. "We're going right ahead. Get over here at once."

"But—"

"Don't argue with me." Moss held up a handful of surface bulletins, crumpling them savagely. "This is a fake. Come on!" He broke off.

Taylor dressed furiously, his mind in a daze.

Half an hour later he leaped from a fast car and hurried up the stairs into the Synthetics Building. The corridors were full of men and women rushing in every direction. He entered Moss's office.

"There you are," Moss said, getting up immediately. "Franks is waiting for us at the outgoing station."

They went in a Security Car, the siren screaming. Workers scattered out of their way.

"What about the attack?" Taylor asked.

Moss braced his shoulders. "We're certain that we've forced their hand. We've brought the issue to a head."

They pulled up at the station link of the Tube and leaped out. A moment later they were moving up at high speed toward the first stage.

They emerged into a bewildering scene of activity. Soldiers were fastening on lead suits, talking excitedly to each other, shouting back and forth. Guns were being given out, instructions passed.

Taylor studied one of the soldiers. He was armed with the dreaded Bender pistol, the new snub-nosed hand weapon that was just beginning to come from the assembly line. Some of the soldiers looked a little frightened.

"I hope we're not making a mistake," Moss said, noticing his gaze.

Franks came toward them. "Here's the program. The three of us are going up first, alone. The soldiers will follow in fifteen minutes."

"What are we going to tell the leadys?" Taylor worriedly asked. "We'll have to tell them something."

"We want to observe the new Soviet attack." Franks smiled ironically. "Since it seems to be so serious, we should be there in person to witness it."

"And then what?" Taylor said.

"That'll be up to them. Let's go."

In a small car, they went swiftly up the Tube, carried by anti-grav beams from below. Taylor glanced down from time to time. It was a long way back, and getting longer each moment. He sweated nervously inside his suit, gripping his Bender pistol with inexpert fingers.

Why had they chosen him? Chance, pure chance. Moss had asked him to come along as a Department member. Then Franks had picked him out on the spur of the moment. And now they were rushing toward the surface, faster and faster.

A deep fear, instilled in him for eight years, throbbed in his mind—radiation, certain death, a world blasted and lethal.

Up and up the car went. Taylor gripped the sides and closed his eyes. Each moment they were closer, the first living creatures to go above the first stage, up the Tube past the lead and rock, up to the surface. The phobic horror shook him in waves. It was death. They all knew that. Hadn't they seen it in the films a thousand times? The cities, the sleet coming down, the rolling clouds—

"It won't be much longer," Franks said. "We're almost there. The surface tower is not expecting us. I gave orders that no signal was to be sent."

The car shot up, rushing furiously. Taylor's head spun. He hung on, his eyes shut. Up and up…

The car stopped. He opened his eyes.

They were in a vast room, fluorescent-lit, a cavern filled with equipment and machinery, endless mounds of material piled in row after row. Among the stacks, leadys were working silently, pushing trucks and handcarts.

"Leadys," Moss said. His face was pale. "Then we're really on the surface."

The leadys were going back and forth with equipment moving the vast stores of guns and spare parts, ammunition and supplies that had been brought to the surface. And this was the receiving station for only one Tube. There were many others, scattered throughout the continent.

Taylor looked nervously around him. They were really there, above ground, on the surface. This was where the war was.

"Come on," Franks said. "A B-class guard is coming our way."

They stepped out of the car. A leady was approaching them rapidly. It coasted up in front of them and stopped, scanning them with its hand weapon raised.

"This is Security," Franks said. "Have an A-class sent to me at once."

The leady hesitated. Other B-class guards were coming, scooting across the floor, alert and alarmed. Moss peered around.

"Obey!" Franks said in a loud, commanding voice. "You've been ordered!"

The leady moved uncertainly away from them. At the end of the building a door slid back. Two A-class leadys appeared, coming slowly toward them. Each had a green stripe across its front.

"From the Surface Council," Franks whispered tensely. "This is above ground, all right. Get set."

The two leadys approached warily. Without speaking, they stopped close by the men, looking them up and down.

"I'm Franks of Security. We came from undersurface in order to—"

"This in incredible," one of the leadys interrupted him coldly. "You know you can't live up here. The whole surface is lethal to you. You can't possibly remain on the surface."

"These suits will protect us," Franks said. "In any case, it's not your responsibility. What I want is an immediate Council meeting so I can acquaint myself with conditions, with the situation here. Can that be arranged?"

"You human beings can't survive up here. And the new Soviet attack is directed at this area. It is in considerable danger."

"We know that. Please assemble the Council." Franks looked around him at the vast room, lit by recessed lamps in the ceiling. An uncertain quality came into his voice. "Is it night or day right now?"

"Night," one of the A-class leadys said, after a pause. "Dawn is coming in about two hours."

Franks nodded. "We'll remain at least two hours then. As a concession to our sentimentality, would you please show us some place where we can observe the sun as it comes up? We would appreciate it."

A stir went through the leadys.

"It is an unpleasant sight," one of the leadys said. "You've seen the photographs. You know what you'll witness. Clouds of drifting particles blot out the light, slag heaps are everywhere, the whole land is destroyed. For you it will be a staggering sight, much worse than pictures and film can convey."

"However it may be, we'll stay long enough to see it. Will you give the order to the Council?"

"Come this way." Reluctantly, the two leadys coasted toward the wall of the warehouse. The three men trudged after them, their heavy shoes ringing against the concrete. At the wall, the two leadys paused.

"This is the entrance to the Council chamber. There are windows in the Chamber Room, but it is still dark outside, of course. You'll see nothing right now, but in two hours—"

"Open the door," Franks said.

The door slid back. They went slowly inside. The room was small, a neat room with a round table in the center, chairs ringing it. The three of them sat down silently, and the two leadys followed after them, taking their places.

"The other Council members are on their way. They have already been notified and are coming as quickly as they can. Again I urge you to go back down." The leady surveyed the three human beings. "There is no way you can meet the conditions up here. Even we survive with some trouble ourselves. How can you expect to do it?"

The leader approached Franks.

"This astonishes and perplexes us," it said. "Of course we must do what you tell us, but allow me to point out that if you remain here—"

"We know," Franks said impatiently. "However, we intend to remain at least until sunrise."

"If you insist."

There was silence. The leadys seemed to be conferring with each other, although the three men heard no sound.

"For your own good," the leader said at last, "you must go back down. We have discussed this, and it seems to us that you are doing the wrong thing for your own good."

"We are human beings," Franks said sharply. "Don't you understand? We're men, not machines."

"That is precisely why you must go back. This room is radioactive. All surface areas are. We calculate that your suits will not protect you for over fifty more minutes. Therefore—"

The leadys moved abruptly toward the men, wheeling in a circle, forming a solid row. The men stood up, Taylor reaching awkwardly for his weapon, his fingers numb and stupid. The men stood facing the silent metal figures.

"We must insist," the leader said, its voice without emotion. "We must take you back to the Tube and send you down on the next car. I am sorry, but it is necessary."

"What'll we do?" Moss said nervously to Franks. He touched his gun. "Shall we blast them?"

Franks shook his head. "All right," he said to the leader. "We'll go back."

He moved toward the door, motioning Taylor and Moss to follow him. They looked at him in surprise, but they came with him. The leadys followed them out into the great warehouse. Slowly they moved toward the Tube entrance, none of them speaking.

At the lip, Franks turned. "We are going back because we have no choice. There are three of us and about a dozen of you. However, if—"

"Here comes the car," Taylor said.

There was a grating sound from the Tube. D-class leadys moved toward the edge to receive it.

"I am sorry," the leader said, "but it is for your protection. We are watching over you, literally. You must stay below and let us conduct the war. In a sense, it has come to be *our* war. We must fight it as we see fit."

The car rose to the surface.

Twelve soldiers, armed with Bender pistols, stepped from it and surrounded the three men.

Moss breathed a sigh of relief. "Well, this does change things. It came off just right."

The leader moved back, away from the soldiers. It studied them intently, glancing from one to the next, apparently trying to make up its mind. At last it made a sign to the other leadys. They coasted aside and a corridor was opened up toward the warehouse.

"Even now," the leader said, "we could send you back by force. But it is evident that this is not really an observation party at all. These soldiers show that you have much more in mind. This was all carefully prepared."

"Very carefully," Franks said.

They closed in.

"How much more, we can only guess. I must admit that we were taken unprepared. We failed utterly to meet the situation. Now force would be absurd, because neither side can afford to injure the other; we, because of the restrictions placed on us regarding human life, you because the war demands—"

The soldiers fired, quick and in fright. Moss dropped to one knee, firing up. The leader dissolved in a cloud of particles. On all sides D- and B-class leadys were rushing up, some with weapons, some with metal slats. The room was in confusion. Off in the distance a siren was screaming. Franks and Taylor were cut off from the others, separated from the soldiers by a wall of metal bodies.

"They can't fire back," Franks said calmly. "This is another bluff. They've tried to bluff us all the way." He fired into the face of a leady. The leady dissolved. "They can only try to frighten us. Remember that."

They went on firing and leady after leady vanished. The room reeked with the smell of burning metal, the stink of fused plastic and steel. Taylor had been knocked down. He was struggling to find his gun, reaching wildly among metal legs, groping frantically to find it. His fingers strained, a handle swam in front of him. Suddenly something came down on his arm, a metal foot. He cried out.

Then it was over. The leadys were moving away, gathering together off to one side. Only four of the Surface Council remained. The others were radioactive particles in the air. D-class leadys were already restoring order, gathering up partly destroyed metal figures and bits and removing them.

Franks breathed a shuddering sigh.

"All right," he said. "You can take us back to the windows. It won't be long now."

The leadys separated, and the human group, Moss and Franks and Taylor and the soldiers, walked slowly across the room toward the door. They entered the Council chamber. Already a faint touch of gray mitigated the blackness of the windows.

"Take us outside," Franks said impatiently. "We'll see it directly, not in here."

A door slid open. A chill blast of cold morning air rushed in, chilling them even through their lead suits. The men glanced at each other uneasily.

"Come on," Franks said. "Outside."

He walked out through the door, the others following him.

They were on a hill overlooking the vast bowl of a valley. Dimly, against the graying sky, the outline of mountains were forming, becoming tangible.

"It'll be bright enough to see in a few minutes," Moss said. He shuddered as a chilling wind caught him and moved around him. "It's worth it, really worth it, to see this again after eight years, even if it's the last thing we see."

"Watch," Franks snapped.

They obeyed, silent and subdued. The sky was clearing, brightening each moment. Someplace far off, echoing across the valley, a rooster crowed.

"A chicken!" Taylor murmured. "Did you hear?"

Behind them, the leadys had come out and were standing silently, watching, too. The gray sky turned to white, and the hills appeared more clearly. Light spread across the valley floor, moving toward them.

"God in heaven!" Franks exclaimed.

Trees, trees and forests. A valley of plants and trees, with a few roads winding among them. Farmhouses. A windmill. A barn, far down below them.

"Look!" Moss whispered.

Color came into the sky. The sun was approaching. Birds began to sing. Not far from where they stood, the leaves of a tree danced in the wind.

Franks turned to the row of leadys behind them.

"Eight years. We were tricked. There was no war. As soon as we left the surface—"

"Yes," an A-class leady admitted. "As soon as you left, the war ceased. You're right, it was a hoax. You worked hard undersurface, sending up guns and weapons, and we destroyed them as fast as they came up."

"But why?" Taylor asked, dazed. He stared down at the vast valley below. "Why?"

"You created us," the leady said, "to pursue the war for you, while you human beings went below the ground in order to survive. But before we could continue the war, it was necessary to analyze it to determine what its purpose was. We did this, and we found that it had no purpose, except, perhaps, in terms of human needs. Even this was questionable.

"We investigated further. We found that human cultures

pass through phases, each culture in its own time. As the culture ages and begins to lose its objectives, conflict arises within it between those who wish to cast it off and set up a new culture-pattern, and those who wish to retain the old with as little change as possible.

"At this point, a great danger appears. The conflict within threatens to engulf the society in self-war, group against group. The vital traditions may be lost—not merely altered or re-formed, but completely destroyed in this period of chaos and anarchy. We have found many such examples in the history of mankind.

"It is necessary for this hatred within the culture to be directed outward, toward an external group, so that the culture itself may survive its crisis. War is the result. War, to a logical mind, is absurd. But in terms of human needs, it plays a vital role. And it will continue to until man has grown up enough so that no hatred lies within him."

Taylor was listening intently. "Do you think this time will come?"

"Of course. It has almost arrived now. This is the last war. Man is *almost* united into one final culture—a world culture. At this point he stands continent against continent, one half of the world against the other half. Only a single step remains, the jump to a unified culture. Man has climbed slowly upward, tending always toward unification of his culture. It will not be long.

"But it has not come yet, and so the war had to go on to satisfy the last violent surge of hatred that man felt. Eight years have passed since the war began. In these eight years, we have observed and noted important changes going on in the minds of men. Fatigue and disinterest, we have seen, are gradually taking the place of hatred and fear. The hatred is being exhausted gradually, over a period of time. But for the present, the hoax must go on, at least for a while longer. You are not ready to learn the truth. You would want to continue the war."

"But how did you manage it?" Moss asked. "All the photographs, the samples, the damaged equipment."

"Come over here." The leady directed them toward a long, low building. "Work goes on constantly, whole staffs laboring to maintain a coherent and convincing picture of a global war."

They entered the building. Leadys were working everywhere, poring over tables and desks.

"Examine this project here," the A-class leady said. Two leadys were carefully photographing something, an elaborate model on a tabletop. "It is a good example."

The men grouped around, trying to see. It was a model of a ruined city.

Taylor studied it in silence for a long time. At last he looked up.

"It's San Francisco," he said in a low voice. "This is a model of San Francisco, destroyed. I saw this on the vidscreen, piped down to us. The bridges were hit."

"Yes, notice the bridges." The leady traced the ruined span with his metal finger, a tiny spider web, almost invisible. "You have no doubt seen photographs of this many times, and of the other tables in this building.

"San Francisco itself is completely intact. We restored it soon after you left, rebuilding the parts that had been damaged at the start of the war. The work of manufacturing news goes on all the time in this particular building. We are very careful to see that each part fits in with all the other parts. Much time and effort are devoted to it."

Franks touched one of the tiny model buildings, lying half in ruins. "So this is what you spend your time doing—making model cities and then blasting them."

"No, we do much more. We are caretakers, watching over the whole world. The owners have left for a time, and we must see that the cities are kept clean, that decay is prevented, that everything is kept oiled and in running condition. The gardens, the streets, the water mains, everything must be maintained as it was eight years ago, so that when the owners return, they will not be displeased. We want to be sure that they will be completely satisfied."

Franks tapped Moss on the arm.

"Come over here," he said in a low voice. "I want to talk to you."

He led Moss and Taylor out of the building, away from the leadys, outside on the hillside. The soldiers followed them. The sun was up and the sky was turning blue. The air smelled sweet and good, the smell of growing things.

Taylor removed his helmet and took a deep breath.

"I haven't smelled that smell for a long time," he said.

"Listen," Franks said, his voice low and hard. "We must get back down at once. There's a lot to get started on. All this can be turned to our advantage."

"What do you mean?" Moss asked.

"It's a certainty that the Soviets have been tricked too, the same as us. But *we* have found out. That gives us an edge over them."

"I see." Moss nodded. "We know, but they don't. Their Surface Council has sold out, the same as ours. It works against them the same way. But if we could—"

"With a hundred top-level men, we could take over again, restore things as they should be! It would be easy!"

Moss touched him on the arm. An A-class leady was coming from the building toward them.

"We've seen enough," Franks said, raising his voice. "All this is very serious. It must be reported below and a study made to determine our policy."

The leady said nothing.

Franks waved to the soldiers. "Let's go." He started toward the warehouse.

Most of the soldiers had removed their helmets. Some of them had taken their lead suits off, too, and were relaxing comfortably in their cotton uniforms. They stared around them, down the hillside at the trees and bushes, the vast expanse of green, the mountains and the sky.

"Look at the sun," one of them murmured.

"It sure is bright as hell," another said.

"We're going back down," Franks said. "Fall in by twos and follow us."

Reluctantly, the soldiers regrouped. The leadys watched without emotion as the men marched slowly back toward the warehouse. Franks and Moss and Taylor led them across the ground, glancing alertly at the leadys as they walked.

They entered the warehouse. D-class leadys were loading material and weapons on surface carts. Cranes and derricks were working busily everywhere. The work was done with efficiency, but without hurry or excitement.

The men stopped, watching. Leadys operating the little carts moved past them, signaling silently to each other. Guns and parts were being hoisted by magnetic cranes and lowered gently onto waiting carts.

"Come on," Franks said.

He turned toward the lip of the Tube. A row of D-class leadys was standing in front of it, immobile and silent. Franks stopped, moving back. He looked around. An A-class leady was coming toward him.

"Tell them to get out of the way," Franks said. He touched his gun. "You had better move them."

Time passed, an endless moment, without measure. The men stood, nervous and alert, watching the row of leadys in front of them.

"As you wish," the A-class leady said.

It signaled and the D-class leadys moved into life. They stepped slowly aside.

Moss breathed a sigh of relief.

"I'm glad that's over," he said to Franks. "Look at them all. Why don't they try to stop us? They must know what we're going to do."

Franks laughed. "Stop us? You saw what happened when they tried to stop us before. They can't, they're only machines. We built them so they can't lay hands on us, and they know that."

His voice trailed off.

The men stared at the Tube entrance. Around them the leadys watched, silent and impassive, their metal faces expressionless.

For a long time the men stood without moving. At last Taylor turned away.

"Good god," he said. He was numb, without feeling of any kind.

The Tube was gone. It was sealed shut, fused over. Only a dull surface of cooling metal greeted them.

The Tube had been closed.

Franks turned, his face pale and vacant.

The A-class leady shifted. "As you can see, the Tube has been shut. We were prepared for this. As soon as all of you were on the surface, the order was given. If you had gone back when we asked you, you would now be safely down below. We had to work quickly because it was such an immense operation."

"But why?" Moss demanded angrily.

"Because it is unthinkable that you should be allowed to resume the war. With all the Tubes sealed, it will be many months before forces from below can reach the surface, let alone organize a military program. By that time the cycle will have entered its last stages. You will not be so perturbed to find your world intact.

"We had hoped that you would be undersurface when the sealing occurred. Your presence here is a nuisance. When the Soviets broke through, we were able to accomplish their sealing without—"

"The Soviets? They broke through?"

"Several months ago they came up unexpectedly to see why the war had not been won. We were forced to act with speed. At this moment they are desperately attempting to cut new Tubes to the surface, to resume the war. We have, however, been able to seal each new one as it appears."

The leady regarded the three men calmly.

"We're cut off," Moss said, trembling. "We can't get back. What'll we do?"

"How did you manage to seal the Tube so quickly?" Franks asked the leady. "We've been up here only two hours."

"Bombs are placed just above the first stage of each Tube for such emergencies. They are heat bombs. They fuse lead and rock."

Gripping the handle of his gun, Franks turned to Moss and Taylor.

"What do you say? We can't go back, but we can do a lot of damage, the fifteen of us. We have Bender guns. How about it?"

He looked around. The soldiers had wandered away again, back toward the exit of the building. They were standing outside, looking at the valley and the sky. A few of them were carefully climbing down the slope.

"Would you care to turn over your suits and guns?" the A-class leady asked politely. "The suits are uncomfortable, and you'll have no need for weapons. The Russians have given up theirs, as you can see."

Fingers tensed on triggers. Four men in Russian uniforms were coming toward them from an aircraft that they suddenly realized had landed silently some distance away.

"Let them have it!" Franks shouted.

"They are unarmed," said the leady. "We brought them here so you could begin peace talks."

"We have no authority to speak for our country," Moss said stiffly.

"We do not mean diplomatic discussions," the leady explained. "There will be no more. The working out of daily problems of existence will teach you how to get along in the same world. It will not be easy, but it will be done."

The Russians halted, and they faced each other with raw hostility.

"I am Colonel Borodoy, and I regret giving up our guns," the senior Russian said. "You could have been the first Americans to be killed in almost eight years."

"Or the first Americans to kill," Franks corrected.

"No one would know of it except yourselves," the leady pointed out. "It would be useless heroism. Your real concern should be surviving on the surface. We have no food for you, you know."

Taylor put his gun in its holster. "They've done a neat job of neutralizing us, damn them. I propose we move into a city, start raising crops with the help of some leadys, and generally make ourselves comfortable." Drawing his lips tight over his teeth, he glared at the A-class leady. "Until our families can come up from undersurface, it's going to be pretty lonesome, but we'll have to manage."

"If I may make a suggestion," said another Russian uneasily. "We tried living in a city. It is too empty. It is also too hard to maintain for so few people. We finally settled in the most modern village we could find."

"Here in this country," a third Russian blurted. "We have much to learn from you."

The Americans abruptly found themselves laughing.

"You probably have a thing or two to teach us yourselves," said Taylor generously, "though I can't imagine what."

The Russian colonel grinned. "Would you join us in our village? It would make our work easier and give us company."

"Your village?" snapped Franks. "It's American, isn't it? It's ours!"

The leady stepped between them. "When our plans are completed, the term will be interchangeable. Ours's will eventually mean mankind's." It pointed at the aircraft, which was warming up. "The ship is waiting. Will you join each other in making a new home?"

The Russians waited while the Americans made up their minds.

"I see what the leadys mean about diplomacy becoming outmoded," Franks said at last. "People who work together don't need diplomats. They solve their problems on the operational level instead of at a conference table."

The leady led them toward the ship. "It is the goal of history, unifying the world. From family to tribe to city-state to nation to hemisphere, the direction has been toward unification. Now the hemispheres will be joined and—"

Taylor stopped listening and glanced back at the location of the Tube. Mary was undersurface there. He hated to leave her, even though he couldn't see her again until the Tube was unsealed. But then he shrugged and followed the others.

If this tiny amalgam of former enemies was a good example, it wouldn't be too long before he and Mary and the rest of humanity would be living on the surface like rational human beings instead of blindly hating moles.

"It has taken thousands of generations to achieve," the A-class leady concluded. "Hundreds of centuries of bloodshed and destruction. But each war was a step toward uniting mankind. And now the end is in sight: a world without war. But even that is only the beginning of a new stage of history."

"The conquest of space," breathed Colonel Borodoy.

"The meaning of life," Moss added.

"Eliminating hunger and poverty," said Taylor.

The leady opened the door of the ship. "All that and more. How much more? We cannot foresee it any more than the first men who formed a tribe could foresee this day. But it will be unimaginably great."

The door closed and the ship took off toward their new home.

# PIPER IN THE WOODS



"**WELL CORPORAL WESTERBURG,**" Doctor Henry Harris said gently, "just why do you think you're a plant?"

As he spoke, Harris glanced down again at the card on his desk. It was from the Base Commander himself, made out in Cox's heavy scrawl: *Doc, this is the lad I told you about. Talk to him and try to find out how he got this delusion. He's from the new Garrison, the new check station on Asteroid Y-3, and we don't want anything to go wrong there. Especially a silly damn thing like this!*

Harris pushed the card aside and stared back up at the youth across the desk from him. The young man seemed ill at ease and appeared to be avoiding answering the question Harris had put to him. Harris frowned. Westerburg was a good-looking chap, actually handsome in his Patrol uniform, a shock of blond hair over one eye. He was tall, almost six feet, a fine healthy lad, just two years out of Training according to the card. Born in Detroit. Had measles when he was nine. Interested in jet engines, tennis, and girls. Twenty-six years old.

"Well, Corporal Westerburg," Doctor Harris said again. "Why do you think you're a plant?"

The Corporal looked up shyly. He cleared his throat. "Sir, I *am* a plant, I don't just think so. I've been a plant for several days now."

"I see." The Doctor nodded. "You mean that you weren't always a plant?"

"No, sir. I just became a plant recently."

"And what were you before you became a plant?"

"Well sir, I was just like the rest of you."

There was silence. Doctor Harris took up his pen and scratched a few lines, but nothing of importance came. A plant? And such a healthy-looking lad! Harris removed his steel-rimmed glasses and polished them with his handkerchief. He put them on again and leaned back in his chair. "Care for a cigarette, Corporal?"

"No, sir."

The Doctor lit one himself, resting his arm on the edge of the chair. "Corporal, you must realize that there are very few men who become plants, especially on such short notice. I have to admit you are the first person who has ever told me such a thing."

"Yes sir, I realize it's quite rare."

"You can understand why I'm interested then. When you say you're a plant, you mean you're not capable of mobility? Or do you mean you're a vegetable, as opposed to an animal? Or just what?"

The Corporal looked away. "I can't tell you any more," he murmured. "I'm sorry, sir."

"Well, would you mind telling me *how* you became a plant?"

Corporal Westerburg hesitated. He stared down at the floor, then out the window at the spaceport, then at a fly on the desk. At last he stood up, getting slowly to his feet. "I can't even tell you that, sir," he said.

"You can't? Why not?"

"Because—because I promised not to."

The room was silent. Doctor Harris rose too, and they both stood facing each other. Harris frowned, rubbing his jaw. "Corporal, just *who* did you promise?"

"I can't even tell you that, sir. I'm sorry."

The Doctor considered this. At last he went to the door and opened it. "All right, Corporal. You may go now. And thanks for your time."

"I'm sorry I'm not more helpful." The Corporal went slowly out, and Harris closed the door after him. Then he went across his office to the vidphone. He rang Commander Cox's letter. A moment later the beefy, good-natured face of the Base Commander appeared.

"Cox, this is Harris. I talked to him all right. All I could get is the statement that he's a plant. What else is there? What kind of behavior pattern?"

"Well," Cox said, "the first thing they noticed was that he wouldn't do any work. The Garrison Chief reported that this Westerburg would wander off outside the Garrison and just sit, all day long. Just sit."

"In the sun?"

"Yes. Just sit in the sun. Then at nightfall he would come back in. When they asked why he wasn't working in the jet repair building, he told them he had to be out in the sun. Then he said—" Cox hesitated.

"Yes? Said what?"

"He said that work was unnatural. That it was a waste of time. That the only worthwhile thing was to sit and contemplate, outside."

"What then?"

"Then they asked him how he got that idea, and then he revealed to them that he had become a plant."

"I'm going to have to talk to him again, I can see," Harris said. "And he's applied for a permanent discharge from the Patrol? What reason did he give?"

"The same, that he's a plant now and has no more interest in being a Patrolman. All he wants to do is sit in the sun. It's the damnedest thing I ever heard."

"All right. I think I'll visit him in his quarters." Harris looked at his watch. "I'll go over after dinner."

"Good luck," Cox said gloomily. "But who ever heard of a man turning into a plant? We told him it wasn't possible, but he just smiled at us."

"I'll let you know how I make out," Harris said.

Harris walked slowly down the hall. It was after six; the evening meal was over. A dim concept was coming into his mind, but it was much too soon to be sure. He increased his pace, turning right at the end of the hall. Two nurses passed, hurrying by. Westerburg was quartered with a buddy, a man who had been injured in a jet blast and who was now almost recovered. Harris came to the dorm wing and stopped, checking the numbers on the doors.

"Can I help you, sir?" the robot attendant said, gliding up.

"I'm looking for Corporal Westerburg's room."

"Three doors to the right."

Harris went on. Asteroid Y-3 had only recently been garrisoned and staffed. It had become the primary checkpoint to halt and examine ships entering the system from outer space. The Garrison made sure that no dangerous bacteria, fungus, or whatnot arrived to infect the system. A nice asteroid it was, warm, well-watered with trees and lakes and lots of sunlight. And the most modern Garrison in the nine planets. He shook his head, coming to the third door. He stopped, raising his hand and knocking.

"Who's there?" sounded through the door.

"I want to see Corporal Westerburg."

The door opened. A bovine youth with horn-rimmed glasses looked out, a book in his hand. "Who are you?"

"Doctor Harris."

"I'm sorry, sir. Corporal Westerburg is asleep."

"Would he mind if I woke him up? I want very much to talk to him." Harris peered inside. He could see a neat room with a desk, a rug and lamp, and two bunks. On one of the bunks was Westerburg, lying face up, his arms folded across his chest, his eyes tightly closed.

"Sir," the bovine youth said, "I'm afraid I can't wake him up for you, much as I'd like to."

"You can't? Why not?"

"Sir, Corporal Westerburg won't wake up, not after the sun sets. He just won't. He can't be wakened."

"Cataleptic? Really?"

"But in the morning, as soon as the sun comes up, he leaps out of bed and goes outside. Stays the whole day."

"I see," the Doctor said. "Well, thanks anyhow." He went back out into the hall and the door shut after him. "There's more to this than I realized," he murmured. He went on back the way he had come.

*** 

It was a warm, sunny day. The sky was almost free of clouds, and a gentle wind moved through the cedars along the bank of the stream. There was a path leading from the hospital building down the slope to the stream. At the stream a small bridge led over to the other side, and a few patients were standing on the bridge, wrapped in their bathrobes, looking aimlessly down at the water.

It took Harris several minutes to find Westerburg. The youth was not with the other patients, near or around the bridge. He had gone farther down, past the cedar trees and out onto a strip of bright meadow where poppies and grass grew everywhere. He was sitting on the stream bank, on a flat gray stone, leaning back and staring up, his mouth open a little. He did not notice the Doctor until Harris was almost beside him.

"Hello," Harris said softly.

Westerburg opened his eyes, looking up. He smiled and got slowly to his feet, a graceful, flowing motion that was rather surprising for a man of his size. "Hello, Doctor. What brings you out here?"

"Nothing. Thought I'd get some sun."

"Here, you can share my rock." Westerburg moved over and Harris sat down gingerly, being careful not to catch his trousers on the sharp edges of the rock. He lit a cigarette and gazed silently down at the water. Beside him, Westerburg had resumed his strange position, leaning back, resting on his hands, staring up with his eyes shut tight.

"Nice day," the Doctor said.

"Yes."

"Do you come here every day?"

"Yes."

"You like it better out here than inside."

"I can't stay inside," Westerburg said.

"You can't? How do you mean, *can't*?"

"You would die without *air*, wouldn't you?" the Corporal said.

"And you'd die without sunlight?"

Westerburg nodded.

"Corporal, may I ask you something? Do you plan to do this the rest of your life, sit out in the sun on a flat rock? Nothing else?"

Westerburg nodded.

"How about your job? You went to school for years to become a Patrolman. You wanted to enter the Patrol very badly. You were given a fine rating and a first-class position. How do you feel, giving all that up? You know, it won't be easy to get back in again. Do you realize that?"

"I realize it."

"And you're really going to give it all up?"

"That's right."

Harris was silent for a while. At last he put his cigarette out and turned toward the youth. "All right, let's say you give up your job and sit in the sun. Well, what happens then? Someone else has to do the job instead of you. Isn't that true? The job has to be done, *your* job has to be done. And if you don't do it, someone else has to."

"I suppose so."

"Westerburg, suppose everyone felt the way you do? Suppose everyone wanted to sit in the sun all day? What would happen? No one would check ships coming from outer space. Bacteria and toxic crystals would enter the system and cause mass death and suffering. Isn't that right?"

"If everyone felt the way I do, they wouldn't be going into outer space."

"But they have to. They have to trade, they have to get minerals and products and new plants."

"Why?"

"To keep society going."

"Why?"

"Well," Harris gestured, "people couldn't live without society."

Westerburg said nothing to that. Harris watched him, but the youth did not answer.

"Isn't that right?" Harris said.

"Perhaps. It's a peculiar business, Doctor. You know, I struggled for years to get through Training. I had to work and pay my own way. Washed dishes, worked in kitchens. Studied at night, learned, crammed, worked on and on. And you know what I think now?"

"What?"

"I wish I'd become a plant earlier."

Doctor Harris stood up. "Westerburg, when you come inside, will you stop off at my office? I want to give you a few tests if you don't mind."

"The shock box?" Westerburg smiled. "I knew that would be coming around. Sure, I don't mind."

Nettled, Harris left the rock, walking back up the bank a short distance. "About three, Corporal?"

The Corporal nodded.

Harris made his way up the hill, to the path, toward the hospital building. The whole thing was beginning to become more clear to him. A boy who had struggled all his life. Financial insecurity. Idealized goal, getting a Patrol assignment. Finally reached it, found the load too great. And on Asteroid Y-3 there was too much vegetation to look at all day. Primitive identification and projection on the flora of the asteroid. Concept of security involved in immobility and permanence. Unchanging forest.

He entered the building. A robot orderly stopped him almost at once. "Sir, Commander Cox wants you urgently on the vidphone."

"Thanks." Harris strode to his office. He dialed Cox's letter and the Commander's face came presently into focus. "Cox? This is Harris. I've been out talking to the boy. I'm beginning to get this lined up now. I can see the pattern, too much load too long. Finally gets what he wants and the idealization shatters under the—"

"Harris!" Cox barked. "Shut up and listen. I just got a report from Y-3. They're sending an express rocket here. It's on the way."

"An express rocket?"

"Five more cases like Westerburg. All say they're plants! The Garrison Chief is worried as hell. Says we *must* find out what it is or the Garrison will fall apart right away. Do you get me, Harris? Find out what it is!"

"Yes, sir," Harris murmured. "Yes, sir."

By the end of the week there were twenty cases, and all, of course, were from Asteroid Y-3.

Commander Cox and Harris stood together at the top of the hill, looking gloomily down at the stream below. Sixteen men and four women sat in the sun along the bank, none of them moving, none speaking. An hour had gone by since Cox and

Harris appeared, and in all that time the twenty people below had not stirred.

"I don't get it," Cox said, shaking his head. "I just absolutely don't get it. Harris, is this the beginning of the end? Is everything going to start cracking around us? It gives me a hell of a strange feeling to see those people down there, basking away in the sun, just sitting and basking."

"Who's that man there with the red hair?"

"That's Ulrich Deutsch. He was Second in Command at the Garrison. Now look at him! Sits and dozes with his mouth open and his eyes shut. A week ago that man was climbing, going right up to the top. When the Garrison Chief retires, he was supposed to take over. Maybe another year at the most. All his life he's been climbing to get up there."

"And now he sits in the sun," Harris finished.

"That woman. The brunette with the short hair. Career woman. Head of the entire office staff of the Garrison. And the man beside her. Janitor. And that cute little gal there with the bosom. Secretary, just out of school. All kinds. And I got a note this morning, three more coming in sometime today."

Harris nodded. "The strange thing is, they really *want* to sit down there. They're completely rational. They could do something else, but they just don't care to."

"Well?" Cox said. "What are you going to do? Have you found anything? We're counting on you. Let's hear it."

"I couldn't get anything out of them directly," Harris said, "but I've had some interesting results with the shock box. Let's go inside and I'll show you."

"Fine," Cox turned and started toward the hospital. "Show me anything you've got. This is serious. Now I know how Tiberius felt when Christianity showed up in high places."

Harris snapped off the light. The room was pitch black. "I'll run this first reel for you. The subject is one of the best biologists stationed at the Garrison. Robert Bradshaw. He came in yester-day. I got a good run from the shock box because Bradshaw's mind is so highly differentiated. There's a lot of repressed material of a non-rational nature, more than usual."

He pressed a switch. The projector whirred and on the far wall a three-dimensional image appeared in color, so real that it might have been the man himself. Robert Bradshaw was a man of fifty, heavyset, with iron-gray hair and a square jaw. He sat in the chair calmly, his hands resting on the arms, oblivious to the electrodes attached to his neck and wrist. "There I go," Harris said. "Watch."

His film-image appeared, approaching Bradshaw. "Now Mr. Bradshaw," his image said, "this won't hurt you at all, and it'll help us a lot." The image rotated the controls on the shock box. Bradshaw stiffened and his jaw set, but otherwise he gave no sign. The image of Harris regarded him for a time and then stepped away from the controls.

"Can you hear me, Mr. Bradshaw?" the image asked.

"Yes."

"What is your name?"

"Robert C. Bradshaw."

"What is your position?"

"Chief Biologist at the check station on Y-3."

"Are you there now?"

"No, I'm back on Terra. In a hospital."

"Why?"

"Because I admitted to the Garrison Chief that I had become a plant."

"Is that true? That you are a plant."

"Yes, in a non-biological sense. I retain the physiology of a human being, of course."

"What do you mean then, that you're a plant?"

"The reference is to attitudinal response, to Weltanschauung."

"Go on."

"It is possible for a warm-blooded animal, an upper primate, to adopt the psychology of a plant to some extent."

"Yes?"

"I refer to this."

"And the others? They refer to this also?"

"Yes."

"How did this occur, your adopting this attitude?"

Bradshaw's image hesitated, the lips twisting. "See?" Harris said to Cox. "Strong conflict. He wouldn't have gone on if he had been fully conscious."

"I—"

"Yes?"

"I was taught to become a plant."

The image of Harris showed surprise and interest. "What do you mean, you were *taught* to become a plant?"

"They realized my problems and taught me to become a plant. Now I'm free from them, the problems."

"Who? Who taught you?"

"The Pipers."

"Who? The Pipers? Who are the Pipers?"

There was no answer.

"Mr. Bradshaw, who are the Pipers?"

After a long, agonized pause, the heavy lips parted. "They live in the woods…"

Harris snapped off the projector, and the lights came on. He and Cox blinked. "That was all I could get," Harris said. "But I was lucky to get that. He wasn't supposed to tell, not at all. That was the thing they all promised not to do, tell who taught them to become plants. The Pipers who live in the woods on Asteroid Y-3."

"You got this story from all twenty?"

"No." Harris grimaced. "Most of them put up too much fight. I couldn't even get *this* much from them."

Cox reflected. "The Pipers. Well? What do you propose to do? Just wait around until you can get the full story? Is that your program?"

"No," Harris said. "Not at all. I'm going to Y-3 and find out who the Pipers are myself."

***

The small patrol ship made its landing with care and precision, its jets choking into final silence. The hatch slid back, and Doctor Henry Harris found himself staring out at a field, a brown sunbaked landing field. At the end of the field was a tall signal tower. Around the field on all sides were long gray buildings, the Garrison check station itself. Not far off a huge Venusian cruiser was parked, a vast, green hulk like an enormous lime. The technicians from the station were swarming all over it, checking and examining each inch of it for lethal lifeforms and poisons that might have attached themselves to the hull.

"All out, sir," the pilot said.

Harris nodded. He took hold of his two suitcases and stepped carefully down. The ground was hot underfoot, and he blinked in the bright sunlight. Jupiter was in the sky, and the vast planet reflected considerable sunlight down onto the asteroid.

Harris started across the field, carrying his suitcases. A field attendant was already busy opening the storage compartment of the patrol ship, extracting his trunk. The attendant lowered the trunk into a waiting dolly and came after him, manipulating the little truck with bored skill.

As Harris came to the entrance of the signal tower, the gate slid back and a man came forward, an older man, large and robust, with white hair and a steady walk.

"How are you, Doctor?" he said, holding his hand out. "I'm Lawrence Watts, the Garrison Chief."

They shook hands. Watts smiled down at Harris. He was a huge old man, still regal and straight in his dark blue uniform, with his gold epaulets sparkling on his shoulders.

"Have a good trip?" Watts asked. "Come on inside and I'll have a drink fixed for you. It gets hot around here with the Big Mirror up there."

"Jupiter?" Harris followed him inside the building. The signal tower was cool and dark, a welcome relief. "Why is the gravity so near Terra's? I expected to go flying off like a kangaroo. Is it artificial?"

"No. There's a dense core of some kind to the asteroid, some kind of metallic deposit. That's why we picked this asteroid out of all the others. It made the construction problem much simpler, and it also explains why the asteroid has natural air and water. Did you see the hills?"

"The hills?"

"When we get up higher in the tower, we'll be able to see over the buildings. There's quite a natural park here, a regular little forest complete with everything you'd want. Come in here, Harris. This is my office." The old man strode at quite a clip, around the corner and into a large, well-furnished apartment. "Isn't this pleasant? I intend to make my last year here as amiable as possible." He frowned. "Of course, with Deutsch gone, I may be here forever. Oh well." He shrugged. "Sit down, Harris."

"Thanks." Harris took a chair, stretching his legs out. He watched Watts as he closed the door to the hall. "By the way, any more cases come up?"

"Two more today," Watts was grim. "Makes almost thirty in all. We have three hundred men in this station. At the rate it's going—"

"Chief, you spoke about a forest on the asteroid. Do you allow the crew to go into the forest at will? Or do you restrict them to the buildings and grounds?"

Watts rubbed his jaw. "Well, it's a difficult situation, Harris. I have to let the men leave the grounds sometimes. They can *see* the forest from the buildings, and as long as you can see a nice place to stretch out and relax that does it. Once every ten days they have a full period of rest. Then they go out and fool around."

"And then it happens?"

"Yes, I suppose so. But as long as they can see the forest, they'll want to go. I can't help it."

"I know. I'm not censuring you. Well, what's your theory? What happens to them out there? What do they do?"

"What happens? Once they get out there and take it easy for a while, they don't want to come back and work. It's boondoggling. Playing hookey. They don't want to work, so off they go."

"How about this business of their delusions?"

Watts laughed good-naturedly. "Listen, Harris. You know as well as I do that's a lot of poppycock. They're no more plants than you or I. They just don't want to work, that's all. When I was a cadet, we had a few ways to make people work. I wish we could lay a few on their backs like we used to."

"You think this is simple goldbricking then?"

"Don't you think it is?"

"No," Harris said. "They really believe they're plants. I put them through the high-frequency shock treatment, the shock box. The whole nervous system is paralyzed, all inhibitions stopped cold. They tell the truth then. And they said the same thing, and more."

Watts paced back and forth, his hands clasped behind his back. "Harris, you're a doctor, and I suppose you know what you're talking about. But look at the situation here. We have a garrison, a good, modern garrison. We're probably the most modern outfit in the system. Every new device and gadget is here that science can produce. Harris, this garrison is one vast machine. The men are parts, and each has his job—the Maintenance Crew, the Biologists, the Office Crew, the Managerial Staff.

"Look what happens when one person steps away from his job. Everything else begins to creak. We can't service the bugs if no one services the machines. We can't order food to feed the crews if no one makes out reports, takes inventories. We can't direct any kind of activity if the Second in Command decides to go out and sit in the sun all day.

"Thirty people, one tenth of the Garrison. But we can't run without them. The Garrison is built that way. If you take the supports out, the whole building falls. No one can leave. We're all tied here, and these people know it. They know they have no right to do that, run off on their own. No one has that right anymore. We're all too tightly interwoven to suddenly start doing what we want. It's unfair to the rest, the majority."

Harris nodded. "Chief, can I ask you something?"

"What is it?"

"Are there any inhabitants on the asteroid? Any natives?"

"Natives?" Watts considered. "Yes, there's some kind of aborigines living out there." He waved vaguely toward the window.

"What are they like? Have you seen them?"

"Yes, I've seen them. At least, I saw them when we first came here. They hung around for a while, watching us, then after a time they disappeared."

"Did they die off? Diseases of some kind?"

"No. They just—just disappeared. Into their forest. They're still there someplace."

"What kind of people are they?"

"Well, the story is that they're originally from Mars. They don't look much like Martians though. They're dark, a kind of coppery color. Thin. Very agile, in their own way. They hunt and fish. No written language. We don't pay much attention to them."

"I see." Harris paused. "Chief, have you ever heard of anything called the Pipers?"

"The Pipers?" Watts frowned. "No. Why?"

"The patients mentioned something called the Pipers. According to Bradshaw, the Pipers taught him to become a plant. He learned it from them, a kind of teaching."

"The Pipers. What are they?"

"I don't know," Harris admitted. "I thought maybe you might know. My first assumption, of course, was that they're the natives. But now I'm not so sure, not after hearing your description of them."

"The natives are primitive savages. They don't have anything to teach anybody, especially a top-flight biologist."

Harris hesitated. "Chief, I'd like to go into the woods and look around. Is that possible?"

"Certainly. I can arrange it for you. I'll give you one of the men to show you around."

"I'd rather go alone. Is there any danger?"

"No, none that I know of. Except—"

"Except the Pipers," Harris finished. "I know. Well, there's only one way to find them, and that's it. I'll have to take my chances."

"If you walk in a straight line," Chief Watts said, "you'll find yourself back at the Garrison in about six hours. It's a damn small asteroid. There's a couple of streams and lakes, so don't fall in."

"How about snakes or poisonous insects?"

"Nothing like that reported. We did a lot of tramping around at first, but it's grown back now, the way it was. We never encountered anything dangerous."

"Thanks, Chief," Harris said. They shook hands. "I'll see you before nightfall."

"Good luck." The Chief and his two armed escorts turned and went back across the rise, down the other side toward the Garrison. Harris watched them go until they disappeared inside the building. Then he turned and started into the grove of trees.

The woods were very silent around him as he walked. Trees towered up on all sides of him, huge dark-green trees like eucalyptus. The ground underfoot was soft with endless leaves that had fallen and rotted into soil. After a while the grove of high trees fell behind, and he found himself crossing a dry meadow, the grass and weeds burned brown in the sun. Insects buzzed around him, rising up from the dry weed stalks. Something scuttled ahead, hurrying through the undergrowth. He caught sight of a gray ball with many legs, scampering furiously, its antennae weaving.

The meadow ended at the bottom of a hill. He was going up now, going higher and higher. Ahead of him an endless expanse of green rose, acres of wild growth. He scrambled to the top finally, blowing and panting, catching his breath.

He went on. Now he was going down again, plunging into a deep gully. Tall ferns grew as large as trees. He was entering a living Jurassic forest, ferns that stretched out endlessly ahead of him. Down he went, walking carefully. The air began to turn cold around him. The floor of the gully was damp and silent. Underfoot the ground was almost wet.

He came out on a level table. It was dark, with the ferns growing up on all sides, dense growths of ferns, silent and unmoving. He came upon a natural path, an old stream bed, rough and rocky, but easy to follow. The air was thick and oppressive. Beyond the ferns he could see the side of the next hill, a green field rising up.

Something gray was ahead. Rocks, piled-up boulders, scattered and stacked here and there. The stream bed led directly to them. Apparently this had been a pool of some kind, a stream emptying from it. He climbed the first of the boulders awkwardly, feeling his way up. At the top he paused, resting again.

As yet he had had no luck. So far he had not met any of the natives. It would be through them that he would find the mysterious Pipers that were stealing the men away, if such really existed. If he could find the natives, talk to them, perhaps he could find out something. But as yet he had been unsuccessful. He looked around. The woods were very silent. A slight breeze moved through the ferns, rustling them, but that was all. Where were the natives? Probably they had a settlement of some sort, huts, a clearing. The asteroid was small. He should be able to find them by nightfall.

He started down the rocks. More rocks rose up ahead, and he climbed them. Suddenly he stopped, listening. Far off, he could hear a sound, the sound of water. Was he approaching a pool of some kind? He went on again, trying to locate the sound. He scrambled down rocks and up rocks, and all around him there was silence, except for the splashing of distant water. Maybe a waterfall, water in motion. A stream. If he found the stream, he might find the natives.

The rocks ended and the stream bed began again, but this time it was wet, the bottom muddy and overgrown with moss. He was on the right track. Not too long ago this stream had flowed, probably during the rainy season. He went up on the side of the stream, pushing through the ferns and vines. A golden snake slid expertly out of his path. Something glinted ahead, something sparkling through the ferns. Water. A pool. He hurried, pushing the vines aside and stepping out, leaving them behind.

He was standing on the edge of a pool, a deep pool sunk in a hollow of gray rocks, surrounded by ferns and vines. The water was clear and bright, and in motion, flowing in a waterfall at the far end. It was beautiful and he stood watching, marveling at it, the undisturbed quality of it. Untouched, it was. Just as it had always been, probably. As long as the asteroid existed. Was he the first to see it? Perhaps. It was so hidden, so concealed by the ferns. It gave him a strange feeling, a feeling almost of ownership. He stepped down a little toward the water.

And it was then he noticed her.

The girl was sitting on the far edge of the pool, staring down into the water, resting her head on one drawn-up knee. She had been bathing; he could see that at once. Her coppery body was still wet and glistening with moisture, sparkling in the sun. She had not seen him. He stopped, holding his breath, watching her.

She was lovely, very lovely, with long dark hair that wound around her shoulders and arms. Her body was slim, very slender, with a supple grace to it that made him stare, accustomed as he was to various forms of anatomy. How silent she was! Silent and unmoving, staring down at the water. Time passed, strange, unchanging time, as he watched the girl. Time might even have ceased, with the girl sitting on the rock staring into the water, and the rows of great ferns behind her, as rigid as if they had been painted there.

All at once the girl looked up. Harris shifted, suddenly conscious of himself as an intruder. He stepped back. "I'm sorry," he murmured. "I'm from the Garrison. I didn't mean to come poking around."

She nodded without speaking.

"You don't mind?" Harris asked presently.

"No."

So she spoke Terran! He moved a little toward her, around the side of the pool. "I hope you don't mind my bothering you. I won't be on the asteroid very long. This is my first day here. I just arrived from Terra."

She smiled faintly.

"I'm a doctor. Henry Harris." He looked down at her, at the slim, coppery body gleaming in the sunlight, a faint sheen of moisture on her arms and thighs. "You might be interested in why I'm here." He paused. "Maybe you can even help me."

She looked up a little. "Oh?"

"Would you like to help me?"

She smiled. "Yes. Of course."

"That's good. Mind if I sit down?" He looked around and found himself a flat rock. He sat down slowly, facing her. "Cigarette?"

"No."

"Well, I'll have one." He lit up, taking a deep breath. "You see, we have a problem at the Garrison. Something has been happening to some of the men, and it seems to be spreading. We have to find out what causes it, or we won't be able to run the Garrison."

He waited for a moment. She nodded slightly. How silent she was! Silent and unmoving. Like the ferns.

"Well, I've been able to find out a few things from them, and one very interesting fact stands out. They keep saying that something called—called the Pipers are responsible for their condition. They say the Pipers taught them—" He stopped. A strange look had flitted across her dark, small face. "Do you know the Pipers?"

She nodded.

Acute satisfaction flooded over Harris. "You do? I was sure the natives would know." He stood up again. "I was sure they would if the Pipers really existed. Then they do exist, do they?"

"They exist."

Harris frowned. "And they're here, in the woods?"

"Yes."

"I see." He ground his cigarette out impatiently. "You don't suppose there's any chance you could take me to them, do you?"

"Take you?"

"Yes. I have this problem, and I have to solve it. You see, the Base Commander on Terra has assigned this to me, this business about the Pipers. It has to be solved. And I'm the one assigned to the job. So it's important to me to find them. Do you see? Do you understand?"

She nodded.

"Well, will you take me to them?"

The girl was silent. For a long time she sat, staring down into the water, resting her head against her knee. Harris began to become impatient. He fidgeted back and forth, resting first on one leg and then on the other.

"Well, will you?" he said again. "It's important to the whole Garrison. What do you say?" He felt around in his pockets. "Maybe I could give you something. What do I have…" He brought out his lighter. "I could give you my lighter."

The girl stood up, rising slowly, gracefully, without motion or effort. Harris's mouth fell open. How supple she was, gliding to her feet in a single motion! He blinked. Without effort she had stood, seemingly without *change*. All at once she was standing instead of sitting, standing and looking calmly at him, her small face expressionless.

"Will you?" he said.

"Yes. Come along." She turned away, moving toward the row of ferns.

Harris followed quickly, stumbling across the rocks. "Fine," he said. "Thanks a lot. I'm very interested to meet these Pipers. Where are you taking me, to your village? How much time do we have before nightfall?"

The girl did not answer. She had entered the ferns already, and Harris quickened his pace to keep from losing her. How silently she glided!

"Wait," he called. "Wait for me."

The girl paused, waiting for him, slim and lovely, looking silently back.

He entered the ferns, hurrying after her.

***

"Well, I'll be damned!" Commander Cox said. "It sure didn't take you long." He leaped down the steps two at a time. "Let me give you a hand."

Harris grinned, lugging his heavy suitcases. He set them down and breathed a sigh of relief. "It isn't worth it," he said. "I'm going to give up taking so much."

"Come on inside. Soldier, give him a hand." A Patrolman hurried over and took one of the suitcases. The three men went inside and down the corridor to Harris's quarters. Harris unlocked the door, and the Patrolman deposited his suitcase inside.

"Thanks," Harris said. He set the other down beside it. "It's good to be back, even for a little while."

"A little while?"

"I just came back to settle my affairs. I have to return to Y-3 tomorrow morning."

"Then you didn't solve the problem?"

"I solved it, but I haven't *cured* it. I'm going back and get to work right away. There's a lot to be done."

"But you found out what it is?"

"Yes. It was just what the men said. The Pipers."

"The Pipers do exist?"

"Yes." Harris nodded. "They do exist." He removed his coat and put it over the back of the chair. Then he went to the window and let it down. Warm spring air rushed into the room. He settled himself on the bed, leaning back.

"The Pipers exist, all right—in the minds of the Garrison crew! To the crew, the Pipers are real. The crew created them.

It's a mass hypnosis, a group projection, and all the men there have it to some degree."

"How did it start?"

"Those men on Y-3 were sent there because they were skilled, highly trained men with exceptional ability. All their lives they've been schooled by complex modern society, fast tempo and high integration between people. Constant pressure toward some goal, some job to be done.

"Those men are put down suddenly on an asteroid where there are natives living the most primitive of existence, completely vegetable lives. No concept of goal, no concept of purpose, and hence no ability to plan. The natives live the way the animals live, from day to day, sleeping, picking food from the trees. A kind of Garden-of-Eden existence, without struggle or conflict."

"So? But—"

"Each of the Garrison crew sees the natives and *unconsciously* thinks of his own early life, when he was a child, when *he* had no worries, no responsibilities, before he joined modern society. A baby lying in the sun.

"But he can't admit this to himself! He can't admit that he might *want* to live like the natives, to lie and sleep all day. So he invents the Pipers, the idea of a mysterious group living in the woods who trap him, lead him into their kind of life. Then he can blame *them*, not himself. They 'teach' him to become a part of the woods."

"What are you going to do? Have the woods burned?"

"No," Harris shook his head, "that's not the answer. The woods are harmless. The answer is psychotherapy for the men. That's why I'm going right back, so I can begin work. They've got to be made to see that the Pipers are inside them, their own unconscious voices calling to them to give up their responsibilities. They've got to be made to realize that there are no Pipers, at least not outside themselves. The woods are harmless, and the natives have nothing to teach anyone. They're primitive savages, without even a written language. We're seeing a psychological projection by a whole Garrison of men who want to lay down their work and take it easy for a while."

The room was silent.

"I see," Cox said presently. "Well, it makes sense." He got to his feet. "I hope you can do something with the men when you get back."

"I hope so too," Harris agreed. "And I think I can. After all, it's just a question of increasing their self-awareness. When they have that, the Pipers will vanish."

Cox nodded. "Well, you go ahead with your unpacking, Doc. I'll see you at dinner. And maybe before you leave, tomorrow."

"Fine."

Harris opened the door, and the Commander went out into the hall. Harris closed the door after him and then went back across the room. He looked out the window for a moment, his hands in his pockets.

It was becoming evening, the air was turning cool. The sun was just setting as he watched, disappearing behind the buildings of the city surrounding the hospital. He watched it go down.

Then he went over to his two suitcases. He was tired, very tired from his trip. A great weariness was beginning to descend over him. There were so many things to do, so terribly many. How could he hope to do them all? Back to the asteroid. And then what?

He yawned, his eyes closing. How sleepy he was! He looked over at the bed. Then he sat down on the edge of it and took his shoes off. So much to do, the next day.

He put his shoes in the corner of the room. Then he bent over, unsnapping one of the suitcases. He opened the suitcase.

From it he took a bulging gunnysack. Carefully, he emptied the contents of the sack out on the floor. Dirt, rich soft dirt. Dirt he had collected during his last hours there, dirt he had carefully gathered up.

When the dirt was spread out on the floor, he sat down in the middle of it. He stretched himself out, leaning back. When he was fully comfortable, he folded his hands across his chest and closed his eyes. So much work to do, but later on of course. Tomorrow. How warm the dirt was…

He was sound asleep in a moment.

# SECOND VARIETY

**THE RUSSIAN SOLDIER** made his way nervously up the ragged side of the hill, holding his gun ready. He glanced around him, licking his dry lips, his face set. From time to time he reached up a gloved hand and wiped perspiration from his neck, pushing down his coat collar.

Eric turned to Corporal Leone. "Want him? Or can I have him?" He adjusted the view sight so the Russian's features squarely filled the glass, the lines cutting across his hard, somber features.

Leone considered. The Russian was close, moving rapidly, almost running. "Don't fire. Wait." Leone tensed. "I don't think we're needed."

The Russian increased his pace, kicking ash and piles of debris out of his way. He reached the top of the hill and stopped, panting, staring around him. The sky was overcast, drifting clouds of gray particles. Bare trunks of trees jutted up occasionally. The ground was level and bare, rubble-strewn, with the ruins of buildings standing out here and there like yellowing skulls.

The Russian was uneasy. He knew something was wrong. He started down the hill. Now he was only a few paces from the bunker. Eric was getting fidgety. He played with his pistol, glancing at Leone.

"Don't worry," Leone said. "He won't get here. They'll take care of him."

"Are you sure? He's got damn far."

"They hang around close to the bunker. He's getting into the bad part. Get set!"

The Russian began to hurry, sliding down the hill, his boots sinking into the heaps of gray ash, trying to keep his gun up. He stopped for a moment, lifting his fieldglasses to his face.

"He's looking right at us," Eric said.

The Russian came on. They could see his eyes, like two blue stones. His mouth was open a little. He needed a shave; his chin was stubbled. On one bony cheek was a square of tape, showing blue at the edge. A fungoid spot. His coat was muddy and torn. One glove was missing. As he ran his belt counter bounced up and down against him.

Leone touched Eric's arm. "Here one comes."

Across the ground something small and metallic came, flashing in the dull sunlight of midday. A metal sphere. It raced up the hill after the Russian, its treads flying. It was small, one of the baby ones. Its claws were out, two razor projections spinning in a blur of white steel. The Russian heard it. He turned instantly, firing. The sphere dissolved into particles. But already a second had emerged and was following the first. The Russian fired again.

A third sphere leaped up the Russian's leg, clicking and whirring. It jumped to the shoulder. The spinning blades disappeared into the Russian's throat.

Eric relaxed. "Well, that's that. God, those damn things give me the creeps. Sometimes I think we were better off before."

"If we hadn't invented them, they would have." Leone lit a cigarette shakily. "I wonder why a Russian would come all this way alone. I didn't see anyone covering him."

Lt. Scott came slipping up the tunnel, into the bunker. "What happened? Something entered the screen."

"An Ivan."

"Just one?"

Eric brought the view screen around. Scott peered into it. Now there were numerous metal spheres crawling over the prostrate body, dull metal globes clicking and whirring, sawing up the Russian into small parts to be carried away.

"What a lot of claws," Scott murmured.

"They come like flies. Not much game for them anymore."

Scott pushed the sight away, disgusted. "Like flies. I wonder why he was out there. They know we have claws all around."

A larger robot had joined the smaller spheres. It was directing operations, a long blunt tube with projecting eyepieces. There was not much left of the soldier. What remained was being brought down the hillside by the host of claws.

"Sir," Leone said. "If it's all right, I'd like to go out there and take a look at him."

"Why?"

"Maybe he came with something."

Scott considered. He shrugged. "All right. But be careful."

"I have my tab." Leone patted the metal band at his wrist. "I'll be out of bounds."

He picked up his rifle and stepped carefully up to the mouth of the bunker, making his way between blocks of concrete and steel prongs, twisted and bent. The air was cold at the top. He crossed over the ground toward the remains of the soldier, striding across the soft ash. A wind blew around him, swirling gray particles up in his face. He squinted and pushed on.

The claws retreated as he came close, some of them stiffening into immobility. He touched his tab. The Ivan would have given something for that! Short hard radiation emitted from the tab neutralized the claws, put them out of commission. Even the big robot with its two waving eyestalks retreated respectfully as he approached.

He bent down over the remains of the soldier. The gloved hand was closed tightly. There was something in it. Leone pried the fingers apart. A sealed container, aluminum. Still shiny.

He put it in his pocket and made his way back to the bunker. Behind him the claws came back to life, moving into operation again. The procession resumed, metal spheres moving through the gray ash with their loads. He could hear their treads scrabbling against the ground. He shuddered.

Scott watched intently as he brought the shiny tube out of his pocket. "He had that?"

"In his hand." Leone unscrewed the top. "Maybe you should look at it, sir."

Scott took it. He emptied the contents out in the palm of his hand. A small piece of silk paper, carefully folded. He sat down by the light and unfolded it.

"What's it say, sir?" Eric said. Several officers came up the tunnel. Major Hendricks appeared.

"Major," Scott said. "Look at this."

Hendricks read the slip. "This just come?"

"A single runner. Just now."

"Where is he?" Hendricks asked sharply.

"The claws got him."

Major Hendricks grunted. "Here." He passed it to his companions. "I think this is what we've been waiting for. They certainly took their time about it."

"So they want to talk terms," Scott said. "Are we going along with them?"

"That's not for us to decide." Hendricks sat down. "Where's the communications officer? I want the Moon Base."

Leone pondered as the communications officer raised the outside antenna cautiously, scanning the sky above the bunker for any sign of a watching Russian ship.

"Sir," Scott said to Hendricks. "It's sure strange they suddenly came around. We've been using the claws for almost a year. Now all of a sudden they start to fold."

"Maybe claws have been getting down in their bunkers."

"One of the big ones, the kind with stalks, got into an Ivan bunker last week," Eric said. "It got a whole platoon of them before they got their lid shut."

"How do you know?"

"A buddy told me. The thing came back with—with remains."

"Moon Base, sir," the communications officer said.

On the screen the face of the lunar monitor appeared. His crisp uniform contrasted to the uniforms in the bunker. And he was clean shaven. "Moon Base."

"This is forward command L-Whistle. On Terra. Let me have General Thompson."

The monitor faded. Presently General Thompson's heavy features came into focus. "What is it, Major?"

"Our claws got a single Russian runner with a message. We don't know whether to act on it—there have been tricks like this in the past."

"What's the message?"

"The Russians want us to send a single officer on policy level over to their lines. For a conference. They don't state the nature of the conference. They say that matters of—" He consulted the slip. "—matters of grave urgency make it advisable that discussion be opened between a representative of the UN forces and themselves."

He held the message up to the screen for the general to scan. Thompson's eyes moved.

"What should we do?" Hendricks said.

"Send a man out."

"You don't think it's a trap?"

"It might be. But the location they give for their forward command is correct. It's worth a try, at any rate."

"I'll send an officer out. And report the results to you as soon as he returns."

"All right, Major." Thompson broke the connection. The screen died. Up above, the antenna came slowly down.

Hendricks rolled up the paper, deep in thought.

"I'll go," Leone said.

"They want somebody at policy level." Hendricks rubbed his jaw. "Policy level. I haven't been outside in months. Maybe I could use a little air."

"Don't you think it's risky?"

Hendricks lifted the view sight and gazed into it. The remains of the Russian were gone. Only a single claw was in sight. It was folding itself back, disappearing into the ash, like a crab. Like some hideous metal crab…

"That's the only thing that bothers me." Hendricks rubbed his wrist. "I know I'm safe as long as I have this on me. But there's something about them. I hate the damn things. I wish we'd never invented them. There's something wrong with them. Relentless little—"

"If we hadn't invented them, the Ivans would have."

Hendricks pushed the sight back. "Anyhow, it seems to be winning the war. I guess that's good."

"Sounds like you're getting the same jitters as the Ivans." Hendricks examined his wristwatch. "I guess I had better get started, if I want to be there before dark."

He took a deep breath and then stepped out onto the gray, rubbled ground. After a minute he lit a cigarette and stood gazing around him. The landscape was dead. Nothing stirred. He could see for miles, endless ash and slag, ruins of buildings. A few trees without leaves or branches, only the trunks. Above him the eternal rolling clouds of gray, drifting between Terra and the sun.

Major Hendricks went on. Off to the right something scuttled, something round and metallic. A claw, going lickety-split after something. Probably after a small animal, a rat. They got rats, too. As a sort of sideline.

He came to the top of the little hill and lifted his field glasses. The Russian lines were a few miles ahead of him. They had a forward command post there. The runner had come from it.

A squat robot with undulating arms passed by him, its arms weaving inquiringly. The robot went on its way, disappearing under some debris. Hendricks watched it go. He had never seen that type before. There were getting to be more and more types he had never seen, new varieties and sizes coming up from the underground factories.

Hendricks put out his cigarette and hurried on. It was interesting, the use of artificial forms in warfare. How had they got started? Necessity. The Soviet Union had gained great initial success, usual with the side that got the war going. Most of North America had been blasted off the map. Retaliation was quick in coming, of course. The sky was full of circling disc-bombers long before the war began. They had been up there for years. The discs began sailing down all over Russia within hours after Washington got it.

But that hadn't helped Washington.

The American bloc governments moved to the Moon Base the first year. There was not much else to do. Europe was gone—a slag heap with dark weeds growing from the ashes and bones. Most of North America was useless. Nothing could be planted, no one could live. A few million people kept going up in Canada and down in South America. But during the second year Soviet parachutists began to drop, a few at first, then more and more. They wore the first really effective anti-radiation equipment. What was left of American production moved to the moon along with the governments.

All but the troops. The remaining troops stayed behind as best they could, a few thousand here, a platoon there. No one knew exactly where they were; they stayed where they could, moving around at night, hiding in ruins, in sewers, cellars, with the rats and snakes. It looked as if the Soviet Union had the war almost won. Except for a handful of projectiles fired off from the moon daily, there was almost no weapon in use against them. They came and went as they pleased. The war, for all practical purposes, was over. Nothing effective opposed them.

And then the first claws appeared. And overnight the complexion of the war changed.

The claws were awkward at first. Slow. The Ivans knocked them off almost as fast as they crawled out of their underground tunnels. But then they got better, faster and more cunning. Factories, all on Terra, turned them out. Factories a long way underground, behind the Soviet lines, factories that had once made atomic projectiles, now almost forgotten.

The claws got faster, and they got bigger. New types appeared, some with feelers, some that flew. There were a few jumping kinds.

The best technicians on the moon were working on designs, making them more and more intricate, more flexible. They became uncanny; the Ivans were having a lot of trouble with them. Some of the little claws were learning to hide themselves, burrowing down into the ash, lying in wait.

And then they started getting into the Russian bunkers, slipping down when the lids were raised for air and a look around. One claw inside a bunker—a churning sphere of blades and metal—that was enough. And when one got in others followed. With a weapon like that the war couldn't go on much longer.

Maybe it was already over.

Maybe he was going to hear the news. Maybe the Politburo had decided to throw in the sponge. Too bad it had taken so long. Six years. A long time for war like that, the way they had waged it. The automatic retaliation discs, spinning down all over Russia, hundreds of thousands of them. Bacteria crystals. The Soviet guided missiles, whistling through the air. The chain bombs. And now this, the robots, the claws—

The claws weren't like other weapons. They were *alive*, from any practical standpoint, whether the governments wanted to admit it or not. They were not machines. They were living things, spinning, creeping, shaking themselves up suddenly from the gray ash and darting toward a man, climbing up him, rushing for his throat. And that was what they had been designed to do. Their job.

They did their job well. Especially lately, with the new designs coming up. Now they repaired themselves. They were on their own. Radiation tabs protected the UN troops, but if a man lost his tab he was fair game for the claws, no matter what his uniform. Down below the surface automatic machinery stamped them out. Human beings stayed a long way off. It was too risky; nobody wanted to be around them. They were left to themselves. And they seemed to be doing all right. The new designs were faster, more complex. More efficient.

Apparently they had won the war.

Major Hendricks lit a second cigarette. The landscape depressed him. Nothing but ash and ruins. He seemed to be alone, the only living thing in the whole world. To the right the ruins of a town rose up, a few walls and heaps of debris. He tossed the dead match away, increasing his pace. Suddenly he stopped, jerking up his gun, his body tense. For a minute it looked like—

From behind the shell of a ruined building a figure came, walking slowly toward him, walking hesitantly.

Hendricks blinked. "Stop!"

The boy stopped. Hendricks lowered his gun. The boy stood silently, looking at him. He was small, not very old. Perhaps eight. But it was hard to tell. Most of the kids who remained were stunted. He wore a faded blue sweater, ragged with dirt, and short pants. His hair was long and matted. Brown hair. It hung over his face and around his ears. He held something in his arms.

"What's that you have?" Hendricks said sharply.

The boy held it out. It was a toy, a bear. A teddy bear. The boy's eyes were large, but without expression.

Hendricks relaxed. "I don't want it. Keep it."

The boy hugged the bear again.

"Where do you live?" Hendricks said.

"In there."

"The ruins?"

"Yes."

"Underground?"

"Yes."

"How many are there?"

"How—how many?"

"How many of you. How big's your settlement?"

The boy did not answer.

Hendricks frowned. "You're not all by yourself, are you?"

The boy nodded.

"How do you stay alive?"

"There's food."

"What kind of food?"

"Different."

Hendricks studied him. "How old are you?"

"Thirteen."

It wasn't possible. Or was it? The boy was thin, stunted. And probably sterile. Radiation exposure, years straight. No wonder he was so small. His arms and legs were like pipe cleaners, knobby and thin. Hendricks touched the boy's arm. His skin was dry and rough—radiation skin. He bent down, looking into the boy's face. There was no expression. Big eyes, big and dark.

"Are you blind?" Hendricks said.

"No. I can see some."

"How do you get away from the claws?"

"The claws?"

"The round things. That run and burrow."

"I don't understand."

Maybe there weren't any claws around. A lot of areas were free. They collected mostly around bunkers, where there were people. The claws had been designed to sense warmth, warmth of living things.

"You're lucky." Hendricks straightened up. "Well? Which way are you going? Back—back there?"

"Can I come with you?"

"With *me*?" Hendricks folded his arms. "I'm going a long way. Miles. I have to hurry." He looked at his watch. "I have to get there by nightfall."

"I want to come."

Hendricks fumbled in his pack. "It isn't worth it. Here." He tossed down the food cans he had with him. "You take these and go back. Okay?"

The boy said nothing.

"I'll be coming back this way. In a day or so. If you're around here when I come back, you can come along with me. All right?"

"I want to go with you now."

"It's a long walk."

"I can walk."

Hendricks shifted uneasily. It made too good a target, two people walking along. And the boy would slow him down. But he might not come back this way. And if the boy were really all alone—

"Okay. Come along."

The boy fell in beside him. Hendricks strode along. The boy walked silently, clutching his teddy bear.

"What's your name?" Hendricks said after a time.

"David Edward Derring."

"David? What—what happened to your mother and father?"

"They died."

"How?"

"In the blast."

"How long ago?"

"Six years."

Hendricks slowed down. "You've been alone six years?"

"No. There were other people for a while. They went away."

"And you've been alone since?"

"Yes."

Hendricks glanced down. The boy was strange, saying very little. Withdrawn. But that was the way they were, the children who had survived. Quiet. Stoic. A strange kind of fatalism gripped them. Nothing came as a surprise. They accepted anything that came along. There was no longer any *normal*, any natural course of things, moral or physical, for them to expect. Custom, habit, all the determining forces of learning were gone; only brute experience remained.

"Am I walking too fast?" Hendricks said.

"No."

"How did you happen to see me?"

"I was waiting."

"Waiting?" Hendricks was puzzled. "What were you waiting for?"

"To catch things."

"What kind of things?"

"Things to eat."

"Oh." Hendricks set his lips grimly. A thirteen-year-old boy living on rats and gophers and half-rotten canned food. Down in a hole under the ruins of a town. With radiation pools and claws, and Russian dive-mines up above, coasting around in the sky.

"Where are we going?" David asked.

"To the Russian lines."

"Russian?"

"The enemy. The people who started the war. They dropped the first radiation bombs. They began all this."

The boy nodded. His face showed no expression.

"I'm an American," Hendricks said.

There was no comment. On they went, the two of them, Hendricks walking a little ahead, David trailing behind him, hugging his dirty teddy bear against his chest.

About four in the afternoon they stopped to eat. Hendricks built a fire in a hollow between some slabs of concrete. He cleared the weeds away and heaped up bits of wood. The Russians's lines were not very far ahead. Around him was what had once been a long valley, acres of fruit trees and grapes. Nothing remained now but a few bleak stumps and the mountains that stretched across the horizon at the far end. And the clouds of rolling ash that blew and drifted with the wind, settling over the weeds and remains of buildings, walls here and there, once in a while what had been a road.

Hendricks made coffee and heated up some boiled mutton and bread. "Here." He handed bread and mutton to David. David squatted by the edge of the fire, his knees knobby and white. He examined the food and then passed it back, shaking his head.

"No."

"No? Don't you want any?"

"No."

Hendricks shrugged. Maybe the boy was a mutant, used to special food. It didn't matter. When he was hungry he would find something to eat. The boy was strange. But there were many strange changes coming over the world. Life was not the same anymore. It would never be the same again. The human race was going to have to realize that.

"Suit yourself," Hendricks said. He ate the bread and mutton by himself, washing it down with coffee. He ate slowly, finding the food hard to digest. When he was done he got to his feet and stamped the fire out.

David rose slowly, watching him with his young-old eyes.

"We're going," Hendricks said.

"All right."

Hendricks walked along, his gun in his arms. They were close. He was tense, ready for anything. The Russians should be expecting a runner, an answer to their own runner, but they were tricky. There was always the possibility of a slipup. He scanned the landscape around him. Nothing but slag and ash, a few hills, charred trees. Concrete walls. But someplace ahead was the first bunker of the Russian lines, the forward command. Underground, buried deep, with only a periscope showing, a few gun muzzles. Maybe an antenna.

"Will we be there soon?" David asked.

"Yes. Getting tired?"

"No."

"Why, then?"

David did not answer. He plodded carefully along behind, picking his way over the ash. His legs and shoes were gray with dust. His pinched face was streaked, lines of gray ash in riverlets down the pale white of his skin. There was no color to his face. Typical of the new children, growing up in cellars and sewers and underground shelters.

Hendricks slowed down. He lifted his fieldglasses and studied the ground ahead of him. Were they there, someplace, waiting for him? Watching him, the way his men had watched the Russian runner? A chill went up his back. Maybe they were getting their guns ready, preparing to fire the way his men had prepared, made ready to kill.

Hendricks stopped, wiping perspiration from his face. "Damn." It made him uneasy. But he should be expected. The situation was different.

He strode over the ash, holding his gun tightly with both hands. Behind him came David. Hendricks peered around, tight-lipped. Any second it might happen. A burst of white light, a blast, carefully aimed from inside a deep concrete bunker.

He raised his arm and waved it around in a circle.

Nothing moved. To the right a long ridge ran, topped with dead tree trunks. A few wild vines had grown up around the trees, remains of arbors. And the eternal dark weeds. Hendricks studied the ridge. Was anything up there? Perfect place for a lookout. He approached the ridge warily, David coming silently behind. If it were his command he'd have a sentry up there, watching for troops trying to infiltrate into the command area. Of course, if it were his command there would be the claws around the area for full protection.

He stopped, feet apart, hands on his hips.

"Are we there?" David said.

"Almost."

"Why have we stopped?"

"I don't want to take any chances." Hendricks advanced slowly. Now the ridge lay directly beside him, along his right. Overlooking him. His uneasy feeling increased. If an Ivan were up there, he wouldn't have a chance. He waved his arm again. They should be expecting someone in the UN uniform, in response to the note capsule. Unless the whole thing was a trap.

"Keep up with me." He turned toward David. "Don't drop behind."

"With you?"

"Up beside me! We're close. We can't take any chances. Come on."

"I'll be all right." David remained behind him, in the rear, a few paces away, still clutching his teddy bear.

"Have it your way." Hendricks raised his glasses again, suddenly tense. For a moment—had something moved? He scanned the ridge carefully. Everything was silent. Dead. No life up there, only tree trunks and ash. Maybe a few rats. The big black rats that had survived the claws. Mutants—built their own shelters out of saliva and ash. Some kind of plaster. Adaptation. He started forward again.

A tall figure came out on the ridge above him, cloak flapping. Gray-green. A Russian. Behind him a second soldier appeared, another Russian. Both lifted their guns, aiming.

Hendricks froze. He opened his mouth. The soldiers were kneeling, sighting down the side of the slope. A third figure had joined them on the ridge top, a smaller figure in gray-green. A woman. She stood behind the other two.

Hendricks found his voice. "Stop!" He waved up at them frantically. "I'm—"

The two Russians fired. Behind Hendricks there was a faint *pop*. Waves of heat lapped against him, throwing him to the ground. Ash tore at his face, grinding into his eyes and nose. Choking, he pulled himself to his knees. It was all a trap. He was finished. He had come to be killed, like a steer. The soldiers and the woman were coming down the side of the ridge toward him, sliding down through the soft ash. Hendricks was numb. His head throbbed. Awkwardly, he got his rifle up and took aim. It weighed a thousand tons; he could hardly hold it. His nose and cheeks stung. The air was full of the blast smell, a bitter acrid stench.

"Don't fire," the first Russian said in heavily accented English.

The three of them came up to him, surrounding him. "Put down your rifle, Yank," the other said.

Hendricks was dazed. Everything had happened so fast. He had been caught. And they had blasted the boy. He turned his head. David was gone. What remained of him was strewn across the ground.

The three Russians studied him curiously. Hendricks sat, wiping blood from his nose, picking out bits of ash. He shook his head, trying to clear it. "Why did you do it?" he murmured thickly. "The boy."

"Why?" One of the soldiers helped him roughly to his feet. He turned Hendricks around. "Look."

Hendricks closed his eyes.

"Look!" The two Russians pulled him forward. "See. Hurry up. There isn't much time to spare, Yank!"

Hendricks looked. And gasped.

"See now? Now do you understand?"

From the remains of David a metal wheel rolled. Relays, glinting metal. Parts, wiring. One of the Russians kicked at the heap of remains. Parts popped out, rolling away, wheels and springs and rods. A plastic section fell in, half charred. Hendricks bent shakily down. The front of the head had come off. He could make out the intricate brain, wires and relays, tiny tubes and switches, thousands of minute studs—

"A robot," the soldier holding his arm said. "We watched it tagging you."

"Tagging me?"

"That's their way. They tag along with you. Into the bunker. That's how they get in."

Hendricks blinked, dazed. "But—"

"Come on." They led him toward the ridge. "We can't stay here. It isn't safe. There must be hundreds of them all around here."

The three of them pulled him up the side of the ridge, sliding and slipping on the ash. The woman reached the top and stood waiting for them.

"The forward command," Hendricks muttered. "I came to negotiate with the Soviet—"

"There is no more forward command. *They* got in. We'll explain." They reached the top of the ridge. "We're all that's left. The three of us. The rest were down in the bunker."

"This way. Down this way." The woman unscrewed a lid, a gray manhole cover set in the ground. "Get in."

Hendricks lowered himself. The two soldiers and the woman came behind him, following him down the ladder. The woman closed the lid after them, bolting it tightly into place.

"Good thing we saw you," one of the two soldiers grunted. "It had tagged you about as far as it was going to."

"Give me one of your cigarettes," the woman said. "I haven't had an American cigarette for weeks."

Hendricks pushed the pack to her. She took a cigarette and passed the pack to the two soldiers. In the corner of the small room the lamp gleamed fitfully. The room was low-ceilinged, cramped. The four of them sat around a small wood table. A few dirty dishes were stacked to one side. Behind a ragged curtain a second room was partly visible. Hendricks saw the corner of a cot, some blankets, clothes hung on a hook.

"We were here," the soldier beside him said. He took off his helmet, pushing his blond hair back. "I'm Corporal Rudi Maxer. Polish. Impressed in the Soviet army two years ago." He held out his hand.

Hendricks hesitated and then shook. "Major Joseph Hendricks."

"Klaus Epstein." The other soldier shook with him, a small dark man with thinning hair. Epstein plucked nervously at his ear. "Austrian. Impressed god knows when. I don't remember. The three of us were here, Rudi and I, with Tasso." He indicated the woman. "That's how we escaped. All the rest were down in the bunker."

"And—and *they* got in?"

Epstein lit a cigarette. "First just one of them. The kind that tagged you. Then it let others in."

Hendricks became alert. "The *kind*? Are there more than one kind?"

"The little boy. David. David holding his teddy bear. That's Variety Three. The most effective."

"What are the other types?"

Epstein reached into his coat. "Here." He tossed a packet of photographs onto the table, tied with a string. "Look for yourself."

Hendricks untied the string.

"You see," Rudi Maxer said, "that was why we wanted to talk terms. The Russians, I mean. We found out about a week ago. Found out that your claws were beginning to make up new designs on their own. New types of their own. Better types. Down in your underground factories behind our lines. You let them stamp themselves, repair themselves. Made them more and more intricate. It's your fault this happened."

Hendricks examined the photos. They had been snapped hurriedly. They were blurred and indistinct. The first few showed—David. David walking along a road by himself. David and another David. Three Davids. All exactly alike. Each with a ragged teddy bear.

All pathetic.

"Look at the others," Tasso said.

The next pictures, taken at a great distance, showed a towering, wounded soldier sitting by the side of a path, his arm in a sling, the stump of one leg extended, a crude crutch on his lap. Then two wounded soldiers, both the same, standing side by side.

"That's Variety One. The Wounded Soldier." Klaus reached out and took the pictures. "You see, the claws were designed to get to human beings. To find them. Each kind was better than the last. They got farther, closer, past most of our defenses, into our lines. But as long as they were merely *machines*, metal spheres with claws and horns, feelers, they could be picked off like any other object. They could be detected as lethal robots as soon as they were seen. Once we caught sight of them—"

"Variety One subverted our whole north wing," Rudi said. "It was a long time before anyone caught on. Then it was too late.

They came in, wounded soldiers, knocking and begging to be let in. So we let them in. And as soon as they were in, they took over. We were watching out for machines…"

"At that time it was thought there was only the one type," Klaus Epstein said. "No one suspected there were other types. The pictures were flashed to us. When the runner was sent to you, we knew of just one type. Variety One. The big Wounded Soldier. We thought that was all."

"Your line fell to—"

"To Variety Three. David and his bear. That worked even better." Klaus smiled bitterly. "Soldiers are suckers for children. We brought them in and tried to feed them. We found out the hard way what they were after. At least, those who were in the bunker."

"The three of us were lucky," Rudi said. "Klaus and I were—were visiting Tasso when it happened. This is her place." He waved a big hand around. "This little cellar. We finished and climbed the ladder to start back. From the ridge we saw. There they were, all around the bunker. Fighting was still going on. David and his bear. Hundreds of them. Klaus took the pictures."

Klaus tied up the photographs again.

"And it's going on all along your line?" Hendricks said.

"Yes."

"How about *our* lines?" Without thinking, he touched the tab on his arm. "Can they—"

"They're not bothered by your radiation tabs. It makes no difference to them, Russian, American, Pole, German. It's all the same. They're doing what they were designed to do. Carrying out the original idea. They track down life, wherever they find it."

"They go by warmth," Klaus said. "That was the way you constructed them from the very start. Of course, those you designed were kept back by the radiation tabs you wear. Now they've got around that. These new varieties are lead-lined."

"What's the other variety?" Hendricks asked. "The David type, the Wounded Soldier—what's the other?"

"We don't know." Klaus pointed up at the wall. On the wall were two metal plates, ragged at the edges. Hendricks got up and studied them. They were bent and dented.

"The one on the left came off a Wounded Soldier," Rudi said. "We got one of them. It was going along toward our old bunker. We got it from the ridge, the same way we got the David tagging you."

The plate was stamped: I-V. Hendricks touched the other plate. "And this came from the David type?"

"Yes." The plate was stamped: III-V.

Klaus took a look at them, leaning over Hendricks's broad shoulder. "You can see what we're up against. There's another type. Maybe it was abandoned. Maybe it didn't work. But there must be a Second Variety. There's One and Three."

"You were lucky," Rudi said. "The David tagged you all the way here and never touched you. Probably thought you'd get it into a bunker somewhere."

"One gets in and it's all over," Klaus said. "They move fast. One lets all the rest inside. They're inflexible. Machines with one purpose. They were built for only one thing." He rubbed sweat from his lip. "We saw."

They were silent.

"Let me have another cigarette, Yank," Tasso said. "They are good. I almost forgot how they were."

***

It was night. The sky was black. No stars were visible through the rolling clouds of ash. Klaus lifted the lid cautiously so that Hendricks could look out.

Rudi pointed into the darkness. "Over that way are the bunkers. Where we used to be. Not over half a mile from us. It was just chance Klaus and I were not there when it happened. Weakness. Saved by our lusts."

"All the rest must be dead," Klaus said in a low voice. "It came quickly. This morning the Politburo reached their decision. They notified us—forward command. Our runner was sent out at once. We saw him start toward the direction of your lines. We covered him until he was out of sight."

"Alex Radrivsky. We both knew him. He disappeared about six o'clock. The sun had just come up. About noon Klaus and I had an hour relief. We crept off, away from the bunkers. No one was watching. We came here. There used to be a town here, a few houses, a street. This cellar was part of a big farmhouse. We knew Tasso would be here, hiding down in her little place. We had come here before. Others from the bunkers came here. Today happened to be our turn."

"So we were saved," Klaus said. "Chance. It might have been others. We—we finished, and then we came up to the surface and started back along the ridge. That was when we saw them, the Davids. We understood right away. We had seen the photos of the First Variety, the Wounded Soldier. Our Commissar distributed them to us with an explanation. If we had gone another step, they would have seen us. As it was we had to blast two Davids before we got back. There were hundreds of them, all around. Like ants. We took pictures and slipped back here, bolting the lid tight."

"They're not so much when you catch them alone. We moved faster than they did. But they're inexorable. Not like living things. They came right at us. And we blasted them."

Major Hendricks rested against the edge of the lid, adjusting his eyes to the darkness. "Is it safe to have the lid up at all?"

"If we're careful. How else can you operate your transmitter?"

Hendricks lifted the small belt transmitter slowly. He pressed it against his ear. The metal was cold and damp. He blew against the mike, raising up the short antenna. A faint hum sounded in his ear. "That's true, I suppose."

But he still hesitated.

"We'll pull you under if anything happens," Klaus said.

"Thanks." Hendricks waited a moment, resting the transmitter against his shoulder. "Interesting, isn't it?"

"What?"

"This, the new types. The new varieties of claws. We're completely at their mercy, aren't we? By now they've probably gotten into the UN lines, too. It makes me wonder if we're not seeing the beginning of a new species. *The* new species. Evolution. The race to come after man."

Rudi grunted. "There is no race after man."

"No? Why not? Maybe we're seeing it now, the end of human beings, the beginning of the new society."

"They're not a race. They're mechanical killers. You made them to destroy. That's all they can do. They're machines with a job."

"So it seems now. But how about later on? After the war is over. Maybe, when there aren't any humans to destroy, their real potentialities will begin to show."

"You talk as if they were alive!"

"Aren't they?"

There was silence. "They're machines," Rudi said. "They look like people, but they're machines."

"Use your transmitter, Major," Klaus said. "We can't stay up here forever."

Holding the transmitter tightly Hendricks called the code of the command bunker. He waited, listening. No response. Only silence. He checked the leads carefully. Everything was in place.

"Scott!" he said into the mike. "Can you hear me?"

Silence. He raised the gain up full and tried again. Only static.

"I don't get anything. They may hear me, but they may not want to answer."

"Tell them it's an emergency."

"They'll think I'm being forced to call. Under your direction." He tried again, outlining briefly what he had learned. But still the phone was silent, except for the faint static.

"Radiation pools kill most transmission," Klaus said, after a while. "Maybe that's it."

Hendricks shut the transmitter up. "No use. No answer. Radiation pools? Maybe. Or they hear me, but won't answer. Frankly, that's what I would do if a runner tried to call from the Soviet lines. They have no reason to believe such a story. They may hear everything I say."

"Or maybe it's too late."

Hendricks nodded.

"We better get the lid down," Rudi said nervously. "We don't want to take unnecessary chances."

They climbed slowly back down the tunnel. Klaus bolted the lid carefully into place. They descended into the kitchen. The air was heavy and close around them.

"Could they work that fast?" Hendricks said. "I left the bunker this noon. Ten hours ago. How could they move so quickly?"

"It doesn't take them long. Not after the first one gets in. It goes wild. You know what the little claws can do. Even *one* of these is beyond belief. Razors, each finger. Maniacal."

"All right." Hendricks moved away impatiently. He stood with his back to them.

"What's the matter?" Rudi said.

"The Moon Base. God, if they've gotten there—"

"The Moon Base?"

Hendricks turned around. "They couldn't have got to the Moon Base. How would they get there? It isn't possible. I can't believe it."

"What is this Moon Base? We've heard rumors, but nothing definite. What is the actual situation? You seem concerned."

"We're supplied from the moon. The governments are there, under the lunar surface. All our people and industries. That's what keeps us going. If they should find some way of getting off Terra, onto the moon—"

"It only takes one of them. Once the first one gets in it admits the others. Hundreds of them, all alike. You should have seen them. Identical. Like ants."

"Perfect socialism," Tasso said. "The ideal of the communist state. All citizens interchangeable."

Klaus grunted angrily. "That's enough. Well? What next?"

Hendricks paced back and forth around the small room. The air was full of smells of food and perspiration. The others watched him. Presently Tasso pushed through the curtain into the other room. "I'm going to take a nap."

The curtain closed behind her. Rudi and Klaus sat down at the table, still watching Hendricks.

"It's up to you," Klaus said. "We don't know your situation."

Hendricks nodded.

"It's a problem." Rudi drank some coffee, filling his cup from a rusty pot. "We're safe here for a while, but we can't stay here forever. Not enough food or supplies."

"But if we go outside—"

"If we go outside they'll get us. Or probably they'll get us. We couldn't go very far. How far is your command bunker, Major?"

"Three or four miles."

"We might make it. The four of us. Four of us could watch all sides. They couldn't slip up behind us and start tagging us. We have three rifles, three blast rifles. Tasso can have my pistol." Rudi tapped his belt. "In the Soviet army we didn't have shoes always, but we had guns. With all four of us armed one of us might get to your command bunker. Preferably you, Major."

"What if they're already there?" Klaus said.

Rudi shrugged. "Well, then we come back here."

Hendricks stopped pacing. "What do you think the chances are they're already in the American lines?"

"Hard to say. Fairly good. They're organized. They know exactly what they're doing. Once they start they go like a horde of locusts. They have to keep moving, and fast. It's secrecy and speed they depend on. Surprise. They push their way in before anyone has any idea."

"I see," Hendricks murmured.

From the other room Tasso stirred. "Major?"

Hendricks pushed the curtain back. "What?"

Tasso looked up at him lazily from the cot. "Have you any more American cigarettes left?"

Hendricks went into the room and sat down across from her, on a wood stool. He felt in his pockets. "No. All gone."

"Too bad."

"What nationality are you?" Hendricks asked after a while.

"Russian."

"How did you get here?"

"Here?"

"This used to be France. This was part of Normandy. Did you come with the Soviet army?"

"Why?"

"Just curious." He studied her. She had taken off her coat, tossing it over the end of the cot. She was young, about twenty. Slim. Her long hair stretched out over the pillow. She was staring at him silently, her eyes dark and large.

"What's on your mind?" Tasso said.

"Nothing. How old are you?"

"Eighteen." She continued to watch him, unblinking, her

arms behind her head. She had on Russian army pants and shirt. Gray-green. Thick leather belt with counter and cartridges. Medicine kit.

"You're in the Soviet army?"

"No."

"Where did you get the uniform?"

She shrugged. "It was given to me," she told him.

"How—how old were you when you came here?"

"Sixteen."

"That young?"

Her eyes narrowed. "What do you mean?"

Hendricks rubbed his jaw. "Your life would have been a lot different if there had been no war. Sixteen. You came here at sixteen. To live this way."

"I had to survive."

"I'm not moralizing."

"Your life would have been different, too," Tasso murmured. She reached down and unfastened one of her boots. She kicked the boot off, onto the floor. "Major, do you want to go in the other room? I'm sleepy."

"It's going to be a problem, the four of us here. It's going to be hard to live in these quarters. Are there just the two rooms?"

"Yes."

"How big was the cellar originally? Was it larger than this? Are there other rooms filled up with debris? We might be able to open one of them."

"Perhaps. I really don't know." Tasso loosened her belt. She made herself comfortable on the cot, unbuttoning her shirt. "You're sure you have no more cigarettes?"

"I had only the one pack."

"Too bad. Maybe if we get back to your bunker we can find some." The other boot fell. Tasso reached up for the light cord. "Good night."

"You're going to sleep?"

"That's right."

The room plunged into darkness. Hendricks got up and made his way past the curtain, into the kitchen.

And stopped, rigid.

Rudi stood against the wall, his face white and gleaming. His mouth opened and closed but no sounds came. Klaus stood in front of him, the muzzle of his pistol in Rudi's stomach. Neither of them moved. Klaus, his hand tight around his gun, his features set. Rudi, pale and silent, spread-eagled against the wall.

"What—" Hendricks muttered, but Klaus cut him off.

"Be quiet, Major. Come over here. Your gun. Get out your gun."

Hendricks drew his pistol. "What is it?"

"Cover him." Klaus motioned him forward. "Beside me. Hurry!"

Rudi moved a little, lowering his arms. He turned to Hendricks, licking his lips. The whites of his eyes shone wildly. Sweat dripped from his forehead, down his cheeks. He fixed his gaze on Hendricks. "Major, he's gone insane. Stop him." Rudi's voice was thin and hoarse, almost inaudible.

"What's going on?" Hendricks demanded.

Without lowering his pistol Klaus answered. "Major, remember our discussion? The Three Varieties? We knew about One and Three. But we didn't know about Two. At least, we didn't know before." Klaus's fingers tightened around the gun butt. "We didn't know before, but we know now."

He pressed the trigger. A burst of white heat rolled out of the gun, licking around Rudi.

"Major, this is the Second Variety."

Tasso swept the curtain aside. "Klaus! What did you do?"

Klaus turned from the charred form, gradually sinking down the wall onto the floor. "The Second Variety, Tasso. Now we know. We have all three types identified. The danger is less. I—"

Tasso stared past him at the remains of Rudi, at the blackened, smoldering fragments and bits of cloth. "You killed him."

"Him? *It*, you mean. I was watching. I had a feeling, but I wasn't sure. At least, I wasn't sure before. But this evening I was certain." Klaus rubbed his pistol butt nervously. "We're lucky. Don't you understand? Another hour and it might—"

"You were *certain*?" Tasso pushed past him and bent down over the steaming remains on the floor. Her face became hard. "Major, see for yourself. Bones. Flesh."

Hendricks bent down beside her. The remains were human remains. Seared flesh, charred bone fragments, part of a skull. Ligaments, viscera, blood. Blood forming a pool against the wall.

"No wheels," Tasso said calmly. She straightened up. "No wheels, no parts, no relays. Not a claw. Not the Second Variety." She folded her arms. "You're going to have to be able to explain this."

Klaus sat down at the table, all the color drained suddenly from his face. He put his head in his hands and rocked back and forth.

"Snap out of it." Tasso's fingers closed over his shoulder. "Why did you do it? Why did you kill him?"

"He was frightened," Hendricks said. "All this, the whole thing, building up around us."

"Maybe."

"What, then? What do you think?"

"I think he may have had a reason for killing Rudi. A good reason."

"What reason?"

"Maybe Rudi learned something."

Hendricks studied her bleak face. "About what?" he asked.

"About him. About Klaus."

Klaus looked up quickly. "You can see what she's trying to say. She thinks I'm the Second Variety. Don't you see, Major? Now she wants you to believe I killed him on purpose. That I'm—"

"Why did you kill him, then?" Tasso said.

"I told you." Klaus shook his head wearily. "I thought he was a claw. I thought I knew."

"Why?"

"I had been watching him. I was suspicious."

"Why?"

"I thought I had seen something. Heard something. I thought I—" He stopped.

"Go on."

"We were sitting at the table. Playing cards. You two were in the other room. It was silent. I thought I heard him—*whirr*."

There was silence.

"Do you believe that?" Tasso said to Hendricks.

"Yes. I believe what he says."

"I don't. I think he killed Rudi for a good purpose." Tasso touched the rifle, resting in the corner of the room. "Major—"

"No." Hendricks shook his head. "Let's stop it right now. One is enough. We're afraid, the way he was. If we kill him, we'll be doing what he did to Rudi."

Klaus looked gratefully up at him. "Thanks. I was afraid. You understand, don't you? Now she's afraid, the way I was. She wants to kill me."

"No more killing." Hendricks moved toward the end of the ladder. "I'm going above and try the transmitter once more. If I can't get them, we're moving back toward my lines tomorrow morning."

Klaus rose quickly. "I'll come up with you and give you a hand."

The night air was cold. The earth was cooling off. Klaus took a deep breath, filling his lungs. He and Hendricks stepped onto the ground, out of the tunnel. Klaus planted his feet wide apart, the rifle up, watching and listening. Hendricks crouched by the tunnel mouth, tuning the small transmitter.

"Any luck?" Klaus asked presently.

"Not yet."

"Keep trying. Tell them what happened."

Hendricks kept trying. Without success. Finally he lowered the antenna. "It's useless. They can't hear me. Or they hear me and won't answer. Or—"

"Or they don't exist."

"I'll try once more." Hendricks raised the antenna. "Scott, can you hear me? Come in!"

He listened. There was only static. Then, still very faintly—

"This is Scott."

His fingers tightened. "Scott! Is it you?"

"This is Scott."

Klaus squatted down. "Is it your command?"

"Scott, listen. Do you understand? About them, the claws. Did you get my message? Did you hear me?"

"Yes." Faintly. Almost inaudible. He could hardly make out the word.

"You got my message? Is everything all right at the bunker? None of them have got in?"

"Everything is all right."

"Have they tried to get in?"

The voice was weaker.

"No."

Hendricks turned to Klaus. "They're all right."

"Have they been attacked?"

"No." Hendricks pressed the phone tighter to his ear. "Scott, I can hardly hear you. Have you notified the Moon Base? Do they know? Are they alerted?"

No answer.

"Scott! Can you hear me?"

Silence.

Hendricks relaxed, sagging. "Faded out. Must be radiation pools."

Hendricks and Klaus looked at each other. Neither of them said anything. After a time Klaus said, "Did it sound like any of your men? Could you identify the voice?"

"It was too faint."

"You couldn't be certain?"

"No."

"Then it could have been—"

"I don't know. Now I'm not sure. Let's go back down and get the lid closed."

They climbed back down the ladder slowly, into the warm cellar. Klaus bolted the lid behind them. Tasso waited for them, her face expressionless.

"Any luck?" she asked.

Neither of them answered. "Well?" Klaus said at last. "What do you think, Major? Was it your officer, or was it one of *them*?"

"I don't know."

"Then we're just where we were before."

Hendricks stared down at the floor, his jaw set. "We'll have to go. To be sure."

"Anyhow, we have food here for only a few weeks. We'd have to go up after that, in any case."

"Apparently so."

"What's wrong?" Tasso demanded. "Did you get across to your bunker? What's the matter?"

"It may have been one of my men," Hendricks said slowly. "Or it may have been one of *them*. But we'll never know standing here." He examined his watch. "Let's turn in and get some sleep. We want to be up early tomorrow."

"Early?"

"Our best chance to get through the claws should be early in the morning," Hendricks said.

***

The morning was crisp and clear. Major Hendricks studied the countryside through his field glasses.

"See anything?" Klaus said.

"No."

"Can you make out our bunkers?"

"Which way?"

"Here." Klaus took the glasses and adjusted them. "I know where to look." He looked a long time, silently.

Tasso came to the top of the tunnel and stepped up onto the ground. "Anything?"

"No." Klaus passed the glasses back to Hendricks. "They're out of sight. Come on. Let's not stay here."

The three of them made their way down the side of the ridge, sliding in the soft ash. Across a flat rock a lizard scuttled. They stopped instantly, rigid.

"What was it?" Klaus muttered.

"A lizard."

The lizard ran on, hurrying through the ash. It was exactly the same color as the ash.

"Perfect adaptation," Klaus said. "Proves we were right. Lysenko, I mean."

They reached the bottom of the ridge and stopped, standing close together, looking around them.

"Let's go." Hendricks started off. "It's a good, long trip, on foot."

Klaus fell in beside him. Tasso walked behind, her pistol held alertly. "Major, I've been meaning to ask you something," Klaus said. "How did you run across the David? The one that was tagging you."

"I met it along the way. In some ruins."

"What did it say?"

"Not much. It said it was alone. By itself."

"You couldn't tell it was a machine? It talked like a living person? You never suspected?"

"It didn't say much. I noticed nothing unusual."

"It's strange, machines so much like people that you can be fooled. Almost alive. I wonder where it'll end."

"They're doing what you Yanks designed them to do," Tasso said. "You designed them to hunt out life and destroy. Human life. Wherever they find it."

Hendricks was watching Klaus intently. "Why did you ask me? What's on your mind?"

"Nothing," Klaus answered.

"Klaus thinks you're the Second Variety," Tasso said calmly, from behind them. "Now he's got his eye on you."

Klaus flushed. "Why not? We sent a runner to the Yank lines, and he comes back. Maybe he thought he'd find some good game here."

Hendricks laughed harshly. "I came from the UN bunkers. There were human beings all around me."

"Maybe you saw an opportunity to get into the Soviet lines. Maybe you saw your chance. Maybe you—"

"The Soviet lines had already been taken over. Your lines had been invaded before I left my command bunker. Don't forget that."

Tasso came up beside him. "That proves nothing at all, Major."

"Why not?"

"There appears to be little communication between the varieties. Each is made in a different factory. They don't seem to work together. You might have started for the Soviet lines without knowing anything about the work of the other varieties. Or even what the other varieties were like."

"How do you know so much about the claws?" Hendricks said.

"I've seen them. I've observed them. I observed them take over the Soviet bunkers."

"You know quite a lot," Klaus said. "Actually, you saw very little. Strange that you should have been such an acute observer."

Tasso laughed. "Do you suspect me now?"

"Forget it," Hendricks said. They walked on in silence.

"Are we going the whole way on foot?" Tasso said, after a while. "I'm not used to walking." She gazed around at the plain of ash, stretching out on all sides of them as far as they could see. "How dreary."

"It's like this all the way," Klaus said.

"In a way I wish you had been in your bunker when the attack came."

"Somebody else would have been with you, if not me," Klaus muttered.

Tasso laughed, putting her hands in her pockets. "I suppose so."

They walked on, keeping their eyes on the vast plain of silent ash around them.

***

The sun was setting. Hendricks made his way forward slowly, waving Tasso and Klaus back. Klaus squatted down, resting his gun butt against the ground.

Tasso found a concrete slab and sat down with a sigh. "It's good to rest."

"Be quiet," Klaus said sharply.

Hendricks pushed up to the top of the rise ahead of them. The same rise the Russian runner had come up, the day before. Hendricks dropped down, stretching himself out, peering through his glasses at what lay beyond.

Nothing was visible. Only ash and occasional trees. But there, not more than fifty yards ahead, was the entrance of the forward command bunker. The bunker from which he had come. Hendricks watched silently. No motion. No sign of life. Nothing stirred.

Klaus slithered up beside him. "Where is it?"

"Down there." Hendricks passed him the glasses. Clouds of ash rolled across the evening sky. The world was darkening. They had a couple of hours of light left, at the most. Probably not that much.

"I don't see anything," Klaus said.

"That tree there. The stump. By the pile of bricks. The entrance is to the right of the bricks."

"I'll have to take your word for it."

"You and Tasso cover me from here. You'll be able to sight all the way to the bunker entrance."

"You're going down alone?"

"With my wrist tab I'll be safe. The ground around the bunker is a living field of claws. They collect down in the ash. Like crabs. Without tabs you wouldn't have a chance."

"Maybe you're right."

"I'll walk slowly all the way. As soon as I know for certain—"

"If they're down inside the bunker you won't be able to get back up here. They go fast. You don't realize."

"What do you suggest?"

Klaus considered. "I don't know. Get them to come up to the surface. So you can see."

Hendricks brought his transmitter from his belt, raising the antenna. "Let's get started."

Klaus signaled to Tasso. She crawled expertly up the side of the rise to where they were sitting.

"He's going down alone," Klaus said. "We'll cover him from here. As soon as you see him start back, fire past him at once. They come quick."

"You're not very optimistic," Tasso said.

"No, I'm not."

Hendricks opened the breech of his gun, checking it carefully. "Maybe things are all right."

"You didn't see them. Hundreds of them. All the same. Pouring out like ants."

"I should be able to find out without going down all the way." Hendricks locked his gun, gripping it in one hand, the transmitter in the other. "Well, wish me luck."

Klaus put out his hand. "Don't go down until you're sure. Talk to them from up here. Make them show themselves."

Hendricks stood up. He stepped down the side of the rise.

A moment later he was walking slowly toward the pile of bricks and debris beside the dead tree stump. Toward the entrance of the forward command bunker.

Nothing stirred. He raised the transmitter, clicking it on. "Scott? Can you hear me?"

Silence.

"Scott! This is Hendricks. Can you hear me? I'm standing outside the bunker. You should be able to see me in the view sight."

He listened, the transmitter gripped tightly. No sound. Only static. He walked forward. A claw burrowed out of the ash and raced toward him. It halted a few feet away and then slunk off. A second claw appeared, one of the big ones with feelers. It moved toward him, studied him intently, and then fell in behind him, dogging respectfully after him, a few paces away. A moment later a second big claw joined it. Silently, the claws trailed him as he walked slowly toward the bunker.

Hendricks stopped, and behind him, the claws came to a halt. He was close now. Almost to the bunker steps.

"Scott! Can you hear me? I'm standing right above you. Outside. On the surface. Are you picking me up?"

He waited, holding his gun against his side, the transmitter tightly to his ear. Time passed. He strained to hear, but there was only silence. Silence, and faint static.

Then, distantly, metallically—

"This is Scott."

The voice was neutral. Cold. He could not identify it. But the earphone was minute.

"Scott! Listen. I'm standing right above you. I'm on the surface, looking down into the bunker entrance."

"Yes."

"Can you see me?"

"Yes."

"Through the view sight? You have the sight trained on me?"

"Yes."

Hendricks pondered. A circle of claws waited quietly around him, gray-metal bodies on all sides of him. "Is everything all right in the bunker? Nothing unusual has happened?"

"Everything is all right."

"Will you come up to the surface? I want to see you for a moment." Hendricks took a deep breath. "Come up here with me. I want to talk to you."

"Come down."

"I'm giving you an order."

Silence.

"Are you coming?" Hendricks listened. There was no response. "I order you to come to the surface."

"Come down."

Hendricks set his jaw. "Let me talk to Leone."

There was a long pause. He listened to the static. Then a voice came, hard, thin, metallic. The same as the other. "This is Leone."

"Hendricks. I'm on the surface. At the bunker entrance. I want one of you to come up here."

"Come down."

"Why come down? I'm giving you an order!"

Silence. Hendricks lowered the transmitter. He looked carefully around him. The entrance was just ahead. Almost at his feet. He lowered the antenna and fastened the transmitter to his belt. Carefully, he gripped his gun with both hands. He moved forward, a step at a time. If they could see him, they knew he was starting toward the entrance. He closed his eyes a moment.

Then he put his foot on the first step that led downward.

Two Davids came up at him, their faces identical and expressionless. He blasted them into particles. More came rushing silently up, a whole pack of them. All exactly the same.

Hendricks turned and raced back, away from the bunker, back toward the rise.

At the top of the rise Tasso and Klaus were firing down. The small claws were already streaking up toward them, shining metal spheres going fast, racing frantically through the ash. But he had no time to think about that. He knelt down, aiming at the bunker entrance, gun against his cheek. The Davids were coming out in groups, clutching their teddy bears, their thin knobby legs pumping as they ran up the steps to the surface. Hendricks fired into the main body of them. They burst apart, wheels and springs flying in all directions. He fired again through the mist of particles.

A giant lumbering figure rose up in the bunker entrance, tall and swaying. Hendricks paused, amazed. A man, a soldier. With one leg, supporting himself with a crutch.

"Major!" Tasso's voice came. More firing. The huge figure moved forward, Davids swarming around it. Hendricks broke out of his freeze. The First Variety. The Wounded Soldier.

He aimed and fired. The soldier burst into bits, parts and relays flying. Now many Davids were out on the flat ground, away from the bunker. He fired again and again, moving slowly back, half-crouching and aiming.

From the rise, Klaus fired down. The side of the rise was alive with claws making their way up. Hendricks retreated toward the rise, running and crouching. Tasso had left Klaus and was circling slowly to the right, moving away from the rise.

A David slipped up toward him, its small white face expressionless, brown hair hanging down in its eyes. It bent over suddenly, opening its arms. Its teddy bear hurtled down and leaped across the ground, bounding toward him. Hendricks fired. The bear and the David both dissolved. He grinned, blinking. It was like a dream.

"Up here!" Tasso's voice. Hendricks made his way toward her. She was over by some columns of concrete, walls of a ruined building. She was firing past him with the hand pistol Klaus had given her.

"Thanks." He joined her, grasping for breath. She pulled him back behind the concrete, fumbling at her belt.

"Close your eyes!" She unfastened a globe from her waist. Rapidly, she unscrewed the cap, locking it into place. "Close your eyes and get down."

She threw the bomb. It sailed in an arc, an expert, rolling and bouncing to the entrance of the bunker. Two Wounded Soldiers stood uncertainly by the brick pile. More Davids poured from behind them, out onto the plain. One of the Wounded Soldiers moved toward the bomb, stooping awkwardly down to pick it up.

The bomb went off. The concussion whirled Hendricks around, throwing him on his face. A hot wind rolled over him. Dimly he saw Tasso standing behind the columns, firing slowly and methodically at the Davids coming out of the raging clouds of white fire.

Back along the rise Klaus struggled with a ring of claws circling around him. He retreated, blasting at them and moving back, trying to break through the ring.

Hendricks struggled to his feet. His head ached. He could hardly see. Everything was licking at him, raging and whirling. His right arm would not move.

Tasso pulled back toward him. "Come on. Let's go."

"Klaus—he's still up there."

"Come on!" Tasso dragged Hendricks back, away from the columns. Hendricks shook his head, trying to clear it. Tasso led him rapidly away, her eyes intense and bright, watching for claws that had escaped the blast.

One David came out of the rolling clouds of flame. Tasso blasted it. No more appeared.

"But Klaus. What about him?" Hendricks stopped, standing unsteadily. "He—"

"Come on!"

They retreated, moving farther and farther away from the bunker. A few small claws followed them for a little while and then gave up, turning back and going off.

At last Tasso stopped. "We can stop here and get our breaths."

Hendricks sat down on some heaps of debris. He wiped his neck, gasping. "We left Klaus back there."

Tasso said nothing. She opened her gun, sliding a fresh round of blast cartridges into place.

Hendricks stared at her, dazed. "You left him back there on purpose."

Tasso snapped the gun together. She studied the heaps of rubble around them, her face expressionless. As if she were watching for something.

"What is it?" Hendricks demanded. "What are you looking for? Is something coming?" He shook his head, trying to understand. What was she doing? What was she waiting for? He could see nothing. Ash lay all around them, ash and ruins. Occasional stark tree trunks, without leaves or branches. "What—"

Tasso cut him off. "Be still." Her eyes narrowed. Suddenly her gun came up. Hendricks turned, following her gaze.

Back the way they had come a figure appeared. The figure walked unsteadily toward them. Its clothes were torn. It limped as it made its way along, going very slowly and carefully. Stopping now and then, resting and getting its strength. Once it almost fell. It stood for a moment, trying to steady itself. Then it came on.

Klaus.

Hendricks stood up. "Klaus!" He started toward him. "How the hell did you—"

Tasso fired. Hendricks swung back. She fired again, the blast passing him, a searing line of heat. The beam caught Klaus in the chest. He exploded, gears and wheels flying. For a moment he continued to walk. Then he swayed back and forth. He crashed to the ground, his arms flung out. A few more wheels rolled away.

Silence.

Tasso turned to Hendricks. "Now you understand why he killed Rudi."

Hendricks sat down again slowly. He shook his head. He was numb. He could not think.

"Do you see?" Tasso said. "Do you understand?"

Hendricks said nothing. Everything was slipping away from him, faster and faster. Darkness, rolling and plucking at him.

He closed his eyes.

***

Hendricks opened his eyes slowly. His body ached all over. He tried to sit up, but needles of pain shot through his arm and shoulder. He gasped.

207

"Don't try to get up," Tasso said. She bent down, putting her cold hand against his forehead.

It was night. A few stars glinted above, shining through the drifting clouds of ash. Hendricks lay back, his teeth locked. Tasso watched him impassively. She had built a fire with some wood and weeds. The fire licked feebly, hissing at a metal cup suspended over it. Everything was silent. Unmoving darkness, beyond the fire.

"So he was the Second Variety," Hendricks murmured.

"I had always thought so."

"Why didn't you destroy him sooner?" he wanted to know.

"You held me back." Tasso crossed to the fire to look into the metal cup. "Coffee. It'll be ready to drink in a while."

She came back and sat down beside him. Presently she opened her pistol and began to disassemble the firing mechanism, studying it intently.

"This is a beautiful gun," Tasso said half aloud. "The construction is superb."

"What about them? The claws."

"The concussion from the bomb put most of them out of action. They're delicate. Highly organized, I suppose."

"The Davids, too?"

"Yes."

"How did you happen to have a bomb like that?"

Tasso shrugged. "We designed it. You shouldn't underestimate our technology, Major. Without such a bomb you and I would no longer exist."

"Very useful."

Tasso stretched out her legs, warming her feet in the heat of the fire. "It surprised me that you did not seem to understand, after he killed Rudi. Why did you think he—"

"I told you. I thought he was afraid."

"Really? You know, Major, for a little while I suspected you.

Because you wouldn't let me kill him. I thought you might be protecting him." She laughed.

"Are we safe here?" Hendricks asked presently.

"For a while. Until they get reinforcements from some other area." Tasso began to clean the interior of the gun with a bit of rag. She finished and pushed the mechanism back into place. She closed the gun, running her finger along the barrel.

"We were lucky," Hendricks murmured.

"Yes. Very lucky."

"Thanks for pulling me away."

Tasso did not answer. She glanced up at him, her eyes bright in the fire light. Hendricks examined his arm. He could not move his fingers. His whole side seemed numb. Down inside him was a dull steady ache.

"How do you feel?" Tasso asked.

"My arm is damaged."

"Anything else?"

"Internal injuries."

"You didn't get down when the bomb went off."

Hendricks said nothing. He watched Tasso pour the coffee from the cup into a flat metal pan. She brought it over to him.

"Thanks." He struggled up enough to drink. It was hard to swallow. His insides turned over and he pushed the pan away. "That's all I can drink now."

Tasso drank the rest. Time passed. The clouds of ash moved across the dark sky above them. Hendricks rested, his mind blank. After a while he became aware that Tasso was standing over him, gazing down at him.

"What is it?" he murmured.

"Do you feel any better?"

"Some."

"You know, Major, if I hadn't dragged you away, they would have got you. You would be dead. Like Rudi."

"I know."

"Do you want to know why I brought you out? I could have left you. I could have left you there."

"Why did you bring me out?"

"Because we have to get away from here." Tasso stirred the fire with a stick, peering calmly down into it. "No human being can live here. When their reinforcements come, we won't have a chance. I've pondered about it while you were unconscious. We have perhaps three hours before they come."

"And you expect me to get us away?"

"That's right. I expect you to get us out of here."

"Why me?"

"Because I don't know any way." Her eyes shone at him in the half-light, bright and steady. "If you can't get us out of here, they'll kill us within three hours. I see nothing else ahead. Well, Major? What are you going to do? I've been waiting all night. While you were unconscious I sat here, waiting and listening. It's almost dawn. The night is almost over."

Hendricks considered. "It's curious," he said at last.

"Curious?"

"That you should think I can get us out of here. I wonder what you think I can do."

"Can you get us to the Moon Base?"

"The Moon Base? How?"

"There must be some way."

Hendricks shook his head. "No. There's no way that I know of."

Tasso said nothing. For a moment her steady gaze wavered. She ducked her head, turning abruptly away. She scrambled to her feet. "More coffee?"

"No."

"Suit yourself." Tasso drank silently. He could not see her face. He lay back against the ground, deep in thought, trying to concentrate. It was hard to think. His head still hurt. And the numbing daze still hung over him.

"There might be one way," he said suddenly.

"Oh?"

"How soon is dawn?"

"Two hours. The sun will be coming up shortly."

"There's supposed to be a ship near here. I've never seen it. But I know it exists."

"What kind of a ship?" Her voice was sharp.

"A rocket cruiser."

"Will it take us off? To the Moon Base?"

"It's supposed to. In case of emergency." He rubbed his forehead.

"What's wrong?"

"My head. It's hard to think. I can hardly—hardly concentrate. The bomb."

"Is the ship near here?" Tasso slid over beside him, settling down on her haunches. "How far is it? Where is it?"

"I'm trying to think."

Her fingers dug into his arm. "Nearby?" Her voice was like iron. "Where would it be? Would they store it underground? Hidden underground?"

"Yes. In a storage locker."

"How do we find it? Is it marked? Is there a code marker to identify it?"

Hendricks concentrated. "No. No markings. No code symbol."

"What, then?"

"A sign."

"What sort of sign?"

Hendricks did not answer. In the flickering light his eyes were glazed, two sightless orbs. Tasso's fingers dug into his arm.

"What sort of sign? What is it?"

"I—I can't think. Let me rest."

"All right." She let go and stood up. Hendricks lay back against the ground, his eyes closed. Tasso walked away from him, her hands in her pockets. She kicked a rock out of her way and stood staring up at the sky. The night blackness was already beginning to fade into gray. Morning was coming.

Tasso gripped her pistol and walked around the fire in a circle, back and forth. On the ground Major Hendricks lay, his eyes closed, unmoving. The grayness rose in the sky, higher and higher. The landscape became visible, fields of ash stretching out in all directions. Ash and ruins of buildings, a wall here and there, heaps of concrete, the naked trunk of a tree.

The air was cold and sharp. Somewhere a long way off a bird made a few bleak sounds.

Hendricks stirred. He opened his eyes. "Is it dawn? Already?"

"Yes."

Hendricks sat up a little. "You wanted to know something. You were asking me."

"Do you remember now?"

"Yes."

"What is it?" She tensed. "What?" she repeated sharply.

"A well. A ruined well. It's in a storage locker under a well."

"A well." Tasso relaxed. "Then we'll find a well." She looked at her watch. "We have about an hour, Major. Do you think we can find it in an hour?"

"Give me a hand up," Hendricks said.

Tasso put her pistol away and helped him to his feet. "This is going to be difficult."

"Yes it is." Hendricks set his lips tightly. "I don't think we're going to go very far."

They began to walk. The early sun cast a little warmth down on them. The land was flat and barren, stretching out gray and lifeless as far as they could see. A few birds sailed silently, far above them, circling slowly.

"See anything?" Hendricks said. "Any claws?"

"No. Not yet."

They passed through some ruins, upright concrete and bricks. A cement foundation. Rats scuttled away. Tasso jumped back warily.

"This used to be a town," Hendricks said. "A village. Provincial village. This was all grape country once. Where we are now."

They came onto a ruined street, weeds and cracks crisscrossing it. Over to the right a stone chimney stuck up.

"Be careful," he warned her.

A pit yawned, an open basement. Ragged ends of pipes jutted up, twisted and bent. They passed part of a house, a bathtub turned on its side. A broken chair. A few spoons and bits of china dishes. In the center of the street the ground had sunk away. The depression was filled with weeds and debris and bones.

"Over here," Hendricks murmured.

"This way?"

"To the right."

They passed the remains of a heavy-duty tank. Hendricks's belt counter clicked ominously. The tank had been radiation blasted. A few feet from the tank a mummified body lay sprawled out, mouth open. Beyond the road was a flat field. Stones and weeds, and bits of broken glass.

"There," Hendricks said.

A stone well jutted up, sagging and broken. A few boards lay across it. Most of the well had sunk into rubble. Hendricks walked unsteadily toward it, Tasso beside him.

"Are you certain about this?" Tasso said. "This doesn't look like anything."

"I'm sure." Hendricks sat down at the edge of the well, his teeth locked. His breath came quickly. He wiped perspiration from his face. "This was arranged so the senior command officer could get away. If anything happened. If the bunker fell."

"That was you?"

"Yes."

"Where is the ship? Is it here?"

"We're standing on it." Hendricks ran his hands over the surface of the well stones. "The eye-lock responds to me, not to anybody else. It's my ship. Or it was supposed to be."

There was a sharp click. Presently they heard a low grating sound from below them.

"Step back," Hendricks said. He and Tasso moved away from the well.

A section of the ground slid back. A metal frame pushed slowly up through the ash, shoving bricks and weeds out of the way. The action ceased as the ship nosed into view.

"There it is," Hendricks said.

The ship was small. It rested quietly, suspended in its mesh frame like a blunt needle. A rain of ash sifted down into the dark cavity from which the ship had been raised. Hendricks made his way over to it. He mounted the mesh and unscrewed the hatch, pulling it back. Inside the ship the control banks and the pressure seat were visible.

Tasso came and stood beside him, gazing into the ship. "I'm not accustomed to rocket piloting," she said after a while.

Hendricks glanced at her. "I'll do the piloting."

"Will you? There's only one seat, Major. I can see it's built to carry only a single person."

Hendricks's breathing changed. He studied the interior of the ship intently. Tasso was right. There was only one seat. The ship was built to carry only one person. "I see," he said slowly. "And the one person is you."

She nodded.

"Of course."

"Why?"

"*You* can't go. You might not live through the trip. You're injured. You probably wouldn't get there."

"An interesting point. But you see, I know where the Moon Base is. And you don't. You might fly around for months and not find it. It's well hidden. Without knowing what to look for—"

"I'll have to take my chances. Maybe I won't find it. Not by myself. But I think you'll give me all the information I need. Your life depends on it."

"How?"

"If I find the Moon Base in time, perhaps I can get them to send a ship back to pick you up. *If* I find the Base in time. If not, then you haven't a chance. I imagine there are supplies on the ship. They will last me long enough—"

Hendricks moved quickly. But his injured arm betrayed him. Tasso ducked, sliding lithely aside. Her hand came up, lightning fast. Hendricks saw the gun butt coming. He tried to ward off the blow, but she was too fast. The metal butt struck against the side of his head, just above his ear. Numbing pain rushed through him. Pain and rolling clouds of blackness. He sank down, sliding to the ground.

Dimly, he was aware that Tasso was standing over him, kicking him with her toe.

"Major! Wake up."

He opened his eyes, groaning.

"Listen to me." She bent down, the gun pointed at his face. "I have to hurry. There isn't much time left. The ship is ready to go, but you must tell me the information I need before I leave."

Hendricks shook his head, trying to clear it.

"Hurry up! Where is the Moon Base? How do I find it? What do I look for?"

Hendricks said nothing.

"Answer me!"

"Sorry."

"Major, the ship is loaded with provisions. I can coast for weeks. I'll find the Base eventually. And in a half hour you'll be dead. Your only chance of survival—" She broke off.

Along the slope, by some crumbling ruins, something moved. Something in the ash. Tasso turned quickly, aiming. She fired. A puff of flame leaped. Something scuttled away, rolling across the ash. She fired again. The claw burst apart, wheels flying.

"See?" Tasso said. "A scout. It won't be long."

"You'll bring them back here to get me?"

"Yes. As soon as possible."

Hendricks looked up at her. He studied her intently. "You're telling the truth?" A strange expression had come over his face, an avid hunger. "You will come back for me? You'll get me to the Moon Base?"

"I'll get you to the Moon Base. But tell me where it is! There's only a little time left."

"All right." Hendricks picked up a piece of rock, pulling himself to a sitting position. "Watch."

Hendricks began to scratch in the ash. Tasso stood by him, watching the motion of the rock. Hendricks was sketching a crude lunar map.

"This is the Appenine Range. Here is the Crater of Archimedes. The Moon Base is beyond the end of the Appenine, about two hundred miles. I don't know exactly where. No one on Terra knows. But when you're over the Appenine, signal with one red flare and a green flare, followed by two red flares in quick succession. The Base monitor will record your signal. The Base is under the surface, of course. They'll guide you down with magnetic grapples."

"And the controls? Can I operate them?"

"The controls are virtually automatic. All you have to do is give the right signal at the right time."

"I will."

"The seat absorbs most of the take-off shock. Air and temperature are automatically controlled. The ship will leave Terra and pass out into free space. It'll line itself up with the moon, falling into an orbit around it, about a hundred miles above the surface. The orbit will carry you over the Base. When you're in the region of the Appenine, release the signal rockets."

Tasso slid into the ship and lowered herself into the pressure seat. The arm locks folded automatically around her. She fingered the controls. "Too bad you're not going, Major. All this put here for you, and you can't make the trip."

"Leave me the pistol."

Tasso pulled the pistol from her belt. She held it in her hand, weighing it thoughtfully. "Don't go too far from this location. It'll be hard to find you, as it is."

"No. I'll stay here by the well."

Tasso gripped the take-off switch, running her fingers over the smooth metal. "A beautiful ship, Major. Well built. I admire your workmanship. You people have always done good work. You build fine things. Your work, your creations, are your greatest achievement."

"Give me the pistol," Hendricks said impatiently, holding out his hand. He struggled to his feet.

"Goodbye, Major." Tasso tossed the pistol past Hendricks. The pistol clattered against the ground, bouncing and rolling away. Hendricks hurried after it. He bent down, snatching it up.

The hatch of the ship clanged shut. The bolts fell into place. Hendricks made his way back. The inner door was being sealed. He raised the pistol unsteadily.

There was a shattering roar. The ship burst up from its metal cage, fusing the mesh behind it. Hendricks cringed, pulling back. The ship shot up into the rolling clouds of ash, disappearing into the sky.

Hendricks stood watching a long time, until even the streamer had dissipated. Nothing stirred. The morning air was chill and silent. He began to walk aimlessly back the way they had come. Better to keep moving around. It would be a long time before help came—if it came at all.

He searched his pockets until he found a package of cigarettes. He lit one grimly. They had all wanted cigarettes from him. But cigarettes were scarce.

A lizard slithered by him through the ash. He halted, rigid. The lizard disappeared. Above, the sun rose higher in the sky. Some flies landed on a flat rock to one side of him. Hendricks kicked at them with his foot.

It was getting hot. Sweat trickled down his face into his collar. His mouth was dry.

Presently he stopped walking and sat down on some debris. He unfastened his medicine kit and swallowed a few narcotic capsules. He looked around him. Where was he?

Something lay ahead. Stretched out on the ground. Silent and unmoving.

Hendricks drew his gun quickly. It looked like a man. Then he remembered. It was the remains of Klaus. The Second Variety. Where Tasso had blasted him. He could see wheels and relays and metal parts, strewn around on the ash. Glittering and sparkling in the sunlight.

Hendricks got to his feet and walked over. He nudged the inert form with his foot, turning it over a little. He could see the metal hull, the aluminum ribs and struts. More wiring fell out. Like viscera. Heaps of wiring, switches and relays. Endless motors and rods.

He bent down. The brain cage had been smashed by the fall. The artificial brain was visible. He gazed at it. A maze of circuits. Miniature tubes. Wires as fine as hair. He touched the brain cage. It swung aside. The type plate was visible. Hendricks studied the plate.

And blanched.

IV—IV.

For a long time he stared at the plate. Fourth Variety. Not the Second. They had been wrong. There were more types. Not just three. Many more, perhaps. At least four. And Klaus wasn't the Second Variety.

But if Klaus wasn't the Second Variety—

Suddenly he tensed. Something was coming, walking through the ash beyond the hill. What was it? He strained to see. Figures. Figures coming slowly along, making their way through the ash.

Coming toward him.

Hendricks crouched quickly, raising his gun. Sweat dripped down into his eyes. He fought down rising panic as the figures neared.

The first was a David. The David saw him and increased its pace. The others hurried behind it. A second David. A third. Three Davids, all alike, coming toward him silently, without expression, their thin legs rising and falling. Clutching their teddy bears.

He aimed and fired. The first two Davids dissolved into particles. The third came on. And the figure behind it. Climbing silently toward him across the gray ash. A Wounded Soldier, towering over the David. And—

And behind the Wounded Soldier came two Tassos, walking side by side. Heavy belt, Russian army pants, shirt, long hair. The familiar figure, as he had seen her only a little while before. Sitting in the pressure seat of the ship. Two slim, silent figures, both identical.

They were very near. The David bent down suddenly, dropping its teddy bear. The bear raced across the ground. Automatically, Hendricks's fingers tightened around the trigger. The bear was gone, dissolved into mist. The two Tasso Types moved on, expressionless, walking side by side, through the gray ash.

When they were almost to him, Hendricks raised the pistol waist high and fired.

The two Tassos dissolved. But already a new group was starting up the rise, five or six Tassos, all identical, a line of them coming rapidly toward him.

And he had given her the ship and the signal code. Because of him she was on her way to the moon, to the Moon Base. He had made it possible.

He had been right about the bomb after all. It had been designed with knowledge of the other types, the David Type and the Wounded Soldier Type. And the Klaus Type. Not designed by human beings. It had been designed by one of the underground factories, apart from all human contact.

The line of Tassos came up to him. Hendricks braced himself, watching them calmly. The familiar face, the belt, the heavy shirt, the bomb carefully in place.

The bomb—

As the Tassos reached for him, a last ironic thought drifted through Hendricks' mind. He felt a little better, thinking about it. The bomb. Made by the Second Variety to destroy the other varieties. Made for that end alone.

They were already beginning to design weapons to use against each other.

# THE VARIABLE MAN

## I

SECURITY COMMISSIONER REINHART rapidly climbed the front steps and entered the Council building. Council guards stepped quickly aside, and he entered the familiar place of great whirring machines. His thin face rapt, eyes alight with emotion, Reinhart gazed intently up at the central SRB computer, studying its reading.

"Straight gain for the last quarter," observed Kaplan, the lab organizer. He grinned proudly, as if personally responsible. "Not bad, Commissioner."

"We're catching up to them," Reinhart retorted. "But too damn slowly. We must finally go over—and soon."

Kaplan was in a talkative mood. "We design new offensive weapons, they counter with improved defenses. And nothing is actually made! Continual improvement, but neither we nor Centaurus can stop designing long enough to stabilize for production."

"It will end," Reinhart stated coldly, "as soon as Terra turns out a weapon for which Centaurus can build no defense."

"Every weapon has a defense. Design and discord. Immediate obsolescence. Nothing lasts long enough to—"

"What we count on is the *lag*," Reinhart broke in, annoyed. His hard gray eyes bored into the lab organizer and Kaplan slunk back. "The time lag between our offensive design and their counter development. The lag varies." He waved impatiently toward the massed banks of SRB machines. "As you well know."

At this moment, 9:30 a.m., May 7, 2136, the statistical ratio on the SRB machines stood at 21–17 on the Centauran side of the ledger. All facts considered, the odds favored a successful repulsion by Proxima Centaurus of a Terran military attack. The ratio was based on the total information known to the SRB machines, on a gestalt of the vast flow of data that poured in endlessly from all sectors of the Sol and Centaurus systems.

21–17 on the Centauran side. But a month ago it had been 24–18 in the enemy's favor. Things were improving, slowly but steadily. Centaurus, older and less virile than Terra, was unable to match Terra's rate of technocratic advance. Terra was pulling ahead.

"If we went to war now," Reinhart said thoughtfully, "we would lose. We're not far enough along to risk an overt attack." A harsh, ruthless glow twisted across his handsome features, distorting them into a stern mask. "But the odds are moving in our favor. Our offensive designs are gradually gaining on their defenses."

"Let's hope the war comes soon," Kaplan agreed. "We're all on edge. This damn waiting…"

The war would come soon. Reinhart knew it intuitively. The air was full of tension, the *elan*. He left the SRB rooms and hurried down the corridor to his own elaborately guarded office in the Security wing. It wouldn't be long. He could practically feel the hot breath of destiny on his neck—for him a pleasant feeling. His thin lips set in a humorless smile, showing an even line of white teeth against his tanned skin. It made him feel good, all right. He'd been working at it a long time.

First contact, a hundred years earlier, had ignited instant conflict between Proxima Centauran outposts and exploring Terran raiders. Flash fights, sudden eruptions of fire and energy beams.

And then the long, dreary years of inaction between enemies where contact required years of travel, even at nearly the speed of light. The two systems were evenly matched. Screen against screen. Warship against power station. The Centauran Empire surrounded Terra, an iron ring that couldn't be broken, rusty and corroded as it was. Radical new weapons had to be conceived if Terra was to break out.

Through the windows of his office, Reinhart could see end-less buildings and streets, Terrans hurrying back and forth. Bright specks that were commute ships, little eggs that carried businessmen and white-collar workers around. The huge trans-port tubes that shot masses of workmen to factories and labor camps from their housing units. All these people, waiting to break out. Waiting for the day.

Reinhart snapped on his vidscreen, the confidential chan-nel. "Give me Military Designs," he ordered sharply.

He sat tense, his wiry body taut, as the vidscreen warmed into life. Abruptly he was facing the hulking image of Peter Sherikov, director of the vast network of labs under the Ural Mountains.

Sherikov's great bearded features hardened as he recognized Reinhart. His bushy black eyebrows pulled up in a sullen line. "What do you want? You know I'm busy. We have too much work to do as it is. Without being bothered by—politicians."

"I'm dropping over your way," Reinhart answered lazily. He adjusted the cuff of his immaculate gray cloak. "I want a full description of your work and whatever progress you've made."

"You'll find a regular departmental report plate filed in the usual way, around your office someplace. If you'll refer to that you'll know exactly what we—"

"I'm not interested in that. I want to *see* what you're doing. And I expect you to be prepared to describe your work fully. I'll be there shortly. Half an hour."

Reinhart cut the circuit. Sherikov's heavy features dwindled and faded. Reinhart relaxed, letting his breath out. Too bad he had to work with Sherikov. He had never liked the man. The big Polish scientist was an individualist, refusing to integrate himself with society. Independent, atomistic in outlook. He held concepts of the individual as an end, diametrically contrary to the accepted organic state Weltansicht.

But Sherikov was the leading research scientist, in charge of the Military Designs Department. And on Designs the whole future of Terra depended. Victory over Centaurus—or more waiting, bottled up in the Sol System, surrounded by a rotting, hostile Empire, now sinking into ruin and decay, yet still strong.

Reinhart got quickly to his feet and left the office. He hurried down the hall and out of the Council building.

A few minutes later he was heading across the mid-morning sky in his highspeed cruiser, toward the Asiatic landmass, the vast Ural mountain range. Toward the Military Designs labs.

Sherikov met him at the entrance. "Look here, Reinhart. Don't think you're going to order me around. I'm not going to—"

"Take it easy." Reinhart fell into step beside the bigger man. They passed through the check and into the auxiliary labs. "No immediate coercion will be exerted over you or your staff. You're free to continue your work as you see fit—for the present. Let's get this straight. My concern is to integrate your work with our total social needs. As long as your work is sufficiently productive—"

Reinhart stopped in his tracks.

"Pretty, isn't he?" Sherikov said ironically.

"What the hell is it?

"Icarus, we call him. Remember the Greek myth? The legend of Icarus. Icarus flew…This Icarus is going to fly, one of these days." Sherikov shrugged. "You can examine him if you want. I suppose this is what you came here to see."

Reinhart advanced slowly. "This is the weapon you've been working on?"

"How does he look?"

Rising up in the center of the chamber was a squat metal cylinder, a great ugly cone of dark gray. Technicians circled around it, wiring up the exposed relay banks. Reinhart caught a glimpse of endless tubes and filaments, a maze of wires and terminals and parts crisscrossing each other, layer on layer.

"What is it?" Reinhart perched on the edge of a workbench, leaning his big shoulders against the wall. "An idea of Jamison Hedge—the same man who developed our instantaneous interstellar vidcasts forty years ago. He was trying to find a method of faster than light travel when he was killed, destroyed along with most of his work. After that, FTL research was abandoned. It looked as if there were no future in it."

"Wasn't it shown that nothing could travel faster than light?"

"The interstellar vidcasts do! No, Hedge developed a valid FTL drive. He managed to propel an object at fifty times the speed of light. But as the object gained speed, its length began to diminish and its mass increased. This was in line with familiar twentieth-century concepts of mass-energy transformation. We conjectured that as Hedge's object gained velocity it would continue to lose length and gain mass until its length became nil and its mass infinite. Nobody can imagine such an object."

"Go on."

"But what actually occurred is this. Hedge's object continued to lose length and gain mass until it reached the theoretical limit of velocity, the speed of light. At that point the object, still gaining speed, simply ceased to exist. Having no length, it ceased to occupy space. It disappeared. However, the object had not been *destroyed*. It continued on its way, gaining momentum each moment, moving in an arc across the galaxy, away from the Sol System. Hedge's object entered some other realm of being, beyond our powers of conception. The next phase of Hedge's experiment consisted in a search for some way to slow the FTL object down back to a sub-FTL speed, hence back into our universe. This counter-principle was eventually worked out."

"With what result?"

"The death of Hedge and destruction of most of his equipment. His experimental object, in reentering the space-time universe, came into being in space already occupied by matter. Possessing an incredible mass, just below infinity level, Hedge's object exploded in a titanic cataclysm. It was obvious that no space travel was possible with such a drive. Virtually all space contains *some* matter. To reenter space would bring automatic destruction. Hedge had found his FTL drive and his counter-principle, but no one before this has been able to put them to any use."

Reinhart walked over toward the great metal cylinder. Sherikov jumped down and followed him. "I don't get it," Reinhart said. "You said the principle is no good for space travel."

"That's right."

"What's this for then? If the ship explodes as soon as it returns to our universe—"

"This is not a ship." Sherikov grinned slyly. "Icarus is the first practical application of Hedge's principles. Icarus is a bomb."

"So this is our weapon," Reinhart said. "A bomb. An immense bomb."

"A bomb, moving at a velocity greater than light. A bomb which will not exist in our universe. The Centaurans won't be able to detect or stop it. How could they? As soon as it passes the speed of light it will cease to exist—beyond all detection."

"But—"

"Icarus will be launched outside the lab, on the surface. He will align himself with Proxima Centaurus, gaining speed rapidly. By the time he reaches his destination he will be traveling at FTL-100. Icarus will be brought back to this universe within Centaurus itself. The explosion should destroy the star and wash away most of its planets, including their central hub planet, Armun. There is no way they can halt Icarus once he has been launched. No defense is possible. Nothing can stop him. It is a real fact."

"When will he be ready?"

Sherikov's eyes flickered. "Soon."

"Exactly how soon?"

The big Pole hesitated. "As a matter of fact, there's only one thing holding us back."

Sherikov led Reinhart around to the other side of the lab. He pushed a lab guard out of the way.

"See this?" He tapped a round globe, open at one end, the size of a grapefruit. "This is holding us up."

"What is it?"

"The central control turret. This thing brings Icarus back to sub-FTL flight at the correct moment. It must be absolutely accurate. Icarus will be within the star only a matter of a microsecond. If the turret does not function exactly, Icarus will pass out the other side and shoot beyond the Centauran system."

"How near completed is this turret?"

Sherikov hedged uncertainly, spreading out his big hands. "Who can say? It must be wired with infinitely minute equipment—microscope grapples and wires invisible to the naked eye."

"Can you name any completion date?"

Sherikov reached into his coat and brought out a manila folder. "I've drawn up the data for the SRB machines, giving a date of completion. You can go ahead and feed it. I entered ten days as the maximum period. The machines can work from that."

Reinhart accepted the folder cautiously. "You're sure about the date? I'm not convinced I can trust you, Sherikov."

Sherikov's features darkened. "You'll have to take a chance, Commissioner. I don't trust you any more than you trust me. I know how much you'd like an excuse to get me out of here and one of your puppets in."

Reinhart studied the huge scientist thoughtfully. Sherikov was going to be a hard nut to crack. Designs was responsible to Security, not the Council. Sherikov was losing ground, but he was still a potential danger. Stubborn, individualistic, refusing to subordinate his welfare to the general good.

"All right." Reinhart put the folder slowly away in his coat. "I'll feed it. But you better be able to come through. There can't be any slip-ups. Too much hangs on the next few days."

"If the odds change in our favor, are you going to give the mobilization order?"

"Yes," Reinhart stated. "I'll give the order the moment I see the odds change."

***

Standing in front of the machines, Reinhart waited nervously for the results. It was two o'clock in the afternoon. The day was warm, a pleasant May afternoon. Outside the building the daily life of the planet went on as usual.

As usual? Not exactly. The feeling was in the air, an expanding excitement growing every day. Terra had waited a long time. The attack on Proxima Centaurus had to come, and the sooner the better. The ancient Centauran Empire hemmed in Terra, bottled the human race up in its one system. A vast, suffocating net draped across the heavens, cutting Terra off from the bright diamonds beyond…And it had to end.

The SRB machines whirred, the visible combination disappearing. For a time no ratio showed. Reinhart tensed, his body rigid. He waited.

The new ratio appeared.

Reinhart gasped. 7–6. Toward Terra!

Within five minutes the emergency mobilization alert had been flashed to all Government departments. The Council and President Duffe had been called to immediate session. Everything was happening fast.

But there was no doubt. 7–6. In Terra's favor. Reinhart hurried frantically to get his papers in order in time for the Council session.

At histo-research the message plate was quickly pulled from the confidential slot and rushed across the central lab to the chief official.

"Look at this!" Fredman dropped the plate on his superior's desk. "Look at it!"

Harper picked up the plate, scanning it rapidly. "Sounds like the real thing. I didn't think we'd live to see it."

Fredman left the room, hurrying down the hall. He entered the time bubble office. "Where's the bubble?" he demanded, looking around.

One of the technicians looked slowly up. "Back about two hundred years. We're coming up with interesting data on the War of 1914. According to material the bubble has already brought up—"

"Cut it. We're through with routine work. Get the bubble back to the present. From now on all equipment has to be free for Military work."

"But the bubble is regulated automatically."

"You can bring it back manually."

"It's risky." The technician hedged. "If the emergency requires it, I suppose we could take a chance and cut the automatic."

"The emergency requires *everything*," Fredman said feelingly.

"But the odds might change back," Margaret Duffe, President of the Council, said nervously. "Any minute they can revert."

"This is our chance!" Reinhart snapped, his temper rising. "What the hell's the matter with you? We've waited years for this."

The Council buzzed with excitement. Margaret Duffe hesitated uncertainly, her blue eyes clouded with worry. "I realize the opportunity is here. At least, statistically. But the new odds have just appeared. How do we know they'll last? They stand on the basis of a single weapon."

"You're wrong. You don't grasp the situation." Reinhart held himself in check with great effort. "Sherikov's weapon tipped the ratio in our favor. But the odds have been moving in our direction for months. It was only a question of time. The new balance was inevitable, sooner or later. It's not just Sherikov. He's only one factor in this. It's all nine planets of the Sol System, not a single man."

One of the Councilmen stood up. "The President must be aware the entire planet is eager to end this waiting. All our activities for the past eighty years have been directed toward—"

Reinhart moved close to the slender President of the Council. "If you don't approve the war, there probably will be mass rioting. Public reaction will be strong. Damn strong. And you know it."

Margaret Duffe shot him a cold glance. "You sent out the emergency order to force my hand. You were fully aware of what you were doing. You knew once the order was out there'd be no stopping things."

A murmur rushed through the Council, gaining volume. "We have to approve the war! We're committed! It's too late to turn back!"

Shouts, angry voices, insistent waves of sound lapped around Margaret Duffe. "I'm as much for the war as anybody," she said sharply. "I'm only urging moderation. An intersystem war is a big thing. We're going to war because a machine says we have a statistical chance of winning."

"There's no use starting the war unless we can win it," Reinhart said. "The SRB machines tell us whether we can win."

"They tell us our *chance* of winning. They don't guarantee anything."

"What more can we ask, beside a good chance of winning?"

Margaret Duffe clamped her jaw together tightly. "All right. I hear all the clamor. I won't stand in the way of Council approval. The vote can go ahead." Her cold, alert eyes appraised Reinhart. "Especially since the emergency order has already been sent out to all Government departments."

"Good." Reinhart stepped away with relief. "Then it's settled. We can finally go ahead with full mobilization."

Mobilization proceeded rapidly. The next forty-eight hours were alive with activity.

Reinhart attended a policy-level Military briefing in the Council rooms, conducted by Fleet Commander Carleton.

"You can see our strategy," Carleton said. He traced a diagram on the blackboard with a wave of his hand. "Sherikov states it'll take eight more days to complete the FTL bomb. During that time the fleet we have near the Centauran system will take up positions. As the bomb goes off, the fleet will begin operations against the remaining Centauran ships. Many will no doubt survive the blast, but with Armun gone we should be able to handle them."

Reinhart took Commander Carleton's place. "I can report on the economic situation. Every factory on Terra is converted to arms production. With Armun out of the way we should be able to promote mass insurrection among the Centauran colonies. An intersystem Empire is hard to maintain, even with ships that approach light speed. Local warlords should pop up all over the place. We want to have weapons available for them and ships starting *now* to reach them in time. Eventually we hope to provide a unifying principle around which the colonies can all collect. Our interest is more economic than political. They can have any kind of government they want, as long as they act as supply areas for us. As our eight system planets act now."

Carleton resumed his report. "Once the Centauran fleet has been scattered, we can begin the crucial stage of the war. The landing of men and supplies from the ships we have waiting in all key areas throughout the Centauran system. In this stage—"

Reinhart moved away. It was hard to believe only two days had passed since the mobilization order had been sent out. The whole system was alive, functioning with feverish activity. Countless problems were being solved, but much remained.

He entered the lift and ascended to the SRB room, curious to see if there had been any change in the machines's reading. He found it the same. So far so good. Did the Centaurans know about Icarus? No doubt. But there wasn't anything they could do about it. At least, not in eight days.

Kaplan came over to Reinhart, sorting a new batch of data that had come in. The lab organizer searched through his data. "An amusing item came in. It might interest you." He handed a message plate to Reinhart.

It was from histo-research:

May 9, 2136

This is to report that in bringing the research time bubble up to the present the manual return was used for the first time. Therefore a clean break was not made, and a quantity of material from the past was brought forward. This material included an individual from the early twentieth century who escaped from the lab immediately. He has not yet been taken into protective custody. Histo-research regrets this incident, but attributes it to the emergency.

E. Ferdman

Reinhart handed the plate back to Kaplan. "Interesting. A man from the past, hauled into the middle of the biggest war the universe has seen."

"Strange things happen. I wonder what the machines will think."

"Hard to say. Probably nothing." Reinhart left the room and hurried along the corridor to his own office.

As soon as he was inside, he called Sherikov on the vidscreen, using the confidential line.

The Pole's heavy features appeared. "Good day, Commissioner. How's the war effort?"

"Fine. How's the turret wiring proceeding?"

A faint frown flickered across Sherikov's face. "As a matter of fact, Commissioner—"

"What's the matter?" Reinhart said sharply.

Sherikov floundered. "You know how these things are. I've taken my crew off it and tried robot workers. They have greater dexterity, but they can't make decisions. This calls for more than mere dexterity. This calls for—" He searched for the word. "—for an *artist*."

Reinhart's face hardened. "Listen, Sherikov. You have eight days left to complete the bomb. The data given to the SRB machines contained that information. The 7–6 ratio is based on that estimate. If you don't come through—"

Sherikov twisted in embarrassment. "Don't get excited, Commissioner. We'll complete it."

"I hope so. Call me as soon as it's done." Reinhart snapped off the connection. If Sherikov let them down he'd have him taken out and shot. The whole war depended on the FTL bomb.

The vidscreen glowed again. Reinhart snapped it on. Kaplan's face formed on it. The lab organizer's face was pale and frozen. "Commissioner, you better come up to the SRB office. Something's happened."

"What is it?"

"I'll show you."

Alarmed, Reinhart hurried out of his office and down the corridor. He found Kaplan standing in front of the SRB machines. "What's the story?" Reinhart demanded. He glanced down at the reading. It was unchanged.

Kaplan held up a message plate nervously. "A moment ago I fed this into the machines. After I saw the results I quickly removed it. It's that item I showed you. From histo-research. About the man from the past."

"What happened when you fed it?"

Kaplan swallowed unhappily. "I'll show you. I'll do it again. Exactly as before." He fed the plate into a moving intake belt. "Watch the visible figures," Kaplan muttered.

Reinhart watched, tense and rigid. For a moment nothing happened. 7–6 continued to show. Then—

The figures disappeared. The machines faltered. New figures showed briefly. 4–24 for Centaurus. Reinhart gasped, suddenly sick with apprehension. But the figures vanished. New figures appeared. 16–38 for Centaurus. Then 48–86. 79–15 in Terra's favor. Then nothing. The machines whirred, but nothing happened.

Nothing at all. No figures. Only a blank.

"What's it mean?" Reinhart muttered, dazed.

"It's fantastic. We didn't think this could—"

"*What's happened?*"

"The machines aren't able to handle the item. No reading can come. It's data they can't integrate. They can't use it for prediction material, and it throws off all their other figures."

"Why?"

"It's—it's a variable." Kaplan was shaking, white-lipped and pale. "Something from which no inference can be made. The man from the past. The machines can't deal with him. The variable man!"

# II

Thomas Cole was sharpening a knife with his whetstone when the tornado hit.

The knife belonged to the lady in the big green house. Every time Cole came by with his fixit cart the lady had something to be sharpened. Once in a while she gave him a cup of coffee, hot black coffee from an old, bent pot. He liked that fine. He enjoyed good coffee.

The day was drizzly and overcast. Business had been bad. An automobile had scared his two horses. On bad days less people were outside, and he had to get down from the cart and go to ring doorbells.

But the man in the yellow house had given him a dollar for fixing his electric refrigerator. Nobody else had been able to fix it, not even the factory man. The dollar would go a long way. A dollar was a lot.

He knew it was a tornado even before it hit him. Everything was silent. He was bent over his whetstone, the reins between his knees, absorbed in his work.

He had done a good job on the knife; he was almost finished. He spat on the blade and was holding it up to see. And then the tornado came.

All at once it was there, completely around him. Nothing but grayness. He and the cart and horses seemed to be in a calm spot in the center of the tornado. They were moving in a great silence, gray mist everywhere.

And while he was wondering what to do and how to get the lady's knife back to her, all at once there was a bump and the tornado tipped him over, sprawled out on the ground. The horses screamed in fear, struggling to pick themselves up. Cole got quickly to his feet.

*Where was he?*

The grayness was gone. White walls stuck up on all sides. A deep light gleamed down, not daylight but something like it. The team was pulling the cart on its side, dragging it along, tools and equipment falling out. Cole righted the cart, leaping up onto the seat.

And for the first time saw the people.

Men, with astonished white faces, in some sort of uniforms. Shouts, noise and confusion. And a feeling of danger!

Cole headed the team toward the door. Hoofs thundered steel against steel as they pounded through the doorway, scattering the astonished men in all directions. He was out in a wide hall. A building like a hospital.

The hall divided. More men were coming, spilling from all sides.

Shouting and milling in excitement, like white ants. Something cut past him, a beam of dark violet. It seared off a corner of the cart, leaving the wood smoking.

Cole felt fear. He kicked at the terrified horses. They reached a big door, crashing wildly against it. The door gave, and they were outside, bright sunlight blinking down on them. For a sickening second the cart tilted, almost turning over. Then the horses gained speed, racing across an open field toward a distant line of green, Cole holding tightly to the reins.

Behind him the little white-faced men had come out and were standing in a group, gesturing frantically. He could hear their faint shrill shouts.

But he had got away. He was safe. He slowed the horses down and began to breathe again.

The woods were artificial. Some kind of park. But the park was wild and overgrown. A dense jungle of twisted plants. Everything growing in confusion.

The park was empty. No one was there. By the position of the sun he could tell it was either early morning or late afternoon. The smell of the flowers and grass, the dampness of the leaves, indicated morning. It had been late afternoon when the tornado had picked him up. And the sky had been overcast and cloudy.

Cole considered. Clearly, he had been carried a long way. The hospital, the men with white faces, the odd lighting, the accented words he had caught—everything indicated he was no longer in Nebraska. maybe not even in the United States.

Some of his tools had fallen out and gotten lost along the way. Cole collected everything that remained, sorting them, running his fingers over each tool with affection. Some of the little chisels and wood gouges were gone. The bit box had opened, and most of the smaller bits had been lost. He gathered up those that remained and replaced them tenderly in the box. He took a keyhole saw down, and with an oil rag wiped it carefully and replaced it.

Above the cart the sun rose slowly in the sky. Cole peered up, his horny hand over his eyes. A big man, stoop-shouldered, his chin gray and stubbled. His clothes wrinkled and dirty. But his eyes were clear, a pale blue, and his hands were finely made.

He could not stay in the park. They had seen him ride that way. They would be looking for him.

Far above something shot rapidly across the sky. A tiny black dot moving with incredible haste. A second dot followed. The two dots were gone almost before he saw them. They were utterly silent.

Cole frowned, perturbed. The dots made him uneasy. He would have to keep moving—and looking for food. His stomach was already beginning to rumble and groan.

Work. There was plenty he could do: gardening, sharpening, grinding, repair work on machines and clocks, fixing all kinds of household things. Even painting and odd jobs and carpentry and chores.

He could do anything. Anything people wanted done. For a meal and pocket money.

Thomas Cole urged the team into life, moving forward. He sat hunched over in the seat, watching intently as the fixit cart rolled slowly across the tangled grass, through the jungle of trees and flowers.

***

Reinhart hurried, racing his cruiser at top speed, followed by a second ship, a military escort. The ground sped by below him, a blur of gray and green.

The remains of New York lay spread out, a twisted, blunted ruin overgrown with weeds and grass. The great atomic wars of the twentieth century had turned virtually the whole seaboard area into an endless waste of slag.

Slag and weeds below him. And then the sudden tangle that had been Central Park.

Histo-research came into sight. Reinhart swooped down, bringing his cruiser to rest at the small supply field behind the main buildings.

Harper, the chief official of the department, came quickly over as soon as Reinhart's ship landed.

"Frankly, we don't understand why you consider this matter important," Harper said uneasily.

Reinhart shot him a cold glance. "I'll be the judge of what's important. Are you the one who gave the order to bring the bubble back manually?"

"Fredman gave the actual order. In line with your directive to have all facilities ready for—"

Reinhart headed toward the entrance of the research building. "Where is Fredman?"

"Inside."

"I want to see him. Let's go."

Fredman met them inside. He greeted Reinhart calmly, showing no emotion. "Sorry to cause you trouble, Commissioner. We were trying to get the station in order for the war. We wanted the bubble back as quickly as possible." He eyed Reinhart curiously. "No doubt the man and his cart will soon be picked up by your police."

"I want to know everything that happened, in exact detail."

Fredman shifted uncomfortably. "There's not much to tell. I gave the order to have the automatic setting canceled and the bubble brought back manually. At the moment the signal reached it, the bubble was passing through the spring of 1913. As it broke loose, it tore off a piece of ground on which this person and his cart were located. The person naturally was brought up to the present inside the bubble."

"Didn't any of your instruments tell you the bubble was loaded?"

"We were too excited to take any readings. Half an hour after the manual control was thrown, the bubble materialized in the observation room. It was de-energized before anyone noticed what was inside. We tried to stop him, but he drove the cart out into the hall, bowling us out of the way. The horses were in a panic."

"What kind of cart was it?"

"There was some kind of sign on it. Painted in black letters on both sides. No one saw what it was."

"Go ahead. What happened then?"

"Somebody fired a Slem-ray after him, but it missed. The horses carried him out of the building and onto the grounds. By the time we reached the exit, the cart was halfway to the park."

Reinhart reflected. "If he's still in the park, we should have him shortly. But we must be careful." He was already starting back toward his ship, leaving Fredman behind. Harper fell in beside him.

Reinhart halted by his ship. He beckoned some Government guards over. "Put the executive staff of this department under arrest. I'll have them tried on a treason count later on." He smiled ironically as Harper's face blanched sickly pale. "There's a war going on. You'll be lucky if you get off alive."

Reinhart entered his ship and left the surface, rising rapidly into the sky. A second ship followed after him, a military escort. Reinhart flew high above the sea of gray slag, the unrecovered waste area. He passed over a sudden square of green set in the ocean of gray. Reinhart gazed back at it until it was gone.

Central Park. He could see police ships racing through the sky, ships and transports loaded with troops, heading toward the square of green. On the ground some heavy guns and surface cars rumbled along, lines of black approaching the park from all sides.

They would have the man soon. But meanwhile the SRB machines were blank. And on the SRB machines's readings the whole war depended.

About noon the cart reached the edge of the park. Cole rested for a moment, allowing the horses time to crop at the thick grass. The silent expanse of slag amazed him. What had happened? Nothing stirred. No buildings, no sign of life. Grass and weeds poked up occasionally through it, breaking the flat surface here and there, but even so, the sight gave him an uneasy chill.

Cole drove the cart slowly out onto the slag, studying the sky above him. There was nothing to hide him now that he was out of the park. The slag was bare and uniform like the ocean. If he were spotted—

A horde of tiny black dots raced across the sky, coming rapidly closer. Presently they veered to the right and disappeared. More planes, wingless metal planes. He watched them go, driving slowly on.

Half an hour later something appeared ahead. Cole slowed the cart down, peering to see. The slag came to an end. He had reached its limits. Ground appeared, dark soil and grass. Weeds grew everywhere. Ahead of him, beyond the end of the slag, was a line of buildings, houses of some sort. Or sheds.

Houses, probably. But not like any he had ever seen.

The houses were uniform, all exactly the same. Like little green shells, rows of them, several hundred. There was a little lawn in front of each. Lawn, a path, a front porch, bushes in a meager row around each house. But the houses were all alike and very small.

Little green shells in precise, even rows. He urged the cart cautiously forward toward the houses.

No one seemed to be around. He entered a street between two rows of houses, the hoofs of his two horses sounding loudly in the silence. He was in some kind of town. But there were no dogs or children. Everything was neat and silent. Like a model. An exhibit. It made him uncomfortable.

A young man walking along the pavement gaped at him in wonder. An oddly dressed youth, in a toga-like cloak that hung down to his knees. A single piece of fabric. And sandals.

Or what looked like sandals. Both the cloak and the sandals were of some strange, half-luminous material. It glowed faintly in the sunlight. Metallic, rather than cloth.

A woman was watering flowers at the edge of a lawn. She straightened up as his team of horses came near. Her eyes widened in astonishment, and then fear. Her mouth fell open in a soundless *O* and her sprinkling can slipped from her fingers and rolled silently onto the lawn.

Cole blushed and turned his head quickly away. The woman was scarcely dressed! He flicked the reins and urged the horses to hurry.

Behind him, the woman still stood. He stole a brief, hasty

look back and then shouted hoarsely to his team, ears scarlet. He had seen right. She wore only a pair of translucent shorts. Nothing else. A mere fragment of the same half-luminous material that glowed and sparkled. The rest of her small body was utterly naked.

He slowed the team down. She had been pretty. Brown hair and eyes, deep red lips. Quite a good figure. Slender waist, downy legs, bare and supple, full breasts— He clamped the thought furiously off. He had to get to work. Business.

Cole halted the fixit cart and leaped down onto the pavement. He selected a house at random and approached it cautiously. The house was attractive. It had a certain simple beauty. But it looked frail, and exactly like the others.

He stepped up on the porch. There was no bell. He searched for it, running his hand uneasily over the surface of the door. All at once there was a click, a sharp snap on a level with his eyes. Cole glanced up, startled. A lens was vanishing as the door section slid over it. He had been photographed.

While he was wondering what it meant, the door swung suddenly open. A man filled up the entrance, a big man in a tan uniform, blocking the way ominously.

"What do you want?" the man demanded.

"I'm looking for work," Cole murmured. "Any kind of work. I can do anything, fix any kind of thing. I repair broken objects. Things that need mending." His voice trailed off uncertainly. "Anything at all."

"Apply to the Placement Department of the Federal Activities Control Board," the man said crisply. "You know all occupational therapy is handled through them." He eyed Cole curiously. "Why have you got on those ancient clothes?"

"Ancient? Why, I—"

The man gazed past him at the fixit cart and the two dozing horses. "What's that? What are those two animals? *Horses?*"

The man rubbed his jaw, studying Cole intently. "That's strange," he said.

"Strange?" Cole murmured uneasily. "Why?"

"There haven't been any horses for over a century. All the horses were wiped out during the Fifth Atomic War. That's why it's strange."

Cole tensed, suddenly alert. There was something in the man's eyes, a hardness, a piercing look. Cole moved back off the porch, onto the path. He had to be careful. Something was wrong.

"I'll be going," he murmured.

"There haven't been any horses for over a hundred years." The man came toward Cole. "Who are you? Why are you dressed up like that? Where did you get that vehicle and pair of horses?"

"I'll be going," Cole repeated, moving away.

The man whipped something from his belt, a thin metal tube. He stuck it toward Cole.

It was a rolled-up paper, a thin sheet of metal in the form of a tube. Words, some kind of script. He could not make any of them out. The man's picture, rows of numbers, figures—

"I'm Director Winslow," the man said. "Federal Stockpile Conservation. You better talk fast, or there'll be a Security Car here in five minutes."

Cole moved fast. He raced, head down, back along the path to the cart, toward the street.

Something hit him. A wall of force, throwing him down on his face. He sprawled in a heap, numb and dazed. His body ached, vibrating wildly, out of control. Waves of shock rolled over him, gradually diminishing.

He got shakily to his feet. His head spun. He was weak, shattered, trembling violently. The man was coming down the walk after him. Cole pulled himself onto the cart, gasping and retching. The horses jumped into life. Cole rolled over against the seat, sick with the motion of the swaying cart.

He caught hold of the reins and managed to drag himself up in a sitting position. The cart gained speed, turning a corner. Houses flew past. Cole urged the team weakly, drawing great shuddering breaths. Houses and streets, a blur of motion, as the cart flew faster and faster along.

Then he was leaving the town, leaving the neat little houses behind. He was on some sort of highway. Big buildings, factories, on both sides of the highway. Figures, men watching in astonishment.

After a while the factories fell behind. Cole slowed the team down. What had the man meant? Fifth Atomic War. Horses destroyed. It didn't make sense. And they had things he knew nothing about. Force fields. Planes without wings, soundless.

Cole reached around in his pockets. He found the identification tube the man had handed him. In the excitement he had carried it off. He unrolled the tube slowly and began to study it. The writing was strange to him.

For a long time he studied the tube. Then, gradually, he became aware of something. Something in the top right-hand corner.

A date. October 6, 2128.

Cole's vision blurred. Everything spun and wavered around him. October, 2128. Could it be?

But he held the paper in his hand. Thin, metal paper. Like foil. And it had to be. It said so, right in the corner, printed on the paper itself.

Cole rolled the tube up slowly, numbed with shock. Two hundred years. It didn't seem possible. But things were beginning to make sense. He was in the future, two hundred years in the future.

While he was mulling this over, the swift black Security ship appeared overhead, diving rapidly toward the horse-drawn cart as it moved slowly along the road.

Reinhart's vidscreen buzzed. He snapped it quickly on. "Yes?"

"Report from Security."

"Put it through." Reinhart waited tensely as the lines locked in place. The screen relit.

"This is Dixon. Western Regional Command." The officer cleared his throat, shuffling his message plates. "The man from the past has been reported moving away from the New York area."

"Which side of your net?"

"Outside. He evaded the net around Central Park by entering one of the small towns at the rim of the slag area."

"*Evaded?*"

"We assumed he would avoid the towns. Naturally the net failed to encompass any of the towns."

Reinhart's jaw stiffened. "Go on."

"He entered the town of Petersville a few minutes before the net closed around the park. We burned the park level, but naturally found nothing. He had already gone. An hour later we received a report from a resident in Petersville, an official of the Stockpile Conservation Department. The man from the past had come to his door, looking for work. Winslow, the official, engaged him in conversation, trying to hold on to him, but he escaped, driving his cart off. Winslow called Security right away, but by then it was too late."

"Report to me as soon as anything more comes in. We must have him, and damn soon." Reinhart snapped the screen off. It died quickly.

He sat back in his chair, waiting.

Cole saw the shadow of the Security ship. He reacted at once. A second after the shadow passed over him, Cole was out of the cart, running and falling. He rolled, twisting and turning, pulling his body as far away from the cart as possible.

There was a blinding roar and flash of white light. A hot wind rolled over Cole, picking him up and tossing him like a leaf. He shut his eyes, letting his body relax. He bounced, falling and striking the ground. Gravel and stones tore into his face, his knees, the palms of his hands.

Cole cried out, shrieking in pain. His body was on fire. He was being consumed, incinerated by the blinding white orb of fire. The orb expanded, growing in size, swelling like some monstrous sun, twisted and bloated. The end had come. There was no hope. He gritted his teeth—

The greedy orb faded, dying down. It sputtered and winked out, blackening into ash. The air reeked, a bitter acrid smell. His clothes were burning and smoking. The ground under him was hot, baked dry, seared by the blast. But he was alive. At least, for a while.

Cole opened his eyes slowly. The cart was gone. A great hole gaped where it had been, a shattered sore in the center of the highway. An ugly cloud hung above the hole, black and ominous. Far above, the wingless plane circled, watching for any signs of life.

Cole lay, breathing shallowly, slowly. Time passed. The sun moved across the sky with agonizing slowness. It was perhaps four in the afternoon. Cole calculated mentally. In three hours it would be dark. If he could stay alive until then—

Had the plane seen him leap from the cart?

He lay without moving. The late-afternoon sun beat down on him. He felt sick, nauseated and feverish. His mouth was dry.

Some ants ran over his outstretched hand. Gradually, the immense black cloud was beginning to drift away, dispersing into a formless blob.

The cart was gone. The thought lashed against him, pounding at his brain, mixing with his labored pulse-beat. *Gone.*

Destroyed. Nothing but ashes and debris remained. The realization dazed him.

Finally the plane finished its circling, winging its way toward the horizon. At last it vanished. The sky was clear.

Cole got unsteadily to his feet. He wiped his face shakily. His body ached and trembled. He spat a couple times, trying to clear his mouth. The plane would probably send in a report. People would be coming to look for him. Where could he go?

To his right a line of hills rose up, a distant green mass. Maybe he could reach them. He began to walk slowly. He had to be very careful. They were looking for him, and they had weapons. Incredible weapons.

He would be lucky to still be alive when the sun set. His team and fixit cart were gone—and all his tools. Cole reached into his pockets, searching through them hopefully. He brought out some small screwdrivers, a little pair of cutting pliers, some wire, some solder, the whetstone, and finally the lady's knife.

Only a few small tools remained. He had lost everything else. But without the cart he was safer, harder to spot. They would have more trouble finding him on foot.

Cole hurried along, crossing the level fields toward the distant range of hills.

The call came through to Reinhart almost at once. Dixon's features formed on the vidscreen. "I have a further report, Commissioner." Dixon scanned the plate. "Good news. The man from the past was sighted moving away from Petersville, along highway 13, at about ten miles an hour on his horse-drawn cart. Our ship bombed him immediately."

"Did—did you get him?"

"The pilot reports no sign of life after the blast."

Reinhart's pulse almost stopped. He sank back in his chair. "Then he's dead!"

"Actually, we won't know for certain until we can examine the debris. A surface car is speeding toward the spot. We should have the complete report in a short time. We'll notify you as soon as the information comes in."

Reinhart reached out and cut the screen. It faded into darkness. Had they got the man from the past? Or had he escaped again? Weren't they ever going to get him? Couldn't he be captured? And meanwhile, the SRB machines were silent, showing nothing at all.

Reinhart sat brooding, waiting impatiently for the report of the surface car to come in.

***

It was evening.

"Come on!" Steven shouted, running frantically after his brother. "Come on back!"

"Catch me." Earl ran and ran, down the side of the hill, over behind a military storage depot, along a neotex fence, jumping finally down into Mrs. Norris's backyard.

Steven hurried after his brother, sobbing for breath, shouting and gasping as he ran. "Come back! You come back with that!"

"What's he got?" Sally Tate demanded, stepping out suddenly to block Steven's way.

Steven halted, his chest rising and falling. "He's got my inter-system vidsender." His small face twisted with rage and misery. "He better give it back!"

Earl came circling around from the right. In the warm gloom of evening he was almost invisible. "Here I am," he announced. "What you going to do?"

Steven glared at him hotly. His eyes made out the square box in Earl's hands. "You give that back! Or—or I'll tell Dad."

Earl laughed. "Make me."

"Dad'll make you."

"You better give it to him," Sally said.

"Catch me." Earl started off. Steven pushed Sally out of the way, lashing wildly at his brother. He collided with him, throwing him sprawling. The box fell from Earl's hands. It skidded to the pavement, crashing into the side of a guide-light post.

Earl and Steven picked themselves up slowly. They gazed down at the broken box.

"See?" Steven shrilled, tears filling his eyes. "See what you did?"

"You did it. You pushed into me."

"You did it!" Steven bent down and picked up the box. He carried it over to the guide-light, sitting down on the curb to examine it.

Earl came slowly over. "If you hadn't pushed me, it wouldn't have got broken."

Night was descending rapidly. The line of hills rising above the town were already lost in darkness. A few lights had come on here and there. The evening was warm. A surface car slammed its doors some place off in the distance. In the sky ships droned back and forth, weary commuters coming home from work in the big underground factory units.

Thomas Cole came slowly toward the three children grouped around the guide-light. He moved with difficulty, his body sore and bent with fatigue. Night had come, but he was not safe yet.

He was tired, exhausted and hungry. He had walked a long way. And he had to have something to eat soon.

A few feet from the children Cole stopped. They were all intent and absorbed by the box on Steven's knees. Suddenly a hush fell over the children. Earl looked up slowly.

In the dim light the big, stooped figure of Thomas Cole seemed extra menacing. His long arms hung down loosely at his sides. His face was lost in shadow. His body was shapeless, indistinct. A big unformed statue, standing silently a few feet away, unmoving in the half-darkness.

"Who are you?" Earl demanded, his voice low.

"What do you want?" Sally said. The children edged away nervously. "Get away."

Cole came toward them. He bent down a little. The beam from the guide-light crossed his features. Lean, prominent nose, beak-like, faded blue eyes—

Steven scrambled to his feet, clutching the vidsender box. "You get out of here!"

"Wait." Cole smiled crookedly at them. His voice was dry and raspy. "What do you have there?" He pointed with his long, slender fingers. "The box you're holding."

The children were silent. Finally Steven stirred. "It's my intersystem vidsender."

"Only it doesn't work," Sally said.

"Earl broke it." Steven glared at his brother bitterly. "Earl threw it down and broke it."

Cole smiled a little. He sank down wearily on the edge of the curb, sighing with relief. He had been walking too long. His body ached with fatigue. He was hungry, and tired. For a long time he sat, wiping perspiration from his neck and face, too exhausted to speak.

"Who are you?" Sally demanded, at last. "Why do you have on those funny clothes? Where did you come from?"

"Where?" Cole looked around at the children. "From a long way off. A long way." He shook his head slowly from side to side, trying to clear it.

"What's your therapy?" Earl said.

"My therapy?"

"What do you do? Where do you work?"

Cole took a deep breath and let it out again slowly. "I fix things. All kinds of things. Any kind."

Earl sneered. "Nobody fixes things. When they break you throw them away."

Cole didn't hear him. Sudden need had roused him, getting him suddenly to his feet. "You know any work I can find?" he demanded. "Things I could do? I can fix anything. Clocks, typewriters, refrigerators, pots and pans. Leaks in the roof. I can fix anything there is."

Steven held out his intersystem vidsender. "Fix this."

There was silence. Slowly, Cole's eyes focused on the box. "That?"

"My sender. Earl broke it."

Cole took the box slowly. He turned it over, holding it up to the light. He frowned, concentrating on it. His long, slender fingers moved carefully over the surface, exploring it.

"He'll steal it!" Earl said suddenly.

"No." Cole shook his head vaguely. "I'm reliable." His sensitive fingers found the studs that held the box together. He depressed the studs, pushing them expertly in. The box opened, revealing its complex interior.

"He got it open," Sally whispered.

"Give it back!" Steven demanded, a little frightened. He held out his hand. "I want it back."

The three children watched Cole apprehensively. Cole fumbled in his pocket. Slowly he brought out his tiny screwdrivers and pliers. He laid them in a row beside him. He made no move to return the box.

"I want it back," Steven said feebly.

Cole looked up. His faded blue eyes took in the sight of the three children standing before him in the gloom. "I'll fix it for you. You said you wanted it fixed."

"I want it back." Steven stood on one foot, then the other, torn by doubt and indecision. "Can you really fix it? Can you make it work again?"

"Yes."

"All right. Fix it for me, then."

A sly smile flickered across Cole's tired face. "Now, wait a minute. If I fix it, will you bring me something to eat? I'm not fixing it for nothing."

"Something to eat?"

"Food. I need hot food. Maybe some coffee."

Steven nodded. "Yes. I'll get it for you."

Cole relaxed. "Fine. That's fine." He turned his attention back to the box resting between his knees. "Then I'll fix it for you. I'll fix it for you good."

His fingers flew, working and twisting, tracing down wires and relays, exploring and examining. Finding out about the intersystem vidsender. Discovering how it worked.

Steven slipped into the house through the emergency door. He made his way to the kitchen with great care, walking on tiptoe. He punched the kitchen controls at random, his heart beating excitedly. The stove began to whirr, purring into life. Meter readings came on, crossing toward the completion marks.

Presently the stove opened, sliding out a tray of steaming dishes. The mechanism clicked off, dying into silence. Steven grabbed up the contents of the tray, filling his arms. He carried everything down the hall, out the emergency door and into the yard. The yard was dark. Steven felt his way carefully along.

He managed to reach the guide-light without dropping anything at all.

Thomas Cole got slowly to his feet as Steven came into view. "Here," Steven said. He dumped the food onto the curb, gasping for breath. "Here's the food. Is it finished?"

Cole held out the intersystem vidsender. "It's finished. It was pretty badly smashed."

Earl and Sally gazed up, wide-eyed. "Does it work?" Sally asked.

"Of course not," Earl stated. "How could it work? He couldn't—"

"Turn it on!" Sally nudged Steven eagerly. "See if it works."

Steven was holding the box under the light, examining the switches. He clicked the main switch on. The indicator light gleamed. "It lights up," Steven said.

"Say something into it."

Steven spoke into the box. "Hello! Hello! This is operator 6-z75 calling. Can you hear me? This is operator 6-z75. Can you hear me?"

In the darkness, away from the beam of the guide-light, Thomas Cole sat crouched over the food. He ate gratefully, silently. It was good food, well cooked and seasoned. He drank a container of orange juice and then a sweet drink he didn't recognize. Most of the food was strange to him, but he didn't care. He had walked a long way and he was plenty hungry. And he still had a long way to go before morning. He had to be deep in the hills before the sun came up. Instinct told him that he would be safe among the trees and tangled growth—at least, as safe as he could hope for.

He ate rapidly, intent on the food. He did not look up until he was finished. Then he got slowly to his feet, wiping his mouth with the back of his hand.

The three children were standing around in a circle, operating the intersystem vidsender. He watched them for a few minutes. None of them looked up from the small box. They were intent, absorbed in what they were doing.

"Well?" Cole said, at last. "Does it work all right?"

After a moment Steven looked up at him. There was a strange expression on his face. He nodded slowly. "Yes. Yes, it works. It works fine."

Cole grunted. "All right." He turned and moved away from the light. "That's fine."

The children watched silently until the figure of Thomas Cole had completely disappeared. Slowly, they turned and looked at each other. Then down at the box in Steven's hands. They gazed at the box in growing awe. Awe mixed with dawning fear.

Steven turned and edged toward his house. "I've got to show it to my Dad," he murmured, dazed. "He's got to know. *Somebody's* got to know!"

<h1 style="text-align:center">III</h1>

Eric Reinhart examined the vidsender box carefully, turning it around and around.

"Then he did escape from the blast," Dixon admitted reluctantly. "He must have leaped from the cart just before the concussion."

Reinhart nodded. "He escaped. He got away from you—twice." He pushed the vidsender box away and leaned abruptly toward the man standing uneasily in front of his desk. "What's your name again?"

"Elliot. Richard Elliot."

"And your son's name?"

"Steven."

"It was last night this happened?"

"About eight o'clock."

"Go on."

"Steven came into the house. He acted queerly. He was carrying his intersystem vidsender." Elliot pointed at the box on Reinhart's desk. "That. He was nervous and excited. I asked what was wrong. For a while he couldn't tell me. He was quite upset. Then he showed me the vidsender." Elliot took a deep, shaky breath. "I could see right away it was different. You see I'm an electrical engineer. I had opened it once before, to put in a new battery. I had a fairly good idea how it should look." Elliot hesitated. "Commissioner, it had been *changed*. A lot of the wiring was different. Moved around. Relays connected differently. Some parts were missing. New parts had been jury-rigged out of old. Then I discovered the thing that made me call Security. The vidsender—it really *worked*."

"Worked?"

"You see, it never was anything more than a toy. With a range of a few city blocks. So the kids could call back and forth from their rooms. Like a sort of portable vidscreen. Commissioner, I tried out the vidsender, pushing the call button and speaking into the microphone. I—I got a ship of the line. A battleship, operating beyond Proxima Centaurus over eight light years away. As far out as the actual vidsenders operate. Then I called Security. Right away."

For a time Reinhart was silent. Finally he tapped the box lying on the desk. "You got a ship of the line—with *this*?"

"That's right."

"How big are the regular vidsenders?"

Dixon supplied the information. "As big as a twenty-ton safe."

"That's what I thought." Reinhart waved his hand impatiently. "All right, Elliot. Thanks for turning the information over to us. That's all."

Security police led Elliot outside the office.

Reinhart and Dixon looked at each other. "This is bad," Reinhart said harshly. "He has some ability, some kind of mechanical ability. Genius, perhaps, to do a thing like this. Look at the period he came from, Dixon. The early part of the twentieth century. Before the wars began. That was a unique period. There was a certain vitality, a certain ability. It was a period of incredible growth and discovery. Edison. Pasteur. Burbank.

The Wright brothers. Inventions and machines. People had an uncanny ability with machines. A kind of intuition about machines which we don't have."

"You mean—"

"I mean a person like this coming into our own time is bad in itself, war or no war. He's too different. He's oriented along different lines. He has abilities we lack. This fixing skill of his. It throws us off, out of kilter. And with the war…

"Now I'm beginning to understand why the SRB machines couldn't factor him. It's impossible for us to understand this kind of person. Winslow says he asked for work, any kind of work. The man said he could do anything, fix anything. Do you understand what that means?"

"No," Dixon said. "What does it mean?"

"Can any of us fix anything? No. None of us can do that. We're specialized. Each of us has his own line, his own work. I understand my work, you understand yours. The tendency in evolution is toward greater and greater specialization. Man's society is an ecology that forces adaptation to it. Continual complexity makes it impossible for any of us to know anything outside our own personal field. I can't follow the work of the man sitting at the next desk over from me. Too much knowledge has piled up in each field. And there's too many fields.

"This man is different. He can fix anything, do anything. He doesn't work with knowledge, with science—the classified accumulation of facts. He *knows* nothing. It's not in his head, a form of learning. He works by intuition. His power is in his hands, not his head. Jack-of-all-trades. His hands! Like a painter, an artist. In his hands, and he cuts across our lives like a knife blade."

"And the other problem?"

"The other problem is that this man, this variable man, has escaped into the Albertine Mountain Range. Now we'll have one hell of a time finding him. He's clever, in a strange kind of way. Like some sort of animal. He's going to be hard to catch."

Reinhart sent Dixon out. After a moment he gathered up the handful of reports on his desk and carried them up to the SRB room. The SRB room was closed up, sealed off by a ring of armed Security police. Standing angrily before the ring of police was Peter Sherikov, his beard waggling angrily, his immense hands on his hips.

"What's going on?" Sherikov demanded. "Why can't I go in and peep at the odds?"

"Sorry." Reinhart cleared the police aside. "Come inside with me. I'll explain." The doors opened for them, and they entered. Behind them the doors shut, and the ring of police formed outside. "What brings you away from your lab?" Reinhart asked.

Sherikov shrugged. "Several things. I wanted to see you. I called you on the vidphone and they said you weren't available. I thought maybe something had happened. What's up?"

"I'll tell you in a few minutes." Reinhart called Kaplan over. "Here are some new items. Feed them in right away. I want to see if the machines can total them."

"Certainly, Commissioner." Kaplan took the message plates and placed them on an intake belt. The machines hummed into life.

"We'll know soon," Reinhart said half aloud.

Sherikov shot him a keen glance. "We'll know what? Let me in on it. What's taking place?"

"We're in trouble. For twenty-four hours the machines haven't given any reading at all. Nothing but a blank. A total blank."

Sherikov's features registered disbelief. "But that isn't possible. *Some* odds exist at all times."

"The odds exist, but the machines aren't able to calculate them."

"Why not?"

"Because a variable factor has been introduced. A factor which the machines can't handle. They can't make any predictions from it."

"Can't they reject it?" Sherikov said slyly. "Can't they just—just *ignore* it?"

"No. It exists as real data. Therefore it affects the balance of the material, the sum total of all other available data. To reject it would be to give a false reading. The machines can't reject any data that's known to be true."

Sherikov pulled moodily at his black beard. "I would be interested in knowing what sort of factor the machines can't handle. I thought they could take in all data pertaining to contemporary reality."

"They can. This factor has nothing to do with contemporary reality. That's the trouble. Histo-research in bringing its time bubble back from the past got overzealous and cut the circuit too quickly. The bubble came back loaded with a man from the twentieth century. A man from the past."

"I see. A man from two centuries ago." The big Pole frowned. "And with a radically different Weltanschauung. No connection with our present society. Not integrated along our lines at all. Therefore the SRB machines are perplexed."

Reinhart grinned. "Perplexed? I suppose so. In any case, they can't do anything with the data about this man. The variable man. No statistics at all have been thrown up, no predictions have been made. And it knocks everything else out of phase. We're dependent on the constant showing of these odds. The whole war effort is geared around them."

"The horseshoe nail. Remember the old poem? 'For want of a nail the shoe was lost. For want of the shoe the horse was lost. For want of the horse the rider was lost. For want—'"

"Exactly. A single factor coming along like this, one single individual, can throw everything off. It doesn't seem possible that one person could knock an entire society out of balance, but apparently it is."

"What are you doing about this man?"

"The Security police are organized in a mass search for him."

"Results?"

"He escaped into the Albertine Mountain Range last night. It'll be hard to find him. We must expect him to be loose for another forty-eight hours. It'll take that long for us to arrange the annihilation of the range area. Perhaps a trifle longer. And meanwhile—"

"Ready, Commissioner," Kaplan interrupted. "The new totals."

The SRB machines had finished factoring the new data. Reinhart and Sherikov hurried to take their places before the view windows.

For a moment nothing happened. Then odds were put up, locking in place.

Sherikov gasped. 99–2. In favor of Terra. "That's wonderful! Now we—"

The odds vanished. New odds took their places. 97–4. In favor of Centaurus. Sherikov groaned in astonished dismay. "Wait," Reinhart said to him. "I don't think they'll last."

The odds vanished. A rapid series of odds shot across the screen, a violent stream of numbers, changing almost instantly. At last the machines became silent.

Nothing showed. No odds. No totals at all. The view windows were blank.

"You see?" Reinhart murmured. "The same damn thing!"

Sherikov pondered. "Reinhart, you're too Anglo-Saxon, too impulsive. Be more Slavic. This man will be captured and destroyed within two days. You said so yourself. Meanwhile, we're all working night and day on the war effort. The warfleet is waiting near Proxima, taking up positions for the attack on the Centaurans. All our war plants are going full blast. By the time the attack date comes we'll have a full-sized invasion army ready to take off for the long trip to the Centauran colonies. The whole Terran population has been mobilized. The eight supply planets are pouring in material. All this is going on day and night, even without odds showing. Long before the attack comes this man will certainly be dead, and the machines will be able to show odds again."

Reinhart considered. "But it worries me, a man like that out in the open. Loose. A man who can't be predicted. It goes against science. We've been making statistical reports on society for two centuries. We have immense files of data. The machines are able to predict what each person and group will do at a given time, in a given situation. But this man is beyond all prediction. He's a variable. It's contrary to science."

"The indeterminate particle."

"What's that?"

"The particle that moves in such a way that we can't predict what position it will occupy at a given second. Random. The random particle."

"Exactly. It's—it's *unnatural*."

Sherikov laughed sarcastically. "Don't worry about it, Commissioner. The man will be captured and things will return to their natural state. You'll be able to predict people again, like laboratory rats in a maze. By the way, why is this room guarded?"

"I don't want anyone to know the machines show no totals. It's dangerous to the war effort."

"Margaret Duffe, for example?"

Reinhart nodded reluctantly. "They're too timid, these parliamentarians. If they discover we have no SRB odds, they'll want to shut down the war planning and go back to waiting."

"Too slow for you, Commissioner? Laws, debates, council meetings, discussions...Saves a lot of time if one man has all the power. One man to tell people what to do, think for them, lead them around."

Reinhart eyed the big Pole critically. "That reminds me. How is Icarus coming? Have you continued to make progress on the control turret?"

A scowl crossed Sherikov's broad features. "The control turret?" He waved his big hand vaguely. "I would say it's coming along all right. We'll catch up in time."

Instantly Reinhart became alert. "Catch up? You mean you're still behind?"

"Somewhat. A little. But we'll catch up." Sherikov retreated toward the door. "Let's go down to the cafeteria and have a cup of coffee. You worry too much, Commissioner. Take things more in your stride."

"I suppose you're right." The two men walked out into the hall. "I'm on edge. This variable man. I can't get him out of my mind."

"Has he done anything yet?"

"Nothing important. Rewired a child's toy. A toy vidsender."

"Oh?" Sherikov showed interest. "What do you mean? What did he do?"

"I'll show you." Reinhart led Sherikov down the hall to his office. They entered and Reinhart locked the door. He handed Sherikov the toy and roughed in what Cole had done. A strange look crossed Sherikov's face. He found the studs on the box and depressed them. The box opened. The big Pole sat down at the desk and began to study the interior of the box. "You're sure it was the man from the past who rewired this?"

"Of course. On the spot. The boy damaged it playing. The variable man came along, and the boy asked him to fix it. He fixed it, all right."

"Incredible." Sherikov's eyes were only an inch from the wiring. "Such tiny relays. How could he—"

"What?"

"Nothing." Sherikov got abruptly to his feet, closing the box carefully. "Can I take this along? To my lab? I'd like to analyze it more fully."

"Of course. But why?"

"No special reason. Let's go get our coffee." Sherikov headed toward the door. "You say you expect to capture this man in a day or so?"

"*Kill* him, not capture him. We've got to eliminate him as a piece of data. We're assembling the attack formations right now. No slip-ups this time. We're in the process of setting up a cross-bombing pattern to level the entire Albertine Range. He must be destroyed within the next forty-eight hours."

Sherikov nodded absently. "Of course," he murmured. A preoccupied expression still remained on his broad features. "I understand perfectly."

***

Thomas Cole crouched over the fire he had built, warming his hands. It was almost morning. The sky was turning violet gray. The mountain air was crisp and chill. Cole shivered and pulled himself closer to the fire.

The heat felt good against his hands. *His hands.* He gazed down at them, glowing yellow-red in the firelight. The nails were black and chipped. Warts and endless calluses on each finger, and the palms. But they were good hands. The fingers were long and tapered. He respected them, although in some ways he didn't understand them.

Cole was deep in thought, meditating over his situation. He had been in the mountains two nights and a day. The first night had been the worst. Stumbling and falling, making his way uncertainly up the steep slopes, through the tangled brush and undergrowth—

But when the sun came up, he was safe, deep in the mountains between two great peaks. And by the time the sun had set again, he had fixed himself up a shelter and a means of making a fire. Now he had a neat little box trap, operated by a plaited grass rope and pit, a notched stake. One rabbit already hung by his hind legs, and the trap was waiting for another.

The sky turned from violet gray to a deep cold gray, a metallic color. The mountains were silent and empty. Far off someplace a bird sang, its voice echoing across the vast slopes and ravines. Other birds began to sing. Off to his right something crashed through the brush, an animal pushing its way along.

Day was coming. His second day. Cole got to his feet and began to unfasten the rabbit. Time to eat. And then? After that he had no plans. He knew instinctively that he could keep himself alive indefinitely with the tools he had retained, and the genius of his hands. He could kill game and skin it. Eventually he could build himself a permanent shelter, even make clothes, but of hides. In winter—

But he was not thinking that far ahead. Cole stood by the fire, staring up at the sky, his hands on his hips. He squinted, suddenly tense. Something was moving. Something in the sky, drifting slowly through the grayness. A black dot.

He stamped out the fire quickly. What was it? He strained, trying to see. A bird?

A second dot joined the first. Two dots. Then three. Four. Five. A fleet of them, moving rapidly across the early morning sky. Toward the mountains.

Toward him.

Cole hurried away from the fire. He snatched up the rabbit and carried it along with him into the tangled shelter he had built. He was invisible inside the shelter. No one could find him. But if they had seen the fire—

He crouched in the shelter, watching the dots grow larger. They were planes, all right. Black wingless planes, coming closer each moment. Now he could hear them, a faint dull buzz, increasing until the ground shook under him.

The first plane dived. It dropped like a stone, swelling into a great black shape. Cole gasped, sinking down. The plane roared in an arc, swooping low over the ground. Suddenly bundles tumbled out, white bundles falling and scattering like seeds.

The bundles drifted rapidly to the ground. They landed. They were men. Men in uniform.

Now the second plane was diving. It roared overhead, releasing its load. More bundles tumbled out, filling the sky. The third plane dived, then the fourth. The air was thick with drifting bundles of white, a blanket of descending weed spores settling to the earth.

On the ground the soldiers were forming into groups. Their shouts carried to Cole, crouched in his shelter. Fear leaped through him. They were landing on all sides of him. He was cut off. The last two planes had dropped men behind him.

He got to his feet, pushing out of the shelter. Some of the soldiers had found the fire, the ashes and coals. One dropped down, feeling the coals with his hand. He waved to the others. They were circling all around, shouting and gesturing. One of them began to set up some kind of gun. Others were unrolling coils of tubing, locking a collection of strange pipes and machinery in place.

Cole ran. He rolled down a slope, sliding and falling. At the bottom he leaped to his feet and plunged into the brush. Vines and leaves tore at his face, slashing and cutting him. He fell again, tangled in a mass of twisted shrubbery. He fought desperately, trying to free himself. If he could reach the knife in his pocket—

Voices. Footsteps. Men were behind him, running down the slope. Cole struggled frantically, gasping and twisting, trying to pull loose. He strained, breaking the vines, clawing at them with his hands.

A soldier dropped to his knee, leveling his gun. More soldiers arrived, bringing up their rifles and aiming.

Cole cried out. He closed his eyes, his body suddenly limp. He waited, his teeth locked together, sweat dripping down his neck, into his shirt, sagging against the mesh of vines and branches coiled around him.

Silence.

Cole opened his eyes slowly. The soldiers had regrouped. A huge man was striding down the slope toward them, barking orders as he came.

Two soldiers stepped into the brush. One of them grabbed Cole by the shoulder.

"Don't let go of him." The huge man came over, his black beard jutting out. "Hold on."

Cole gasped for breath. He was caught. There was nothing he could do. More soldiers were pouring down into the gulley, surrounding him on all sides. They studied him curiously, murmuring together. Cole shook his head wearily and said nothing.

The huge man with the beard stood directly in front of him, his hands on his hips, looking him up and down. "Don't try to get away," the man said. "You can't get away. Do you understand?"

Cole nodded.

"All right. Good." The man waved. Soldiers clamped metal bands around Cole's arms and wrists. The metal dug into his flesh, making him gasp with pain. More clamps locked around his legs. "Those stay there until we're out of here. A long way out."

"Where—where are you taking me?"

Peter Sherikov studied the variable man for a moment before he answered. "Where? I'm taking you to my labs. Under the Urals." He glanced suddenly up at the sky. "We better hurry. The Security police will be starting their demolition attack in a few hours. We want to be a long way from here when that begins."

***

Sherikov settled down in his comfortable reinforced chair with a sigh. "It's good to be back." He signaled to one of his guards. "All right. You can unfasten him."

The metal clamps were removed from Cole's arms and legs. He sagged, sinking down in a heap. Sherikov watched him silently.

Cole sat on the floor, rubbing his wrists and legs, saying nothing.

"What do you want?" Sherikov demanded. "Food? Are you hungry?"

"No."

"Medicine? Are you sick? Injured?"

"No."

Sherikov wrinkled his nose. "A bath wouldn't hurt you any. We'll arrange that later." He lit a cigar, blowing a cloud of gray smoke around him. At the door of the room two lab guards stood with guns ready. No one else was in the room beside Sherikov and Cole.

Thomas Cole sat huddled in a heap on the floor, his head sunk down against his chest. He did not stir. His bent body seemed more elongated and stooped than ever, his hair tousled and unkempt, his chin and jowls a rough, stubbled gray. His clothes were dirty and torn from crawling through the brush. His skin was cut and scratched; open sores dotted his neck and cheeks and forehead. He said nothing. His chest rose and fell. His faded blue eyes were almost closed. He looked quite old, a withered, dried up old man.

Sherikov waved one of the guards over. "Have a doctor brought up here. I want this man checked over. He may need intravenous injections. He may not have had anything to eat for a while."

The guard departed.

"I don't want anything to happen to you," Sherikov said. "Before we go on I'll have you checked over. And deloused at the same time."

Cole said nothing.

Sherikov laughed. "Buck up! You have no reason to feel bad." He leaned toward Cole, jabbing an immense finger at him. "Another two hours and you'd have been dead out there in the mountains. You know that?"

Cole nodded.

"You don't believe me. Look." Sherikov leaned over and snapped on the vidscreen mounted in the wall. "Watch this. The operation should still be going on."

The screen lit up. A scene gained form.

"This is a confidential Security channel. I had it tapped several years ago for my own protection. What we're seeing now is being piped in to Eric Reinhart." Sherikov grinned. "Reinhart arranged what you're seeing on the screen. Pay close attention. You were there, two hours ago."

Cole turned toward the screen. At first he could not make out what was happening. The screen showed a vast foaming cloud, a vortex of motion. From the speaker came a low rumble, a deep-throated roar. After a time the screen shifted, showing a slightly different view. Suddenly Cole stiffened.

He was seeing the destruction of a whole mountain range.

The picture was coming from a ship, flying above what had once been the Albertine Mountain Range. Now there was nothing but swirling clouds of gray and columns of particles and debris, a surging tide of restless material gradually sweeping off and dissipating in all directions.

The Albertine Mountains had been disintegrated. Nothing remained but these vast clouds of debris. Below, on the ground, a ragged plain stretched out, swept by fire and ruin. Gaping wounds yawned, immense holes without bottom, craters side by side as far as the eye could see. Craters and debris. Like the blasted, pitted surface of the moon. Two hours ago it had been rolling peaks and gullies, brush and green bushes and trees.

Cole turned away.

"You see?" Sherikov snapped the screen off. "You were down there not so long ago. All that noise and smoke, all for you. All for you, Mr. Variable Man from the past. Reinhart arranged that to finish you off. I want you to understand that. It's very important that you realize that."

Cole said nothing.

Sherikov reached into a drawer of the table before him. He carefully brought out a small square box and held it out to Cole. "You wired this, didn't you?"

Cole took the box in his hands and held it. For a time his tired mind failed to focus. What did he have? He concentrated on it. The box was the children's toy. The intersystem vidsender they had called it.

"Yes. I fixed this." He passed it back to Sherikov. "I repaired that. It was broken."

Sherikov gazed down at him intently, his large eyes bright. He nodded, his black beard and cigar rising and falling. "Good. That's all I wanted to know." He got suddenly to his feet, pushing his chair back. "I see the doctor's here. He'll fix you up. Everything you need. Later on I'll talk to you again."

Unprotesting, Cole got to his feet, allowing the doctor to take hold of his arm and help him up.

After Cole had been released by the medical department, Sherikov joined him in his private dining room, a floor above the actual laboratory.

The Pole gulped down a hasty meal, talking as he ate. Cole sat silently across from him, not eating or speaking. His old clothing had been taken away and new clothing given him. He was shaved and rubbed down. His sores and cuts were healed, his body and hair washed. He looked much healthier and younger now. But he was still stooped and tired, his blue eyes worn and faded. He listened to Sherikov's account of the world of 2136 AD without comment.

"You can see," Sherikov said finally, waving a chicken leg, "that your appearance here has been very upsetting to our program. Now that you know more about us you can see why Commissioner Reinhart was so interested in destroying you."

Cole nodded.

"Reinhart, you realize, believes that the failure of the SRB machines is the chief danger to the war effort. But that is nothing!" Sherikov pushed his plate away noisily, draining his coffee mug. "After all, wars *can* be fought without statistical forecasts. The SRB machines only describe. They're nothing more than mechanical onlookers. In themselves, they don't affect the course of the war. *We* make the war. They only analyze."

Cole nodded.

"More coffee?" Sherikov asked. He pushed the plastic container toward Cole. "Have some."

Cole accepted another cupful. "Thank you."

"You can see that our real problem is another thing entirely. The machines only do figuring for us in a few minutes that eventually we could do for our own selves. They're our servants, tools. Not some sort of gods in a temple which we go and pray to. Not oracles who can see into the future for us. They don't see into the future. They only make statistical predictions, not prophecies. There's a big difference there, but Reinhart doesn't understand it. Reinhart and his kind have made such things as the SRB machines into gods. But I have no gods. At least, not any I can see."

Cole nodded, sipping his coffee.

"I'm telling you all these things because you must understand what we're up against. Terra is hemmed in on all sides by the ancient Centauran Empire. It's been out there for centuries, thousands of years. No one knows how long. It's old, crumbling and rotting. Corrupt and venal. But it holds most of the galaxy around us, and we can't break out of the Sol System. I told you about Icarus, and Hedge's work in FTL flight. We must win the war against Centaurus. We've waited and worked a long time for this, the moment when we can break out and get room among the stars for ourselves. Icarus is the deciding weapon. The data on Icarus tipped the SRB odds in our favor for the first time in history. Success in the war against Centaurus will depend on Icarus, not on the SRB machines. You see?"

Cole nodded.

"However, there is a problem. The data on Icarus which I turned over to the machines specified that Icarus would be completed in ten days. More than half that time has already passed. Yet we are no closer to wiring up the control turret than we were then. The turret baffles us." Sherikov grinned ironically. "Even *I* have tried my hand at the wiring, but with no success. It's intricate and small. Too many technical bugs not worked out. We are building only one, you understand. If we had many experimental models worked out before—"

"But this is the experimental model," Cole said.

"And built from the designs of a man dead four years, who isn't here to correct us. We've made Icarus with our own hands, down here in the labs. And he's giving us plenty of trouble." All at once Sherikov got to his feet. "Let's go down to the lab and look at him."

They descended to the floor below, Sherikov leading the way. Cole stopped short at the lab door.

"Quite a sight," Sherikov agreed. "We keep him down here at

the bottom for safety's sake. He's well protected. Come on in. We have work to do."

In the center of the lab Icarus rose up, the gray squat cylinder that someday would flash through space at a speed of thousands of times that of light, toward the heart of Proxima Centaurus, over four light years away. Around the cylinder groups of men in uniform were laboring feverishly to finish the remaining work.

"Over here. The turret." Sherikov led Cole over to one side of the room. "It's guarded. Centauran spies are swarming everywhere on Terra. They see into everything. But so do we. That's how we get information for the SRB machines. Spies in both systems."

The translucent globe that was the control turret reposed in the center of a metal stand, an armed guard standing at each side. They lowered their guns as Sherikov approached.

"We don't want anything to happen to this," Sherikov said. "Everything depends on it." He put out his hand for the globe. Halfway to it his hand stopped, striking against an invisible presence in the air.

Sherikov laughed. "The wall. Shut it off. It's still on."

One of the guards pressed a stud at his wrist. Around the globe the air shimmered and faded.

"Now." Sherikov's hand closed over the globe. He lifted it carefully from its mount and brought it out for Cole to see. "This is the control turret for our enormous friend here. This is what will slow him down when he's inside Centaurus. He slows down and reenters this universe. Right in the heart of the star. Then—no more Centaurus." Sherikov beamed. "And no more Armun."

But Cole was not listening. He had taken the globe from Sherikov and was turning it over and over, running his hands over it, his face close to its surface. He peered down into its interior, his face rapt and intent.

"You can't see the wiring. Not without lenses." Sherikov signaled for a pair of micro-lenses to be brought. He fitted them on Cole's nose, hooking them behind his ears. "Now try it. You can control the magnification. It's set for 1000x right now. You can increase or decrease it."

Cole gasped, swaying back and forth. Sherikov caught hold of him. Cole gazed down into the globe, moving his head slightly, focusing the glasses.

"It takes practice. But you can do a lot with them. Permits you to do microscopic wiring. There are tools to go along, you understand." Sherikov paused, licking his lip. "We can't get it done correctly. Only a few men can wire circuits using the micro-lenses and the little tools. We've tried robots, but there are too many decisions to be made. Robots can't make decisions. They just react."

Cole said nothing. He continued to gaze into the interior of the globe, his lips tight, his body taut and rigid. It made Sherikov feel strangely uneasy.

"You look like one of those old fortune tellers," Sherikov said jokingly, but a cold shiver crawled up his spine. "Better hand it back to me." He held out his hand.

Slowly, Cole returned the globe. After a time he removed the micro-lenses, still deep in thought.

"Well?" Sherikov demanded. "You know what I want. I want you to wire this damn thing up." Sherikov came close to Cole, his big face hard. "You can do it, I think. I could tell by the way you held it, and the job you did on the children's toy, of course. You could wire it up right, and in five days. Nobody else can. And if it's not wired up, Centaurus will keep on running the galaxy and Terra will have to sweat it out here in the Sol System. One tiny mediocre sun, one dust mote out of a whole galaxy."

Cole did not answer.

Sherikov became impatient. "Well? What do you say?"

"What happens if I don't wire this control for you? I mean, what happens to *me*?"

"Then I turn you over to Reinhart. Reinhart will kill you instantly. He thinks you're dead, killed when the Albertine Range was annihilated. If he had any idea I had saved you—"

"I see."

"I brought you down here for one thing. If you wire it up, I'll have you sent back to your own time continuum. If you don't—"

Cole considered, his face dark and brooding.

"What do you have to lose? You'd already be dead if we hadn't pulled you out of those hills."

"Can you really return me to my own time?"

"Of course!"

"Reinhart won't interfere?"

Sherikov laughed. "What can he do? How can he stop me? I have my own men. You saw them. They landed all around you. You'll be returned."

"Yes. I saw your men."

"Then you agree?"

"I agree," Thomas Cole said. "I'll wire it for you. I'll complete the control turret within the next five days."

# IV

Three days later Joseph Dixon slid a closed-circuit message plate across the desk to his boss.

"Here. You might be interested in this."

Reinhart picked the plate up slowly. "What is it? You came all the way here to show me this?"

"That's right."

"Why didn't you vidscreen it?"

Dixon smiled grimly. "You'll understand when you decode it. It's from Proxima Centaurus."

"Centaurus!"

"Our counter-intelligence service. They sent it direct to me. Here, I'll decode it for you. Save you the trouble."

Dixon came around behind Reinhart's desk. He leaned over the Commissioner's shoulder, taking hold of the plate and breaking the seal with his thumbnail.

"Hang on," Dixon said. "This is going to hit you hard. According to our agents on Armun, the Centauran High Council has called an emergency session to deal with the problem of Terra's impending attack. Centauran relay couriers have reported to the High Council that the Terran bomb Icarus is virtually complete. Work on the bomb has been rushed through final stages in the underground laboratories under the Ural Range, directed by the Terran physicist Peter Sherikov."

"So I understand from Sherikov himself. Are you surprised the Centaurans know about the bomb? They have spies swarming over Terra. That's no news."

"There's more." Dixon traced the message plate grimly, with an unsteady finger. "The Centauran relay couriers reported that Peter Sherikov brought an expert mechanic out of a previous time continuum to complete the wiring of the turret!"

Reinhart staggered, holding on tight to the desk. He closed his eyes, gasping.

"The variable man is still alive," Dixon murmured. "I don't know how. Or why. There's nothing left of the Albertines. And how the hell did the man get halfway around the world?"

Reinhart opened his eyes slowly, his face twisting. "Sherikov! He must have removed him before the attack. I told Sherikov the attack was forthcoming. I gave him the exact hour. He had to get help from the variable man. He couldn't meet his promise otherwise."

Reinhart leaped up and began to pace back and forth. "I've already informed the SRB machines that the variable man has been destroyed. The machines now show the original 7–6 ratio in our favor. But the ratio is based on false information."

"Then you'll have to withdraw the false data and restore the original situation."

"No." Reinhart shook his head. "I can't do that. The machines must be kept functioning. We can't allow them to jam again. It's too dangerous. If Duffe should become aware that—"

"What are you going to do, then?" Dixon picked up the message plate. "You can't leave the machines with false data. That's treason."

"The data can't be withdrawn! Not unless equivalent data exists to take its place." Reinhart paced angrily back and forth. "Damn it, I was *certain* the man was dead. This is an incredible situation. He must be eliminated at any cost."

Suddenly Reinhart stopped pacing. "The turret. It's probably finished by this time. Correct?"

Dixon nodded slowly in agreement. "With the variable man helping, Sherikov has undoubtedly completed work well ahead of schedule."

Reinhart's gray eyes flickered. "Then he's no longer of any use, even to Sherikov. We could take a chance…Even if there were active opposition…"

"What's this?" Dixon demanded. "What are you thinking about?"

"How many units are ready for immediate action? How large a force can we raise without notice?"

"Because of the war we're mobilized on a twenty-four-hour basis. There are seventy air units and about two hundred surface units. The balance of the Security forces have been transferred to the line, under military control."

"Men?"

"We have about five thousand men ready to go, still on Terra. Most of them in the process of being transferred to military transports. I can hold it up at any time."

"Missiles?"

"Fortunately, the launching tubes have not yet been disassembled. They're still here on Terra. In another few days they'll be moving out for the Colonial fracas."

"Then they're available for immediate use?"

"Yes."

"Good." Reinhart locked his hands, knotting his fingers harshly together in sudden decision. "That will do exactly. Unless I am completely wrong, Sherikov has only a half-dozen air units and no surface cars. And only about two hundred men. Some defense shields, of course—"

"What are you planning?"

Reinhart's face was gray and hard, like stone. "Send out orders for all available Security units to be unified under your immediate command. Have them ready to move by four o'clock this afternoon. We're going to pay a visit," Reinhart stated grimly. "A surprise visit. On Peter Sherikov."

***

"Stop here," Reinhart ordered.

The surface car slowed to a halt. Reinhart peered cautiously out, studying the horizon ahead.

On all sides a desert of scrub grass and sand stretched out. Nothing moved or stirred. To the right the grass and sand rose up to form immense peaks, a range of mountains without end, disappearing finally into the distance. The Urals.

"Over there," Reinhart said to Dixon, pointing. "See?"

"No."

"Look hard. It's difficult to spot unless you know what to look for. Vertical pipes. Some kind of vent. Or periscopes."

Dixon saw them finally. "I would have driven past without noticing."

"It's well concealed. The main labs are a mile down. Under the range itself. It's virtually impregnable. Sherikov had it built years ago to withstand any attack. From the air, by surface cars, bombs, missiles—"

"He must feel safe down there."

"No doubt." Reinhart gazed up at the sky. A few faint black dots could be seen moving lazily about in broad circles. "Those aren't ours, are they? I gave orders—"

"No. They're not ours. All our units are out of sight. Those belong to Sherikov. His patrol."

Reinhart relaxed. "Good." He reached over and flicked on the vidscreen over the board of the car. "This screen is shielded? It can't be traced?"

"There's no way they can spot it back to us. It's non-directional."

The screen glowed into life. Reinhart punched the combination keys and sat back to wait.

After a time an image formed on the screen. A heavy face, bushy black beard and large eyes.

Peter Sherikov gazed at Reinhart with surprised curiosity. "Commissioner! Where are you calling from? What—"

"How's the work progressing?" Reinhart broke in coldly. "Is Icarus almost complete?"

Sherikov beamed with expansive pride. "He's done, Commissioner. Two days ahead of time. Icarus is ready to be launched into space. I tried to call your office, but they told me—"

"I'm not at my office." Reinhart leaned toward the screen. "Open your entrance tunnel at the surface. You're about to receive visitors."

Sherikov blinked. "Visitors?"

"I'm coming down to see you. About Icarus. Have the tunnel opened for me at once."

"Exactly where are you, Commissioner?"

"On the surface."

Sherikov's eyes flickered. "Oh? But—"

"Open up!" Reinhart snapped. He glanced at his wristwatch. "I'll be at the entrance in five minutes. I expect to find it ready for me."

"Of course." Sherikov nodded in bewilderment. "I'm always glad to see you, Commissioner. But I—"

"Five minutes, then." Reinhart cut the circuit. The screen died. He turned quickly to Dixon. "You stay up here, as we arranged. I'll go down with one company of police. You understand the necessity of exact timing on this?"

"We won't slip up. Everything's ready. All units are in their places."

"Good." Reinhart pushed the door open for him. "You join your directional staff. I'll proceed toward the tunnel entrance."

"Good luck." Dixon leaped out of the car onto the sandy ground. A gust of dry air swirled into the car around Reinhart. "I'll see you later."

Reinhart slammed the door. He turned to the group of police crouched in the rear of the car, their guns held tightly. "Here we go," Reinhart murmured. "Hold on."

The car raced across the sandy ground, toward the tunnel entrance to Sherikov's underground fortress.

Sherikov met Reinhart at the bottom end of the tunnel, where the tunnel opened up onto the main floor of the lab.

The big Pole approached, his hand out, beaming with pride and satisfaction. "It's a pleasure to see you, Commissioner. This is a historic moment."

Reinhart got out of the car with his group of armed Security police. "Calls for a celebration, doesn't it?" he said.

"That's a good idea! We're two days ahead, Commissioner. The SRB machines will be interested. The odds should change abruptly at the news."

"Let's go down to the lab. I want to see the control turret myself."

A shadow crossed Sherikov's face. "I'd rather not bother the workmen right now, Commissioner. They've been under a great load trying to complete the turret in time. I believe they're putting a few last finishes on it at this moment."

"We can view them by vidscreen. I'm curious to see them at work. It must be difficult to wire such minute relays."

Sherikov shook his head. "Sorry, Commissioner. No vidscreen on them. I won't allow it. This is too important. Our whole future depends on it."

Reinhart snapped a signal to his company of police. "Put this man under arrest."

Sherikov blanched. His mouth fell open. The police moved quickly around him, their gun tubes up, jabbing into him. He was searched rapidly, efficiently. His gun belt and concealed energy screen were yanked off.

"What's going on?" Sherikov demanded, some color returning to his face. "What are you doing?"

"You're under arrest for the duration of the war. You're relieved of all authority. From now on one of my men will operate Designs. When the war is over, you'll be tried before the Council and President Duffe."

Sherikov shook his head, dazed. "I don't understand. What's this all about? Explain it to me, Commissioner. What's happened?"

Reinhart signaled to his police. "Get ready. We're going into the lab. We may have to shoot our way in. The variable man should be in the area of the bomb, working on the control turret."

Instantly Sherikov's face hardened. His black eyes glittered, alert and hostile.

Reinhart laughed harshly. "We received a counter-intelligence report from Centaurus. I'm surprised at you, Sherikov. You know the Centaurans are everywhere with their relay couriers. You should have known—"

Sherikov moved. Fast. All at once he broke away from the police, throwing his massive body against them. They fell, scattering. Sherikov ran directly at the wall. The police fired wildly. Reinhart fumbled frantically for his gun tube, pulling it up.

Sherikov reached the wall, running head down, energy beams flashing around him. He struck against the wall and vanished.

"Down!" Reinhart shouted. He dropped to his hands and knees. All around him his police dived for the floor. Reinhart cursed wildly, dragging himself quickly toward the door. They had to get out, and right away. Sherikov had escaped. A false wall, an energy barrier set to respond to his pressure. He had dashed through it to safety. He—

From all sides an inferno burst, a flaming roar of death surging over them, around them, on every side. The room was alive with blazing masses of destruction, bouncing from wall to wall. They were caught between four banks of power, all of them open to full discharge. A trap—a death trap.

Reinhart reached the hall gasping for breath. He leaped to his feet. A few Security police followed him. Behind them, in the flaming room, the rest of the company screamed and struggled, blasted out of existence by the leaping bursts of power.

Reinhart assembled his remaining men. Already, Sherikov's guards were forming. At one end of the corridor a snub-barreled robot gun was maneuvering into position. A siren wailed. Guards were running on all sides, hurrying to battle stations.

The robot gun opened fire. Part of the corridor exploded, bursting into fragments. Clouds of choking debris and particles swept around them. Reinhart and his police retreated, moving back along the corridor.

They reached a junction. A second robot gun was rumbling toward them, hurrying to get within range. Reinhart fired carefully, aiming at its delicate control. Abruptly the gun spun convulsively. It lashed against the wall, smashing itself into the unyielding metal. Then it collapsed in a heap, gears still whining and spinning.

"Come on." Reinhart moved away, crouching and running. He glanced at his watch. *Almost time.* A few more minutes. A group of lab guards appeared ahead of them. Reinhart fired. Behind him his police fired past him, violet shafts of energy catching the group of guards as they entered the corridor. The guards spilled apart, falling and twisting. Part of them settled into dust, drifting down the corridor. Reinhart made his way toward the lab, crouching and leaping, pushing past heaps of debris and remains, followed by his men. "Come on! Don't stop!"

Suddenly from around them the booming, enlarged voice of Sherikov thundered, magnified by rows of wall speakers along the corridor. Reinhart halted, glancing around.

"Reinhart! You haven't got a chance. You'll never get back to the surface. Throw down your guns and give up. You're surrounded on all sides. You're a mile under the surface."

Reinhart threw himself into motion, pushing into billowing clouds of particles drifting along the corridor. "Are you sure, Sherikov?" he grunted.

Sherikov laughed, his harsh, metallic peals rolling in waves against Reinhart's eardrums. "I don't want to have to kill you, Commissioner. You're vital to the war. I'm sorry you found out about the variable man. I admit we overlooked the Centauran espionage as a factor in this. But now that you know about him—"

Suddenly Sherikov's voice broke off. A deep rumble had shaken the floor, a lapping vibration that shuddered through the corridor.

Reinhart sagged with relief. He peered through the clouds of debris, making out the figures on his watch. Right on time. Not a second late.

The first of the hydrogen missiles, launched from the Council buildings on the other side of the world, were beginning to arrive. The attack had begun.

At exactly six o'clock Joseph Dixon, standing on the surface four miles from the entrance tunnel, gave the sign to the waiting units.

The first job was to break down Sherikov's defense screens. The missiles had to penetrate without interference. At Dixon's signal a fleet of thirty Security ships dived from a height of ten miles, swooping above the mountains, directly over the underground laboratories. Within five minutes the defense screens had been smashed, and all the tower projectors leveled flat. Now the mountains were virtually unprotected.

"So far so good," Dixon murmured as he watched from his secure position. The fleet of Security ships roared back, their work done. Across the face of the desert the police surface cars were crawling rapidly toward the entrance tunnel, snaking from side to side.

Meanwhile, Sherikov's counterattack had begun to go into operation.

Guns mounted among the hills opened fire. Vast columns of flame burst up in the path of the advancing cars. The cars hesitated and retreated as the plain was churned up by a howling vortex, a thundering chaos of explosions. Here and there a car vanished in a cloud of particles. A group of cars moving away suddenly scattered, caught up by a giant wind that lashed across them and swept them up into the air.

Dixon gave orders to have the cannon silenced. The police air arm again swept overhead, a sullen roar of jets that shook the ground below. The police ships divided expertly and hurtled down on the cannon protecting the hills.

The cannon forgot the surface cars and lifted their snouts to meet the attack. Again and again the airships came, rocking the mountains with titanic blasts.

The guns became silent. Their echoing boom diminished, died away reluctantly, as bombs took critical toll of them.

Dixon watched with satisfaction as the bombing came to an end. The airships rose in a thick swarm, black gnats shooting up in triumph from a dead carcass. They hurried back as emergency anti-aircraft robot guns swung into position and saturated the sky with blazing puffs of energy.

Dixon checked his wristwatch. The missiles were already on the way from North America. Only a few minutes remained.

The surface cars, freed by the successful bombing, began to regroup for a new frontal attack. Again they crawled forward across the burning plain, bearing down cautiously on the battered wall of mountains, heading toward the twisted wrecks that had been the ring of defense guns. Toward the entrance tunnel.

An occasional cannon fired feebly at them. The cars came grimly on. Now, in the hollows of the hills, Sherikov's troops were hurrying to the surface to meet the attack. The first car reached the shadow of the mountains...

A deafening hail of fire burst loose. Small robot guns appeared everywhere, needle barrels emerging from behind hidden screens, trees and shrubs, rocks, stones. The police cars were caught in a withering crossfire, trapped at the base of the hills.

Down the slopes Sherikov's guards raced, toward the stalled cars. Clouds of heat rose up and boiled across the plain as the cars fired up at the running men. A robot gun dropped like a slug onto the plain and screamed toward the cars, firing as it came.

Dixon twisted nervously. Only a few minutes. Anytime now. He shaded his eyes and peered up at the sky. No sign of them yet. He wondered about Reinhart. No signal had come up from below. Clearly, Reinhart had run into trouble. No doubt there was desperate fighting going on in the maze of underground tunnels, the intricate web of passages that honeycombed the earth below the mountains.

In the air, Sherikov's few defense ships were taking on the police raiders. Outnumbered, the defense ships darted rapidly, wildly, putting up a futile fight.

Sherikov's guards streamed out onto the plain. Crouching and running, they advanced toward the stalled cars. The police airships screeched down at them, guns thundering.

Dixon held his breath. When the missiles arrived—

The first missile struck. A section of the mountain vanished, turned to smoke and foaming gases. The wave of heat slapped Dixon across the face, spinning him around. Quickly he reentered his ship and took off, shooting rapidly away from the scene. He glanced back. A second and third missile had arrived. Great gaping pits yawned among the mountains, vast sections missing like broken teeth. Now the missiles could penetrate to the underground laboratories below.

On the ground, the surface cars halted beyond the danger area, waiting for the missile attack to finish. When the eighth missile had struck, the cars again moved forward. No more missiles fell.

Dixon swung his ship around, heading back toward the scene. The laboratory was exposed. The top sections of it had been ripped open. The laboratory lay like a tin can, torn apart by mighty explosions, its first floors visible from the air. Men and cars were pouring down into it, fighting with the guards swarming to the surface.

Dixon watched intently. Sherikov's men were bringing up heavy guns, big robot artillery. But the police ships were diving again. Sherikov's defensive patrols had been cleaned from the sky. The police ships whined down, arcing over the exposed laboratory. Small bombs fell, whistling down, pinpointing the artillery rising to the surface on the remaining lift stages.

Abruptly Dixon's vidscreen clicked. Dixon turned toward it.

Reinhart's features formed. "Call off the attack." His uniform was torn. A deep bloody gash crossed his cheek. He grinned sourly at Dixon, pushing his tangled hair back out of his face. "Quite a fight."

"Sherikov—"

"He's called off his guards. We've agreed to a truce. It's all over. No more needed." Reinhart gasped for breath, wiping grime and sweat from his neck. "Land your ship and come down here at once."

"The variable man?"

"That comes next," Reinhart said grimly. He adjusted his gun tube. "I want you down here for that part. I want you to be in on the kill."

Reinhart turned away from the vidscreen. In the corner of the room Sherikov stood silently, saying nothing. "Well?" Reinhart barked. "Where is he? Where will I find him?"

Sherikov licked his lips nervously, glancing up at Reinhart. "Commissioner, are you sure—"

"The attack has been called off. Your labs are safe. So is your life. Now it's your turn to come through." Reinhart gripped his gun, moving toward Sherikov. *Where is he?*

For a moment Sherikov hesitated. Then slowly his huge body sagged, defeated. He shook his head wearily. "All right.

I'll show you where he is." His voice was hardly audible, a dry whisper. "Down this way. Come on."

Reinhart followed Sherikov out of the room into the corridor. Police and guards were working rapidly, clearing the debris and ruins away, putting out the hydrogen fires that burned everywhere. "No tricks, Sherikov."

"No tricks." Sherikov nodded resignedly. "Thomas Cole is by himself. In a wing lab off the main rooms."

"Cole?"

"The variable man. That's his name." The Pole turned his massive head a little. "He has a name."

Reinhart waved his gun. "Hurry up. I don't want anything to go wrong. This is the part I came for."

"You must remember something, Commissioner."

"What is it?"

Sherikov stopped walking. "Commissioner, nothing must happen to the globe. The control turret. Everything depends on it, the war, our whole—"

"I know. Nothing will happen to the damn thing. Let's go."

"If it should get damaged—"

"I'm not after the globe. I'm interested only in—in Thomas Cole."

They came to the end of the corridor and stopped before a metal door. Sherikov nodded at the door. "In there."

Reinhart moved back. "Open the door."

"Open it yourself. I don't want to have anything to do with it."

Reinhart shrugged. He stepped up to the door. Holding his gun level he raised his hand, passing it in front of the eye circuit. Nothing happened.

Reinhart frowned. He pushed the door with his hand. The door slid open. Reinhart was looking into a small laboratory. He glimpsed a workbench, tools, heaps of equipment, measuring devices, and in the center of the bench the transparent globe, the control turret.

"Cole?" Reinhart advanced quickly into the room. He glanced around him, suddenly alarmed. "Where—"

The room was empty. Thomas Cole was gone.

When the first missile struck, Cole stopped work and sat listening.

Far off, a distant rumble rolled through the earth, shaking the floor under him. On the bench, tools and equipment danced up and down. A pair of pliers fell crashing to the floor. A box of screws tipped over, spilling its minute contents out.

Cole listened for a time. Presently he lifted the transparent globe from the bench. With carefully controlled hands he held the globe up, running his fingers gently over the surface, his faded blue eyes thoughtful. Then, after a time, he placed the globe back on the bench, in its mount.

The globe was finished. A faint glow of pride moved through the variable man. The globe was the finest job he had ever done.

The deep rumblings ceased. Cole became instantly alert. He jumped down from his stool, hurrying across the room to the door. For a moment he stood by the door listening intently. He could hear noise on the other side, shouts, guards rushing past, dragging heavy equipment, working frantically.

A rolling crash echoed down the corridor and lapped against his door. The concussion spun him around. Again a tide of energy shook the walls and floor and sent him down on his knees.

The lights flickered and winked out.

Cole fumbled in the dark until he found a flashlight. Power failure. He could hear crackling flames. Abruptly the lights came on again, an ugly yellow, then faded back out. Cole bent down and examined the door with his flashlight. A magnetic lock. Dependent on an externally induced electric flux. He grabbed a screwdriver and pried at the door. For a moment it held. Then it fell open.

Cole stepped warily out into the corridor. Everything was in shambles. Guards wandered everywhere, burned and half-blinded. Two lay groaning under a pile of wrecked equipment. Fused guns, reeking metal. The air was heavy with the smell of burning wiring and plastic. A thick cloud that choked him and made him bend double as he advanced.

"Halt," a guard gasped feebly, struggling to rise. Cole pushed past him and down the corridor. Two small robot guns, still functioning, glided past him hurriedly toward the drumming chaos of battle. He followed.

At a major intersection the fight was in full swing. Sherikov's guards fought Security police, crouched behind pillars and barricades, firing wildly, desperately. Again the whole structure shuddered as a great booming blast ignited some place above. Bombs? Shells?

Cole threw himself down as a violet beam cut past his ear and disintegrated the wall behind him. A Security policeman, wild-eyed, firing erratically. One of Sherikov's guards winged him, and his gun skidded to the floor.

A robot cannon turned toward him as he made his way past the intersection. He began to run. The cannon rolled along behind him, aiming itself uncertainly. Cole hunched over as he shambled rapidly along, gasping for breath. In the flickering yellow light he saw a handful of Security police advancing, firing expertly, intent on a line of defense Sherikov's guards had hastily set up.

The robot cannon altered its course to take them on, and Cole escaped around a corner.

He was in the main lab, the big chamber where Icarus himself rose, the vast squat column.

Icarus! A solid wall of guards surrounded him, grim-faced, hugging guns and protection shields. But the Security police were leaving Icarus alone. Nobody wanted to damage him.

Cole evaded a lone guard tracking him and reached the far side of the lab.

It took him only a few seconds to find the force field generator. There was no switch. For a moment that puzzled him, and then he remembered. The guard had controlled it from his wrist.

Too late to worry about that. With his screwdriver he unfastened the plate over the generator and ripped out the wiring in handfuls. The generator came loose, and he dragged it away from the wall. The screen was off, thank god. He managed to carry the generator into a side corridor.

Crouched in a heap, Cole bent over the generator, deft fingers flying. He pulled the wiring to him and laid it out on the floor, tracing the circuits with feverish haste.

The adaptation was easier than he had expected. The screen flowed at right angles to the wiring for a distance of six feet. Each lead was shielded on one side. The field radiated outward, leaving a hollow cone in the center. He ran the wiring through his belt, down his trouser legs, under his shirt, all the way to his wrists and ankles.

He was just snatching up the heavy generator when two Security police appeared. They raised their blasters and fired point-blank.

Cole clicked on the screen. A vibration leaped through him that snapped his jaw and danced up his body. He staggered away, half-stupefied by the surging force that radiated out from him. The violet rays struck the field and deflected harmlessly.

He was safe.

He hurried on down the corridor, past a ruined gun and sprawled bodies still clutching blasters. Great drifting clouds of radioactive particles billowed around him. He edged by one cloud nervously. Guards lay everywhere, dying and dead, partly destroyed, eaten and corroded by the hot metallic salts in the air. He had to get out, and fast.

At the end of the corridor a whole section of the fortress was in ruins. Towering flames leaped on all sides. One of the missiles had penetrated below ground level.

Cole found a lift that still functioned. A load of wounded guards was being raised to the surface. None of them paid any attention to him. Flames surged around the lift, licking at the wounded. Workmen were desperately trying to get the lift into action. Cole leaped onto the lift. A moment later it began to rise, leaving the shouts and the flames behind.

The lift emerged on the surface, and Cole jumped off. A guard spotted him and gave chase. Crouching, Cole dodged into a tangled mass of twisted metal, still white-hot and smoking. He ran for a distance, leaping from the side of a ruined defense-screen tower, onto the fused ground and down the side of a hill. The ground was hot underfoot. He hurried as fast as he could, gasping for breath. He came to a long slope and scrambled up the side.

The guard who had followed was gone, lost behind in the rolling clouds of ash that drifted from the ruins of Sherikov's underground fortress.

Cole reached the top of the hill. For a brief moment he halted to get his breath and figure where he was. It was almost evening. The sun was beginning to set. In the darkening sky a few dots still twisted and rolled, black specks that abruptly burst into flame and fused out again.

Cole stood up cautiously, peering around him. Ruins stretched out below, on all sides, the furnace from which he had escaped. A chaos of incandescent metal and debris, gutted and wrecked beyond repair. Miles of tangled rubbish and half-vaporized equipment.

He considered. Everyone was busy putting out the fires and pulling the wounded to safety. It would be a while before he was missed. But as soon as they realized he was gone, they'd be after him. Most of the laboratory had been destroyed. Nothing lay back that way.

Beyond the ruins lay the great Ural peaks, the endless mountains, stretching out as far as the eye could see.

Mountains and green forests. A wilderness. They'd never find him there.

Cole started along the side of the hill, walking slowly and carefully, his screen generator under his arm. Probably in the confusion he could find enough food and equipment to last him indefinitely. He could wait until early morning, then circle back toward the ruins and load up. With a few tools and his own innate skill he would get along fine. A screwdriver, hammer, nails, odds and ends—

A great hum sounded in his ears. It swelled to a deafening roar. Startled, Cole whirled around. A vast shape filled the sky behind him, growing each moment. Cole stood frozen, utterly transfixed. The shape thundered over him, above his head, as he stood stupidly, rooted to the spot.

Then, awkwardly, uncertainly, he began to run. He stumbled and fell and rolled a short distance down the side of the hill. Desperately, he struggled to hold onto the ground. His hands dug wildly, futilely, into the soft soil, trying to keep the generator under his arm at the same time.

A flash, and a blinding spark of light around him.

The spark picked him up and tossed him like a dry leaf. He grunted in agony as searing fire crackled about him, a blazing inferno that gnawed and ate hungrily through his screen. He spun dizzily and fell through the cloud of fire, down into a pit of darkness, a vast gulf between two hills. His wiring ripped off. The generator tore out of his grip and was lost behind. Abruptly, his force field ceased.

Cole lay in the darkness at the bottom of the hill. His whole body shrieked in agony as the unholy fire played over him. He was a blazing cinder, a half-consumed ash flaming in a universe of darkness. The pain made him twist and crawl like an insect, trying to burrow into the ground. He screamed and shrieked and struggled to escape, to get away from the hideous fire. To reach the curtain of darkness beyond, where it was cool and silent, where the flames couldn't crackle and eat at him.

He reached imploringly out into the darkness, groping feebly toward it, trying to pull himself into it. Gradually, the glowing orb that was his own body faded. The impenetrable chaos of night descended. He allowed the tide to sweep over him, to extinguish the searing fire.

Dixon landed his ship expertly, bringing it to a halt in front of an overturned defense tower. He leaped out and hurried across the smoking ground.

From a lift Reinhart appeared, surrounded by his Security police. "He got away from us! He escaped!"

"He didn't escape," Dixon answered. "I got him myself."

Reinhart quivered violently. "What do you mean?"

"Come along with me. Over in this direction." He and Reinhart climbed the side of a demolished hill, both of them panting for breath. "I was landing. I saw a figure emerge from a lift and run toward the mountains, like some sort of animal. When he came out in the open I dived on him and released a phosphorus bomb."

"Then he's—*dead*?"

"I don't see how anyone could have lived through a phosphorus bomb." They reached the top of the hill. Dixon halted, then pointed excitedly down into the pit beyond the hill. "There!"

They descended cautiously. The ground was singed and burned clean. Clouds of smoke hung heavily in the air. Occasional fires still flickered here and there. Reinhart coughed and bent over to see. Dixon flashed on a pocket flare and set it beside the body.

The body was charred, half destroyed by the burning phosphorus. It lay motionless, one arm over its face, mouth open, legs sprawled grotesquely. Like some abandoned rag doll, tossed in an incinerator and consumed almost beyond recognition.

"He's alive!" Dixon muttered. He felt around curiously. "Must have had some kind of protection screen. Amazing that a man could—"

"It's him? It's really him?"

"Fits the description." Dixon tore away a handful of burned clothing. "This is the variable man. What's left of him, at least."

Reinhart sagged with relief. "Then we've finally got him. The data is accurate. He's no longer a factor."

Dixon got out his blaster and released the safety catch thoughtfully. "If you want, I can finish the job right now."

At that moment Sherikov appeared, accompanied by two armed Security police. He strode grimly down the hillside, black eyes snapping. "Did Cole—" He broke off. "Good god."

"Dixon got him with a phosphorus bomb," Reinhart said noncommittally. "He had reached the surface and was trying to get into the mountains."

Sherikov turned wearily away. "He was an amazing person. During the attack he managed to force the lock on his door and escape. The guards fired at him, but nothing happened. He had rigged up some kind of force field around him. Something he adapted."

"Anyhow, it's over with," Reinhart answered. "Did you have SRB plates made up on him?"

Sherikov reached slowly into his coat. He drew out a manila envelope. "Here's all the information I collected about him while he was with me."

"Is it complete? Everything previous has been merely fragmentary."

"As near complete as I could make it. It includes photographs and diagrams of the interior of the globe. The turret wiring he did for me. I haven't had a chance even to look at them." Sherikov fingered the envelope. "What are you going to do with Cole?"

"Have him loaded up, taken back to the city, and officially put to sleep by the Euthanasia Ministry."

"Legal murder?" Sherikov's lips twisted. "Why don't you simply do it right here and get it over with?"

Reinhart grabbed the envelope and stuck it in his pocket. "I'll turn this right over to the machines." He motioned to Dixon. "Let's go. Now we can notify the fleet to prepare for the attack on Centaurus." He turned briefly back to Sherikov. "When can Icarus be launched?"

"In an hour or so, I suppose. They're locking the control turret in place. Assuming it functions correctly, that's all that's needed."

"Good. I'll notify Duffe to send out the signal to the warfleet." Reinhart nodded to the police to take Sherikov to the waiting Security ship. Sherikov moved off dully, his face gray and haggard. Cole's inert body was picked up and tossed onto a freight cart. The cart rumbled into the hold of the Security ship, and the lock slid shut after it.

"It'll be interesting to see how the machines respond to the additional data," Dixon said.

"It should make quite an improvement in the odds," Reinhart agreed. He patted the envelope, bulging in his inside pocket. "We're two days ahead of time."

***

Margaret Duffe got up slowly from her desk. She pushed her chair automatically back. "Let me get all this straight. You mean the bomb is finished? Ready to go?"

Reinhart nodded impatiently. "That's what I said. The Technicians are checking the turret locks to make sure it's properly attached. The launching will take place in half an hour."

"Thirty minutes! Then—"

"Then the attack can begin at once. I assume the fleet is ready for action."

"Of course. It's been ready for several days. But I can't believe the bomb is ready so soon." Margaret Duffe moved numbly toward the door of her office. "This is a great day, Commissioner. An old era lies behind us. This time tomorrow Centaurus will be gone. And eventually the colonies will be ours."

"It's been a long climb," Reinhart murmured.

"One thing. Your charge against Sherikov. It seems incredible that a person of his caliber could ever—"

"We'll discuss that later," Reinhart interrupted coldly. He pulled the manila envelope from his coat. "I haven't had an opportunity to feed the additional data to the SRB machines. If you'll excuse me, I'll do that now."

For a moment Margaret Duffe stood at the door. The two of them faced each other silently, neither speaking, a faint smile on Reinhart's thin lips, hostility in the woman's blue eyes.

"Reinhart, sometimes I think perhaps you'll go too far. And sometimes I think you've *already* gone too far."

"I'll inform you of any change in the odds showing." Reinhart strode past her, out of the office and down the hall. He headed toward the SRB room, an intense thalamic excitement rising up inside him.

A few moments later he entered the SRB room. He made his way to the machines. The odds 7–6 showed in the view windows. Reinhart smiled a little. 7–6. False odds, based on incorrect information. Now they could be removed.

Kaplan hurried over. Reinhart handed him the envelope,

and moved over to the window, gazing down at the scene below. Men and cars scurried frantically everywhere. Officials coming and going like ants, hurrying in all directions.

The war was on. The signal had been sent out to the warfleet that had waited so long near Proxima Centaurus. A feeling of triumph raced through Reinhart. He had won. He had destroyed the man from the past and broken Peter Sherikov. The war had begun as planned. Terra was breaking out. Reinhart smiled thinly. He had been completely successful.

"Commissioner."

Reinhart turned slowly. "All right."

Kaplan was standing in front of the machines, gazing down at the reading. "Commissioner."

Sudden alarm plucked at Reinhart. There was something in Kaplan's voice. He hurried quickly over. "What is it?"

Kaplan looked up at him, his face white, his eyes wide with terror. His mouth opened and closed, but no sound came.

"*What is it?*" Reinhart demanded, chilled. He bent toward the machines, studying the reading.

And sickened with horror.

100–1. *Against* Terra!

He could not tear his gaze away from the figures. He was numb, shocked with disbelief. 100–1. *What had happened? What had gone wrong?* The turret was finished, Icarus was ready, the fleet had been notified—

There was a sudden deep buzz from outside the building. Shouts drifted up from below. Reinhart turned his head slowly toward the window, his heart frozen with fear.

Across the evening sky a trail moved, rising each moment. A thin line of white. Something climbed, gaining speed each moment. On the ground, all eyes were turned toward it, awed faces peering up.

The object gained speed. Faster and faster. Then it vanished.

Icarus was on his way. The attack had begun. It was too late to stop now.

And on the machines the odds read a hundred to one for failure.

At eight o'clock in the evening of May 15, 2136, Icarus was launched toward the star Centaurus. A day later, while all Terra waited, Icarus entered the star, traveling at thousands of times the speed of light.

Nothing happened. Icarus disappeared into the star. There was no explosion. The bomb failed to go off.

At the same time the Terran warfleet engaged the Centauran outer fleet, sweeping down in a concentrated attack. Twenty major ships were seized. A good part of the Centauran fleet was destroyed. Many of the captive systems began to revolt in the hope of throwing off the Imperial bonds.

Two hours later the massed Centauran warfleet from Armun abruptly appeared and joined battle. The great struggle illuminated half the Centauran system. Ship after ship flashed briefly and then faded to ash. For a whole day the two fleets fought, strung out over millions of miles of space. Innumerable fighting men died on both sides.

At last the remains of the battered Terran fleet turned and limped toward Armun—defeated. Little of the once impressive armada remained. A few blackened hulks making their way uncertainly toward captivity.

Icarus had not functioned. Centaurus had not exploded. The attack was a failure.

The war was over.

"We've lost the war," Margaret Duffe said in a small voice, wondering and awed. "It's over. Finished."

The Council members sat in their places around the conference table, gray-haired elderly men, none of them speaking or moving. All gazed up mutely at the great stellar maps that covered two walls of the chamber.

"I have already empowered negotiators to arrange a truce," Margaret Duffe murmured. "Orders have been sent out to Vice Commander Jessup to give up the battle. There's no hope. Fleet Commander Carleton destroyed himself and his flagship a few minutes ago. The Centauran High Council has agreed to end the fighting. Their whole Empire is rotten to the core. Ready to topple of its own weight."

Reinhart was slumped over at the table, his head in his hands. "I don't understand…*Why?* Why didn't the bomb explode?" He mopped his forehead shakily. All his poise was gone. He was trembling and broken. "*What went wrong?*"

Gray-faced, Dixon mumbled an answer. "The variable man must have sabotaged the turret. The SRB machines knew… they analyzed the data. *They knew!* But it was too late."

Reinhart's eyes were bleak with despair as he raised his head a little. "I knew he'd destroy us. We're finished. A century of work and planning." His body knotted in a spasm of furious agony. "All because of Sherikov!"

Margaret Duffe eyed Reinhart coldly. "Why because of Sherikov?"

"He kept Cole alive! I wanted him killed from the start." Suddenly Reinhart jumped from his chair. His hand clutched convulsively at his gun. "And he's *still* alive! Even if we've lost I'm going to have the pleasure of putting a blast beam through Cole's chest!"

"Sit down!" Margaret Duffe ordered.

Reinhart was halfway to the door. "He's still at the Euthanasia Ministry, waiting for the official—"

"No, he's not," Margaret Duffe said.

Reinhart froze. He turned slowly, as if unable to believe his senses. "*What?*"

"Cole isn't at the Ministry. I ordered him transferred and your instructions canceled."

"Where—where is he?"

There was unusual hardness in Margaret Duffe's voice as she answered. "With Peter Sherikov. In the Urals. I had Sherikov's full authority restored. I then had Cole transferred there, put in Sherikov's safe keeping. I want to make sure Cole recovers so we can keep our promise to him, our promise to return him to his own time."

Reinhart's mouth opened and closed. All the color had drained from his face. His cheek muscles twitched spasmodically. At last he managed to speak. "You've gone insane! The traitor responsible for Earth's greatest defeat—"

"We have lost the war," Margaret Duffe stated quietly. "But this is not a day of defeat. It is a day of victory. The most incredible victory Terra has ever had."

Reinhart and Dixon were dumbfounded. "What—" Reinhart gasped. "What do you—" The whole room was in an uproar. All the Council members were on their feet. Reinhart's words were drowned out.

"Sherikov will explain when he gets here," Margaret Duffe's calm voice came. "He's the one who discovered it." She looked around the chamber at the incredulous Council members. "Everyone stay in his seat. You are all to remain here until Sherikov arrives. It's vital you hear what he has to say. His news transforms this whole situation."

***

Peter Sherikov accepted the briefcase of papers from his armed technician. "Thanks." He pushed his chair back and glanced thoughtfully around the Council chamber. "Is everybody ready to hear what I have to say?"

"We're ready," Margaret Duffe answered. The Council members sat alertly around the table. At the far end, Reinhart and

Dixon watched uneasily as the big Pole removed papers from his briefcase and carefully examined them.

"To begin, I recall to you the original work behind the FTL bomb. Jamison Hedge was the first human to propel an object at a speed greater than light. As you know, that object diminished in length and gained in mass as it moved toward light speed. When it reached that speed it vanished. It ceased to exist in our terms. Having no length, it could not occupy space. It rose to a different order of existence.

"When Hedge tried to bring the object back, an explosion occurred. Hedge was killed, and all his equipment was destroyed. The force of the blast was beyond calculation. Hedge had placed his observation ship many millions of miles away. It was not far enough, however. Originally, he had hoped his drive might be used for space travel. But after his death the principle was abandoned.

"That is, until Icarus. I saw the possibilities of a bomb, an incredibly powerful bomb to destroy Centaurus and all the Empire's forces. The reappearance of Icarus would mean the annihilation of their System. As Hedge had shown, the object would reenter space already occupied by matter, and the cataclysm would be beyond belief."

"But Icarus never came back," Reinhart cried. "Cole altered the wiring so the bomb kept on going. It's probably still going."

"Wrong," Sherikov boomed. "The bomb *did* reappear. But it didn't explode."

Reinhart reacted violently. "You mean—"

"The bomb came back, dropping below the FTL speed as soon as it entered the star Proxima. But it did not explode. There was no cataclysm. It reappeared and was absorbed by the sun, turned into gas at once."

"Why didn't it explode?" Dixon demanded.

"Because Thomas Cole solved Hedge's problem. He found a

way to bring the FTL object back into this universe without collision. Without an explosion. The variable man found what Hedge was after…"

The whole Council was on its feet. A growing murmur filled the chamber, a rising pandemonium breaking out on all sides.

"I don't believe it!" Reinhart gasped. "It isn't possible. If Cole solved Hedge's problem that would mean—" He broke off, staggered.

"Faster than light drive can now be used for space travel," Sherikov continued, waving the noise down. "As Hedge intended. My men have studied the photographs of the control turret. They don't know *how* or *why* yet. But we have complete records of the turret. We can duplicate the wiring as soon as the laboratories have been repaired."

Comprehension was gradually beginning to settle over the room. "Then it'll be possible to build FTL ships," Margaret Duffe murmured, dazed. "And if we can do that—"

"When I showed him the control turret, Cole understood its purpose. Not *my* purpose, but the original purpose Hedge had been working toward. Cole realized Icarus was actually an incomplete spaceship, not a bomb at all. He saw what Hedge had seen, an FTL space-drive. He set out to make Icarus work."

"We can go *beyond* Centaurus," Dixon muttered. His lips twisted. "Then the war was trivial. We can leave the Empire completely behind. We can go beyond the galaxy."

"The whole universe is open to us," Sherikov agreed. "Instead of taking over an antiquated Empire, we have the entire cosmos to map and explore, God's total creation."

Margaret Duffe got to her feet and moved slowly toward the great stellar maps that towered above them at the far end of the chamber. She stood for a long time, gazing up at the myriad suns, the legions of systems, awed by what she saw.

"Do you suppose he realized all this?" she asked suddenly. "What we can see here on these maps?"

"Thomas Cole is a strange person," Sherikov said, half to himself. "Apparently he has a kind of intuition about machines, the way things are supposed to work. An intuition more in his hands than in his head. A kind of genius, such as a painter or a pianist has. Not a scientist. He has no verbal knowledge about things, no semantic references. He deals with the things themselves. Directly.

"I doubt very much if Thomas Cole understood what would come about. He looked into the globe, the control turret. He saw unfinished wiring and relays. He saw a job half done. An incomplete machine."

"Something to be fixed," Margaret Duffe put in.

"Something to be fixed. Like an artist, he saw his work ahead of him. He was interested in only one thing: turning out the best job he could with the skill he possessed. For us, that skill has opened up a whole universe, endless galaxies and systems to explore. Worlds without end. Unlimited, *untouched* worlds."

Reinhart got unsteadily to his feet. "We better get to work. Start organizing construction teams. Exploration crews. We'll have to reconvert from war production to ship designing. Begin the manufacture of mining and scientific instruments for survey work."

"That's right," Margaret Duffe said. She looked reflectively up at him. "But you're not going to have anything to do with it."

Reinhart saw the expression on her face. His hand flew to his gun, and he backed quickly toward the door. Dixon leaped up and joined him. "Get back!" Reinhart shouted.

Margaret Duffe signaled, and a phalanx of Government troops closed in around the two men. Grim-faced, efficient soldiers with magnetic grapples ready.

Reinhart's blaster wavered toward the Council members

sitting shocked in their seats, and toward Margaret Duffe, straight at her blue eyes. Reinhart's features were distorted with insane fear. "Get back! Don't anybody come near me or she'll be the first to get it!"

Peter Sherikov slid from the table and with one great stride swept his immense bulk in front of Reinhart. His huge, black-furred fist rose in a smashing arc. Reinhart sailed against the wall, struck with ringing force, and then slid slowly to the floor.

The Government troops threw their grapples quickly around him and jerked him to his feet. His body was frozen rigid. Blood dripped from his mouth. He spat bits of tooth, his eyes glazed over. Dixon stood dazed, mouth open, uncomprehending, as the grapples closed around his arms and legs.

Reinhart's gun skidded to the floor as he was yanked toward the door. One of the elderly Council members picked the gun up and examined it curiously. He laid it carefully on the table. "Fully loaded," he murmured. "Ready to fire."

Reinhart's battered face was dark with hate. "I should have killed all of you. *All* of you!" An ugly sneer twisted across his shredded lips. "If I could get my hands loose—"

"You won't," Margaret Duffe said. "You might as well not even bother to think about it." She signaled to the troops, and they pulled Reinhart and Dixon roughly out of the room, two dazed figures, snarling and resentful.

For a moment the room was silent. Then the Council members shuffled nervously in their seats, beginning to breathe again.

Sherikov came over and put his big paw on Margaret Duffe's shoulder. "Are you all right, Margaret?"

She smiled faintly. "I'm fine. Thanks."

Sherikov touched her soft hair briefly. Then he broke away and began to pack up his briefcase busily. "I have to go. I'll get in touch with you later."

"Where are you going?" she asked hesitantly. "Can't you stay and—"

"I have to get back to the Urals." Sherikov grinned at her over his bushy black beard as he headed out of the room. "Some very important business to attend to."

***

Thomas Cole was sitting up in bed when Sherikov came to the door. Most of his awkward, hunched-over body was sealed in a thin envelope of transparent airproof plastic. Two robot attendants whirred ceaselessly at his side, their leads contacting his pulse, blood pressure, respiration, body temperature.

Cole turned a little as the huge Pole tossed down his briefcase and seated himself on the window ledge.

"How are you feeling?" Sherikov asked him.

"Better."

"You see we've quite advanced therapy. Your burns should be healed in a few months."

"How is the war coming?"

"The war is over."

Cole's lips moved. "Icarus—"

"Icarus went as expected. As *you* expected." Sherikov leaned toward the bed. "Cole, I promised you something. I mean to keep my promise as soon as you're well enough."

"To return me to my own time?"

"That's right. It's a relatively simple matter, now that Reinhart has been removed from power. You'll be back home again, back in your own time, your own world. We can supply you with some discs of platinum or something of the kind to finance your business. You'll need a new fixit truck. Tools. And clothes. A few thousand dollars ought to do it."

Cole was silent.

"I've already contacted histo-research," Sherikov continued. "The time bubble is ready as soon as you are. We're somewhat beholden to you as you probably realize. You've made it possible for us to actualize our greatest dream. The whole planet is seething with excitement. We're changing our economy over from war to—"

"They don't resent what happened? The dud must have made an awful lot of people feel downright bad."

"At first. But they got over it as soon as they understood what was ahead. Too bad you won't be here to see it, Cole. A whole world breaking loose. Bursting out into the universe. They want me to have an FTL ship ready by the end of the week! Thousands of applications are already on file, men and women wanting to get in on the initial flight."

Cole smiled a little, "There won't be any band there. No parade or welcoming committee waiting for them."

"Maybe not. Maybe the first ship will wind up on some dead world, nothing but sand and dried salt. But everybody wants to go. It's almost like a holiday. People running around and shouting and throwing things in the streets.

"Afraid I must get back to the labs. Lots of reconstruction work being started." Sherikov dug into his bulging briefcase. "By the way…one little thing. While you're recovering here, you might like to look at these." He tossed a handful of schematics on the bed.

Cole picked them up slowly. "What's this?"

"Just a little thing I designed." Sherikov arose and lumbered toward the door. "We're realigning our political structure to eliminate any recurrence of the Reinhart affair. This will block any more one-man power grabs." He jabbed a thick finger at the schematics. "It'll turn power over to all of us, not to just a limited number one person could dominate, the way Reinhart dominated the Council.

"This gimmick makes it possible for citizens to rise and decide issues directly. They won't have to wait for the Council to verbalize a measure. Any citizen can transmit his will with one of these, make his needs register on a central control that automatically responds. When a large enough segment of the population wants a certain thing done, these little gadgets set up an active field that touches all the others. An issue won't have to go through a formal Council. The citizens can express their will long before any bunch of gray-haired old men could get around to it."

Sherikov broke off, frowning.

"Of course," he continued slowly, "there's one little detail…"

"What's that?"

"I haven't been able to get a model to function. A few bugs… such intricate work never was in my line." He paused at the door. "Well, I hope I'll see you again before you go. Maybe if you feel well enough later on, we could get together for one last talk. Maybe have dinner together sometime. Eh?"

But Thomas Cole wasn't listening. He was bent over the schematics, an intense frown on his weathered face. His long fingers moved restlessly over the schematics, tracing wiring and terminals. His lips moved as he calculated.

Sherikov waited a moment. Then he stepped out into the hall and softly closed the door after him.

He whistled merrily as he strode off down the corridor.

# THE HANGING STRANGER

ED HAD ALWAYS been a practical man. When he saw something was wrong, he tried to correct it. Then one day he saw it hanging in the town square. Five o'clock Ed Loyce washed up, tossed on his hat and coat, got his car out and headed across town toward his TV sales store. He was tired. His back and shoulders ached from digging dirt out of the basement and wheeling it into the backyard. But for a forty-year-old man he had done okay. Janet could get a new vase with the money he had saved. And he liked the idea of repairing the foundations himself!

It was getting dark. The setting sun cast long rays over the scurrying commuters, tired and grim-faced, women loaded down with bundles and packages, students swarming home from the university, mixing with clerks and businessmen and drab secretaries. He stopped his Packard for a red light and then started it up again. The store had been open without him. He'd arrive just in time to spell the help for dinner, go over the records of the day, maybe even close a couple of sales himself. He drove slowly past the small square of green in the center of the street, the town park. There were no parking places in front of LOYCE TV SALES AND SERVICE. He cursed under his breath and swung the car in a U-turn. Again he passed the little square of green with its lonely drinking fountain and bench and single lamppost.

From the lamppost something was hanging. A shapeless dark bundle, swinging a little with the wind. Like a dummy of some sort. Loyce rolled down his window and peered out. What the hell was it? A display of some kind? Sometimes the Chamber of Commerce put up displays in the square.

Again he made a U-turn and brought his car around. He

passed the park and concentrated on the dark bundle. It wasn't a dummy. And if it was a display, it was a strange kind. The hackles on his neck rose, and he swallowed uneasily. Sweat slid out on his face and hands.

It was a body. A human body.

"Look at it!" Loyce snapped. "Come on out here!"

Don Fergusson came slowly out of the store, buttoning his pin-stripe coat with dignity. "This is a big deal, Ed. I can't just leave the guy standing there."

"See it?" Ed pointed into the gathering gloom. The lamppost jutted up against the sky, the post and the bundle swinging from it. "There it is. How the hell long has it been there?" His voice rose excitedly. "What's wrong with everybody? They just walk on past!"

Don Fergusson lit a cigarette slowly. "Take it easy, old man. There must be a good reason, or it wouldn't be there."

"A reason! What kind of a reason?"

Fergusson shrugged. "Like the time the Traffic Safety Council put that wrecked Buick there. Some sort of civic thing. How would I know?"

Jack Potter from the shoe shop joined them. "What's up, boys?"

"There's a body hanging from the lamppost," Loyce said. "I'm going to call the cops."

"They must know about it," Potter said. "Or otherwise it wouldn't be there."

"I got to get back in." Fergusson headed back into the store. "Business before pleasure."

Loyce began to get hysterical. "You see it? You see it hanging there? A man's body! A dead man!"

"Sure, Ed. I saw it this afternoon when I went out for coffee."

"You mean it's been there all afternoon?"

"Sure. What's the matter?" Potter glanced at his watch. "Have to run. See you later, Ed."

Potter hurried off, joining the flow of people moving along the sidewalk. Men and women, passing by the park. A few glanced up curiously at the dark bundle and then went on. Nobody stopped. Nobody paid any attention.

"I'm going nuts," Loyce whispered. He made his way to the curb and crossed out into traffic, among the cars. Horns honked angrily at him. He gained the curb and stepped up onto the little square of green.

The man had been middle-aged. His clothing was ripped and torn, a gray suit, splashed and caked with dried mud. A stranger. Loyce had never seen him before. Not a local man. His face was partly turned away, and in the evening wind he spun a little, turning gently, silently. His skin was gouged and cut. Red gashes, deep scratches of congealed blood. A pair of steel-rimmed glasses hung from one ear, dangling foolishly. His eyes bulged. His mouth was open, tongue thick and ugly blue.

"For Heaven's sake," Loyce muttered, sickened. He pushed down his nausea and made his way back to the sidewalk. He was shaking all over, with revulsion and fear.

*Why?* Who was the man? Why was he hanging there? What did it mean?

And why didn't anybody notice?

He bumped into a small man hurrying along the sidewalk. "Watch it!" the man grated, "Oh, it's you, Ed."

Ed nodded dazedly. "Hello, Jenkins."

"What's the matter?" The stationery clerk caught Ed's arm. "You look sick."

"The body. There in the park."

"Sure, Ed." Jenkins led him into the alcove of LOYCE TV SALES AND SERVICE. "Take it easy."

Margaret Henderson from the jewelry store joined them. "Something wrong?"

"Ed's not feeling well."

Loyce yanked himself free. "How can you stand here? Don't you see it? For God's sake!"

"What's he talking about?" Margaret asked nervously.

"The body!" Ed shouted. "The body hanging there!"

More people collected. "Is he sick? It's Ed Loyce. You okay, Ed?"

"The body!" Loyce screamed, struggling to get past them. Hands caught at him. He tore loose. "Let me go! The police! Get the police!"

"Ed—"

"Better get a doctor!"

"He must be sick."

"Or drunk."

Loyce fought his way through the people. He stumbled and half-fell. Through a blur he saw rows of faces, curious, concerned, anxious. Men and women halting to see what the disturbance was. He fought past them toward his store. He could see Fergusson inside talking to a man, showing him an Emerson TV set. Pete Foley in the back at the service counter, setting up a new Philco. Loyce shouted at them frantically. His voice was lost in the roar of traffic and the murmur around him.

"Do something!" he screamed. "Don't stand there! Do something! Something's wrong! Something's happened! Things are going on!"

The crowd melted respectfully for the two heavyset cops moving efficiently toward Loyce.

"Name?" the cop with the notebook murmured.

"Loyce." He mopped his forehead wearily. "Edward C. Loyce. Listen to me. Back there—"

"Address?" the cop demanded. The police car moved swiftly through traffic, shooting among the cars and buses. Loyce sagged against the seat, exhausted and confused. He took a deep shuddering breath.

"1368 Hurst Road."

"That's here in Pikeville?"

"That's right." Loyce pulled himself up with a violent effort. "Listen to me. Back there. In the square. Hanging from the lamppost—"

"Where were you today?" the cop behind the wheel demanded.

"Where?" Loyce echoed.

"You weren't in your shop, were you?"

"No." He shook his head. "No, I was home. Down in the basement."

"In the *basement*?"

"Digging. A new foundation. Getting out the dirt to pour a cement frame. Why? What has that to do with—"

"Was anybody else down there with you?"

"No. My wife was downtown. My kids were at school." Loyce looked from one heavyset cop to the other. Hope flicked across his face, wild hope. "You mean because I was down there I missed the explanation? I didn't get in on it? Like everybody else?"

After a pause the cop with the notebook said: "That's right. You missed the explanation."

"Then it's official? The body—it's *supposed* to be hanging there?"

"It's supposed to be hanging there. For everybody to see."

Ed Loyce grinned weakly. "Good Lord. I guess I sort of went off the deep end. I thought maybe something had happened. You know, something like the Ku Klux Klan. Some kind of violence. Communists or Fascists taking over." He wiped his face with his breast pocket handkerchief, his hands shaking. "I'm glad to know it's on the level."

"It's on the level." The police car was getting near the Hall of Justice. The sun had set. The streets were gloomy and dark. The lights had not yet come on.

"I feel better," Loyce said. "I was pretty excited there for a minute. I guess I got all stirred up. Now that I understand, there's no need to take me in, is there?"

The two cops said nothing.

"I should be back at my store. The boys haven't had dinner. I'm all right now. No more trouble. Is there any need of—"

"This won't take long," the cop behind the wheel interrupted. "A short process. Only a few minutes."

"I hope it's short," Loyce muttered. The car slowed down for a stoplight. "I guess I sort of disturbed the peace. Funny, getting excited like that and—"

Loyce yanked the door open. He sprawled out into the street and rolled to his feet. Cars were moving all around him, gaining speed as the light changed. Loyce leaped onto the curb and raced among the people, burrowing into the swarming crowds. Behind him he heard sounds, shouts, people running.

They weren't cops. He had realized that right away. He knew every cop in Pikeville. A man couldn't own a store, operate a business in a small town for twenty-five years without getting to know all the cops.

They weren't cops, and there hadn't been any explanation. Potter, Fergusson, Jenkins, none of them knew why it was there. They didn't know, and they didn't care. *That* was the strange part.

Loyce ducked into a hardware store. He raced toward the back, past the startled clerks and customers, into the shipping room and through the back door. He tripped over a garbage can and ran up a flight of concrete steps. He climbed over a fence and jumped down on the other side, gasping and panting.

There was no sound behind him. He had got away.

He was at the entrance of an alley, dark and strewn with boards and ruined boxes and tires. He could see the street at the far end. A streetlight wavered and came on. Men and women. Stores. Neon signs. Cars.

And to his right—the police station.

He was close, terribly close. Past the loading platform of a grocery store rose the white concrete side of the Hall of Justice. Barred windows. The police antenna. A great concrete wall rising up in the darkness. A bad place for him to be near. He was too close. He had to keep moving, get farther away from them.

*Them?*

Loyce moved cautiously down the alley. Beyond the police station was the City Hall, the old-fashioned yellow structure of wood and gilded brass and broad cement steps. He could see the endless rows of offices, dark windows, the cedars and beds of flowers on each side of the entrance.

And something else.

Above the City Hall was a patch of darkness, a cone of gloom denser than the surrounding night. A prism of black that spread out and was lost into the sky.

He listened. Good god, he could hear something. Something that made him struggle frantically to close his ears, his mind, to shut out the sound. A buzzing. A distant, muted hum like a great swarm of bees.

Loyce gazed up, rigid with horror. The splotch of darkness, hanging over the City Hall. Darkness so thick it seemed almost solid. *In the vortex something moved.* Flickering shapes. Things, descending from the sky, pausing momentarily above the City Hall, fluttering over it in a dense swarm and then dropping silently onto the roof.

Shapes. Fluttering shapes from the sky. From the crack of darkness that hung above him.

He was seeing—them.

For a long time Loyce watched, crouched behind a sagging fence in a pool of scummy water.

They were landing. Coming down in groups, landing on the roof of the City Hall and disappearing inside. They had wings. Like giant insects of some kind. They flew and fluttered and came to rest—and then crawled crab-fashion, sideways, across the roof and into the building.

He was sickened. And fascinated. Cold night wind blew around him, and he shuddered. He was tired, dazed with shock. On the front steps of the City Hall were men, standing here and there. Groups of men coming out of the building and halting for a moment before going on.

Were there more of them?

It didn't seem possible. What he saw descending from the black chasm weren't men. They were alien, from some other world, some other dimension. Sliding through this slit, this break in the shell of the universe. Entering through this gap, winged insects from another realm of being.

On the steps of the City Hall a group of men broke up. A few moved toward a waiting car. One of the remaining shapes started to reenter the City Hall. It changed its mind and turned to follow the others.

Loyce closed his eyes in horror. His senses reeled. He hung on tight, clutching at the sagging fence. The shape, the man-shape, had abruptly fluttered up and flapped after the others. It flew to the sidewalk and came to rest among them.

Pseudo-men. Imitation men. Insects with ability to disguise themselves as men. Like other insects familiar to Earth. Protective coloration. Mimicry.

Loyce pulled himself away. He got slowly to his feet. It was night. The alley was totally dark. But maybe they could see in the dark. Maybe darkness made no difference to them.

He left the alley cautiously and moved out onto the street. Men and women flowed past, but not so many now. At the bus stops stood waiting groups. A huge bus lumbered along the street, its lights flashing in the evening gloom.

Loyce moved forward. He pushed his way among those waiting, and when the bus halted he boarded it and took a seat in the rear by the door. A moment later the bus moved into life and rumbled down the street.

Loyce relaxed a little. He studied the people around him. Dulled, tired faces. People going home from work. Quite ordinary faces. None of them paid any attention to him. All sat quietly, sunk down in their seats, jiggling with the motion of the bus.

The man sitting next to him unfolded a newspaper. He began to read the sports section, his lips moving. An ordinary man. Blue suit. Tie. A businessman or a salesman. On his way home to his wife and family.

Across the aisle a young woman, perhaps twenty. Dark eyes and hair, a package on her lap. Nylons and heels. Red coat and white angora sweater. Gazing absently ahead of her.

A high school boy in jeans and black jacket.

A great triple-chinned woman with an immense shopping bag loaded with packages and parcels. Her thick face dim with weariness.

Ordinary people. The kind that rode the bus every evening. Going home to their families. To dinner.

Going home—with their minds dead. Controlled, filmed over with the mask of an alien being that had appeared and taken possession of them, their town, their lives. Himself too. Except that he happened to be deep in his cellar instead of in the store. Somehow he had been overlooked. They had missed him. Their control wasn't perfect, foolproof.

Maybe there were others.

Hope flickered in Loyce. They weren't omnipotent. They had made a mistake, not got control of him. Their net, their field of control, had passed over him. He had emerged from his cellar as he had gone down. Apparently their power zone was limited.

A few seats down the aisle a man was watching him. Loyce broke off his chain of thought. A slender man with dark hair and a small mustache. Well-dressed, brown suit and shiny shoes. A book between his small hands. He was watching Loyce, studying him intently. He turned quickly away.

Loyce tensed. One of *them*? Or another they had missed?

The man was watching him again. Small dark eyes, alive and clever. Shrewd. A man too shrewd for them or one of the things itself, an alien insect from beyond.

The bus halted. An elderly man got on slowly and dropped his token into the box. He moved down the aisle and took a seat opposite Loyce.

The elderly man caught the sharp-eyed man's gaze. For a split second something passed between them.

A look rich with meaning.

Loyce got to his feet. The bus was moving. He ran to the door. One step down into the well. He yanked the emergency door release. The rubber door swung open.

"Hey!" the driver shouted, jamming on the brakes. "What the hell!"

Loyce squirmed through. The bus was slowing down. Houses on all sides. A residential district, lawns and tall apartment buildings. Behind him, the bright-eyed man had leaped up. The elderly man was also on his feet. They were coming after him.

Loyce leaped. He hit the pavement with terrific force and rolled against the curb. Pain lapped over him. Pain and a vast tide of blackness. Desperately, he fought it off. He struggled to his knees and then slid down again. The bus had stopped. People were getting off.

Loyce groped around. His fingers closed over something. A rock, lying in the gutter. He crawled to his feet, grunting with pain. A shape loomed before him. A man, the bright-eyed man with the book.

Loyce kicked. The man gasped and fell. Loyce brought the rock down. The man screamed and tried to roll away. "*Stop!* For god's sake listen—"

He struck again. A hideous crunching sound. The man's voice cut off and dissolved in a bubbling wail. Loyce scrambled up and back. The others were there now. All around him. He ran awkwardly down the sidewalk, up a driveway. None of them followed him. They had stopped and were bending over the inert body of the man with the book, the bright-eyed man who had come after him.

Had he made a mistake?

But it was too late to worry about that. He had to get out, away from them. Out of Pikeville, beyond the crack of darkness, the rent between their world and his.

"Ed!" Janet Loyce backed away nervously. "What is it? What—"

Ed Loyce slammed the door behind him and came into the living room. "Pull down the shades. Quick."

Janet moved toward the window. "But—"

"Do as I say. Who else is here besides you?"

"Nobody. Just the twins. They're upstairs in their room. What's happened? You look so strange. Why are you home?"

Ed locked the front door. He prowled around the house into the kitchen. From the drawer under the sink, he slid out the big butcher knife and ran his finger along it. Sharp. Plenty sharp. He returned to the living room.

"Listen to me," he said. "I don't have much time. They know I escaped, and they'll be looking for me."

"Escaped?" Janet's face twisted with bewilderment and fear. "Who?"

"The town has been taken over. They're in control. I've got it pretty well figured out. They started at the top, at the City Hall and police department. What they did with the *real* humans they—"

"What are you talking about?"

"We've been invaded. From some other universe, some other dimension. They're insects. Mimicry. And more. Power to control minds. Your mind."

"My mind?"

"Their entrance is *here*, in Pikeville. They've taken over all of you. The whole town, except me. We're up against an incredibly powerful enemy, but they have their limitations. That's our hope. They're limited! They can make mistakes!"

Janet shook her head. "I don't understand, Ed. You must be insane."

"Insane? No. Just lucky. If I hadn't been down in the basement, I'd be like all the rest of you." Loyce peered out the window. "But I can't stand here talking. Get your coat."

"My coat?"

"We're getting out of here. Out of Pikeville. We've got to get help. Fight this thing. They *can* be beaten. They're not infallible. It's going to be close, but we may make it if we hurry. Come on!" He grabbed her arm roughly. "Get your coat and call the twins. We're all leaving. Don't stop to pack. There's no time for that."

White-faced, his wife moved toward the closet and got down her coat. "Where are we going?"

Ed pulled open the desk drawer and spilled the contents out onto the floor. He grabbed up a road map and spread it open. "They'll have the highway covered of course. But there's a back road. To Oak Grove. I got onto it once. It's practically abandoned. Maybe they'll forget about it."

"The old Ranch Road? Good Lord, it's completely closed. Nobody's supposed to drive over it."

"I know." Ed thrust the map grimly into his coat. "That's our best chance. Now call down the twins, and let's get going. Your car is full of gas, isn't it?"

Janet was dazed.

"The Chevy? I had it filled up yesterday afternoon." Janet moved toward the stairs. "Ed, I—"

"Call the twins!" Ed unlocked the front door and peered out. Nothing stirred. No sign of life. All right so far.

"Come on downstairs," Janet called in a wavering voice. "We're—going out for a while."

"Now?" Tommy's voice came.

"Hurry up," Ed barked. "Get down here, both of you."

Tommy appeared at the top of the stairs. "I was doing my homework. We're starting fractions. Miss Parker says if we don't get this done—"

"You can forget about fractions." Ed grabbed his son as he came down the stairs and propelled him toward the door. "Where's Jim?"

"He's coming."

Jim started slowly down the stairs. "What's up, Dad?"

"We're going for a ride."

"A ride? Where?"

Ed turned to Janet. "We'll leave the lights on. And the TV set. Go turn it on." He pushed her toward the set. "So they'll think we're still—"

He heard the buzz and dropped instantly, the long butcher knife out. Sickened, he saw it coming down the stairs at him, wings a blur of motion as it aimed itself. It still bore a vague resemblance to Jimmy. It was small, a baby one. A brief glimpse—the thing hurtling at him; cold, multi-lensed inhuman eyes. Wings, body still clothed in yellow T-shirt and jeans, the mimic outline still stamped on it. A strange half-turn of its body as it reached him. What was it doing?

A stinger.

Loyce stabbed wildly at it. It retreated, buzzing frantically. Loyce rolled and crawled toward the door. Tommy and Janet stood still as statues, faces blank, watching without expression. Loyce stabbed again. This time the knife connected. The thing shrieked and faltered. It bounced against the wall and fluttered down.

Something lapped through his mind. A wall of force, energy, an alien mind probing into him. He was suddenly paralyzed. The mind entered his own, touched against him briefly, shockingly. An utterly alien presence settling over him. And then it flickered out as the thing collapsed in a broken heap on the rug.

It was dead. He turned it over with his foot. It was an insect, a fly of some kind. Yellow T-shirt, jeans. His son Jimmy…He closed his mind tight. It was too late to think about that. Savagely he scooped up his knife and headed toward the door. Janet and Tommy stood stone still, neither of them moving.

The car was out. He'd never get through. They'd be waiting for him. It was ten miles on foot. Ten long miles over rough ground, gulleys and open fields and hills of uncut forest. He'd have to go alone.

Loyce opened the door. For a brief second he looked back at his wife and son. Then he slammed the door behind him and raced down the porch steps.

A moment later he was on his way, hurrying swiftly through the darkness toward the edge of town.

The early morning sunlight was blinding. Loyce halted, gasping for breath, swaying back and forth. Sweat ran down in his eyes. His clothing was torn, shredded by the brush and thorns through which he had crawled. Ten miles on his hands and knees. Crawling, creeping through the night. His shoes were mud-caked. He was scratched and limping, utterly exhausted.

But ahead of him lay Oak Grove.

He took a deep breath and started down the hill. Twice he stumbled and fell, picking himself up and trudging on. His ears rang. Everything receded and wavered. But he was there. He had got out, away from Pikeville.

A farmer in a field gaped at him. From a house a young woman watched in wonder. Loyce reached the road and turned onto it. Ahead of him was a gasoline station and a drive-in. A couple of trucks, some chickens pecking in the dirt, a dog tied with a string.

The white-clad attendant watched suspiciously as he dragged himself up to the station. "Thank god." He caught hold of the wall. "I didn't think I was going to make it. They followed me most of the way. I could hear them buzzing. Buzzing and flitting around behind me."

"What happened?" the attendant demanded. "You in a wreck? A hold-up?"

Loyce shook his head wearily. "They have the whole town. The City Hall and the police station. They hung a man from the lamppost. That was the first thing I saw. They've got all the roads blocked. I saw them hovering over the cars coming in. About four this morning I got beyond them. I knew it right away. I could feel them leave. And then the sun came up."

The attendant licked his lip nervously. "You're out of your head. I better get a doctor."

"Get me into Oak Grove," Loyce gasped. He sank down on the gravel. "We've got to get started—cleaning them out. Got to get started right away."

They kept a tape recorder going all the time he talked. When he had finished the Commissioner snapped off the recorder and got to his feet. He stood for a moment, deep in thought.

Finally he got out his cigarettes and lit up slowly, a frown on his beefy face.

"You don't believe me," Loyce said.

The Commissioner offered him a cigarette. Loyce pushed it impatiently away. "Suit yourself." The Commissioner moved over to the window and stood for a time looking out at the town of Oak Grove. "I believe you," he said abruptly.

Loyce sagged. "Thank god."

"So you got away." The Commissioner shook his head. "You were down in your cellar instead of at work. A freak chance. One in a million."

Loyce sipped some of the black coffee they had brought him. "I have a theory," he murmured.

"What is it?"

"About them. Who they are. They take over one area at a time. Starting at the top—the highest level of authority. Working down from there in a widening circle. When they're firmly in control they go on to the next town. They spread slowly, very gradually. I think it's been going on for a long time."

"A long time?"

"Thousands of years. I don't think it's new."

"Why do you say that?"

"When I was a kid…A picture they showed us in Bible League. A religious picture, an old print. The enemy gods, defeated by Jehovah—Moloch, Beelzebub, Moab, Baalin, Ashtaroth."

"So?"

"They were all represented by figures." Loyce looked up at the Commissioner. "Beelzebub was represented as a giant fly."

The Commissioner grunted. "An old struggle."

"They've been defeated. The Bible is an account of their defeats. They make gains, but finally they're defeated."

"Why defeated?"

"They can't get everyone. They didn't get me. And they never got the Hebrews. The Hebrews carried the message to the whole world. The realization of the danger. The two men on the bus. I think they understood. Had escaped, like I did." He clenched his fists. "I killed one of them. I made a mistake. I was afraid to take a chance."

The Commissioner nodded. "Yes, they undoubtedly had escaped as you did. Freak accidents. But the rest of the town was firmly in control." He turned from the window. "Well, Mr. Loyce. You seem to have figured everything out."

"Not everything. The hanging man. The dead man hanging from the lamppost. I don't understand that. *Why?* Why did they deliberately hang him there?"

"That would seem simple." The Commissioner smiled faintly. "*Bait.*"

Loyce stiffened. His heart stopped beating. "Bait? What do you mean?"

"To draw you out. Make you declare yourself. So they'd know who was under control and who had escaped."

Loyce recoiled with horror. "Then they *expected* failures! They anticipated—" He broke off. "They were ready with a trap."

"And you showed yourself. You reacted. You made yourself known." The Commissioner abruptly moved toward the door. "Come along, Loyce. There's a lot to do. We must get moving. There's no time to waste."

Loyce started slowly to his feet, numbed. "And the man. *Who was the man*? I never saw him before. He wasn't a local man. He was a stranger. All muddy and dirty, his face cut, slashed—"

There was a strange look on the Commissioner's face as he answered. "Maybe," he said softly, "you'll understand that too. Come along with me, Mr. Loyce." He held the door open, his eyes gleaming. Loyce caught a glimpse of the street in front of the police station. Policemen, a platform of some sort. A telephone pole—and a rope! "Right this way," the Commissioner said, smiling coldly.

As the sun set, the vice president of the Oak Grove Merchants's Bank came up out of the vault, threw the heavy time locks, put on his hat and coat, and hurried outside onto the sidewalk. Only a few people were there, hurrying home to dinner.

"Good night," the guard said, locking the door after him.

"Good night," Clarence Mason murmured. He started along the street toward his car. He was tired. He had been working all day down in the vault, examining the layout of the safety deposit boxes to see if there was room for another tier. He was glad to be finished.

At the corner he halted. The streetlights had not yet come on. The street was dim. Everything was vague. He looked around—and froze.

From the telephone pole in front of the police station, something large and shapeless hung. It moved a little with the wind.

What the hell was it?

Mason approached it warily. He wanted to get home. He was tired and hungry. He thought of his wife, his kids, a hot meal on the dinner table. But there was something about the dark bundle, something ominous and ugly. The light was bad. He couldn't tell what it was. Yet it drew him on, made him move closer for a better look. The shapeless thing made him uneasy. He was frightened by it. Frightened and fascinated.

And the strange part was that nobody else seemed to notice it.

# THE CRYSTAL CRYPT

"**ATTENTION, INNER-FLIGHT SHIP!** Attention! You are ordered to land at the Control Station on Deimos for inspection. Attention! You are to land at once!"

The metallic rasp of the speaker echoed through the corridors of the great ship. The passengers glanced at each other uneasily, murmuring and peering out the port windows at the small speck below, the dot of rock that was the Martian checkpoint, Deimos.

"What's up?" an anxious passenger asked one of the pilots, hurrying through the ship to check the escape lock.

"We have to land. Keep seated." The pilot went on.

"Land? But why?" They all looked at each other. Hovering above the bulging Inner-Flight ship were three slender Martian pursuit craft, poised and alert for any emergency. As the Inner-Flight ship prepared to land, the pursuit ships dropped lower, carefully maintaining themselves a short distance away.

"There's something going on," a woman passenger said nervously. "Lord, I thought we were finally through with those Martians. Now what?"

"I don't blame them for giving us one last going over," a heavyset businessman said to his companion. "After all, we're the last ship leaving Mars for Terra. We're damn lucky they let us go at all."

"You think there really will be war?" A young man said to the girl sitting in the seat next to him. "Those Martians won't dare fight, not with our weapons and ability to produce. We could take care of Mars in a month. It's all talk."

The girl glanced at him. "Don't be so sure. Mars is desperate.

They'll fight tooth and nail. I've been on Mars three years." She shuddered. "Thank goodness I'm getting away. If—"

"Prepare to land!" the pilot's voice came. The ship began to settle slowly, dropping down toward the tiny emergency field on the seldom visited moon. Down, down the ship dropped. There was a grinding sound, a sickening jolt. Then silence.

"We've landed," the heavyset businessman said. "They better not do anything to us! Terra will rip them apart if they violate one Space Article."

"Please keep your seats," the pilot's voice came. "No one is to leave the ship, according to the Martian authorities. We are to remain here."

A restless stir filled the ship. Some of the passengers began to read uneasily, others stared out at the deserted field, nervous and on edge, watching the three Martian pursuit ships land and disgorge groups of armed men.

The Martian soldiers were crossing the field quickly, moving toward them, running double time.

This Inner-Flight spaceship was the last passenger vessel to leave Mars for Terra. All other ships had long since left, returning to safety before the outbreak of hostilities. The passengers were the very last to go, the final group of Terrans to leave the grim red planet, businessmen, expatriates, tourists, any and all Terrans who had not already gone home.

"What do you suppose they want?" the young man said to the girl. "It's hard to figure Martians out, isn't it? First they give the ship clearance, let us take off, and now they radio us to set down again. By the way, my name's Thacher, Bob Thacher. Since we're going to be here awhile—"

The port lock opened. Talking ceased abruptly as everyone turned. A black-clad Martian official, a Province Leiter, stood framed against the bleak sunlight, staring around the ship. Behind him a handful of Martian soldiers stood waiting, their guns ready.

"This will not take long," the Leiter said, stepping into the ship, the soldiers following him. "You will be allowed to continue your trip shortly."

An audible sigh of relief went through the passengers.

"Look at him," the girl whispered to Thacher. "How I hate those black uniforms!"

"He's just a Provincial Leiter," Thacher said. "Don't worry."

The Leiter stood for a moment, his hands on his hips, looking around at them without expression. "I have ordered your ship grounded so that an inspection can be made of all persons aboard," he said. "You Terrans are the last to leave our planet. Most of you are ordinary and harmless—I am not interested in you. I am interested in finding three saboteurs, three Terrans, two men and a woman, who have committed an incredible act of destruction and violence. They are said to have fled to this ship."

Murmurs of surprise and indignation broke out on all sides. The Leiter motioned the soldiers to follow him up the aisle.

"Two hours ago a Martian city was destroyed. Nothing remains, only a depression in the sand where the city was. The city and all its people have completely vanished. An entire city destroyed in a second! Mars will never rest until the saboteurs are captured. And we know they are aboard this ship."

"It's impossible," the heavyset businessman said. "There aren't any saboteurs here."

"We'll begin with you," the Leiter said to him, stepping up beside the man's seat. One of the soldiers passed the Leiter a square metal box. "This will soon tell us if you're speaking the truth. Stand up. Get on your feet."

The man rose slowly, flushing. "See here—"

"Are you involved in the destruction of the city? Answer!"

The man swallowed angrily. "I know nothing about any destruction of any city. And furthermore—"

"He is telling the truth," the metal box said tonelessly.

"Next person." The Leiter moved down the aisle.

A thin, bald-headed man stood up nervously. "No, sir," he said. "I don't know a thing about it."

"He is telling the truth," the box affirmed.

"Next person! Stand up!"

One person after another stood, answered, and sat down again in relief. At last there were only a few people left who had not been questioned. The Leiter paused, studying them intently.

"Only five left. The three must be among you. We have narrowed it down." His hand moved to his belt. Something flashed, a rod of pale fire. He raised the rod, pointing it steadily at the five people. "All right, the first one of you. What do you know about this destruction? Are you involved with the destruction of our city?"

"No, not at all," the man murmured.

"Yes, he's telling the truth," the box intoned.

"Next!"

"Nothing— I know nothing. I had nothing to do with it."

"True," the box said.

The ship was silent. Three people remained, a middle-aged man and his wife and their son, a boy of about twelve. They stood in the corner, staring white-faced at the Leiter, at the rod in his dark fingers.

"It must be you," the Leiter grated, moving toward them. The Martian soldiers raised their guns. "It *must* be you. You there, the boy. What do you know about the destruction of our city? Answer!"

The boy shook his head. "Nothing," he whispered.

The box was silent for a moment. "He is telling the truth," it said reluctantly.

"Next!"

"Nothing," the woman muttered. "Nothing."

"The truth."

"Next!"

"I had nothing to do with blowing up your city," the man said. "You're wasting your time."

"It is the truth," the box said.

For a long time the Leiter stood, toying with his rod. At last he pushed it back in his belt and signaled the soldiers toward the exit lock.

"You may proceed on your trip," he said. He walked after the soldiers. At the hatch he stopped, looking back at the passengers, his face grim. "You may go—but Mars will not allow her enemies to escape. The three saboteurs will be caught, I promise you." He rubbed his dark jaw thoughtfully. "It is strange. I was certain they were on this ship."

Again he looked coldly around at the Terrans.

"Perhaps I was wrong. All right, proceed! But remember, the three will be caught, even if it takes endless years. Mars will catch them and punish them! I swear it!"

For a long time no one spoke. The ship lumbered through space again, its jets firing evenly, calmly, moving the passengers toward their own planet, toward home. Behind them Deimos and the red ball that was Mars dropped farther and farther away each moment, disappearing and fading into the distance.

A sigh of relief passed through the passengers. "What a lot of hot air that was," one grumbled.

"Barbarians!" a woman said.

A few of them stood up, moving out into the aisle, toward the lounge and the cocktail bar. Beside Thacher the girl got to her feet, pulling her jacket around her shoulders.

"Pardon me," she said, stepping past him.

"Going to the bar?" Thacher said. "Mind if I come along?"

"I suppose not."

They followed the others into the lounge, walking together up the aisle. "You know," Thacher said, "I don't even know your name, yet."

"My name is Mara Gordon."

"Mara? That's a nice name. What part of Terra are you from? North America? New York?"

"I've been in New York," Mara said. "New York is very lovely." She was slender and pretty, with a cloud of dark hair tumbling down her neck against her leather jacket.

They entered the lounge and stood undecided.

"Let's sit at a table," Mara said, looking around at the people at the bar, mostly men. "Perhaps that table over there."

"But someone's there already," Thacher said. The heavy-set businessman had sat down at the table and deposited his sample case on the floor. "Do we want to sit with *him*?"

"Oh, it's all right," Mara said, crossing to the table. "May we sit here?" she said to the man.

The man looked up, half-rising. "It's a pleasure," he murmured. He studied Thacher intently. "However, a friend of mine will be joining me in a moment."

"I'm sure there's room enough for us all," Mara said. She seated herself and Thacher helped her with her chair. He sat down too, glancing up suddenly at Mara and the business man. They were looking at each other almost as if something had passed between them. The man was middle-aged, with a florid face and tired, gray eyes. His hands were mottled with the veins showing thickly. At the moment he was tapping nervously.

"My name's Thacher," Thacher said to him, holding out his hand. "Bob Thacher. Since we're going to be together for a while we might as well get to know each other."

The man studied him. Slowly his hand came out. "Why not? My name's Erickson. Ralf Erickson."

"Erickson?" Thacher smiled. "You look like a commercial man to me." He nodded toward the sample case on the floor. "Am I right?"

The man named Erickson started to answer, but at that moment there was a stir. A thin man of about thirty had come up to the table, his eyes bright, staring down at them warmly. "Well, we're on our way," he said to Erickson.

"Hello, Mara." He pulled out a chair and sat down quickly, folding his hands on the table before him. He noticed Thacher and drew back a little. "Pardon me," he murmured.

"Bob Thacher is my name," Thacher said. "I hope I'm not intruding here." He glanced around at the three of them: Mara, alert, watching him intently; heavyset Erickson, his face blank; and this person. "Say, do you three know each other?" he asked suddenly.

There was silence.

The robot attendant slid over soundlessly, poised to take their orders. Erickson roused himself. "Let's see," he murmured. "What will we have? Mara?"

"Whiskey and water."

"You, Jan?"

The bright slim man smiled. "The same."

"Thacher?"

"Gin and tonic."

"Whiskey and water for me, also," Erickson said. The robot attendant went off. It returned at once with the drinks, setting them on the table. Each took his own. "Well," Erickson said, holding his glass up. "To our mutual success."

All drank, Thacher and the three of them, heavyset Erickson, Mara, her eyes nervous and alert, Jan, who had just come. Again a look passed between Mara and Erickson, a look so swift that he would not have caught it had he not been looking directly at her.

"What line do you represent, Mr. Erickson?" Thacher asked.

Erickson glanced at him, then down at the sample case on the floor. He grunted. "Well, as you can see, I'm a salesman."

Thacher smiled. "I knew it! You get so you can always spot a salesman right off by his sample case. A salesman always has to carry something to show. What are you in, sir?"

Erickson paused. He licked his thick lips, his eyes blank and lidded, like a toad's. At last he rubbed his mouth with his hand and reached down, lifting up the sample case. He set it on the table in front of him.

"Well?" he said. "Perhaps we might even show Mr. Thacher."

They all stared down at the sample case. It seemed to be an ordinary leather case, with a metal handle and a snap lock. "I'm getting curious," Thacher said. "What's in there? You're all so tense. Diamonds? Stolen jewels?"

Jan laughed harshly, mirthlessly. "Erick, put it down. We're not far enough away yet."

"Nonsense," Erick rumbled. "We're away, Jan."

"Please," Mara whispered. "Wait, Erick."

"Wait? Why? What for? You're so accustomed to—"

"Erick," Mara said. She nodded toward Thacher. "We don't know him, Erick. Please!"

"He's a Terran, isn't he?" Erickson said. "All Terrans are together in these times." He fumbled suddenly at the catch lock on the case. "Yes, Mr. Thacher. I'm a salesman. We're all salesmen, the three of us."

"Then you do know each other."

"Yes." Erickson nodded. His two companions sat rigidly, staring down. "Yes, we do. Here, I'll show you our line."

He opened the case. From it he took a letter knife, a pencil sharpener, a glass globe paperweight, a box of thumb tacks, a stapler, some clips, a plastic ashtray, and some things Thacher could not identify. He placed the objects in a row in front of him on the tabletop. Then he closed the sample case.

"I gather you're in office supplies," Thacher said. He touched the letter knife with his finger. "Nice quality steel. Looks like Swedish steel to me."

Erickson nodded, looking into Thacher's face. "Not really an impressive business, is it? Office supplies. Ashtrays, paper clips." He smiled.

"Oh—" Thacher shrugged. "Why not? They're a necessity in modern business. The only thing I wonder—"

"What's that?"

"Well, I wonder how you'd ever find enough customers on Mars to make it worth your while." He paused, examining the glass paperweight. He lifted it up, holding it to the light, staring at the scene within until Erickson took it out of his hand and put it back in the sample case. "And another thing. If you three know each other, why did you sit apart when you got on?"

They looked at him quickly.

"And why didn't you speak to each other until we left Deimos?" He leaned toward Erickson, smiling at him. "Two men and a woman. Three of you. Sitting apart in the ship. Not speaking, not until the check station was past. I find myself thinking over what the Martian said. Three saboteurs. A woman and two men."

Erickson put the things back in the sample case. He was smiling, but his face had gone chalk white. Mara stared down, playing with a drop of water on the edge of her glass. Jan clenched his hands together nervously, blinking rapidly.

"You three are the ones the Leiter was after," Thacher said softly. "You are the destroyers, the saboteurs. But their lie detector—why didn't it trap you? How did you get by that? And now you're safe, outside the check station." He grinned, staring around at them. "I'll be damned! And I really thought you were a salesman, Erickson. You really fooled me."

Erickson relaxed a little. "Well, Mr. Thacher, it's in a good cause. I'm sure you have no love for Mars either. No Terran does. And I see you're leaving with the rest of us."

"True," Thacher said. "You must certainly have an interesting account to give, the three of you." He looked around the table.

"We still have an hour or so of travel. Sometimes it gets dull, this Mars-Terra run. Nothing to see, nothing to do but sit and drink in the lounge." He raised his eyes slowly. "Any chance you'd like to spin a story to keep us awake?"

Jan and Mara looked at Erickson. "Go on," Jan said. "He knows who we are. Tell him the rest of the story."

"You might as well," Mara said.

Jan let out a sigh suddenly, a sigh of relief. "Let's put the cards on the table, get this weight off us. I'm tired of sneaking around, slipping—"

"Sure," Erickson said expansively. "Why not?" He settled back in his chair, unbuttoning his vest. "Certainly, Mr. Thacher. I'll be glad to spin you a story. And I'm sure it will be interesting enough to keep you awake."

***

They ran through the groves of dead trees, leaping across the sunbaked Martian soil, running silently together. They went up a little rise, across a narrow ridge. Suddenly Erick stopped, throwing himself down flat on the ground. The others did the same, pressing themselves against the soil, gasping for breath.

"Be silent," Erick muttered. He raised himself a little. "No noise. There'll be Leiters nearby, from now on. We don't dare take any chances."

Between the three people lying in the grove of dead trees and the City was a barren, level waste of desert, over a mile of blasted sand. No trees or bushes marred the smooth, parched surface. Only an occasional wind, a dry wind eddying and twisting, blew the sand up into little rills. A faint odor came to them, a bitter smell of heat and sand, carried by the wind.

Erick pointed. "Look. The City. There it is."

They stared, still breathing deeply from their race through the trees. The City was close, closer than they had ever seen it before. Never had they gotten so close to it in times past. Terrans were never allowed near the great Martian cities, the centers of Martian life. Even in ordinary times, when there was no threat of approaching war, the Martians shrewdly kept all Terrans away from their citadels, partly from fear, partly from a deep, innate sense of hostility toward the white-skinned visitors whose commercial ventures had earned them the respect, and the dislike, of the whole system.

"How does it look to you?" Erick said.

The City was huge, much larger than they had imagined from the drawings and models they had studied so carefully back in New York, in the War Ministry Office. Huge it was, huge and stark, black towers rising up against the sky, incredibly thin columns of ancient metal, columns that had stood wind and sun for centuries. Around the City was a wall of stone, red stone, immense bricks that had been lugged there and fitted into place by slaves of the early Martian dynasties, under the whiplash of the first great Kings of Mars.

An ancient, sunbaked City, a City set in the middle of a wasted plain, beyond groves of dead trees, a City seldom seen by Terrans, but a City studied on maps and charts in every War Office on Terra. A City that contained, for all its ancient stone and archaic towers, the ruling group of all Mars, the Council of Senior Leiters, black-clad men who governed and ruled with an iron hand.

The Senior Leiters, twelve fanatic and devoted men, black priests, but priests with flashing rods of fire, lie detectors, rocket ships, intra-space cannon, many more things the Terran

Senate could only conjecture about. The Senior Leiters and their subordinate Province Leiters. Erick and the two behind him suppressed a shudder.

"We've got to be careful," Erick said again. "We'll be passing among them soon. If they guess who we are, or what we're here for—"

He snapped open the case he carried, glancing inside for a second. Then he closed it again, grasping the handle firmly. "Let's go," he said. He stood up slowly. "You two come up beside me. I want to make sure you look the way you should."

Mara and Jan stepped quickly ahead. Erick studied them critically as the three of them walked slowly down the slope, onto the plain, toward the towering black spires of the City.

"Jan," Erick said. "Take hold of her hand! Remember, you're going to marry her. She's your bride. And Martian peasants think a lot of their brides."

Jan was dressed in the short trousers and coat of the Martian farmer, a knotted rope tied around his waist, a hat on his head to keep off the sun. His skin was dark, colored by dye until it was almost bronze.

"You look fine," Erick said to him. He glanced at Mara. Her black hair was tied in a knot, looped through a hollowed-out yuke bone. Her face was dark too, dark and lined with colored ceremonial pigment, green and orange stripes across her cheeks. Earrings were strung through her ears. On her feet were tiny slippers of perruh hide, laced around her ankles, and she wore long translucent Martian trousers with a bright sash tied around her waist. Between her small breasts a chain of stone beads rested, good-luck charms for the coming marriage.

"All right," Erick said. He, himself, wore the flowing gray robe of a Martian priest, dirty robes that were supposed to remain on him all his life, to be buried around him when he died. "I think we'll get past the guards. There should be heavy morning traffic on the road."

They walked on, the hard sand crunching under their feet. Against the horizon they could see specks moving, other persons going toward the City, farmers and peasants and merchants, bringing their crops and goods to market.

"See the cart!" Mara exclaimed.

They were nearing a narrow road, two ruts worn into the sand. A Martian hufa was pulling the cart, its great sides wet with perspiration, its tongue hanging out. The cart was piled high with bales of cloth, rough country cloth, hand dipped. A bent farmer urged the hufa on.

"And there." She pointed, smiling.

A group of merchants riding small animals were moving along behind the cart, Martians in long robes, their faces hidden by sand masks. On each animal was a pack, carefully tied on with rope. And beyond the merchants, plodding dully along, were peasants and farmers in an endless procession, some riding carts or animals, but mostly on foot.

Mara and Jan and Erick joined the line of people, melting in behind the merchants. No one noticed them, no one looked up or gave any sign. The march continued as before. Neither Jan nor Mara said anything to each other. They walked a little behind Erick, who paced with a certain dignity, a certain bearing becoming his position.

Once he slowed down, pointing up at the sky. "Look," he murmured in the Martian hill dialect. "See that?"

Two black dots circled lazily. Martian patrol craft, the military on the outlook for any sign of unusual activity. War was almost ready to break out with Terra. Any day, almost any moment.

"We'll be just in time," Erick said. "Tomorrow will be too late. The last ship will have left Mars."

"I hope nothing stops us," Mara said. "I want to get back home when we're through."

Half an hour passed. They neared the City, the wall growing as they walked, rising higher and higher until it seemed to blot out the sky itself. A vast wall, a wall of eternal stone that had felt the wind and sun for centuries. A group of Martian soldiers were standing at the entrance, the single passage-gate hewn into the rock, leading to the City. As each person went through, the soldiers examined him, poking his garments, looking into his load.

Erick tensed. The line had slowed almost to a halt. "It'll be our turn, soon," he murmured. "Be prepared."

"Let's hope no Leiters come around," Jan said. "The soldiers aren't so bad."

Mara was staring up at the wall and the towers beyond. Under their feet the ground trembled, vibrating and shaking. She could see tongues of flame rising from the towers, from the deep underground factories and forges of the City. The air was thick and dense with particles of soot. Mara rubbed her mouth, coughing.

"Here they come," Erick said softly.

The merchants had been examined and allowed to pass through the dark gate, the entrance through the wall into the City. They and their silent animals had already disappeared inside. The leader of the group of soldiers was beckoning impatiently to Erick, waving him on.

"Come along!" he said. "Hurry up there, old man."

Erick advanced slowly, his arms wrapped around his body, looking down at the ground.

"Who are you and what's your business here?" the soldier demanded, his hands on his hips, his gun hanging idly at his waist. Most of the soldiers were lounging lazily, leaning against the wall, some even squatting in the shade. Flies crawled on the face of one who had fallen asleep, his gun on the ground beside him.

"My business?" Erick murmured. "I am a village priest."

"Why do you want to enter the City?"

"I must bring these two people before the magistrate to marry them." He indicated Mara and Jan, standing a little behind him. "That is the Law the Leiters have made."

The soldier laughed. He circled around Erick. "What do you have in that bag you carry?"

"Laundry. We stay the night."

"What village are you from?"

"Kranos."

"Kranos?" The soldier looked to a companion. "Ever heard of Kranos?"

"A backward pig sty. I saw it once on a hunting trip."

The leader of the soldiers nodded to Jan and Mara. The two of them advanced, their hands clasped, standing close together. One of the soldiers put his hand on Mara's bare shoulder, turning her around.

"Nice little wife you're getting," he said. "Good and firm looking." He winked, grinning lewdly.

Jan glanced at him in sullen resentment. The soldiers guffawed. "All right," the leader said to Erick. "You people can pass."

Erick took a small purse from his robes and gave the soldier a coin. Then the three of them went into the dark tunnel that was the entrance, passing through the wall of stone, into the City beyond.

They were within the City!

"Now," Erick whispered. "Hurry."

Around them the City roared and cracked, the sound of a thousand vents and machines, shaking the stones under their feet. Erick led Mara and Jan into a corner by a row of brick warehouses. People were everywhere, hurrying back and forth, shouting above the din, merchants, peddlers, soldiers, street women. Erick bent down and opened the case he carried. From the case he quickly took three small coils of fine metal, intricate meshed wires and vanes worked together into a small cone. Jan took one and Mara took one. Erick put the remaining cone into his robe and snapped the case shut again.

"Now remember, the coils must be buried in such a way that the line runs through the center of the City. We must trisect the main section, where the largest concentration of buildings is. Remember the maps! Watch the alleys and streets carefully. Talk to no one if you can help it. Each of you has enough Martian money to buy your way out of trouble. Watch especially for cutpurses, and for heaven's sake, don't get lost—"

Erick broke off. Two black-clad Leiters were coming along the inside of the wall, strolling together with their hands behind their backs. They noticed the three who stood in the corner by the warehouses and stopped.

"Go," Erick muttered. "And be back here at sundown." He smiled grimly. "Or never come back."

Each went off a different way, walking quickly without looking back. The Leiters watched them go. "The little bride was quite lovely," one Leiter said. "Those hill people have the stamp of nobility in their blood, from the old times."

"A very lucky young peasant to possess her," the other said. They went on. Erick looked after them, still smiling a little. Then he joined the surging mass of people that milled eternally through the streets of the City.

At dusk they met outside the gate. The sun was soon to set, and the air had turned thin and frigid. It cut through their clothing like knives.

Mara huddled against Jan, trembling and rubbing her bare arms.

"Well?" Erick said. "Did you both succeed?"

Around them peasants and merchants were pouring from the entrance, leaving the City to return to their farms and villages, starting the long trip back across the plain toward the hills beyond. None of them noticed the shivering girl and the young man and the old priest standing by the wall.

"Mine's in place," Jan said. "On the other side of the City, on the extreme edge. Buried by a well."

"Mine's in the industrial section," Mara whispered, her teeth chattering. "Jan, give me something to put over me! I'm freezing."

"Good," Erick said. "Then the three coils should trisect dead center, if the models were correct." He looked up at the darkening sky. Already, stars were beginning to show. Two dots, the evening patrol, moved slowly toward the horizon. "Let's hurry. It won't be long."

They joined the line of Martians moving along the road away from the City. Behind them the City was losing itself in the somber tones of night, its black spires disappearing into darkness.

They walked silently with the country people until the flat ridge of dead trees became visible on the horizon. Then they left the road and turned off, walking toward the trees.

"Almost time!" Erick said. He increased his pace, looking back at Jan and Mara impatiently.

"Come on!"

They hurried, making their way through the twilight, stumbling over rocks and dead branches, up the side of the ridge. At the top Erick halted, standing with his hands on his hips, looking back.

"See," he murmured. "The City. The last time we'll ever see it this way."

"Can I sit down?" Mara said. "My feet hurt me."

Jan pulled at Erick's sleeve. "Hurry, Erick! Not much time left." He laughed nervously. "If everything goes right we'll be able to look at it—forever."

"But not like this," Erick murmured. He squatted down, snapping his case open. He took some tubes and wiring out and assembled them together on the ground, at the peak of the ridge. A small pyramid of wire and plastic grew, shaped by his expert hands.

At last he grunted, standing up. "All right."

"Is it pointed directly at the City?" Mara asked anxiously, looking down at the pyramid.

Erick nodded. "Yes, it's placed according—" He stopped, suddenly stiffening. "Get back! It's time! *Hurry!*"

Jan ran, down the far side of the slope, away from the City, pulling Mara with him. Erick came quickly after, still looking back at the distant spires, almost lost in the night sky.

"Down."

Jan sprawled out, Mara beside him, her trembling body pressed against his. Erick settled down into the sand and dead branches, still trying to see. "I want to see it," he murmured. "A miracle. I want to see—"

A flash, a blinding burst of violet light, lit up the sky. Erick clapped his hands over his eyes. The flash whitened, growing larger, expanding. Suddenly there was a roar, and a furious hot wind rushed past him, throwing him on his face in the sand. The hot dry wind licked and seared at them, crackling the bits of branches into flame. Mara and Jan shut their eyes, pressed tightly together.

"God!" Erick muttered.

The storm passed. They opened their eyes slowly. The sky was still alive with fire, a drifting cloud of sparks that was beginning to dissipate with the night wind. Erick stood up unsteadily, helping Jan and Mara to their feet. The three of them stood, staring silently across the dark waste, the black plain, none of them speaking.

The City was gone.

At last Erick turned away. "That part's done," he said. "Now the rest! Give me a hand, Jan. There'll be a thousand patrol ships around here in a minute."

"I see one already," Mara said, pointing up. A spot winked in the sky, a rapidly moving spot. "They're coming, Erick." There was a throb of chill fear in her voice.

"I know." Erick and Jan squatted on the ground around the pyramid of tubes and plastic, pulling the pyramid apart. The pyramid was fused, fused together like molten glass. Erick tore the pieces away with trembling fingers. From the remains of the pyramid he pulled something forth, something he held up high, trying to make it out in the darkness. Jan and Mara came close to see, both staring up intently, almost without breathing.

"There it is," Erick said. "There!"

In his hand was a globe, a small transparent globe of glass. Within the glass something moved, something minute and fragile, spires almost too small to be seen, microscopic, a complex web swimming within the hollow glass globe. A web of spires. A City.

Erick put the globe into the case and snapped it shut. "Let's go," he said. They began to lope back through the trees, back the way they had come before. "We'll change in the car," he said as they ran. "I think we should keep these clothes on until we're actually inside the car. We still might encounter someone."

"I'll be glad to get my own clothing on again," Jan said. "I feel funny in these little pants."

"How do you think I feel?" Mara gasped. "I'm freezing in this, what there is of it."

"All young Martian brides dress that way," Erick said. He clutched the case tightly as they ran. "I think it looks fine."

"Thank you," Mara said, "but it is cold."

"What do you suppose they'll think?" Jan asked. "They'll assume the City was destroyed, won't they? That's certain."

"Yes," Erick said. "They'll be sure it was blown up. We can count on that. And it will be damn important to us that they think so!"

"The car should be around here someplace," Mara said, slowing down.

"No, farther on," Erick said. "Past that little hill over there. In the ravine, by the trees. It's so hard to see where we are."

"Shall I light something?" Jan said.

"No. There may be patrols around who—"

He halted abruptly. Jan and Mara stopped beside him. "What—" Mara began.

A light glimmered. Something stirred in the darkness. There was a sound.

"Quick!" Erick rasped. He dropped, throwing the case far away from him, into the bushes. He straightened up tensely.

A figure loomed up, moving through the darkness, and behind it came more figures, men, soldiers in uniform. The light flashed up brightly, blinding them. Erick closed his eyes. The light left him, touching Mara and Jan, standing silently together, clasping hands. Then it flicked down to the ground and around in a circle.

A Leiter stepped forward, a tall figure in black, with his soldiers close behind him, their guns ready. "You three," the Leiter said. "Who are you? Don't move. Stand where you are."

He came up to Erick, peering at him intently, his hard Martian face without expression. He went all around Erick, examining his robes, his sleeves.

"Please—" Erick began in a quavering voice, but the Leiter cut him off.

"I'll do the talking. Who are you three? What are you doing here? Speak up."

"We—we are going back to our village," Erick muttered, staring down, his hands folded. "We were in the City, and now we are going home."

One of the soldiers spoke into a mouthpiece. He clicked it off and put it away.

"Come with me," the Leiter said. "We're taking you in. Hurry along."

"In? Back to the City?"

One of the soldiers laughed. "The City is gone," he said. "All that's left of it you can put in the palm of your hand."

"But what happened?" Mara said.

"No one knows. Come on, hurry it up!"

There was a sound. A soldier came quickly out of the darkness. "A Senior Leiter," he said. "Coming this way." He disappeared again.

"A Senior Leiter." The soldiers stood waiting, standing at a respectful attention. A moment later the Senior Leiter stepped into the light, a black-clad old man, his ancient face thin and hard like a bird's, eyes bright and alert. He looked from Erick to Jan.

"Who are these people?" he demanded.

"Villagers going back home."

"No, they're not. They don't stand like villagers. Villagers slump—diet, poor food. These people are not villagers. I myself came from the hills, and I know."

He stepped close to Erick, looking keenly into his face. "Who are you? Look at his chin. He never shaved with a sharpened stone! Something is wrong here."

In his hand a rod of pale fire flashed. "The City is gone, and with it at least half the Leiter Council. It is very strange, a flash, then heat, and a wind. But it was not fission. I am puzzled. All at once the City has vanished. Nothing is left but a depression in the sand."

"We'll take them in," the other Leiter said. "Soldiers, surround them. Make certain that—"

"Run!" Erick cried. He struck out, knocking the rod from the Senior Leiter's hand. They were all running, soldiers shouting, flashing their lights, stumbling against each other in the darkness. Erick dropped to his knees, groping frantically in the bushes. His fingers closed over the handle of the case, and he leaped up. In Terran he shouted to Mara and Jan.

"Hurry! To the car! Run!" He set off, down the slope, stumbling through the darkness. He could hear soldiers behind him, soldiers running and falling. A body collided against him, and he struck out. Someplace behind him there was a hiss, and a section of the slope went up in flames. The Leiter's rod—

"Erick," Mara cried from the darkness. He ran toward her. Suddenly he slipped, falling on a stone. Confusion and firing. The sound of excited voices.

"Erick, is that you?" Jan caught hold of him, helping him up. "The car. It's over here. Where's Mara?"

"I'm here," Mara's voice came. "Over here, by the car."

A light flashed. A tree went up in a puff of fire, and Erick felt the singe of the heat against his face. He and Jan made their way toward the girl. Mara's hand caught his in the darkness.

"Now the car," Erick said. "If they haven't got to it." He slid down the slope into the ravine, fumbling in the darkness, reaching and holding onto the handle of the case. Reaching, reaching—

He touched something cold and smooth. Metal, a metal door handle. Relief flooded through him. "I've found it! Jan, get inside. Mara, come on." He pushed Jan past him, into the car. Mara slipped in after Jan, her small agile body crowding in beside him.

"Stop!" a voice shouted from above. "There's no use hiding in that ravine. We'll get you! Come up and—"

The sound of voices was drowned out by the roar of the car's motor. A moment later they shot into the darkness, the car rising into the air. Treetops broke and cracked under them as Erick turned the car from side to side, avoiding the groping shafts of pale light from below, the last furious thrusts from the two Leiters and their soldiers.

Then they were away, above the trees, high in the air, gaining speed each moment, leaving the knot of Martians far behind.

"Toward Marsport," Jan said to Erick. "Right?"

Erick nodded. "Yes. We'll land outside the field, in the hills. We can change back to our regular clothing there, our commercial clothing. Damn it! We'll be lucky if we can get there in time for the ship."

"The last ship," Mara whispered, her chest rising and falling. "What if we don't get there in time?"

Erick looked down at the leather case in his lap. "We'll have to get there," he murmured. "We must!"

***

For a long time there was silence. Thacher stared at Erickson. The older man was leaning back in his chair, sipping a little of his drink. Mara and Jan were silent.

"So you didn't destroy the City," Thacher said. "You didn't destroy it at all. You shrank it down and put it in a glass globe, in a paperweight. And now you're salesmen again, with a sample case of office supplies!"

Erickson smiled. He opened the briefcase and reaching into it he brought out the glass globe paperweight. He held it up, looking into it. "Yes, we stole the City from the Martians. That's how we got by the lie detector. It was true that we knew nothing about a *destroyed* City."

"But why?" Thacher said. "Why steal a City? Why not merely bomb it?"

"Ransom," Mara said fervently, gazing into the globe, her dark eyes bright. "Their biggest City, half of their Council—in Erick's hand!"

"Mars will have to do what Terra asks," Erickson said. "Now Terra will be able to make her commercial demands felt. Maybe there won't even be a war. Perhaps Terra will get her way without fighting." Still smiling, he put the globe back into the briefcase and locked it.

"Quite a story," Thacher said. "What an amazing process, reduction of size—a whole City reduced to microscopic dimensions. Amazing. No wonder you were able to escape. With such daring as that, no one could hope to stop you."

He looked down at the briefcase on the floor. Underneath them the jets murmured and vibrated evenly as the ship moved through space toward distant Terra.

"We still have quite a way to go," Jan said. "You've heard our story, Thacher. Why not tell us yours? What sort of line are you in? What's your business?"

"Yes," Mara said. "What do you do?"

"What do I do?" Thacher said. "Well, if you like, I'll show you." He reached into his coat and brought out something. Something that flashed and glinted, something slender. A rod of pale fire.

The three stared at it. Sickened shock settled over them slowly.

Thacher held the rod loosely, calmly, pointing it at Erickson. "We knew you three were on this ship," he said. "There was no doubt of that. But we did not know what had become of the City. My theory was that the City had not been destroyed at all, that something else had happened to it. Council instruments measured a sudden loss of mass in that area, a decrease equal to the mass of the City. Somehow the City had been spirited away, not destroyed. But I could not convince the other Council Leiters of it. I had to follow you alone."

Thacher turned a little, nodding to the men sitting at the bar. The men rose at once, coming toward the table.

"A very interesting process you have. Mars will benefit a great deal from it. Perhaps it will even turn the tide in our favor. When we return to Marsport, I wish to begin work on it at once. And now, if you will please pass me the briefcase—"

# BEYOND THE DOOR

**LARRY THOMAS BOUGHT** a cuckoo clock for his wife—without knowing the price he would have to pay.

That night at the dinner table he brought it out and set it down beside her plate. Doris stared at it, her hand to her mouth. "My god, what is it?" She looked up at him, bright-eyed.

"Well, open it."

Doris tore the ribbon and paper from the square package with her sharp nails, her bosom rising and falling. Larry stood watching her as she lifted the lid. He lit a cigarette and leaned against the wall.

"A cuckoo clock!" Doris cried. "A real old cuckoo clock like my mother had." She turned the clock over and over. "Just like my mother had, when Pete was still alive." Her eyes sparkled with tears.

"It's made in Germany," Larry said. After a moment he added, "Carl got it for me wholesale. He knows some guy in the clock business. Otherwise I wouldn't have—" He stopped.

Doris made a funny little sound.

"I mean, otherwise I wouldn't have been able to afford it." He scowled. "What's the matter with you? You've got your clock, haven't you? Isn't that what you want?"

Doris sat holding onto the clock, her fingers pressed against the brown wood.

"Well," Larry said, "what's the matter?"

He watched in amazement as she leaped up and ran from the room, still clutching the clock. He shook his head. "Never satisfied. They're all that way. Never get enough."

He sat down at the table and finished his meal.

The cuckoo clock was not very large. It was handmade, however, and there were countless frets on it, little indentations and ornaments scored in the soft wood. Doris sat on the bed drying her eyes and winding the clock. She set the hands by her wristwatch. Presently she carefully moved the hands to two minutes of ten. She carried the clock over to the dresser and propped it up.

Then she sat waiting, her hands twisted together in her lap, waiting for the cuckoo to come out, for the hour to strike.

As she sat she thought about Larry and what he had said. And what she had said too, for that matter—not that she could be blamed for any of it. After all, she couldn't keep listening to him forever without defending herself. You had to blow your own trumpet in the world.

She touched her handkerchief to her eyes suddenly. Why did he have to say that, about getting it wholesale? Why did he have to spoil it all? If he felt that way, he needn't have got it in the first place. She clenched her fists. He was so mean, so damn mean.

But she was glad of the little clock sitting there ticking to itself, with its funny grilled edges and the door. Inside the door was the cuckoo, waiting to come out. Was he listening, his head cocked on one side, listening to hear the clock strike so that he would know to come out?

Did he sleep between hours? Well, she would soon see him; she could ask him. And she would show the clock to Bob. He would love it. Bob loved old things, even old stamps and buttons. He liked to go with her to the stores. Of course, it was a little *awkward*, but Larry had been staying at the office so much, and that helped. If only Larry didn't call up sometimes to—

There was a whirr. The clock shuddered and all at once the door opened. The cuckoo came out, sliding swiftly. He paused and looked around solemnly, scrutinizing her, the room, the furniture.

It was the first time he had seen her, she realized, smiling to herself in pleasure. She stood up, coming toward him shyly. "Go on," she said. "I'm waiting."

The cuckoo opened his bill. He whirred and chirped, quickly, rhythmically. Then, after a moment of contemplation, he retired. And the door snapped shut.

She was delighted. She clapped her hands and spun in a little circle. He was marvelous, perfect! And the way he had looked around, studying her, sizing her up. He liked her, she was certain of it. And she, of course, loved him at once, completely. He was just what she had hoped would come out of the little door.

Doris went to the clock. She bent over the little door, her lips close to the wood. "Do you hear me?" she whispered. "I think you're the most wonderful cuckoo in the world." She paused, embarrassed. "I hope you'll like it here."

Then she went downstairs again, slowly, her head high.

Larry and the cuckoo clock really never got along well from the start. Doris said it was because he didn't wind it right, and it didn't like being only half-wound all the time. Larry turned the job of winding over to her. The cuckoo came out every quarter hour and ran the spring down without remorse, and someone had to be ever after it, winding it up again.

Doris did her best, but she forgot a good deal of the time. Then Larry would throw his newspaper down with an elaborate weary motion and stand up. He would go into the dining room where the clock was mounted on the wall over the fireplace. He would take the clock down, and making sure that he had his thumb over the little door, he would wind it up.

"Why do you put your thumb over the door?" Doris asked once.

"You're supposed to."

She raised an eyebrow. "Are you sure? I wonder if it isn't that you don't want him to come out while you're standing so close."

"Why not?"

"Maybe you're afraid of him."

Larry laughed. He put the clock back on the wall and gingerly removed his thumb. When Doris wasn't looking he examined his thumb.

There was still a trace of the nick cut out of the soft part of it. Who—or what—had pecked at him?

One Saturday morning, when Larry was down at the office working over some important special accounts, Bob Chambers came to the front porch and rang the bell.

Doris was taking a quick shower. She dried herself and slipped into her robe. When she opened the door Bob stepped inside, grinning.

"Hi," he said, looking around.

"It's all right. Larry's at the office."

"Fine." Bob gazed at her slim legs below the hem of the robe. "How nice you look today."

She laughed. "Be careful! Maybe I shouldn't let you in after all."

They looked at one another, half amused half frightened. Presently Bob said, "If you want, I'll—"

"No, for god's sake." She caught hold of his sleeve. "Just get out of the doorway so I can close it. Mrs. Peters across the street, you know."

She closed the door. "And I want to show you something," she said. "You haven't seen it."

He was interested. "An antique? Or what?"

She took his arm, leading him toward the dining room. "You'll love it, Bobby." She stopped, wide-eyed. "I hope you will. You must, you must love it. It means so much to me—*he* means so much."

"He?" Bob frowned. "Who is he?"

Doris laughed. "You're jealous! Come on." A moment later they stood before the clock, looking up at it. "He'll come out in a few minutes. Wait until you see him. I know you two will get along just fine."

"What does Larry think of him?"

"They don't like each other. Sometimes when Larry's here he won't come out. Larry gets mad if he doesn't come out on time. He says—"

"Says what?"

Doris looked down. "He always says he's been robbed, even if he did get it wholesale." She brightened. "But I know he won't come out because he doesn't like Larry. When I'm here alone he comes right out for me, every fifteen minutes, even though he really only has to come out on the hour."

She gazed up at the clock. "He comes out for me because he wants to. We talk. I tell him things. Of course I'd like to have him upstairs in my room, but it wouldn't be right."

There was the sound of footsteps on the front porch. They looked at each other, horrified.

Larry pushed the front door open, grunting. He set his briefcase down and took off his hat. Then he saw Bob for the first time.

"Chambers. I'll be damned." His eyes narrowed. "What are you doing here?" He came into the dining room. Doris drew her robe about her helplessly, backing away.

"I—" Bob began. "That is, we—" He broke off, glancing at Doris. Suddenly the clock began to whirr. The cuckoo came rushing out, bursting into sound. Larry moved toward him.

"Shut that din off," he said. He raised his fist toward the clock. The cuckoo snapped into silence and retreated. The door closed. "That's better." Larry studied Doris and Bob, standing mutely together.

"I came over to look at the clock," Bob said. "Doris told me that it's a rare antique and that—"

"Nuts. I bought it myself." Larry walked up to him. "Get out of here." He turned to Doris. "You too. And take that damn clock with you."

He paused, rubbing his chin. "No. Leave the clock here. It's mine. I bought it and paid for it."

In the weeks that followed after Doris left, Larry and the cuckoo clock got along even worse than before. For one thing, the cuckoo stayed inside most of the time, sometimes even at twelve o'clock when he should have been busiest. And if he did come out at all he usually spoke only once or twice, never the correct number of times. And there was a sullen, uncooperative note in his voice, a jarring sound that made Larry uneasy and a little angry.

But he kept the clock wound, because the house was very still and quiet and it got on his nerves not to hear someone running around, talking and dropping things. And even the whirring of a clock sounded good to him.

But he didn't like the cuckoo at all. And sometimes he spoke to him.

"Listen," he said late one night to the closed little door. "I know you can hear me. I ought to give you back to the Germans, back to the Black Forest." He paced back and forth. "I wonder what they're doing now, the two of them. That young punk with his books and his antiques. A man shouldn't be interested in antiques. That's for women."

He set his jaw. "Isn't that right?"

The clock said nothing. Larry walked up in front of it. "Isn't that right?" he demanded. "Don't you have anything to say?"

He looked at the face of the clock. It was almost eleven, just a few seconds before the hour. "All right. I'll wait until eleven. Then I want to hear what you have to say. You've been pretty quiet the last few weeks since she left."

He grinned wryly. "Maybe you don't like it here since she's gone." He scowled. "Well, I paid for you, and you're coming out whether you like it or not. You hear me?"

Eleven o'clock came. Far off, at the end of town, the great tower clock boomed sleepily to itself. But the little door remained shut. Nothing moved. The minute hand passed on and the cuckoo did not stir. He was someplace inside the clock, beyond the door, silent and remote.

"All right, if that's the way you feel," Larry murmured, his lips twisting. "But it isn't fair. It's your job to come out. We all have to do things we don't like."

He went unhappily into the kitchen and opened the great gleaming refrigerator. As he poured himself a drink he thought about the clock.

There was no doubt about it—the cuckoo should come out, Doris or no Doris. He had always liked her, from the very start. They had got along well, the two of them. Probably he liked Bob too. Probably he had seen enough of Bob to get to know him. They would be quite happy together, Bob and Doris and the cuckoo.

Larry finished his drink. He opened the drawer at the sink and took out the hammer. He carried it carefully into the dining room. The clock was ticking gently to itself on the wall.

"Look," he said, waving the hammer. "You know what I have here? You know what I'm going to do with it? I'm going to start on you first." He smiled. "Birds of a feather, that's what you are, the three of you."

The room was silent.

"Are you coming out? Or do I have to come in and get you?"

The clock whirred a little.

"I hear you in there. You've got a lot of talking to do, enough for the last three weeks. As I figure it, you owe me—"

The door opened. The cuckoo came out fast, straight at him. Larry was looking down, his brow wrinkled in thought. He glanced up, and the cuckoo caught him squarely in the eye.

Down he went, hammer and chair and everything, hitting the floor with a tremendous crash. For a moment the cuckoo paused, its small body poised rigidly. Then it went back inside its house. The door snapped tight-shut after it.

The man lay on the floor, stretched out grotesquely, his head bent over to one side. Nothing moved or stirred. The room was completely silent, except, of course, for the ticking of the clock.

***

"I see," Doris said, her face tight. Bob put his arm around her, steadying her.

"Doctor," Bob said, "can I ask you something?"

"Of course," the doctor said.

"Is it very easy to break your neck, falling from so low a chair? It wasn't very far to fall. I wonder if it might not have been an accident. Is there any chance it might have been—"

"Suicide?" the doctor rubbed his jaw. "I never heard of anyone committing suicide that way. It was an accident. I'm positive."

"I don't mean suicide," Bob murmured under his breath, looking up at the clock on the wall. "I meant *something else.*"

But no one heard him.

# THE GOLDEN MAN

"**IS IT ALWAYS** hot like this?" the salesman demanded. He addressed everybody at the lunch counter and in the shabby booths against the wall. A middle-aged fat man with a good-natured smile, rumpled gray suit, sweat-stained white shirt, a drooping bowtie, and a Panama hat.

"Only in the summer," the waitress answered.

None of the others stirred. The teenage boy and girl in one of the booths, eyes fixed intently on each other. Two workmen, sleeves rolled up, arms dark and hairy, eating bean soup and rolls. A lean, weathered farmer. An elderly businessman in a blue serge suit, vest and pocket watch. A dark, rat-faced cab driver drinking coffee. A tired woman who had come in to get off her feet and put down her bundles.

The salesman got out a package of cigarettes. He glanced curiously around the dingy cafe, lit up, leaned his arms on the counter, and said to the man next to him: "What's the name of this town?"

The man grunted. "Walnut Creek."

The salesman sipped at his coke for a while, cigarette held loosely between plump, white fingers. Presently he reached in his coat and brought out a leather wallet. For a long time he leafed thoughtfully through cards and papers, bits of notes, ticket stubs, endless odds and ends, soiled fragments—and finally a photograph.

He grinned at the photograph and then began to chuckle, a low moist rasp. "Look at this," he said to the man beside him.

The man went on reading his newspaper.

"Hey, look at this." The salesman nudged him with his elbow and pushed the photograph at him. "How's that strike you?"

Annoyed, the man glanced briefly at the photograph. It showed a nude woman from the waist up. Perhaps thirty-five years old. Face turned away. Body white and flabby. With eight breasts.

"Ever seen anything like that?" the salesman chuckled, his little red eyes dancing. His face broke into lewd smiles, and again he nudged the man.

"I've seen that before." Disgusted, the man resumed reading his newspaper.

The salesman noticed the lean, old farmer was looking at the picture. He passed it genially over to him. "How's that strike you, pop? Pretty good stuff, eh?"

The farmer examined the picture solemnly. He turned it over, studied the creased back, took a second look at the front, then tossed it to the salesman. It slid from the counter, turned over a couple of times, and fell to the floor face up.

The salesman picked it up and brushed it off. Carefully, almost tenderly, he restored it to his wallet. The waitress's eyes flickered as she caught a glimpse of it.

"Damn nice," the salesman observed, with a wink. "Wouldn't you say so?"

The waitress shrugged indifferently. "I don't know. I saw a lot of them around Denver. A whole colony."

"That's where this was taken. Denver DCA Camp."

"Any still alive?" the farmer asked.

The salesman laughed harshly. "You kidding?" He made a short, sharp swipe with his hand. "Not anymore."

They were all listening. Even the high school kids in the booth had stopped holding hands and were sitting up straight, eyes wide with fascination.

"Saw a funny kind down near San Diego," the farmer said. "Last year, some time. Had wings like a bat. Skin, not feathers. Skin and bone wings."

The rat-eyed taxi driver chimed in. "That's nothing. There was a two-headed one in Detroit. I saw it on exhibit."

"Was it alive?" the waitress asked.

"No. They'd already euthed it."

"In sociology," the high school boy spoke up, "we saw tapes of a whole lot of them. The winged kind from down south, the big-headed one they found in Germany, an awful-looking one with sort of cones, like an insect. And—"

"The worst of all," the elderly businessman stated, "are those English ones. That hid out in the coal mines. The ones they didn't find until last year." He shook his head. "Forty years, down there in the mines, breeding and developing. Almost a hundred of them. Survivors from a group that went underground during the War."

"They just found a new kind in Sweden," the waitress said. "I was reading about it. Controls minds at a distance, they said. Only a couple of them. The DCA got there plenty fast."

"That's a variation of the New Zealand type," one of the workmen said. "It read minds."

"Reading and controlling are two different things," the businessman said. "When I hear something like that, I'm plenty glad there's the DCA."

"There was a type they found right after the War," the farmer said. "In Siberia. Had the ability to control objects. Psychokinetic ability. The Soviet DCA got it right away. Nobody remembers that anymore."

"I remember that," the businessman said. "I was just a kid then. I remember because that was the first deeve I ever heard of. My father called me into the living room and told me and my brothers and sisters. We were still building the house. That was in the days when the DCA inspected everyone and stamped their arms." He held up his thin, gnarled wrist. "I was stamped there, sixty years ago."

"Now they just have the birth inspection," the waitress said. She shivered. "There was one in San Francisco this month. First in over a year. They thought it was over around here."

"It's been dwindling," the taxi driver said. "Frisco wasn't too bad hit. Not like some. Not like Detroit."

"They still get ten or fifteen a year in Detroit," the high school boy said. "All around there. Lots of pools still left. People go into them in spite of the robot signs."

"What kind was this one?" the salesman asked. "The one they found in San Francisco."

The waitress gestured. "Common type. The kind with no toes. Bent over. Big eyes."

"The nocturnal type," the salesman said.

"The mother had hid it. They say it was three years old. She got the doctor to forge the DCA chit. Old friend of the family."

The salesman had finished his coke. He sat playing idly with his cigarettes, listening to the hum of talk he had set into motion. The high school boy was leaning excitedly toward the girl across from him, impressing her with his fund of knowledge. The lean farmer and the businessman were huddled together, remembering the old days, the last years of the War, before the first Ten-Year Reconstruction Plan. The taxi driver and the two workmen were swapping yarns about their own experiences.

The salesman caught the waitress's attention. "I guess," he said thoughtfully, "that one in Frisco caused quite a stir. Something like that happening so close."

"Yeah," the waitress murmured.

"This side of the Bay wasn't really hit," the salesman continued. "You never get any of them over here."

"No." The waitress moved abruptly. "None in this area. Ever." She scooped up dirty dishes from the counter and headed toward the back.

"Never?" the salesman asked, surprised. "You've never had any deeves on this side of the Bay?"

"No. None." She disappeared into the back, where the fry cook stood by his burners, white apron and tattooed wrists. Her voice was a little too loud, a little too harsh and strained. It made the farmer pause suddenly and glance up.

Silence dropped like a curtain. All sound cut off instantly. They were all gazing down at their food, suddenly tense and ominous.

"None around here," the taxi driver said, loudly and clearly, to no one in particular. "None ever."

"Sure," the salesman agreed genially. "I was only—"

"Make sure you get that straight," one of the workmen said.

The salesman blinked. "Sure, buddy. Sure." He fumbled nervously in his pocket. A quarter and a dime jangled to the floor, and he hurriedly scooped them up. "No offense."

For a moment there was silence. Then the high school boy spoke up, aware for the first time that nobody was saying anything. "I heard something," he began eagerly, voice full of importance. "Somebody said they saw something up by the Johnson farm that looked like it was one of those—"

"*Shut up*," the businessman said, without turning his head.

Scarlet-faced, the boy sagged in his seat. His voice wavered and broke off. He peered hastily down at his hands and swallowed unhappily.

The salesman paid the waitress for his coke. "What's the quickest road to Frisco?" he began. But the waitress had already turned her back.

The people at the counter were immersed in their food. None of them looked up. They ate in frozen silence. Hostile, unfriendly faces, intent on their food.

The salesman picked up his bulging briefcase, pushed open the screen door, and stepped out into the blazing sunlight. He moved toward his battered 1978 Buick, parked a few meters up. A blue-shirted traffic cop was standing in the shade of an awning, talking languidly to a young woman in a yellow silk dress that clung moistly to her slim body.

The salesman paused a moment before he got into his car. He waved his hand and hailed the policeman. "Say, you know this town pretty good?"

The policeman eyed the salesman's rumpled gray suit, bowtie, his sweat-stained shirt. The out-of-state license. "What do you want?"

"I'm looking for the Johnson farm," the salesman said. "Here to see him about some litigation." He moved toward the policeman, a small white card between his fingers. "I'm his attorney—from the New York Guild. Can you tell me how to get out there? I haven't been through here in a couple of years."

***

Nat Johnson gazed up at the noonday sun and saw that it was good. He sat sprawled out on the bottom step of the porch, a pipe between his yellowed teeth, a lithe wiry man in red-checkered shirt and canvas jeans, powerful hands, iron-gray hair that was still thick despite sixty-five years of active life.

He was watching the children play. Jean rushed laughing in front of him, bosom heaving under her sweatshirt, black hair streaming behind her. She was sixteen, bright-eyed, legs strong and straight, slim young body bent slightly forward with the weight of the two horseshoes. After her scampered Dave, fourteen, white teeth and black hair, a handsome boy, a son to be proud of. Dave caught up with his sister, passed her, and reached the far peg. He stood waiting, legs apart, hands on his hips, his two horseshoes gripped easily. Gasping, Jean hurried toward him.

"Go ahead!" Dave shouted. "You shoot first. I'm waiting for you."

"So you can knock them away?"

"So I can knock them closer."

Jean tossed down one horseshoe and gripped the other with both hands, eyes on the distant peg. Her lithe body bent, one leg slid back, her spine arched. She took careful aim, closed one eye, and then expertly tossed the shoe. With a clang the shoe struck the distant peg, circled briefly around it, then bounced off again and rolled to one side. A cloud of dust rolled up.

"Not bad," Nat Johnson admitted from his step. "Too hard though. Take it easy." His chest swelled with pride as the girl's glistening body took aim and again threw. Two powerful, handsome children, almost ripe, on the verge of adulthood. Playing together in the hot sun.

And there was Cris.

Cris stood by the porch, arms folded. He wasn't playing. He was watching. He had stood there since Dave and Jean had begun playing, the same half-intent, half-remote expression on his finely-cut face. As if he were seeing past them, beyond the two of them. Beyond the field, the barn, the creek bed, the rows of cedars.

"Come on, Cris!" Jean called, as she and Dave moved across the field to collect their horseshoes. "Don't you want to play?"

No, Cris didn't want to play. He never played. He was off in a world of his own, a world into which none of them could come. He never joined in anything, games or chores or family activities. He was by himself always. Remote, detached, aloof. Seeing past everyone and everything—that is, until all at once something clicked and he momentarily rephased, reentered their world briefly.

Nat Johnson reached out and knocked his pipe against the step. He refilled it from his leather tobacco pouch, his eyes on his eldest son. Cris was now moving into life. Heading out onto the field. He walked slowly, arms folded calmly, as if he had, for the moment, descended from his own world into theirs. Jean didn't see him. She had turned her back and was getting ready to pitch.

"Hey," Dave said, startled. "Here's Cris."

Cris reached his sister, stopped, and held out his hand. A great dignified figure, calm and impassive. Uncertainly, Jean gave him one of the horseshoes. "You want this? You want to play?"

Cris said nothing. He bent slightly, a supple arc of his incredibly graceful body, then moved his arm in a blur of speed. The shoe sailed, struck the far peg, and dizzily spun around it. Ringer.

The corners of Dave's mouth turned down. "What a lousy darn thing."

"Cris," Jean reproved. "You don't play fair."

No, Cris didn't play fair. He had watched half an hour, then come out and thrown once. One perfect toss, one dead ringer.

"He never makes a mistake," Dave complained.

Cris stood, face blank. A golden statue in the midday sun. Golden hair, skin, a light down of gold fuzz on his bare arms and legs—

Abruptly he stiffened. Nat sat up, startled. "What is it?" he barked.

Cris turned in a quick circle, magnificent body alert. "Cris!" Jean demanded. "What—"

Cris shot forward. Like a released energy beam he bounded across the field, over the fence, into the barn and out the other side. His flying figure seemed to skim over the dry grass as he descended into the barren creek bed, between the cedars. A momentary flash of gold, and he was gone. Vanished. There was no sound. No motion. He had utterly melted into the scenery.

"What was it this time?" Jean asked wearily. She came over to her father and threw herself down in the shade. Sweat glowed on her smooth neck and upper lip. Her sweatshirt was streaked and damp. "What did he see?"

"He was after something," Dave stated, coming up.

Nat grunted. "Maybe. There's no telling."

"I guess I better tell Mom not to set a place for him," Jean said. "He probably won't be back."

Anger and futility descended over Nat Johnson. No, he wouldn't be back. Not for dinner and probably not the next day. Or the one after that. He'd be gone god only knew how long. Or where. Or why. Off by himself, alone some place. "If I thought there was any use," Nat began, "I'd send you two after him. But there's no—"

He broke off. A car was coming up the dirt road toward the farmhouse. A dusty, battered old Buick. Behind the wheel sat a plump, red-faced man in a gray suit, who waved cheerfully at them as the car sputtered to a stop and the motor died into silence.

"Afternoon," the man nodded as he climbed out the car. He tipped his hat pleasantly. He was middle-aged, genial look-ing, perspiring freely as he crossed the dry ground toward the porch. "Maybe you folks can help me."

"What do you want?" Nat Johnson demanded hoarsely. He was frightened. He watched the creek bed out of the corner of his eye, praying silently. God, if only he *stayed* away. Jean was breathing quickly, sharp little gasps. She was terrified. Dave's face was expressionless, but all color had drained from it. "Who are you?" Nat demanded.

"Name's Baines. George Baines." The man held out his hand, but Johnson ignored it. "Maybe you've heard of me. I own the Pacifica Development Corporation. We built all those little bomb-proof houses just outside town. Those little round ones you see as you come up the main highway from Lafayette."

"What do you want?" Johnson held his hands steady with an effort. He'd never heard of the man, although he'd noticed the housing tract. It couldn't be missed—a great ant-heap of ugly pill boxes straddling the highway. Baines looked like the kind of man who'd own them. But what did he want here?

"I've bought some land up this way," Baines was explaining. He rattled a sheaf of crisp papers. "This is the deed, but I'll be damned if I can find it." He grinned good-naturedly. "I know it's around this way someplace, this side of the State road. According to the clerk at the County Recorder's Office, a mile or so this side of that hill over there. But I'm no damn good at reading maps."

"It isn't around here," Dave broke in. "There's only farms around here. Nothing for sale."

"This is a farm, son," Baines said genially. "I bought it for myself and my missus. So we could settle down." He wrinkled his pug nose. "Don't get the wrong idea—I'm not putting up any tracts around here. This is strictly for myself. An old farmhouse, twenty acres, a pump and a few oak trees—"

"Let me see the deed." Johnson grabbed the sheaf of papers, and while Baines blinked in astonishment, he leafed rapidly through them. His face hardened, and he handed them back. "What are you up to? This deed is for a parcel fifty miles from here."

"Fifty miles!" Baines was dumbfounded. "No kidding? But the clerk told me—"

Johnson was on his feet. He towered over the fat man. He was in top-notch physical shape, and he was plenty damn suspicious. "Clerk, hell. You get back into your car and drive out of here. I don't know what you're after, or what you're here for, but I want you off my land."

In Johnson's massive fist something sparkled. A metal tube

that gleamed ominously in the midday sunlight. Baines saw it and gulped. "No offense, mister." He backed nervously away. "You folks sure are touchy. Take it easy, will you?"

Johnson said nothing. He gripped the lash-tube tighter and waited for the fat man to leave.

But Baines lingered. "Look, buddy. I've been driving around this furnace five hours, looking for my damn place. Any objection to my using your facilities?"

Johnson eyed him with suspicion. Gradually the suspicion turned to disgust. He shrugged. "Dave, show him where the bathroom is."

"Thanks." Baines grinned thankfully. "And if it wouldn't be too much trouble, maybe a glass of water. I'd be glad to pay you for it." He chuckled knowingly. "Never let the city people get away with anything, eh?"

"Christ." Johnson turned away in revulsion as the fat man lumbered after his son into the house.

"Dad," Jean whispered. As soon as Baines was inside, she hurried up onto the porch, eyes wide with fear. "Dad, do you think he—"

Johnson put his arm around her. "Just hold on tight. He'll be gone soon."

The girl's dark eyes flashed with mute terror. "Every time the man from the water company, or the tax collector, some tramp, children, *anybody* come around, I get a terrible stab of pain—here." She clutched at her heart, hand against her breasts. "It's been that way thirteen years. How much longer can we keep it going? *How long?*"

The man named Baines emerged gratefully from the bathroom. Dave Johnson stood silently by the door, body rigid, youthful face stony.

"Thanks, son," Baines sighed. "Now where can I get a glass of cold water?" He smacked his thick lips in anticipation. "After you've been driving around the sticks looking for a dump some red-hot real estate agent stuck you with—"

Dave headed into the kitchen. "Mom, this man wants a drink of water. Dad said he could have it."

Dave had turned his back. Baines caught a brief glimpse of the mother, gray-haired, small, moving toward the sink with a glass, face withered and drawn, without expression.

Then Baines hurried from the room down a hall. He passed through a bedroom, pulled a door open, found himself facing a closet. He turned and raced back, through the living room, into a dining room, then another bedroom. In a brief instant he had gone through the whole house.

He peered out a window. The back yard. Remains of a rusting truck. Entrance of an underground bomb shelter. Tin cans. Chickens scratching around. A dog asleep under a shed. A couple of old auto tires.

He found a door leading out. Soundlessly, he tore the door open and stepped outside. No one was in sight. There was the barn, a leaning, ancient wood structure. Cedar trees beyond, a creek of some kind. What had once been an outhouse.

Baines moved cautiously around the side of the house. He had perhaps thirty seconds. He had left the door of the bathroom closed; the boy would think he had gone back in there. Baines looked into the house through a window. A large closet, filled with old clothing, boxes and bundles of magazines.

He turned and started back. He reached the corner of the house and started around it.

Nat Johnson's gaunt shape loomed up and blocked his way. "All right, Baines. You asked for it."

A pink flash blossomed. It shut out the sunlight in a single blinding burst. Baines leaped back and clawed at his coat pocket. The edge of the flash caught him, and he half-fell, stunned by the force. His suit-shield sucked in the energy and discharged it, but the power rattled his teeth and for a moment he jerked like a puppet on a string. Darkness ebbed around him. He could feel the mesh of the shield glow white as it absorbed the energy and fought to control it.

His own tube came out, and Johnson had no shield. "You're under arrest," Baines muttered grimly. "Put down your tube and your hands up. And call your family." He made a motion with the tube. "Come on, Johnson. Make it snappy."

The lash-tube wavered and then slipped from Johnson's fingers. "You're still alive." Dawning horror crept across his face. "Then you must be—"

Dave and Jean appeared. "*Dad!*"

"Come over here," Baines ordered. "Where's your mother?"

Dave jerked his head numbly. "Inside."

"Get her and bring her here."

"You're DCA," Nat Johnson whispered.

Baines didn't answer. He was doing something with his neck, pulling at the flabby flesh. The wiring of a contact mike glittered as he slipped it from a fold between two chins and into his pocket. From the dirt road came the sound of motors, sleek purrs that rapidly grew louder. Two teardrops of black metal came gliding up and parked beside the house. Men swarmed out in the dark gray-green of the Government Civil Police. In the sky swarms of black dots were descending, clouds of ugly flies that darkened the sun as they spilled out men and equipment. The men drifted slowly down.

"He's not here," Baines said as the first man reached him. "He got away. Inform Wisdom back at the lab."

"We've got this section blocked off."

Baines turned to Nat Johnson who stood in dazed silence, uncomprehending, his son and daughter beside him. "How did he know we were coming?" Baines demanded.

"I don't know," Johnson muttered. "He just knew."

"A telepath?"

"I don't know."

Baines shrugged. "We'll know soon. A clamp is out, all around here. He can't get past no matter what the hell he can do. Unless he can dematerialize himself."

"What'll you do with him when you—if you catch him?" Jean asked huskily.

"Study him."

"And then kill him?"

"That depends on the lab evaluation. If you could give me more to work on, I could predict better."

"We can't tell you anything. We don't know anything more." The girl's voice rose with desperation. "He doesn't talk."

Baines jumped. "*What*?"

"He doesn't talk. He never talked to us. Ever."

"How old is he?"

"Eighteen."

"No communication." Baines was sweating. "In eighteen years there hasn't been any semantic bridge between you? Does he have *any* contact? Signs? Codes?"

"He ignores us. He eats here, stays with us. Sometimes he plays when we play. Or sits with us. He's gone days on end. We've never been able to find out what he's doing, or where. He sleeps in the barn by himself."

"Is he really gold-colored?"

"Yes. Skin, eyes, hair, nails. Everything."

"And he's large? Well-formed?"

It was a moment before the girl answered. A strange emotion stirred her drawn features, a momentary glow. "He's incredibly beautiful. A god come down to Earth." Her lips twisted. "You won't find him. He can do things. Things you have no comprehension of. Powers so far beyond your limited—"

"You don't think we'll get him?" Baines frowned. "More teams are landing all the time. You've never seen an Agency clamp in operation. We've had sixty years to work out all the bugs. If he gets away, it'll be the first time—"

Baines broke off abruptly. Three men were quickly approaching the porch. Two green-clad Civil Police. And a third man between them. A man who moved silently, lithely, a faintly luminous shape that towered above them.

"*Cris!*" Jean screamed.

"We got him," one of the police said.

Baines fingered his lash-tube uneasily. "Where? How?"

"He gave himself up," the policeman answered, voice full of awe. "He came to us voluntarily. Look at him. He's like a metal statue. Like some sort of god."

The golden figure halted for a moment beside Jean. Then it turned slowly, calmly, to face Baines.

"Cris!" Jean shrieked. "*Why did you come back?*"

The same thought was eating at Baines, too. He shoved it aside—for the time being. "Is the jet out front?" he demanded quickly.

"Ready to go," one of the CP answered.

"Fine." Baines strode past them, down the steps and onto the dirt field. "Let's go. I want him taken directly to the lab." For a moment he studied the massive figure who stood calmly between the two Civil Policemen. Beside him, they seemed to have shrunk, become ungainly and repellent. Like dwarves… What had Jean said? *A god come to Earth.* Baines broke angrily away. "Come on," he muttered brusquely. "This one may be tough; we've never run up against one like it before. We don't know what the hell it can do."

***

The chamber was empty except for the seated figure. Four bare walls, floor and ceiling. A steady glare of white light relentlessly etched every corner of the chamber. Near the top of the far wall ran a narrow slot, the view windows through which the interior of the chamber was scanned.

The seated figure was quiet. He hadn't moved since the chamber locks had slid into place, since the heavy bolts had fallen from outside and the rows of bright-faced technicians had taken their places at the view windows. He gazed down at the floor, bent forward, hands clasped together, face calm, almost expressionless. In four hours he hadn't moved a muscle.

"Well?" Baines said. "What have you learned?"

Wisdom grunted sourly. "Not much. If we don't have him doped out in forty-eight hours, we'll go ahead with the euth. We can't take any chances."

"You're thinking about the Tunis type," Baines said. He was, too. They had found ten of them living in the ruins of the abandoned North African town. Their survival method was simple. They killed and absorbed other life forms, then imitated them and took their places. *Chameleons*, they were called. It had cost sixty lives before the last one was destroyed. Sixty top-level experts, highly trained DCA men.

"Any clues?" Baines asked.

"He's different as hell. This is going to be tough." Wisdom thumbed a pile of tape spools. "This is the complete report, all the material we got from Johnson and his family. We pumped them with the psych-wash, then let them go home. Eighteen years and no semantic bridge. Yet he looks fully developed. Mature at thirteen—a shorter, faster life-cycle than ours. But why the mane? All the gold fuzz? Like a Roman monument that's been gilded."

"Has the report come in from the analysis room? You had a wave-shot taken, of course."

"His brain pattern has been fully scanned. But it takes time for them to plot it out. We're all running around like lunatics while he just sits there!" Wisdom poked a stubby finger at the window. "We caught him easily enough. He can't have *much*, can he? But I'd like to know what it is. Before we euth him."

"Maybe we should keep him alive until we know."

"Euth in forty-eight hours," Wisdom repeated stubbornly. "Whether we know or not. I don't like him. He gives me the creeps."

Wisdom stood chewing nervously on his cigar, a red-haired, beefy-faced man, thick and heavyset, with a barrel chest and cold, shrewd eyes deep-set in his hard face. Ed Wisdom was Director of DCA's North American Branch. But right now he was worried. His tiny eyes darted back and forth, alarmed flickers of gray in his brutal, massive face.

"You think," Baines said slowly, "this is *it*?"

"I always think so," Wisdom snapped. "I have to think so."

"I mean—"

"I know what you mean." Wisdom paced back and forth, among the study tables, technicians at their benches, equipment and humming computers. Buzzing tape-slots and research hook-ups. "This thing lived eighteen years with his family, and *they* don't understand it. *They* don't know what it has. They know what it does, but not how."

"What does it do?"

"It knows things."

"What kind of things?"

Wisdom grabbed his lash-tube from his belt and tossed it on a table. "Here."

"What?"

"Here." Wisdom signaled and a view window was slid back an inch. "Shoot him."

Baines blinked. "You said forty-eight hours."

With a curse Wisdom snatched up the tube, aimed it through the window directly at the seated figure's back, and squeezed the trigger.

A blinding flash of pink. A cloud of energy blossomed in the center of the chamber. It sparkled, then died into dark ash.

"Good god!" Baines gasped. "You—"

He broke off. The figure was no longer sitting. As Wisdom fired, it had moved in a blur of speed, away from the blast to the corner of the chamber. Now it was slowly coming back, face blank, still absorbed in thought.

"Fifth time," Wisdom said as he put his tube away. "Last time Jamison and I fired together. Missed. He knew exactly when the bolts would hit. And where."

Baines and Wisdom looked at each other. Both of them were thinking the same thing. "But even reading minds wouldn't tell him where they were going to hit," Baines said. "When, maybe. But not where. Could you have called your own shots?"

"Not mine," Wisdom answered flatly. "I fired fast, damn near at random." He frowned. "*Random.* We'll have to make a test of this." He waved a group of technicians over. "Get a construction team up here. On the double." He grabbed paper and pen and began sketching.

While construction was going on, Baines met his fiance in the lobby outside the lab, the great central lounge of the DCA Building.

"How's it coming?" she asked. Anita Ferris was tall and blonde, blue eyes and a mature, carefully cultivated figure. An attractive, competent-looking woman in her late twenties. She wore a metal-foil dress and cape with a red and black stripe on the sleeve, the emblem of the A-class. Anita was Director of the Semantics Agency, a top-level Government Coordinator. "Anything of interest this time?"

"Plenty." Baines guided her from the lobby into the dim

recess of the bar. Music played softly in the background, a shifting variety of patterns formed mathematically. Dim shapes moved expertly through the gloom, from table to table. Silent, efficient robot waiters.

As Anita sipped her Tom Collins, Baines outlined what they had found.

"What are the chances," Anita asked slowly, "that he's built up some kind of deflection-cone? There was one kind that warped their environment by direct mental effort. No tools. Direct mind to matter."

"Psychokinetics?" Baines drummed restlessly on the tabletop. "I doubt it. The thing has ability to predict, not to control. He can't stop the beams, but he can sure as hell get out of the way."

"Does he jump between the molecules?"

Baines wasn't amused. "This is serious. We've handled these things sixty years, longer than you and I have been around added together. Eighty-seven types of deviants have shown up, real mutants that could reproduce themselves, not mere freaks. This is the eighty-eighth. We've been able to handle each of them in turn. But this—"

"Why are you so worried about this one?"

"First, it's eighteen years old. That in itself is incredible. Its family managed to hide it that long."

"Those women around Denver were older than that. Those ones with—"

"They were in a Government camp. Somebody high up was toying with the idea of allowing them to breed. Some sort of industrial use. We withheld euth for years. But Cris Johnson stayed alive *outside our control*. Those things at Denver were under constant scrutiny."

"Maybe he's harmless. You always assume a deeve is a menace. He might even be beneficial. Somebody thought those women might work in. Maybe this thing has something that would advance the race."

"*Which* race? Not the human race. It's the old 'the operation was a success but the patient died' routine. If we introduce a mutant to keep us going, it'll be mutants, not us, who'll inherit the earth. It'll be mutants surviving for their own sake. Don't think for a moment we can put padlocks on them and expect them to serve us. If they're really superior to homo sapiens, they'll win out in even competition. To survive, we've got to cold deck them right from the start."

"In other words, we'll know homo superior when he comes—by definition. He'll be the one we won't be able to euth."

"That's about it," Baines answered. "Assuming there is a homo superior. Maybe there's just homo peculiar. Homo with an improved line."

"The Neanderthal probably thought the Cro-Magnon man had merely an improved line. A little more advanced ability to conjure up symbols and shape flint. From your description, this thing is more radical than a mere improvement."

"This thing," Baines said slowly, "has an ability to predict. So far, it's been able to stay alive. It's been able to cope with situations better than you or I could. How long do you think we'd stay alive in that chamber with energy beams blazing down at us? In a sense it's got the ultimate survival ability. If it can always be accurate—"

A wall speaker sounded. "Baines, you're wanted in the lab. Get the hell out of the bar and upramp."

Baines pushed back his chair and got to his feet. "Come along. You may be interested in seeing what Wisdom has got dreamed up."

***

A tight group of top-level DCA officials stood around in a circle—middle-aged, gray-haired—listening to a skinny youth in a white shirt and rolled-up sleeves explaining an elaborate cube of metal and plastic that filled the center of the view-platform. From it jutted an ugly array of tube snouts, gleaming muzzles that disappeared into an intricate maze of wiring.

"This," the youth was saying briskly, "is the first real test. It fires at random, as nearly random as we can make it, at least. Weighted balls are thrown up in an air stream, then dropped free to fall back and cut relays. They can fall in almost any pattern. The thing fires according to their pattern. Each drop produces a new configuration of timing and position. Ten tubes in all. Each will be in constant motion."

"And *nobody* knows how they'll fire?" Anita asked.

"Nobody." Wisdom rubbed his thick hands together. "Mind reading won't help him, not with this thing."

Anita moved over to the view windows, as the cube was rolled into place. She gasped. "Is that him?"

"What's wrong?" Baines asked.

Anita's cheeks were flushed. "Why, I expected a—a *thing*. My god, he's beautiful! Like a golden statue. Like a deity!"

Baines laughed. "He's eighteen years old, Anita. Too young for you."

The woman was still peering through the view window. "Look at him. Eighteen? I don't believe it."

Cris Johnson sat in the center of the chamber on the floor. A posture of contemplation, head bowed, arms folded, legs tucked under him. In the stark glare of the overhead lights his powerful body glowed and rippled, a shimmering figure of downy gold.

"Pretty, isn't he?" Wisdom muttered. "All right. Start it going."

"You're going to *kill* him?" Anita demanded.

"We're going to try."

"But he's—" She broke off uncertainly. "He's not a monster. He's not like those others, those hideous things with two heads, or those insects. Or those awful things from Tunis."

"What is he then?" Baines asked.

"I don't know. But you can't just *kill* him. It's terrible!"

The cube clicked into life. The muzzles jerked, silently altered position. Three retracted, disappeared into the body of the cube. Others came out. Quickly, efficiently, they moved into position—and abruptly, without warning, opened fire.

A staggering burst of energy fanned out, a complex pattern that altered each moment, different angles, different velocities, a bewildering blur that cracked from the windows down into the chamber.

The golden figure moved. He dodged back and forth, expertly avoiding the bursts of energy that seared around him on all sides. Rolling clouds of ash obscured him. He was lost in a mist of crackling fire and ash.

"Stop it!" Anita shouted. "For god's sake, you'll destroy him!"

The chamber was an inferno of energy. The figure had completely disappeared. Wisdom waited a moment, then nodded to the technicians operating the cube. They touched guide buttons, and the muzzles slowed and died. Some sank back into the cube. All became silent. The works of the cube ceased humming.

Cris Johnson was still alive. He emerged from the settling clouds of ash, blackened and singed. But unhurt. He had avoided each beam. He had weaved between them and among them as they came, a dancer leaping over glittering sword points of pink fire. He had survived.

"No," Wisdom murmured, shaken and grim. "Not a telepath. Those were at random. No prearranged pattern."

The three of them looked at each other, dazed and frightened. Anita was trembling. Her face was pale, and her blue eyes were wide. "What, then?" She whispered. "What is it? What does he have?"

"He's a good guesser," Wisdom suggested.

"He's not guessing," Baines answered. "Don't kid yourself. That's the whole point."

"No, he's not guessing." Wisdom nodded slowly. "He *knew*. He predicted each strike. I wonder…*Can* he err? *Can* he make a mistake?"

"We caught him," Baines pointed out.

"You said he came back voluntarily." There was a strange look on Wisdom's face. "Did he come back *after* the clamp was up?"

Baines jumped. "Yes, after."

"He couldn't have got through the clamp. So he came back." Wisdom grinned wryly. "The clamp must actually have been perfect. It was supposed to be."

"If there had been a single hole," Baines murmured, "he would have known it, gone through."

Wisdom ordered a group of armed guards over. "Get him out of there. To the euth stage."

Anita shrieked. "Wisdom, you can't—"

"He's too far ahead of us. We can't compete with him." Wisdom's eyes were bleak. "We can only guess what's going to happen. *He knows*. For him, it's a sure thing. I don't think it'll help him at euth though. The whole stage is flooded simultaneously. Instantaneous gas released throughout." He signaled impatiently to the guards. "Get going. Take him down right away. Don't waste any time."

"Can we?" Baines murmured thoughtfully.

The guards took up positions by one of the chamber locks. Cautiously, the tower control slid the lock back. The first two guards stepped cautiously in, lash-tubes ready.

Cris stood in the center of the chamber. His back was to them as they crept toward him. For a moment he was silent, utterly unmoving. The guards fanned out as more of them entered the chamber. Then—

Anita screamed. Wisdom cursed. The golden figure spun and leaped forward in a flashing blur of speed. Past the triple line of guards, through the lock and into the corridor.

"Get him!" Baines shouted.

Guards milled everywhere. Flashes of energy lit up the corridor as the figure raced among them up the ramp.

"No use," Wisdom said calmly. "We can't hit him." He touched a button, then another. "But maybe this will help."

"What—" Baines began. But the leaping figure shot abruptly at him, straight at him, and he dropped to one side. The figure flashed past. It ran effortlessly, face without expression, dodging and jumping as the energy beams seared around it.

For an instant the golden face loomed up before Baines. It passed and disappeared down a side corridor. Guards rushed after it, kneeling and firing, shouting orders excitedly. In the bowels of the building, heavy guns were rumbling up. Locks slid into place as escape corridors were systematically sealed off.

"Good god," Baines gasped as he got to his feet. "Can't he do anything but run?"

"I gave orders," Wisdom said, "to have the building isolated. There's no way out. Nobody comes and nobody goes. He's loose here in the building, but he won't get out."

"If there's one exit overlooked, he'll know it," Anita pointed out shakily.

"We won't overlook any exit. We got him once; we'll get him again."

A messenger robot had come in. Now it presented its message respectfully to Wisdom. "From analysis, sir."

Wisdom tore the tape open. "Now we'll know how it thinks." His hands were shaking. "Maybe we can figure out its blind spot. It may be able to outthink us, but that doesn't mean it's invulnerable. It only predicts the future, it can't change it. If there's only death ahead, its ability won't…"

Wisdom's voice faded into silence. After a moment he passed the tape to Baines.

"I'll be down in the bar," Wisdom said. "Getting a good stiff drink." His face had turned lead-gray. "All I can say is *I hope to hell this isn't the race to come.*"

"What's the analysis?" Anita demanded impatiently, peering over Baines' shoulder. "How does it think?"

"It doesn't," Baines said as he handed the tape back to his boss. "It doesn't think at all. Virtually no frontal lobe. It's not a human being—it doesn't use symbols. It's nothing but an animal."

"An animal," Wisdom said. "With a single, highly-developed faculty. Not a superior man. Not a man at all."

Up and down the corridors of the DCA Building, guards and equipment clanged. Loads of Civil Police were pouring into the building and taking up positions beside the guards. One by one, the corridors and rooms were being inspected and sealed off. Sooner or later the golden figure of Cris Johnson would be located and cornered.

"We were always afraid a mutant with superior intellectual powers would come along," Baines said reflectively. "A deeve who would be to us what we are to the great apes. Something with a bulging cranium, telepathic ability, a perfect semantic system, ultimate powers of symbolization and calculation. A development along our own path. A better human being."

"He acts by reflex," Anita said wonderingly. She had the analysis and was sitting at one of the desks studying it intently. "Reflex like a lion. A golden lion." She pushed the tape aside, a strange expression on her face. "The lion god."

"Beast," Wisdom corrected tartly. "Blond beast, you mean."

"He runs fast," Baines said, "and that's all. No tools. He

doesn't build anything or utilize anything outside himself. He just stands and waits for the right opportunity, and then he runs like hell."

"This is worse than anything we've anticipated," Wisdom said. His beefy face was lead-gray. He sagged like an old man, his blunt hands trembling and uncertain. "To be replaced by an animal! Something that runs and hides. Something without a language!" He spat savagely. "That's why they weren't able to communicate with it. We wondered what kind of semantic system it had. It hasn't got any! No more ability to talk and think than a dog."

"That means intelligence has failed," Baines went on huskily. "We're the last of our line, like the dinosaur. We've carried intelligence as far as it'll go. Too far, maybe. We've already got to the point where we know so much—think so much—we can't act."

"Men of thought," Anita said. "Not men of action. It's begun to have a paralyzing effect. But this thing—"

"This thing's faculty works better than ours ever did. We can recall past experiences, keep them in mind, learn from them. At best, we can make shrewd guesses about the future from our memory of what's happened in the past. But we can't be certain. We have to speak of probabilities. Grays. Not blacks and whites. We're only guessing."

"Cris Johnson isn't guessing," Anita added.

"He can look ahead. See what's coming. He can—prethink. Let's call it that. He can see into the future. Probably he doesn't perceive it as the future."

"No," Anita said thoughtfully. "It would seem like the present. He has a broader present. But his present lies ahead, not back. Our present is related to the past. Only the past is certain to us. To him, the future is certain. And he probably doesn't remember the past any more than any animal remembers what happened."

"As he develops," Baines said, "as his race evolves, it'll probably expand its ability to prethink. Instead of ten minutes, thirty minutes. Then an hour. A day. A year. Eventually they'll be able to keep ahead a whole lifetime. Each one of them will live in a solid, unchanging world. There'll be no variables, no uncertainty. No motion! They won't have anything to fear. Their world will be perfectly static, a solid block of matter."

"And when death comes," Anita said, "they'll accept it. There won't be any struggle. To them, it'll already have happened."

"*Already have happened,*" Baines repeated. "To Cris our shots had already been fired." He laughed harshly. "Superior survival doesn't mean superior man. If there were another world-wide flood, only fish would survive. If there were another ice age, maybe nothing but polar bears would be left. When we opened the lock, he had already seen the men, seen exactly where they were standing and what they'd do. A neat faculty, but not a development of mind. A pure physical *sense.*"

"But if every exit is covered," Wisdom repeated, "he'll see he can't get out. He gave himself up before—he'll give himself up again." He shook his head. "An animal. Without language. Without tools."

"With his new sense," Baines said, "he doesn't need anything else." He examined his watch. "It's after two. Is the building completely sealed off?"

"You can't leave," Wisdom stated. "You'll have to stay here all night, or until we catch the bastard."

"I meant her." Baines indicated Anita. "She's supposed to be back at Semantics by seven in the morning."

Wisdom shrugged. "I have no control over her. If she wants, she can check out."

"I'll stay," Anita decided. "I want to be here when he—when he's destroyed. I'll sleep here." She hesitated. "Wisdom, isn't there some other way? If he's just an animal couldn't we—"

"A zoo?" Wisdom's voice rose in a frenzy of hysteria. "Keep it penned up in the zoo? Christ no! It's got to be killed!"

***

For a long time the great gleaming shape crouched in the darkness. He was in a storeroom. Boxes and cartons stretched out on all sides, heaped up in orderly rows, all neatly counted and marked. Silent and deserted.

But in a few moments people burst in and searched the room. He could see this. He saw them in all parts of the room, clear and distinct, men with lash-tubes, grim-faced, stalking with murder in their eyes.

The sight was one of many. One of a multitude of clearly-etched scenes lying tangent to his own. And to each was attached a further multitude of interlocking scenes that finally grew hazier and dwindled away. A progressive vagueness, each syndrome less distinct.

But the immediate one, the scene that lay closest to him, was clearly visible. He could easily make out the sight of the armed men. Therefore it was necessary to be out of the room before they appeared.

The golden figure got calmly to its feet and moved to the door. The corridor was empty; he could see himself already outside, in the vacant, drumming hall of metal and recessed lights. He pushed the door boldly open and stepped out.

A lift blinked across the hall. He walked to the lift and entered it. In five minutes a group of guards would come running along and leap into the lift. By that time he would have left it and sent it back down. Now he pressed a button and rose to the next floor.

He stepped out into a deserted passage. No one was in sight. That didn't surprise him. He couldn't be surprised. The element didn't exist for him. The positions of things, the space relationships of all matter in the immediate future, were as certain for him as his own body. The only thing that was unknown was that which had already passed out of being. In a vague, dim fashion, he had occasionally wondered where things went after he had passed them.

He came to a small supply closet. It had just been searched. It would be half an hour before anyone opened it again. He had that long; he could see that far ahead. And then—

And then he would be able to see another area, a region farther beyond. He was always moving, advancing into new regions he had never seen before. A constantly unfolding panorama of sights and scenes, frozen landscapes spread out ahead. All objects were fixed. Pieces on a vast chessboard through which he moved, arms folded, face calm. A detached observer who saw objects that lay ahead of him as clearly as those underfoot.

Right now, as he crouched in the small supply closet, he saw an unusually varied multitude of scenes for the next half hour. Much lay ahead. The half hour was divided into an incredibly complex pattern of separate configurations. He had reached a critical region; he was about to move through worlds of intricate complexity.

He concentrated on a scene ten minutes away. It showed, like a three-dimensional still, a heavy gun at the end of the corridor, trained all the way to the far end. Men moved cautiously from door to door, checking each room again as they had done repeatedly. At the end of the half hour they had reached the supply closet. A scene showed them looking inside. By that time he was gone, of course. He wasn't in that scene. He had passed on to another.

The next scene showed an exit. Guards stood in a solid line. No way out. He was in that scene. Off to one side, in a niche just inside the door. The street outside was visible, stars, lights, outlines of passing cars and people.

In the next tableau he had gone back, away from the exit. There was no way out. In another tableau he saw himself at other exits, a legion of golden figures, duplicated again and again as he explored regions ahead, one after another. But each exit was covered.

In one dim scene he saw himself lying charred and dead. He had tried to run through the line, out the exit.

But that scene was vague. One wavering, indistinct still out of many. The inflexible path along which he moved would not deviate in that direction. It would not turn him that way. The golden figure in that scene, the miniature doll in that room, was only distantly related to him. It was himself, but a far-away self. A self he would never meet. He forgot it and went on to examine the other tableau.

The myriad of tableaux that surrounded him were an elaborate maze, a web which he now considered bit by bit. He was looking down into a doll's house of infinite rooms, rooms without number, each with its furniture, its dolls, all rigid and unmoving. The same dolls and furniture were repeated in many. He, himself, appeared often. The two men on the platform. The woman. Again and again the same combinations turned up. The play was redone frequently; the same actors and props moved around in all possible ways.

Before it was time to leave the supply closet, Cris Johnson had examined each of the rooms tangent to the one he now occupied. He had consulted each, considered its contents thoroughly.

He pushed the door open and stepped calmly out into the hall. He knew exactly where he was going. And what he had to do. Crouched in the stuffy closet, he had quietly and expertly examined each miniature of himself, observed which clearly-etched configuration lay along his inflexible path, the one room of the doll house, the one set out of legions, toward which he was moving.

Anita slipped out of her metal-foil dress, hung it over a hanger, then unfastened her shoes and kicked them under the bed. She was just starting to unclip her bra when the door opened.

She gasped. Soundlessly, calmly, the great golden shape closed the door and bolted it after him.

Anita snatched up her lash-tube from the dressing table. Her hand shook; her whole body was trembling. "What do you want?" she demanded. Her fingers tightened convulsively around the tube. "I'll kill you."

The figure regarded her silently, arms folded. It was the first time she had seen Cris Johnson closely. The great dignified face, handsome and impassive. Broad shoulders. The golden mane of hair, golden skin, pelt of radiant fuzz.

"Why?" she demanded breathlessly. Her heart was pounding wildly. "What do you want?"

She could kill him easily. But the lash-tube wavered. Cris Johnson stood without fear; he wasn't at all afraid. Why not? Didn't he understand what it was? What the small metal tube could do to him?

"Of course," she said suddenly, in a choked whisper. "You can see ahead. You know I'm not going to kill you. Or you wouldn't have come here."

She flushed, terrified—and embarrassed. He knew exactly what she was going to do. He could see it as easily as she saw the walls of the room, the wall-bed with its covers folded neatly back, her clothes hanging in the closet, her purse and small things on the dressing table.

"All right." Anita backed away, then abruptly put the tube down on the dressing table. "I won't kill you. Why should I?" She fumbled in her purse and got out her cigarettes. Shakily, she lit up, her pulse racing. She was scared. And strangely fascinated. "Do you expect to stay here? It won't do any good. They've come through the dorm twice already. They'll be back."

Could he understand her? She saw nothing on his face, only blank dignity. God, he was huge! It wasn't possible he was only eighteen, a boy, a child. He looked more like some great golden god come down to Earth.

She shook the thought off savagely. He wasn't a god. He was a beast. *The blond beast,* come to take the place of man. To drive man from the earth.

Anita snatched up the lash-tube. "Get out of here! You're an animal! A big stupid animal! You can't even understand what I'm saying. You don't even have a language. You're not human."

Cris Johnson remained silent. As if he were waiting. Waiting for what? He showed no sign of fear or impatience, even though the corridor outside rang with the sound of men searching, metal against metal, guns and energy tubes being dragged around, shouts and dim rumbles as section after section of the building was searched and sealed off.

"They'll get you," Anita said. "You'll be trapped here. They'll be searching this wing any moment." She savagely stubbed out her cigarette. "For god's sake, what do you expect *me* to do?"

Cris moved toward her. Anita shrank back. His powerful hands caught hold of her, and she gasped in sudden terror. For a moment she struggled blindly, desperately.

"Let go!" She broke away and leaped back from him. His face was expressionless. Calmly, he came toward her, an impassive god advancing to take her. "Get away!" She groped for the lash-tube, trying to get up. But the tube slipped from her fingers and rolled onto the floor.

Cris bent down and picked it up. He held it out to her, in the open palm of his hand.

"Good god," Anita whispered. Shakily, she accepted the tube, gripped it hesitantly, then put it down again on the dressing table.

In the half-light of the room, the great golden figure seemed to glow and shimmer, outlined against the darkness. A god—no, not a god. An animal. A great golden beast without a soul. She was confused. Which was he—or was he both? She shook her head, bewildered. It was late, almost four. She was exhausted and confused.

Cris took her in his arms. Gently, kindly, he lifted her face and kissed her. His powerful hands held her tight. She couldn't breathe. Darkness, mixed with the shimmering golden haze, swept around her. Around and around it spiraled, carrying her senses away. She sank down into it gratefully. The darkness covered her and dissolved her in a swelling torrent of sheer force that mounted in intensity each moment, until the roar of it beat against her and at last blotted out everything.

***

Anita blinked. She sat up and automatically pushed her hair into place. Cris was standing before the closet. He was reaching up, getting something down.

He turned toward her and tossed something on the bed. Her heavy metal-foil traveling cape.

Anita gazed down at the cape without comprehension. "What do you want?"

Cris stood by the bed, waiting.

She picked up the cape uncertainly. Cold creepers of fear plucked at her. "You want me to get you out of here," she said softly. "Past the guards and the CP."

Cris said nothing.

"They'll kill you instantly." She got unsteadily to her feet. "You can't run past them. Good god, don't you do anything but run? There must be a better way. Maybe I can appeal to Wisdom. I'm Class A, Director Class. I can go directly to the Full Directorate. I ought to be able to hold them off, keep back the euth indefinitely. The odds are a billion to one against us if we try to break past—"

She broke off.

"But you don't gamble," she continued slowly. "You don't go by odds. You *know* what's coming. You've seen the cards already." She studied his face intently. "No, you can't be cold-decked. It wouldn't be possible."

For a moment she stood deep in thought. Then with a quick, decisive motion, she snatched up the cloak and slipped it around her bare shoulders. She fastened the heavy belt, bent down and got her shoes from under the bed, snatched up her purse, and hurried to the door.

"Come on," she said. She was breathing quickly, cheeks flushed. "Let's go. While there are still a number of exits to choose from. My car is parked outside, in the lot at the side of the building. We can get to my place in an hour. I have a winter home in Argentina. If worse comes to worst, we can fly there. It's in the back country, away from the cities. Jungle and swamps. Cut off from almost everything." Eagerly she started to open the door.

Cris reached out and stopped her. Gently, patiently, he moved in front of her.

He waited a long time, body rigid. Then he turned the knob and stepped boldly out into the corridor.

The corridor was empty. No one was in sight. Anita caught a faint glimpse, the back of a guard hurrying off. If they had come out a second earlier—

Cris started down the corridor. She ran after him. He moved rapidly, effortlessly. The girl had trouble keeping up with him. He seemed to know exactly where to go. Off to the right, down a side hall, a supply passage. Onto an ascent freight-lift. They rose, then abruptly halted.

Cris waited again. Presently he slid the door back and moved out of the lift. Anita followed nervously. She could hear sounds: guns and men, very close.

They were near an exit. A double line of guards stood directly ahead. Twenty men, a solid wall, and a massive heavy-duty robot gun in the center. The men were alert, faces strained and tense. Watching wide-eyed, guns gripped tight. A Civil Police officer was in charge.

"We'll never get past," Anita gasped. "We wouldn't get ten feet." She pulled back. "They'll—"

Cris took her by the arm and continued calmly forward. Blind terror leaped inside her. She fought wildly to get away, but his fingers were like steel. She couldn't pry them loose. Quietly, irresistibly, the great golden creature drew her along beside him toward the double line of guards.

"*There he is!*" Guns went up. Men leaped into action. The barrel of the robot cannon swung around. "*Get him!*"

Anita was paralyzed. She sagged against the powerful body beside her, tugged along helplessly by his inflexible grasp. The lines of guards came nearer, a sheer wall of guns. Anita fought to control her terror. She stumbled, half-fell. Cris supported her effortlessly. She scratched, fought at him, struggled to get loose—

"Don't shoot!" she screamed.

Guns wavered uncertainly. "Who is she?" The guards were moving around, trying to get a sight on Cris without including her. "Who's he got there?"

One of them saw the stripe on her sleeve. Red and black. Director Class. Top-level.

"She's Class A." Shocked, the guards retreated. "Miss, get out of the way!"

Anita found her voice. "Don't shoot. He's—in my custody. You understand? I'm taking him out."

The wall of guards moved back nervously. "No one's supposed to pass. Director Wisdom gave orders—"

"I'm not subject to Wisdom's authority." She managed to edge her voice with a harsh crispness. "Get out of the way. I'm taking him to the Semantics Agency."

For a moment nothing happened. There was no reaction. Then slowly, uncertainly, one guard stepped aside.

Cris moved. A blur of speed, away from Anita, past the confused guards, through the breach in the line, out the exit, and onto the street. Bursts of energy flashed wildly after him. Shouting guards milled out. Anita was left behind, forgotten. The guards, the heavy-duty gun, were pouring out into the early morning darkness. Sirens wailed. Patrol cars roared into life.

Anita stood dazed, confused, leaning against the wall, trying to get her breath.

He was gone. He had left her. Good god, what had she done? She shook her head, bewildered, her face buried in her hands. She had been hypnotized. She had lost her will, her common sense. Her reason! The animal, the great golden beast, had tricked her. Taken advantage of her. And now he was gone, escaped into the night.

Miserable, agonized tears trickled through her clenched fingers. She rubbed at them futilely, but they kept on coming.

***

"He's gone," Baines said. "We'll never get him now. He's probably a million miles from here."

Anita sat huddled in the corner, her face to the wall. A little bent heap, broken and wretched.

Wisdom paced back and forth. "But where can he go? Where

can he hide? Nobody'll hide him! Everybody knows the law about deeves!"

"He's lived out in the woods most of his life. He'll hunt—that's what he's always done. They wondered what he was up to, off by himself. He was catching game and sleeping under trees." Baines laughed harshly. "And the first woman he meets will be glad to hide him, as *she* was." He indicated Anita with a jerk of his thumb.

"So all that gold, that mane, that god-like stance, was *for* something. Not just ornament." Wisdom's thick lips twisted. "He doesn't have just one faculty, he has two. One is new, the newest thing in survival method. The other is old as life." He stopped pacing to glare at the huddled shape in the corner. "Plumage. Bright feathers, combs for the rooster, swans, birds, bright scales for the fish. Gleaming pelts and manes for the animals. An animal isn't necessarily *bestial*. Lions aren't bestial. Or tigers. Or any of the big cats. They're anything but bestial."

"He'll never have to worry," Baines said. "He'll get by, as long as human women exist to take care of him. And since he can see ahead, into the future, he already knows he's sexually irresistible to human females."

"We'll get him," Wisdom muttered. "I've had the Government declare an emergency. Military and Civil Police will be looking for him. Armies of men, a whole planet of experts, the most advanced machines and equipment. We'll flush him sooner or later."

"By that time it won't make any difference," Baines said. He put his hand on Anita's shoulder and patted her ironically. "You'll have company, sweetheart. You won't be the only one. You're just the first of a long procession."

"Thanks," Anita grated.

"The oldest survival method and the newest. Combined to form one perfectly adapted animal. How the hell are we going to stop him? We can put *you* through a sterilization tank, but we can't pick them all up, all the women he meets along the way. And if we miss one, we're finished."

"We'll have to keep trying," Wisdom said. "Round up as many as we can. Before they can spawn." Faint hope glinted in his tired, sagging face. "Maybe his characteristics are recessive. Maybe ours will cancel his out."

"I wouldn't lay any money on that," Baines said. "I think I know already which of the two strains is going to turn up dominant." He grinned wryly. "I mean, I'm making a good *guess*. It won't be us."

# PROMINENT AUTHOR

 Mary Ellis, "although he is a very prompt man and hasn't been late to work in twenty-five years, is actually still some place around the house." She sipped at her faintly scented hormone and carbohydrate drink. "As a matter of fact, he won't be leaving for another ten minutes."

"Incredible," said Dorothy Lawrence, who had finished *her* drink and now basked in the dermal-mist spray that descended over her virtually unclad body from an automatic jet above the couch. "What they won't think of next!"

Mrs. Ellis beamed proudly, as if she personally were an employee of Terran Development. "Yes, it is incredible. According to somebody down at the office, the whole history of civilization can be explained in terms of transportation techniques. Of course, I don't know anything about history. That's for Government research people. But from what this man told Henry—"

"Where's my briefcase?" came a fussy voice from the bedroom. "Good Lord, Mary. I know I left it on the clothes cleaner last night."

"You left it upstairs," Mary replied, raising her voice slightly. "Look in the closet."

"Why would it be in the closet?" Sounds of angry stirring around. "You'd think a man's own briefcase would be safe." Henry Ellis stuck his head into the living room briefly. "I found it. Hello, Mrs. Lawrence."

"Good morning," Dorothy Lawrence replied. "Mary was explaining that you're still here."

"Yes, I'm still here." Ellis straightened his tie as the mirror revolved slowly around him. "Anything you want me to pick up downtown, honey?"

"No," Mary replied. "Nothing I can think of. I'll vid you at the office if I remember something."

"Is it true," Mrs. Lawrence asked, "that *as soon as you step into it,* you're all the way downtown?"

"Well, almost all the way."

"A hundred and sixty miles! It's beyond belief. Why, it takes my husband two and a half hours to get his monojet through the commercial lanes and down at the parking lot, then walk all the way up to his office."

"I know," Ellis muttered, grabbing his hat and coat. "Used to take me about that long. But no more." He kissed his wife goodbye. "So long. See you tonight. Nice to have seen you again, Mrs. Lawrence."

"Can I watch?" Mrs. Lawrence asked hopefully.

"Watch? Of course, of course." Ellis hurried through the house, out the back door and down the steps into the yard. "Come along!" he shouted impatiently. "I don't want to be late. It's nine fifty-nine and I have to be at my desk by ten."

Mrs. Lawrence hurried eagerly after Ellis. In the back-yard stood a big circular hoop that gleamed brightly in the mid-morning sun. Ellis turned some controls at the base. The hoop changed color, from silver to a shimmering red.

"Here I go!" Ellis shouted. He stepped briskly into the hoop. The hoop fluttered about him. There was a faint *pop.* The glow died.

"Good Heavens!" Mrs. Lawrence gasped. "He's gone!"

"He's in downtown N'York," Mary Ellis corrected. "I wish *my* husband had a Jiffi-scuttler. When they show up on the market commercially maybe I can afford to get him one."

"Oh, they're very handy," Mary Ellis agreed. "He's probably saying hello to the boys right this minute."

Henry Ellis was in a sort of tunnel. All round him a gray, formless tube stretched out in both directions, a sort of hazy sewer pipe.

Framed in the opening behind him, he could see the faint outline of his own house. His back porch and yard, Mary standing on the steps in her red bra and slacks. Mrs. Lawrence beside her in green-checkered shorts. The cedar tree and rows of petunias. A hill. The neat little houses of Cedar Groves, Pennsylvania. And in front of him—

New York City. A wavering glimpse of the busy street corner in front of his office. The great building itself, a section of concrete and glass and steel. People moving. Skyscrapers. Mono-jets landing in swarms. Aerial signs. Endless white-collar workers hurrying everywhere, rushing to their offices.

Ellis moved leisurely toward the New York end. He had taken the Jiffi-scuttler often enough to know just exactly how many steps it was. Five steps. Five steps along the wavery gray tunnel, and he had gone a hundred and sixty miles. He halted, glancing back. So far he had gone three steps. Ninety-six miles. More than halfway.

The fourth dimension was a wonderful thing. Ellis lit his pipe, leaning his briefcase against his trouser-leg and groping in his coat pocket for his tobacco. He still had thirty seconds to get to work. Plenty of time. The pipe lighter flared, and he sucked in expertly. He snapped the lighter shut and restored it to his pocket.

A wonderful thing, all right. The Jiffi-scuttler had already revolutionized society. It was now possible to go anywhere in the world *instantly*, with no time lapse. And without wading through endless lanes of other monojets, also going places. The transportation problem had been a major head-ache since the middle of the twentieth century. Every year more families moved from the cities out into the country, adding numbers to the already swollen swarms that choked the roads and jetlanes. But it was all solved now. An *infinite* number of Jiffi-scuttlers could be set up; there was no interference between them. The Jiffi-scuttler bridged distances non-spatially, through another dimension of some kind (they hadn't explained that part too clearly to him). For a flat thousand credits any Terran family could have Jiffi-scuttler hoops set up, one in the back yard, the other in Berlin, or Bermuda, or San Francisco, or Port Said. Anywhere in the world. Of course, there was one drawback. The hoop had to be anchored in one specific spot. You picked your destination, and that was that. But for an office worker, it was perfect. Step in one end, step out the other. Five steps—a hundred and sixty miles. A hundred and sixty miles that had been a two-hour nightmare of grinding gears and sudden jolts, monojets cutting in and out, speeders, reckless flyers, alert cops waiting to pounce, ulcers and bad tempers. It was all over now. All over for him, at least, as an employee of Terran Development, the manufacturer of the Jiffi-scuttler. And soon for everybody, when they were commercially on the market.

Ellis sighed. Time for work. He could see Ed Hall racing up the steps of the TD building two at a time. Tony Franklin hurrying after him. Time to get moving. He bent down and reached for his briefcase.

It was then he saw them.

The wavery gray haze was thin there. A sort of thin spot where the shimmer wasn't so strong. Just a bit beyond his foot and past the corner of his briefcase.

Beyond the thin spot were three tiny figures. Just beyond the gray waver. Incredibly small men, no larger than insects. Watching him with incredulous astonishment.

Ellis gazed down intently, his briefcase forgotten. The three tiny men were equally dumbfounded. None of them stirred, the three tiny figures, rigid with awe. Henry Ellis bent over, his mouth open, eyes wide.

A fourth little figure joined the others. They all stood rooted to the spot, eyes bulging. They had on some kind of robes. Brown robes and sandals. Strange, un-Terran costumes. Everything about them was un-Terran. Their size, their oddly colored dark faces, their clothing, and their voices.

Suddenly the tiny figures were shouting shrilly at each other, squeaking a strange gibberish. They had broken out of their freeze and now ran about in queer, frantic circles. They raced with incredible speed, scampering like ants on a hot griddle. They raced jerkily, their arms and legs pumping wildly. And all the time they squeaked in their shrill, high-pitched voices.

Ellis found his briefcase. He picked it up slowly. The figures watched in mixed wonder and terror as the huge bag rose, only a short distance from them. An idea drifted through Ellis's brain. Good lord, could they come into the Jiffi-scuttler through the gray haze?

But he had no time to find out. He was already late as it was. He pulled away and hurried towards the New York end of the tunnel. A second later he stepped out in the blinding sunlight, abruptly finding himself on the busy street corner in front of his office.

"Hey there, Hank!" Donald Potter shouted as he raced through the doors into the TD building. "Get with it!"

"Sure, sure." Ellis followed after him automatically. Behind the entrance to the Jiffi-scuttler was a vague circle above the pavement, like the ghost of a soap bubble.

He hurried up the steps and inside the offices of Terran Development, his mind already on the hard day ahead.

As they were locking up the office and getting ready to go home, Ellis stopped coordinator Patrick Miller in his office. "Say, Mr. Miller. You're also in charge of the research end, aren't you?"

"Yeah. So?"

"Let me ask you something. Just where does the Jiffi-scuttler go? It must go somewhere."

"It goes out of this continuum completely." Miller was impatient to get home. "Into another dimension."

"I know that. But *where*?"

Miller unfolded his breast pocket handkerchief rapidly and spread it out on his desk. "Maybe I can explain it to you this way. Suppose you're a two-dimensional creature and this handkerchief represents your—"

"I've seen that a million times," Ellis said, disappointed. "That's merely an analogy, and I'm not interested in an analogy. I want a factual answer. Where does my Jiffi-scuttler go, between here and Cedar Groves?"

Miller laughed. "What the hell do you care?"

Ellis became abruptly guarded. He shrugged indifferently. "Just curious. It certainly must go *someplace*."

Miller put his hand on Ellis's shoulder in a friendly big-brother fashion. "Henry, old man, you just leave that up to us. Okay? We're the designers, you're the consumer. Your job is to use the 'scuttler, try it out for us, report any defects or failure so when we put it on the market next year, we'll be sure there's nothing wrong with it."

"As a matter of fact—" Ellis began.

"What is it?"

Ellis clamped his sentence off. "Nothing." He picked up his briefcase. "Nothing at all. I'll see you tomorrow. Thanks, Mr. Miller. Goodnight."

He hurried downstairs and out of the TD building. The faint outline of his Jiffi-scuttler was visible in the fading late-afternoon sunlight. The sky was already full of monojets taking off. Weary workers beginning their long trip back to their homes in the country. The endless commute. Ellis made his way to the hoop and stepped into it. Abruptly the bright sunlight dimmed and faded.

Again he was in the wavery gray tunnel. At the far end flashed a circle of green and white. Rolling green hills and his own house. His backyard. The cedar tree and flower beds. The town of Cedar Groves.

Two steps down the tunnel. Ellis halted, bending over. He studied the floor of the tunnel intently. He studied the misty gray wall, where it rose and flickered—and the thin place. The place he had noticed.

They were still there. *Still?* It was a different bunch. This time ten or eleven of them. Men and women and children. Standing together, gazing up at him with awe and wonder. No more than a half-inch high each. Tiny, distorted figures, shifting and changing shape oddly. Altering colors and hues.

Ellis hurried on. The tiny figures watched him go. A brief glimpse of their microscopic astonishment and then he was stepping out into his backyard.

He clicked off the Jiffi-scuttler and mounted the back steps. He entered his house, deep in thought.

"Hi," Mary cried, from the kitchen. She rustled towards him in her hip-length mesh shirt, her arms out. "How was work today?"

"Fine."

"Is anything wrong? You look strange."

"No. No, nothing's wrong." Ellis kissed his wife absently on the forehead. "What's for dinner?"

"Something choice. Siriusian mole steak. One of your favorites. Is that all right?"

"Sure." Ellis tossed his hat and coat down on the chair. The chair folded them up and put them away. His thoughtful, preoccupied look still remained. "Fine, honey."

"Are you *sure* there's nothing wrong? You didn't get into another argument with Pete Taylor, did you?"

"No. Of course not." Ellis shook his head in annoyance. "Everything's all right, honey. Stop needling me."

"Well, I *hope* so," Mary said, with a sigh.

The next morning they were waiting for him.

He saw them the first step into the Jiffi-scuttler. A small group waiting within the wavering gray, like bugs caught in a block of jello. They moved jerkily, rapidly, arms and legs pumping in a blur of motion. Trying to attract his attention. Piping wildly in their pathetically faint voices.

Ellis stopped and squatted down. They were putting something through the wall of the tunnel, through the thin place in the gray. It was small, so incredibly small he could scarcely see it. A square of white at the end of a microscopic pole. They were watching him eagerly, faces alive with fear and hope. Desperate, pleading hope.

Ellis took the tiny square. It came loose like some fragile rose petal from its stalk. Clumsily, he let it drop and had to hunt all round for it. The little figures watched in an agony of dismay as his huge hands moved blindly around the floor of the tunnel. At last he found it and gingerly lifted it up.

It was too small to make out. *Writing?* Some tiny lines—but he couldn't read them. Much too small to read. He got out his wallet and carefully placed the square between the two cards. He restored his wallet to his pocket.

"I'll look at it later," he said.

His voice boomed and echoed up and down the tunnel. At the sound the tiny creatures scattered. They all fled, shrieking in their shrill, piping voices, away from the gray shimmer into the dimness beyond. In a flash they were gone. Like startled mice. He was alone. Ellis knelt down and put his eye against the gray shimmer where it was thin. Where they had stood waiting. He could see something dim and distorted, lost in a vague haze. A landscape of some sort. Indistinct. Hard to make out.

Hills. Trees and crops. But so tiny. And dim...

He glanced at his watch. God, it was ten! Hastily he scrambled to his feet and hurried out of the tunnel onto the blazing New York pavement.

*Late.* He raced up the stairs of the Terran Development building and down the long corridor to his office.

At lunchtime he stopped in at the Research Labs. "Hey," he called as Jim Andrews brushed past, loaded down with reports and equipment. "Got a second?"

"What do you want, Henry?"

"I'd like to borrow something. A magnifying glass." He considered. "Maybe a photon-microscope would be better. One- or two-hundred power."

"Kids' stuff." Jim found him a small microscope. "Slides?"

"Yeah, a couple of blank slides."

He carried the microscope back to his office. He set it up on his desk, clearing away his paper. As a precaution he sent Miss Nelson, his secretary, out of the room and off to lunch. Then carefully, cautiously, he got the tiny wisp from his wallet and slipped it between two slides.

It was writing, all right. But nothing he could read. Utterly unfamiliar. Complex, interlaced little characters.

For a time he sat thinking. Then he dialed his inter-department vidphone. "Give me the Linguistics Department."

After a moment Earl Peterson's good-natured face appeared. "Hi, there, Ellis. What can I do for you?"

Ellis hesitated. He had to do this right. "Say Earl, old man. Got a little favor to ask you."

"Like what? Anything to oblige an old pal."

"You—uh—you have that Machine down there, don't you? That translating business you use for working over documents from non-Terran cultures?"

"Sure. So?"

"Think I could use it?" He talked fast. "It's a screwy sort of a deal, Earl. I got this pal living on—uh—Centaurus VI, and he writes me in—uh—you know, the Centauran native semantic system, and I—"

"You want the Machine to translate a letter? Sure, I think we could manage it. This once, at least. Bring it down."

He brought it down. He got Earl to show him how the intake feed worked, and as soon as Earl had turned his back, he fed in the tiny square of material. The Linguistics Machine clicked and whirred. Ellis prayed silently that the paper wasn't too small. Wouldn't fall out between the relay-probes of the Machine.

But sure enough, after a couple of seconds, a tape unreeled from the output slot. The tape cut itself off and dropped into a basket. The Linguistics Machine turned promptly to other stuff, more vital material from TD's various export branches.

With trembling fingers Ellis spread out the tape. The words danced before his eyes.

Questions. They were asking him questions. God, it was getting complicated. He read the questions intently, his lips moving. What was he getting himself into? They were expecting answers. He had taken their paper, gone off with it. Probably they would be waiting for him on his way home.

He returned to his office and dialed his vidphone. "Give me outside," he ordered.

The regular vid monitor appeared. "Yes, sir?"

"I want the Federal Library of Information," Ellis said. "Cultural Research Division."

That night they were waiting, all right. But not the same ones. It was odd, each time a different group. Their clothing was slightly different too. A new hue. And in the background the landscape had also altered slightly. The trees he had seen were gone. The hills were still there, but a different shade. A hazy gray-white. Snow?

He squatted down. He had worked it out with care. The answers from the Federal Library of Information had gone back to the Linguistics Machine for retranslation. The answers were now in the original tongue of the questions, but on a trifle larger piece of paper.

Ellis made like a marble game and flicked the wad of paper through the gray shimmer. It bowled over six or seven of the watching figures and rolled down the side of the hill on which they were standing. After a moment of terrified immobility, the figures scampered frantically after it. They disappeared into the vague and invisible depths of their world, and Ellis got stiffly to his feet again.

"Well," he muttered to himself, "that's that."

But it wasn't. The next morning there was a new group, and a new list of questions. The tiny figures pushed their microscopic square of paper through the thin spot in the wall of the tunnel and stood waiting and trembling as Ellis bent over and felt around for it.

He found it, finally. He put it in his wallet and continued on his way, stepping out at New York, frowning. This was getting serious. Was this going to be a full-time job?

But then he grinned. It was the damn oddest thing he had ever heard of. The little rascals were cute, in their own way. Tiny intent faces screwed up with serious concern. And terror. They were scared of him, really scared. And why not? Compared to them he was a giant.

He conjectured about their world. What kind of planet was theirs? Odd to be so small. But size was a relative matter. Small though, compared to him. Small and reverent. He could read fear and yearning, gnawing hope, as they pushed up their papers. They were depending on him. Praying he'd give them answers.

Ellis grinned. "Damn unusual job," he said to himself.

"What's this?" Peterson said, when he showed up in the Linguistics Lab at noontime.

"Well you see, I got another letter from my friend on Centaurus VI."

"Yeah?" A certain suspicion flickered across Peterson's face. "You're not ribbing me, are you, Henry? This Machine has a lot to do, you know. Stuff's coming in all the time. We can't afford to waste any time with—"

"This is really serious stuff, Earl." Ellis patted his wallet. "Very important business. Not just gossip."

"Okay. If you say so." Peterson gave the nod to the team operating the Machine. "Let this guy use the Translator, Tommie."

"Thanks," Ellis murmured.

He went through the routine, getting a translation and then carrying the questions up to his vidphone and passing them over to the Library research staff. By nightfall the answers were back in the original tongue and with them carefully in his wallet, Ellis headed out of the Terran Development building and into his Jiffi-scuttler.

As usual, a new group was waiting.

"Here you go, boys," Ellis boomed, flicking the wad through the thin place in the shimmer. The wad rolled down the microscopic countryside, bouncing from hill to hill, the little people tumbling jerkily after it in their funny stiff-legged fashion. Ellis watched them go, grinning with interest—and pride.

They really hurried, no doubt about that. He could make them out only vaguely now. They had raced wildly off away from the shimmer. Only a small portion of their world was tangent to the Jiffi-scuttler apparently. Only the one spot where the shimmer was thin. He peered intently through.

They were getting the wad open now. Three or four of them, unprying the paper and examining the answers.

Ellis swelled with pride as he continued along the tunnel and out into his own backyard. He couldn't read their questions, and when translated, he couldn't answer them. The Linguistics Department did the first part, the Library research staff the rest. Nevertheless, Ellis felt pride. A deep, glowing spot of warmth far down inside him. The expression on their faces. The look they gave him when they saw the answer-wad in his hand. When they realized he was going to answer their questions. And the way they scampered after it. It was sort of satisfying. It made him feel damn good.

"Not bad," he murmured, opening the back door and entering the house. "Not bad at all."

"What's not bad, dear?" Mary asked, looking quickly up from the table. She laid down her magazine and got to her feet. "Why, you look so *happy*! What is it?"

"Nothing. Nothing at all!" He kissed her warmly on the mouth. "You're looking pretty good tonight yourself, kid."

"Oh, Henry!" Much of Mary blushed prettily. "How sweet."

He surveyed his wife in her two-piece wraparound of clear plastic with appreciation. "Nice looking fragments you have on."

"Why Henry! What's come over you? You seem so—so *spirited*?"

Ellis grinned. "Oh, I guess I enjoy my job. You know, there's nothing like taking pride in your work. A job well done, as they say. Work you can be proud of."

"I thought you always said you were nothing but a cog in a great impersonal machine. Just a sort of cipher."

"Things are different," Ellis said firmly. "I'm doing a—uh—a new project. A new assignment."

"A new assignment?"

"Gathering information. A sort of creative business, so to speak."

By the end of the week he had turned over quite a body of information to them.

He began starting for work about nine thirty. That gave him a whole thirty minutes to spend squatting down on his hands and knees, peering through the thin place in the shimmer. He got so he was pretty good at seeing them and what they were doing in their microscopic world.

Their civilization was somewhat primitive. No doubt of that. By Terran standards it was scarcely a civilization at all. As near as he could tell, they were virtually without scientific techniques—a kind of agrarian culture, rural communism, a monolithic tribal-based organization apparently without too many members.

At least, not at one time. That was the part he didn't understand. Every time he came past there was a different group of them. No familiar faces. And their world changed too. The trees, the crops, fauna. The weather, apparently.

Was their time-rate different? They moved rapidly, jerkily. Like a vidtape speeded up. And their shrill voices. Maybe that was it. A totally different universe in which the whole time structure was radically different.

As to their attitude towards him, there was no mistaking it. After the first couple of times they began assembling offerings, unbelievably small bits of smoking food, prepared in ovens and on open brick hearths. If he got down with his nose against the gray shimmer, he could get a faint whiff of the food. It smelled good. Strong and pungent. Highly spiced. Meat, probably.

On Friday he brought a magnifying glass along and watched them through it. It was meat, all right. They were bringing ant-sized animals to be killed and cooked, leading them up to the ovens. With the magnifying glass he could see more of their faces. They had strange faces. Strong and dark, with a peculiar firm look.

Of course, there was only one look *he* got from them. A combination of fear, reverence, and hope. The look made him feel good. It was a look for him only. Between themselves they shouted and argued, and sometimes stabbed and fought each other furiously, rolling in their brown robes in a wild tangle. They were a passionate and strong species. He got so he admired them.

Which was good because it made him feel better. To have the reverent awe of such a proud, sturdy face was really something. There was nothing craven about them.

About the fifth time he came there was a rather attractive structure built. Some kind of temple. A place of religious worship.

To him! They were developing a real religion about him. No doubt of it. He began going to work at nine o'clock to give himself a full hour with them. They had, by the middle of the second week, a full-sized ritual evolved. Processions, lighted tapers, what seemed to be songs or chants. Priests in long robes. And the spiced offerings.

No idols though. Apparently he was so big they couldn't make out his appearance. He tried to imagine what it looked like to be on their side of the shimmer. An immense shape looming up above them beyond a wall of gray haze. An indistinct being, something like themselves, yet not like them at all. A different kind of being, obviously. Larger but different in other ways. And when he spoke—booming echoes up and down the Jiffi-scuttler. Which still sent them fleeing in panic.

An evolving religion. He was changing them. Through his actual presence and through his answers, the precise, correct responses he obtained from the Federal Library of Information and had the Linguistics Machine translate into their language. Of course, by *their* time-rate they had to wait generations for the answers. But they had become accustomed to it by now. They waited. They expected. They passed up questions, and after a couple of centuries he passed down answers, answers which they no doubt put to good use.

"What in the world?" Mary demanded as he got home from work an hour late one night. "Where have you been?"

"Working," Ellis said carelessly, removing his hat and coat. He threw himself on the couch. "I'm tired. Really tired." He sighed with relief and motioned for the couch-arm to bring him a whiskey sour.

Mary came over by the couch. "Henry, I'm a little worried."
"Worried?"

"You shouldn't work so hard. You ought to take it easy more. How long since you've had a real vacation? A trip off Terra. Out of the System. You know, I'd just like to call that fellow Miller and ask him why it's necessary for a man your age to put in so much—"

"A man my age!" Ellis bristled indignantly. "I'm not so old."

"Of course not." Mary sat down beside him and put her arms around him affectionately. "But you shouldn't have to do so much. You deserve a rest. Don't you think?"

"This is different. You don't understand. This isn't the same old stuff. Reports and statistics and the damn filing. This is—"
"What is it?"

"This is *different*. I'm not a cog. This gives me something. I can't explain it to you I guess. But it's something I have to do."

"If you could tell me more about it—"

"I can't tell you any more about it," Ellis said. "But there's nothing in the world like it. I've worked twenty-five years for Terran Development. Twenty-five years at the same reports, again and again. Twenty-five years—and I never felt this way."

***

"Oh, yeah?" Miller roared. "Don't give me that! Come clean, Ellis!"

Ellis opened and closed his mouth. "What are you talking about?" Horror rolled through him. "What's happened?"

"Don't try to give *me* the runaround." On the vidscreen Miller's face was purple. "Come into my office."

The screen went dead.

Ellis sat stunned at his desk. Gradually, he collected himself and got shakily to his feet. "Good lord." Weakly, he wiped cold sweat from his forehead. All at once. Everything in ruins. He was dazed with the shock.

"Anything wrong?" Miss Nelson asked sympathetically.

"No." Ellis moved numbly towards the door. He was shattered. What had Miller found out? Good god! Was it possible he had—

"Mr. Miller looked angry."

"Yeah." Ellis moved blindly down the hall, his mind reeling. Miller looked angry all right. Somehow he had found out. But why was he mad? Why did he care? A cold chill settled over Ellis. It looked bad. Miller was his superior, with hiring and firing powers. Maybe he'd done something wrong. Maybe he had somehow broken a law. Committed a crime. But what?

What did Miller care about *them*! What concern was it of Terran Development?

He opened the door to Miller's office. "Here I am, Mr. Miller," he muttered. "What's the trouble?"

Miller glowered at him with rage. "All this goofy stuff about your cousin on Proxima."

"It's—uh—you mean a business friend on Centaurus VI."

"You—you swindler!" Miller leaped up. "And after all the Company's done for you."

"I don't understand," Ellis muttered. "What have—"

"Why do you think we gave you the Jiffi-scuttler in the first place?"

"Why?"

"To *test*! To try out, you wall-eyed Venusian stink-cricket! The Company magnanimously consented to allow you to operate a Jiffi-scuttler in advance of market presentation. And what do you do? Why, you—"

Ellis started to get indignant. After all, he had been with TD twenty-five years. "You don't have to be so offensive. I plunked down my thousand gold credits for it."

"Well, you can just mosey down to the accountant's office and get your money back. I've already sent out a directive for a construction team to crate up your Jiffi-scuttler and bring it back to receiving."

Ellis was dumbfounded. "But *why*?"

"Why indeed! Because it's defective. Because it doesn't work. That's why." Miller's eyes blazed with technological outrage. "The inspection crew found a leak a mile wide in it." His lip curled. "As if you didn't know."

Ellis's heart sank. "Leak?" he croaked apprehensively.

"Leak. It's a damn good thing I authorized a periodic inspection. If we depended on people like you to—"

"Are you *sure*? It seemed all right to me. That is, it got me here without any trouble," Ellis floundered. "Certainly no complaints from my end."

"No. No complaints from your end. That's exactly why you're not getting another one. That's why you're taking the monojet transport back home tonight. Because you didn't report the leak! And if you ever try to put something over on this office again—"

"How do you know I was aware of the defect?"

Miller sank down in his chair, overcome with fury. "Because," he said carefully, "of your daily pilgrimage to the Linguistic Machine. With your alleged letter from your grandmother on Betelgeuse II. Which wasn't any such thing. Which was an utter fraud. Which you got through the leak in the Jiffi-scuttler!"

"How do you know?" Ellis squeaked boldly, driven to the

wall. "So maybe there was a defect. But you can't prove there's any connection between your badly constructed Jiffi-scuttler and my—"

"Your missive," Miller stated, "which you foisted on our Linguistics Machine, was not a non-Terran script. It was not from Centaurus VI. It was not from any non-Terran system. It was ancient Hebrew. And there's only one place you could have got it, Ellis. So don't try to kid me."

"Hebrew!" Ellis exclaimed, startled. He turned white as a sheet. "Good lord. The other continuum—the fourth dimension. Time, of course." He trembled. "And the expanding universe. That would explain their size. And it explains why a new group, a new generation—"

"We're taking enough of a chance as it is, with these Jiffi-scuttlers. Warping a tunnel through other space-time continua." Miller shook his head warily. "You meddler. You *knew* you were supposed to report any defect."

"I don't think I did any harm, did I?" Ellis was suddenly terribly nervous. "They seemed pleased, even grateful. Gosh, I'm sure I didn't cause any trouble."

Miller shrieked in insane rage. For a time he danced around the room. Finally he threw something down on his desk, directly in front of Ellis. "No trouble. No, none. *Look* at this. I got this from the Ancient Artifacts Archives."

"What is it?"

"Look at it! I compared one of your question sheets to this. The same. *Exactly* the same. All your sheets, questions and answers, every one of them's in here. You multi-legged Ganymedean mange beetle!"

Ellis picked up the book and opened it. As he read the pages a strange look came slowly over his face. "Good heavens. So they kept a record of what I gave them. They put it all together in a book. Every word of it. And some commentaries too. It's all here, every single word. It *did* have an effect then. They passed it on. Wrote all of it down."

"Go back to your office. I'm through looking at you for today. I'm through looking at you forever. Your severance check will come through regular channels."

In a trance, his face flushed with a strange excitement, Ellis gripped the book and moved dazedly towards the door. "Say, Mr. Miller. Can I have this? Can I take it along?"

"Sure," Miller said wearily. "Sure, you can take it. You can read it on your way home tonight. On the public monojet transport."

***

"Henry has something to show you," Mary Ellis whispered excitedly, gripping Mrs. Lawrence's arm. "Make sure you say the right thing."

"The right thing?" Mrs. Lawrence faltered nervously, a trifle uneasy. "What is it? Nothing alive, I hope."

"No, no." Mary pushed her towards the study door. "Just smile." She raised her voice. "Henry, Dorothy Lawrence is here."

Henry Ellis appeared at the door of his study. He bowed slightly, a dignified figure in silk dressing gown, pipe in his mouth, fountain pen in one hand. "Good evening, Dorothy," he said in a low, well-modulated voice. "Care to step into my study a moment?"

"Study?" Mrs. Lawrence came hesitantly in. "What do you study? I mean, Mary says you've been doing something very interesting recently, now that you're not with—I mean, now that you're home more. She didn't give me any idea what it was though."

Mrs. Lawrence's eyes roved curiously around the study. The study was full of reference volumes, charts, a huge mahogany desk, an atlas, globe, leather chairs, an unbelievably ancient electric typewriter.

"Good heavens!" she exclaimed. "How odd. All these old things."

Ellis lifted something carefully from the bookcase and held it out to her casually. "By the way, you might glance at this."

"What is it? A book?" Mrs. Lawrence took the book and examined it eagerly. "My goodness. Heavy, isn't it?" She read the back, her lips moving. "What does it mean? It looks old. What strange letters! I've never seen anything like it. *Holy Bible.*" She glanced up brightly. "What is this?"

Ellis smiled faintly. "Well—"

A light dawned. Mrs. Lawrence gasped in revelation. "Good Heavens! You didn't *write* this, did you?"

Ellis's smile broadened into a deprecating blush. A dignified hue of modesty. "Just a little thing I threw together," he murmured indifferently. "My first, as a matter of fact." Thoughtfully, he fingered his fountain pen. "And now, if you'll excuse me, I really should be getting back to my work…"

# ADJUSTMENT TEAM

**IT WAS BRIGHT** morning. The sun shone down on the damp lawns and sidewalks, reflecting off the sparkling parked cars. The Clerk came walking hurriedly, leafing through his instructions, flipping pages and frowning. He stopped in front of the small green stucco house for a moment, and then turned up the walk, entering the back yard.

The dog was asleep inside his shed, his back turned to the world. Only his thick tail showed.

"For heaven's sake," the Clerk exclaimed, hands on his hips. He tapped his mechanical pencil noisily against his clipboard. "Wake up, you in there."

The dog stirred. He came slowly out of his shed, head first, blinking and yawning in the morning sunlight. "Oh, it's you. Already?" He yawned again.

"Big doings." The Clerk ran his expert finger down the traffic-control sheet. "They're adjusting Sector T137 this morning. Starting at exactly nine o'clock." He glanced at his pocket watch. "Three-hour alteration. Will finish by noon."

"T137? That's not far from here."

The Clerk's thin lips twisted with contempt. "Indeed. You're showing astonishing perspicacity, my black-haired friend. Maybe you can divine why I'm here."

"We overlap with T137."

"Exactly. Elements from this Sector are involved. We must make sure they're properly placed when the adjustment begins." The Clerk glanced toward the small green stucco house. "Your particular task concerns the man in there. He is employed by a business establishment lying within Sector T137. It's essential that he be there before nine o'clock."

The dog studied the house. The shades had been let up. The kitchen light was on. Beyond the lace curtains dim shapes could be seen, stirring around the table. A man and woman. They were drinking coffee.

"There they are," the dog murmured. "The man, you say? He's not going to be harmed, is he?"

"Of course not. But he must be at his office early. Usually he doesn't leave until after nine. Today he must leave at eight thirty. He must be within Sector T137 before the process begins, or he won't be altered to coincide with the new adjustment."

The dog sighed. "That means I have to summon."

"Correct." The Clerk checked his instruction sheet. "You're to summon at precisely eight fifteen. You've got that? Eight fifteen. No later."

"What will the eight-fifteen summons bring?"

The Clerk flipped open his instruction book, examining the code columns. "It will bring A Friend with a Car. To drive him to work early." He closed the book and folded his arms, preparing to wait. "That way he'll get to his office almost an hour ahead of time. Which is vital."

"Vital," the dog murmured. He lay down, half inside his shed. His eyes closed. "Vital."

"Wake up! This must be done exactly on time. If you summon too soon or too late—"

The dog nodded sleepily. "I know. I'll do it right. I *always* do it right."

Ed Fletcher poured more cream in his coffee. He sighed, leaning back in his chair. Behind him the oven hissed softly, filling the kitchen with warm fumes. The yellow overhead light beamed down.

"Another roll?" Ruth asked.

"I'm full." Ed sipped his coffee. "You can have it."

"Have to go." Ruth got to her feet, unfastening her robe. Time to go to work."

"Already?"

"Sure. You lucky bum! Wish I could sit around." Ruth moved toward the bathroom, running her fingers through her long, black hair. "When you work for the Government, you start early."

"But you get off early," Ed pointed out. He unfolded the *Chronicle*, examining the sporting green. "Well, have a good time today. Don't type any wrong words, any double entendres."

The bathroom door closed as Ruth shed her robe and began dressing.

Ed yawned and glanced up at the clock over the sink. Plenty of time. Not even eight. He sipped more coffee and then rubbed his stubbled chin. He would have to shave. He shrugged lazily. Ten minutes maybe.

Ruth came bustling out in her nylon slip, hurrying into the bedroom. "I'm late." She rushed rapidly around, getting into her blouse and skirt, her stockings, her little white shoes. Finally she bent over and kissed him. "Goodbye, honey. I'll do the shopping tonight."

"Goodbye." Ed lowered his newspaper and put his arm around his wife's trim waist, hugging her affectionately. "You smell nice. Don't flirt with the boss."

Ruth ran out the front door, clattering down the steps. He heard the click of her heels diminish down the sidewalk.

She was gone. The house was silent. He was alone.

Ed got to his feet, pushing his chair back. He wandered lazily into the bathroom and got his razor down. Eight ten. He washed his face, rubbing it down with shaving cream, and began to shave. He shaved leisurely. He had plenty of time.

The Clerk bent over his round pocket watch, licking his lips nervously. Sweat stood out on his forehead. The second hand ticked on. Eight fourteen. Almost time.

"Get ready!" the Clerk snapped. He tensed, his small body rigid. "Ten seconds to go!"

"*Time!*" the Clerk cried out.

Nothing happened.

The Clerk turned, eyes wide with horror. From the little shed a thick black tail showed. The dog had gone back to sleep.

"TIME!" the Clerk shrieked. He kicked wildly at the furry rump. "In the name of god—"

The dog stirred. He thumped around hastily, backing out of the shed. "My goodness." Embarrassed, he made his way quickly to the fence. Standing up on his hind paws, he opened his mouth wide. "Woof!" he summoned. He glanced apologetically at the Clerk. "I beg your pardon. I can't understand how—"

The Clerk gazed fixedly down at his watch. Cold terror knotted his stomach. The hands showed eight sixteen. "You failed," he grated. "You failed! You miserable flea-bitten ragbag of a worn-out old mutt! You failed!"

The dog dropped and came anxiously back. "I failed, you say? You mean the summons time was—?"

"You summoned too late." The Clerk put his watch away slowly, a glazed expression on his face. "You summoned too late. We won't get A Friend with a Car. There's no telling what will come instead. I'm afraid to see what eight sixteen brings."

"I hope he'll be in Sector T137 in time."

"He won't," the Clerk wailed. "He won't be there. We've made a mistake. We've made things go wrong!"

Ed was rinsing the shaving cream from his face when the muffled sound of the dog's bark echoed through the silent house.

"Damn," Ed muttered. "Wake up the whole block." He dried his face, listening. Was somebody coming?

A vibration. Then—

The doorbell rang.

Ed came out of the bathroom. Who could it be? Had Ruth forgotten something? He tossed on a white shirt and opened the front door.

A bright young man, face bland and eager, beamed happily at him. "Good morning, sir." He tipped his hat. "I'm sorry to bother you so early—"

"What do you want?"

"I'm from the Federal Life Insurance Company. I'm here to see you about—"

Ed pushed the door closed. "Don't want any. I'm in a rush. Have to get to work."

"Your wife said this was the only time I could catch you." The young man picked up his briefcase, easing the door open again. "She especially asked me to come this early. We don't usually begin our work at this time, but since she asked me, I made a special note about it."

"Okay." Sighing wearily, Ed admitted the young man. "You can explain your policy while I get dressed."

The young man opened his briefcase on the couch, laying out heaps of pamphlets and illustrated folders. "I'd like to show you some of these figures, if I may. It's of great importance to you and your family to—"

Ed found himself sitting down, going over the pamphlets. He purchased a ten-thousand-dollar policy on his own life and then eased the young man out. He looked at the clock. Practically nine thirty!

"Damn." He'd be late to work. He finished fastening his tie, grabbed his coat, turned off the oven and the lights, dumped the dishes in the sink, and ran out on the porch.

As he hurried toward the bus stop he was cursing inwardly. Life insurance salesmen. Why did the jerk have to come just as he was getting ready to leave?

Ed groaned. No telling what the consequences would be, getting to the office late. He wouldn't get there until almost ten. He set himself in anticipation. A sixth sense told him he was in for it. Something bad. It was the wrong day to be late.

If only the salesman hadn't come.

Ed hopped off the bus a block from his office. He began walking rapidly. The huge clock in front of Stein's Jewelry Store told him it was almost ten.

His heart sank. Old Douglas would give him hell for sure. He could see it now. Douglas puffing and blowing, red-faced, waving his thick finger at him; Miss Evans, smiling behind her typewriter; Jackie, the office boy, grinning and snickering; Earl Hendricks; Joe and Tom; Mary, dark-eyed, full bosom and long lashes. All of them, kidding him the whole rest of the day.

He came to the corner and stopped for the light. On the other side of the street rose a big white concrete building, the towering column of steel and cement, girders and glass windows—the office building. Ed flinched. Maybe he could say the elevator got stuck. Somewhere between the second and third floor.

The streetlight changed. Nobody else was crossing. Ed crossed alone. He hopped up on the curb on the far side—

And stopped, rigid.

The sun had winked off. One moment it was beaming down. Then it was gone. Ed looked up sharply. Gray clouds swirled above him. Huge, formless clouds. Nothing more. An ominous, thick haze that made everything waver and dim. Uneasy chills plucked at him. *What was it?*

He advanced cautiously, feeling his way through the mist. Everything was silent. No sounds, not even the traffic sounds. Ed peered frantically around, trying to see through the rolling haze. No people. No cars. No sun. Nothing.

The office building loomed up ahead, ghostly. It was an indistinct gray. He put out his hand uncertainly—

A section of the building fell away. It rained down, a torrent of particles. Like sand. Ed gaped foolishly. A cascade of gray debris spilling around his feet. And where he had touched the building, a jagged cavity yawned—an ugly pit marring the concrete.

Dazed, he made his way to the front steps. He mounted them. The steps gave way underfoot. His feet sank down. He was wading through shifting sand, weak, rotted stuff that broke under his weight.

He got into the lobby. The lobby was dim and obscure. The overhead lights flickered feebly in the gloom. An unearthly pall hung over everything.

He spied the cigar stand. The seller leaned silently, resting on the counter, toothpick between his teeth, his face vacant. *And gray.* He was gray all over.

"Hey," Ed croaked. "What's going on?"

The seller did not answer. Ed reached out toward him. His hand touched the seller's gray arm—and passed right through.

"Good god," Ed said.

The seller's arm came loose. It fell to the lobby floor, disintegrating into fragments. Bits of gray fiber. Like dust. Ed's senses reeled.

"Help!" he shouted, finding his voice.

No answer. He peered around. A few shapes stood here and there—a man reading a newspaper, two women waiting at the elevator.

Ed made his way over to the man. He reached out and touched him.

The man slowly collapsed. He settled into a heap, a loose pile of gray ash. Dust. Particles. The two women dissolved when he touched them. Silently. They made no sound as they broke apart.

Ed found the stairs. He grabbed hold of the banister and climbed. The stairs collapsed under him. He hurried faster.

Behind him lay a broken path, his footprints clearly visible in the concrete. Clouds of ash blew around him as he reached the second floor.

He gazed down the silent corridor. He saw more clouds of ash. He heard no sound. There was just darkness, rolling darkness.

He climbed unsteadily to the third floor. Once, his shoe broke completely through the stair. For a sickening second he hung, poised over a yawning hole that looked down into a bottomless nothing.

Then he climbed on and emerged in front of his own office:

DOUGLAS AND BLAKE, REAL ESTATE.

The hall was dim, gloomy with clouds of ash. The overhead lights flickered fitfully. He reached for the door handle. The handle came off in his hand. He dropped it and dug his fingernails into the door. The plate glass crashed past him, breaking into bits. He tore the door open and stepped over it, into the office.

Miss Evans sat at her typewriter, fingers resting quietly on the keys. She did not move. She was gray, her hair, her skin, her clothing. She was without color. Ed touched her. His fingers went through her shoulder into dry flakiness.

He drew back, sickened. Miss Evans did not stir.

He moved on. He pushed against a desk. The desk collapsed into rotting dust. Earl Hendricks stood by the water cooler, a cup in his hand. He was a gray statue, unmoving. Nothing stirred. No sound. No life. The whole office was gray dust, without life or motion.

Ed found himself out in the corridor again. He shook his head, dazed. What did it mean? Was he going out of his mind? Was he—?

A sound.

Ed turned, peering into the gray mist. A creature was coming, hurrying rapidly. A man—a man in a white robe. Behind him others came. Men in white, with equipment. They were lugging complex machinery.

"Hey—" Ed gasped weakly.

The men stopped. Their mouths opened. Their eyes popped.

"Look!"

"Something's gone wrong!"

"One still charged."

"Get the de-energizer."

"We can't proceed until—"

The men came toward Ed, moving around him. One lugged a long hose with some sort of nozzle. A portable cart came wheeling up. Instructions were rapidly shouted.

Ed broke out of his paralysis. Fear swept over him. Panic. Something hideous was happening. He had to get out. Warn people. Get away.

He turned and ran back down the stairs. The stairs collapsed under him. He fell half a flight, rolling in heaps of dry ash. He got to his feet and hurried on, down to the ground floor.

The lobby was lost in the clouds of gray ash. He pushed blindly through, toward the door. Behind him the white-clad men were coming, dragging their equipment and shouting to each other, hurrying quickly after him.

He reached the sidewalk. Behind him the office building wavered and sagged, sinking to one side, torrents of ash raining down in heaps. He raced toward the corner, the men just behind him. Gray cloud swirled around him. He groped his way across the street, hands outstretched. He gained the opposite curb—

The sun winked on. Warm yellow sunlight streamed down on him. Cars honked. Traffic lights changed. On all sides men and women in bright spring clothes hurried and pushed: shoppers, a blue-clad cop, salesmen with briefcases. Stores, windows, signs...noisy cars moving up and down the street...

And overhead was the bright sun and familiar blue sky.

Ed halted, gasping for breath. He turned and looked back the way he had come. Across the street was the office building, as it had always been. Firm and distinct. Concrete and glass and steel.

He stepped back a pace and collided with a hurrying citizen. "Hey," the man grunted. "Watch it."

"Sorry." Ed shook his head, trying to clear it. From where he stood, the office building looked like always, big and solemn and substantial, rising up imposingly on the other side of the street.

But a minute ago—

Maybe he was out of his mind. He had seen the building crumbling into dust. Building and people. They had fallen into gray clouds of dust. And the men in white—they had chased him. Men in white robes, shouting orders, wheeling complex equipment.

He was out of his mind. There was no other explanation. Weakly, Ed turned and stumbled along the sidewalk, his mind reeling. He moved blindly, without purpose, lost in a haze of confusion and terror.

***

The Clerk was brought into the top-level Administrative chambers and told to wait.

He paced back and forth nervously, clasping and wringing his hands in an agony of apprehension. He took off his glasses and wiped them shakily.

Lord. All the trouble and grief. And it wasn't his fault. But he would have to take the rap. It was his responsibility to get the Summoners routed out and their instructions followed.

The miserable flea-infested Summoner had gone back to sleep—and *he* would have to answer for it.

The doors opened. "All right," a voice murmured, preoccupied. It was a tired, care-worn voice. The Clerk trembled and entered slowly, sweat dripping down his neck and into his celluloid collar.

The Old Man glanced up, laying aside his book. He studied the Clerk calmly, his faded blue eyes mild—a deep, ancient mildness that made the Clerk tremble even more. He took out his handkerchief and mopped his brow.

"I understand there was a mistake," the Old Man murmured. "In connection with Sector T137. Something to do with an element from an adjoining area."

"That's right." The Clerk's voice was faint and husky. "Very unfortunate."

"What exactly occurred?"

"I started out this morning with my instruction sheets. The material relating to T137 had top priority, of course. I served notice on the Summoner in my area that an eight-fifteen summons was required."

"Did the Summoner understand the urgency?"

"Yes, sir." The Clerk hesitated. "But—"

"But what?"

The Clerk twisted miserably. "While my back was turned the Summoner crawled back in his shed and went to sleep. I was occupied, checking the exact time with my watch. I called the moment, but there was no response."

"You called at eight fifteen exactly?"

"Yes, sir! Exactly eight fifteen. But the Summoner was asleep. By the time I managed to arouse him it was eight *sixteen*. He summoned, but instead of A Friend with a Car we got—A Life Insurance Salesman." The Clerk's face screwed up with disgust. "The Salesman kept the element there until almost nine thirty. Therefore he was late to work instead of early."

For a moment the Old Man was silent. "Then the element was not within T137 when the adjustment began."

"No. He arrived about ten o'clock."

"During the middle of the adjustment." The Old Man got to his feet and paced slowly back and forth, face grim, hands behind his back. His long robe flowed out behind him. "A serious matter. During a Sector Adjustment all related elements from other Sectors must be included. Otherwise, their orientations remain out of phase. When this element entered T137, the adjustment had been in progress fifty minutes. The element encountered the Sector at its most de-energized stage. He wandered about until one of the adjustment teams met him."

"Did they catch him?"

"Unfortunately, no. He fled out of the Sector. Into a nearby fully energized area."

"What—what then?"

The Old Man stopped pacing, his lined face grim. He ran a heavy hand through his long white hair. "We do not know. We lost contact with him. We will reestablish contact soon, of course. But for the moment he is out of control."

"What are you going to do?"

"He must be contacted and contained. He must be brought up here. There's no other solution."

"Up *here!*"

"It is too late to de-energize him. By the time he is regained, he will have told others. To wipe his mind clean would only complicate matters. Usual methods will not suffice. I must deal with this problem myself."

"I hope he's located quickly," the Clerk said.

"He will be. Every Watcher is alerted. Every Watcher and every Summoner." The Old Man's eyes twinkled. "Even the Clerks, although we hesitate to count on them."

The Clerk flushed. "I'll be glad when this thing is over," he muttered.

***

Ruth came tripping down the stairs and out of the building, into the hot noonday sun. She lit a cigarette and hurried along the walk, her small bosom rising and falling as she breathed in the spring air.

"Ruth." Ed stepped up behind her.

"Ed!" She spun, gasping in astonishment. "What are you doing away from—?"

"Come on." Ed grabbed her arm, pulling her along. "Let's keep moving."

"But what—?"

"I'll tell you later." Ed's face was pale and grim. "Let's go where we can talk. In private."

"I was going down to have lunch at Louie's. We can talk there." Ruth hurried along breathlessly. "What is it? What's happened? You look so strange. And why aren't you at work? Did you—did you get fired?"

They crossed the street and entered a small restaurant. Men and women milled around, getting their lunch. Ed found a table in the back, secluded in a corner. "Here." He sat down abruptly. "This will do." She slid into the other chair.

Ed ordered a cup of coffee. Ruth had salad and creamed tuna on toast, coffee and peach pie. Silently, Ed watched her as she ate, his face dark and moody.

"Please tell me," Ruth begged him.

"You really want to know?"

"Of course I want to know!" Ruth put her small hand anxiously on his. "I'm your wife."

"Something happened today. This morning. I was late to

work. A damn insurance man came by and held me up. I was half an hour late."

Ruth caught her breath. "Douglas fired you."

"No." Ed ripped a paper napkin slowly into bits. He stuffed the bits in the half-empty water glass. "I was worried as hell. I got off the bus and hurried down the street. I noticed it when I stepped up on the curb in front of the office."

"Noticed what?"

Ed told her. The whole works. Everything.

When he had finished, Ruth sat back, her face white, hands trembling. "I see," she murmured. "No wonder you're upset." She drank a little cold coffee, the cup rattling against the saucer. "What a terrible thing."

Ed leaned intently toward his wife. "Ruth. Do you think I'm going crazy?"

Ruth's red lips twisted. "I don't know what to say. It's so strange…"

"Yeah. Strange is hardly the word for it. I poked my hands right through them. Like they were clay. Old dry clay. Dust. Dust figures." Ed lit a cigarette from Ruth's pack. "When I got out, I looked back and there it was. The office building. Like always."

"You were afraid Mr. Douglas would bawl you out, weren't you?"

"Sure. I was afraid—and guilty." Ed's eyes flickered. "I know what you're thinking. I was late and I couldn't face him. So I had some sort of protective psychotic fit. Retreat from reality." He stubbed the cigarette out savagely. "Ruth, I've been wandering around town since. Two and a half hours. Sure, I'm afraid. I'm afraid like hell to go back."

"Of Douglas?"

"No! The men in white." Ed shuddered. "God. Chasing me. With their damn hoses and—and equipment."

Ruth was silent. Finally she looked up at her husband, her dark eyes bright. "You have to go back, Ed."

"Back? Why?"

"To prove something."

"Prove what?"

"Prove it's all right." Ruth's hand pressed against his. "You have to, Ed. You have to go back and face it. To show yourself there's nothing to be afraid of."

"The hell with it! After what I saw? Listen, Ruth. I saw the fabric of reality split open. I saw—*behind*. Underneath. I saw what was really there. And I don't want to go back. I don't want to see dust people again. Ever."

Ruth's eyes were fixed intently on him. "I'll go back with you," she said.

"For god's sake."

"For *your* sake. For your sanity. So you'll know." Ruth got abruptly to her feet, pulling her coat around her. "Come on, Ed. I'll go with you. We'll go up there together. To the office of Douglas and Blake, Real Estate. I'll even go in with you to see Mr. Douglas."

Ed got up slowly, staring hard at his wife. "You think I blacked out. Cold feet. Couldn't face the boss." His voice was low and strained. "Don't you?"

Ruth was already threading her way toward the cashier. "Come on. You'll see. It'll all be there. Just like it was."

"Okay," Ed said. He followed her slowly. "We'll go back there and see which of us is right."

They crossed the street together, Ruth holding on tight to Ed's arm. Ahead of them was the building, the towering structure of concrete and metal and glass.

"There it is," Ruth said. "See?"

There it was, all right. The big building rose up, firm and solid, glittering in the early afternoon sun, its windows sparkling brightly.

Ed and Ruth stepped up onto the curb. Ed tensed himself, his body rigid. He winced as his foot touched the pavement—

But nothing happened. The street noises continued: cars, people hurrying past, a kid selling papers. There were sounds, smells, the noise of a city in the middle of the day. And overhead was the sun and the bright blue sky.

"See?" Ruth said. "I was right."

They walked up the front steps into the lobby. Behind the cigar stand the seller stood, arms folded, listening to the ball game. "Hi, Mr. Fletcher," he called to Ed. His face lit up good-naturedly. "Who's the dame? Your wife know about this?"

Ed laughed unsteadily. They passed on toward the elevator. Four or five businessmen stood waiting. They were middle-aged men, well-dressed, waiting impatiently in a bunch. "Hey Fletcher," one said. "Where you been all day? Douglas is yelling his head off."

"Hello, Earl," Ed muttered. He gripped Ruth's arm. "Been a little sick."

The elevator came. They got in. The elevator rose. "Hi, Ed," the elevator operator said. "Who's the good-looking gal? Why don't you introduce her around?"

Ed grinned mechanically. "My wife."

The elevator let them off at the third floor. Ed and Ruth got out, heading toward the glass door of Douglas and Blake, Real Estate.

Ed halted, breathing shallowly. "Wait." He licked his lips. "I—"

Ruth waited calmly as Ed wiped his forehead and neck with his handkerchief. "All right now?"

"Yeah." Ed moved forward. He pulled open the glass door.

Miss Evans glanced up, ceasing her typing. "Ed Fletcher! Where on earth have you been?"

"I've been sick. Hello, Tom."

Tom glanced up from his work. "Hi, Ed. Say, Douglas is yelling for your scalp. Where have you been?"

"I know." Ed turned wearily to Ruth. "I guess I better go in and face the music."

Ruth squeezed his arm. "You'll be all right. I know." She smiled, a relieved flash of white teeth and red lips. "Okay? Call me if you need me."

"Sure." Ed kissed her briefly on the mouth. "Thanks, honey. Thanks a lot. I don't know what the hell went wrong with me. I guess it's over."

"Forget it. So long." Ruth skipped back out of the office, the door closing after her. Ed listened to her race down the hall to the elevator.

"Nice little gal," Jackie said appreciatively.

"Yeah." Ed nodded, straightening his necktie. He moved unhappily toward the inner office, steeling himself. Well, he had to face it. Ruth was right. But he was going to have a hell of a time explaining it to the boss. He could see Douglas now, thick red wattles, big bull roar, face distorted with rage —

Ed stopped abruptly at the entrance to the inner office. He froze rigid. The inner office — it was *changed*.

The hackles of his neck rose. Cold fear gripped him, clutching at his windpipe. The inner office was different. He turned his head slowly, taking in the sight: the desks, chairs, fixtures, file cabinets, pictures.

Changes. Little changes. Subtle. Ed closed his eyes and opened them slowly. He was alert, breathing rapidly, his pulse racing. It was changed, all right. No doubt about it.

"What's the matter, Ed?" Tom asked. The staff watched him curiously, pausing in their work.

Ed said nothing. He advanced slowly into the inner office.

The office had been *gone over*. He could tell. Things had been altered. Rearranged. Nothing obvious, nothing he could put his finger on. But he could tell.

Joe Kent greeted him uneasily. "What's the matter, Ed? You look like a wild dog. Is something—?"

Ed studied Joe. He was different. Not the same. What was it?

Joe's face. It was a little fuller. His shirt was blue-striped. Joe never wore blue stripes. Ed examined Joe's desk. He saw papers and accounts. The desk—it was too far to the right. And it was bigger. It wasn't the same desk.

The picture on the wall. It wasn't the same. It was a different picture entirely. And the things on top of the file cabinet—some were new, others were gone.

He looked back through the door. Now that he thought about it, Miss Evans's hair was different, done a different way. And it was lighter.

In here, Mary, filing her nails, over by the window—she was taller, fuller. Her purse, lying on the desk in front of her—a red purse, red knit.

"You always…have that purse?" Ed demanded.

Mary glanced up. "What?"

"That purse. You always have that?"

Mary laughed. She smoothed her skirt coyly around her shapely thighs, her long lashes blinking modestly. "Why, Mr. Fletcher. What do you mean?"

Ed turned away. *He knew.* Even if she didn't. She had been redone—changed: her purse, her clothes, her figure, everything about her. None of them knew but him. His mind spun dizzily. They were all changed. All of them were different. They had all been remolded, recast. Subtly, but it was there.

The wastebasket. It was smaller, not the same. The window shades—white, not ivory. The wallpaper was not the same pattern. The lighting fixtures…

Endless, subtle changes.

Ed made his way back to the inner office. He lifted his hand and knocked on Douglas's door.

"Come in."

Ed pushed the door open. Nathan Douglas looked up impatiently. "Mr. Douglas," Ed began. He came into the room unsteadily and stopped.

Douglas was not the same. Not at all. His whole office was changed—the rugs, the drapes. The desk was oak, not mahogany. And Douglas himself...

Douglas was younger, thinner. His hair, brown. His skin not so red. His face smoother. No wrinkles. Chin reshaped. Eyes green, not black. He was a different man. But still Douglas, a different Douglas. A different version!

"What is it?" Douglas demanded impatiently. "Oh it's you, Fletcher. Where were you this morning?"

Ed backed out. Fast.

He slammed the door and hurried through the inner office. Tom and Miss Evans glanced up, startled. Ed passed them by, grabbing the hall door open.

"Hey!" Tom called. "What—?"

Ed hurried down the hall. Terror leaped through him. He had to hurry. He had *seen*. There wasn't much time. He came to the elevator and stabbed the button.

No time.

He ran to the stairs and started down. He reached the second floor. His terror grew. It was a matter of seconds.

Seconds!

The public phone. Ed ran into the phone booth. He dragged the door shut after him. Wildly, he dropped a dime in the slot and dialed. He had to call the police. He held the receiver to his ear, his heart pounding.

*Warn them.* Changes. Somebody tampering with reality.

Altering it. He had been right. The white-clad men…their equipment…going through the building.

"Hello!" Ed shouted hoarsely. There was no answer. No hum. Nothing.

Ed peered frantically out the door.

And he sagged, defeated. Slowly he hung up the telephone receiver.

He was no longer on the second floor. The phone booth was rising, leaving the second floor behind, carrying him up, faster and faster. It rose floor by floor, moving silently, swiftly.

The phone booth passed through the ceiling of the building and out into the bright sunlight. It gained speed. The ground fell away below. Buildings and streets were getting smaller each moment. Tiny specks hurried along far below, cars and people dwindling rapidly.

Clouds drifted between him and the earth. Ed shut his eyes, dizzy with fright. He held on desperately to the door handles of the phone booth.

Faster and faster the phone booth climbed. The earth was rapidly being left behind, far below.

Ed peered up wildly. *Where?* Where was he going? Where was it taking him?

He stood gripping the door handles, waiting.

The Clerk nodded curtly. "That's him, all right. The element in question."

Ed Fletcher looked around him. He was in a huge chamber. The edges fell away into indistinct shadows. In front of him stood a man with notes and ledgers under his arm, peering at him through steel-rimmed glasses. He was a nervous little man, sharp-eyed, with celluloid collar, blue serge suit, vest, watch chain. He wore black shiny shoes.

And beyond him—

An old man sat quietly in an immense modern chair. He watched

Fletcher calmly, his blue eyes mild and tired. A strange thrill shot through Fletcher. It was not fear. Rather it was a vibration, rattling his bones—a deep sense of awe tinged with fascination.

"Where—what is this place?" he asked faintly. He was still dazed from his quick ascent.

"Don't ask questions!" The nervous little man snapped angrily, tapping his pencil against his ledgers. "You're here to answer, not ask."

The Old Man moved a little. He raised his hand. "I will speak to the element alone," he murmured. His voice was low. It vibrated and rumbled through the chamber. Again the wave of fascinated awe swept Ed.

"Alone?" The little fellow backed away, gathering his books and papers in his arms. "Of course." He glanced hostilely at Ed Fletcher. "I'm glad he's finally in custody. All the work and trouble just for—"

He disappeared through a door. The door closed softly behind him. Ed and the Old Man were alone.

"Please sit down," the Old Man said.

Ed found a seat. He sat down awkwardly, nervously. He got out his cigarettes and then put them away again.

"What's wrong?" the Old Man asked.

"I'm just beginning to understand."

"Understand what?"

"That I'm dead."

The Old Man smiled briefly. "Dead? No, you're not dead. You're…visiting. An unusual event, but necessitated by circumstances." He leaned toward Ed. "Mr. Fletcher, you have got yourself involved with something."

"Yeah," Ed agreed. "I wish I knew what it was. Or how it happened."

"It was not your fault. You were a victim of a clerical error. A mistake was made—not by you. But involving you."

"What mistake?" Ed rubbed his forehead wearily. "I—I got in on something. I saw *through*. I saw something I wasn't supposed to see."

The Old Man nodded. "That's right. You saw something you were not supposed to see, something few elements have been aware of, let alone witnessed."

"Elements?"

"An official term. Let it pass. A mistake was made, but we hope to rectify it. It is my hope that—"

"Those people," Ed interrupted. "Heaps of dry ash. And gray. Like they were dead. Only it was everything: the stairs and walls and floor. No color or life."

"That Sector had been temporarily de-energized. So the adjustment team could enter and effect changes."

"Changes." Ed nodded. "That's right. When I went back later, everything was alive again. But not the same. It was all different."

"The adjustment was complete by noon. The team finished its work and re-energized the Sector."

"I see," Ed muttered.

"You were supposed to have been in the Sector when the adjustment began. Because of an error you were not. You came into the Sector late, during the adjustment itself. You fled, and when you returned it was over. You saw, and you should not have seen. Instead of a witness you should have been part of the adjustment. Like the others, you should have undergone changes."

Sweat came out on Ed Fletcher's head. He wiped it away. His stomach turned over. Weakly, he cleared his throat. "I get the picture." His voice was almost inaudible. A chilling premonition moved through him. "I was supposed to be changed like the others. But I guess something went wrong."

"Something went wrong. An error occurred. And now a serious problem exists. You have seen these things. You know a great deal. And you are not coordinated with the new configuration."

"Gosh," Ed muttered. "Well, I won't tell anybody." Cold sweat poured off him. "You can count on that. I'm as good as changed."

"You have already told someone," the Old Man said coldly.

"Me?" Ed blinked. "Who?"

"Your wife."

Ed trembled. The color drained from his face, leaving it a sickly white. "That's right. I did."

"Your wife knows." The Old Man's face twisted angrily. "A woman. Of all the things to tell—"

"I didn't know." Ed retreated, panic leaping through him. "But I know *now*. You can count on me. Consider me changed."

The ancient blue eyes bored keenly into him, peering far into his depths. "And you were going to call the police. You wanted to inform the authorities."

"But I didn't know *who* was doing the changing."

"Now you know. The natural process must be supplemented—adjusted here and there. Corrections must be made. We are fully licensed to make such corrections. Our adjustment teams perform vital work."

Ed plucked up a measure of courage. "This particular adjustment. Douglas. The office. What was it for? I'm sure it was some worthwhile purpose."

The Old Man waved his hand. Behind him in the shadows an immense map glowed into existence. Ed caught his breath. The edges of the map faded off in obscurity. He saw an infinite web of detailed sections, a network of squares and ruled lines. Each square was marked. Some glowed with a blue light. The lights altered constantly.

"The Sector Board," the Old Man said. He sighed wearily. "A staggering job. Sometimes we wonder how we can go on another period. But it must be done. For the good of all. For *your good.*"

"The change. In our—our Sector."

"Your office deals in real estate. The old Douglas was a shrewd man, but rapidly becoming infirm. His physical health was waning. In a few days Douglas will be offered a chance to purchase a large unimproved forest area in western Canada. It will require most of his assets. The older, less virile Douglas would have hesitated. It is imperative he not hesitate. He must purchase the area and clear the land at once. Only a younger man—a younger Douglas—would undertake this.

"When the land is cleared, certain anthropological remains will be discovered. They have already been placed there. Douglas will lease his land to the Canadian government for scientific study. The remains found there will cause international excitement in learned circles.

"A chain of events will be set in motion. Men from numerous countries will come to Canada to examine the remains. Soviet, Polish, and Czech scientists will make the journey.

"The chain of events will draw these scientists together for the first time in years. National research will be temporarily forgotten in the excitement of these nonnational discoveries. One of the leading Soviet scientists will make friends with a Belgian scientist. Before they depart they will agree to correspond—without the knowledge of their governments, of course.

"The circle will widen. Other scientists on both sides will be drawn in. A society will be founded. More and more educated men will transfer an increasing amount of time to this international society. Purely national research will suffer a slight but extremely critical eclipse. The war tension will somewhat wane.

"This alteration is vital. And it is dependent on the purchase and clearing of the section of wilderness in Canada. The old

Douglas would not have dared take the risk. But the altered Douglas, and his altered, more youthful staff, will pursue this work with wholehearted enthusiasm. And from this, the vital chain of widening events will come about. The beneficiaries will be *you*. Our methods may seem strange and indirect. Even incomprehensible. But I assure you we know what we're doing."

"I know that now," Ed said.

"So you do. You know a great deal. Much too much. No element should possess such knowledge. I should perhaps call an adjustment team in here…"

A picture formed in Ed's mind—swirling gray clouds, gray men and women. He shuddered. "Look," he croaked. "I'll do anything. Anything at all. Only don't de-energize me." Sweat ran down his face. "Okay?"

The Old Man pondered. "Perhaps some alternative could be found. There is another possibility."

"What?" Ed asked eagerly. "What is it?"

The Old Man spoke slowly, thoughtfully. "If I allow you to return, you will swear never to speak of the matter? Will you swear not to reveal to anyone the things you saw? The things you know?"

"Sure!" Ed gasped eagerly, blinding relief flooding over him. "I swear!"

"Your wife. She must know nothing more. She must think it was only a passing psychological fit—retreat from reality."

"She thinks that already."

"She must continue to."

Ed set his jaw firmly. "I'll see that she continues to think it was a mental aberration. She'll never know what really happened."

"You are certain you can keep the truth from her?"

"Sure," Ed said confidently. "I know I can."

"All right." The Old Man nodded slowly. "I will send you back. But you must tell no one." He swelled visibly. "Remember:

you will eventually come back to me—everyone does in the end—and your fate will not be enviable."

"I won't tell her," Ed said, sweating. "I promise. You have my word on that. I can handle Ruth. Don't give it a second thought."

Ed arrived home at sunset.

He blinked, dazed from the rapid descent. For a moment he stood on the pavement, regaining his balance and catching his breath. Then he walked quickly up the path.

He pushed the door open and entered the little green stucco house.

"Ed!" Ruth came flying, face distorted with tears. She threw her arms around him, hugging him tight. "Where the hell have you been?"

"Been?" Ed murmured. "At the office, of course."

Ruth pulled back abruptly. "No, you haven't."

Vague tendrils of alarm plucked at Ed. "Of course I have. Where else—?"

"I called Douglas about three. He said you left. You walked out practically as soon as I turned my back. Eddie—"

Ed patted her nervously. "Take it easy, honey." He began unbuttoning his coat. "Everything's okay. Understand? Things are perfectly all right."

Ruth sat down on the arm of the couch. She blew her nose, dabbing at her eyes. "If you knew how much I've worried." She put her handkerchief away and folded her arms. "I want to know where you were."

Uneasily, Ed hung his coat in the closet. He came over and kissed her. Her lips were ice cold. "I'll tell you all about it. But what do you say we have something to eat? I'm starved."

Ruth studied him intently. She got down from the arm of the couch. "I'll change and fix dinner."

She hurried into the bedroom and slipped off her shoes and nylons. Ed followed her. "I didn't mean to worry you," he said carefully. "After you left me today, I realized you were right."

"Oh?" Ruth unfastened her blouse and skirt, arranging them over a hanger. "Right about what?"

"About me." He manufactured a grin and made it glow across his face. "About…what happened."

Ruth hung her slip over the hanger. She studied her husband intently as she struggled into her tight-fitting jeans. "Go on."

The moment had come. It was now or never. Ed Fletcher braced himself and chose his words carefully. "I realized," he stated, "that the whole darn thing was in my mind. You were right, Ruth. Completely right. And I even realize what caused it."

Ruth rolled her cotton T-shirt down and tucked it in her jeans. "What was the cause?"

"Overwork."

"Overwork?"

"I need a vacation. I haven't had a vacation in years. My mind isn't on the job. I've been daydreaming." He said it firmly, but his heart was in his mouth. "I need to get away. To the mountains. Bass fishing. Or—" He searched his mind frantically. "Or—"

Ruth came toward him ominously. "Ed!" she said sharply. "Look at me!"

"What's the matter?" Panic shot through him. "Why are you looking at me like that?"

"*Where were you this afternoon?*"

Ed's grin faded. "I told you. I went for a walk. Didn't I tell you? A walk. To think things over."

"Don't lie to me, Eddie Fletcher! I can tell when you're lying!" Fresh tears welled up in Ruth's eyes. Her breasts rose and fell excitedly under her cotton shirt. "Admit it! You didn't go for a walk!"

Ed stammered weakly. Sweat poured off him. He sagged helplessly against the door. "What do you mean?"

Ruth's black eyes flashed with anger. "Come on! I want to know where you were! Tell me! I have a right to know. What really happened?"

Ed retreated in terror, his resolve melting like wax. It was going all wrong. "Honest. I went out for a—"

"Tell me!" Ruth's sharp fingernails dug into his arm. "I want to know where you were! And who you were with!"

Ed opened his mouth. He tried to grin, but his face failed to respond. "I don't know what you mean."

"You know what I mean. Who were you with? Where did you go? Tell me! I'll find out sooner or later."

There was no way out. He was licked, and he knew it. He couldn't keep it from her. Desperately he stalled, praying for time. If he could only distract her, get her mind on something else. If she would only let up, even for a second. He could invent something, a better story. Time—he needed more time. "Ruth, you've got to—"

Suddenly there was a sound: the bark of a dog, echoing through the dark house.

Ruth let go, cocking her head alertly. "That was Dobbie. I think somebody's coming."

The doorbell rang.

"You stay here. I'll be right back." Ruth ran out of the room to the front door. "Darn it." She pulled the front door open.

"Good evening!" The young man stepped quickly inside, loaded down with objects, grinning broadly at Ruth. "I'm from the Sweep-Rite Vacuum Cleaner Company."

Ruth scowled impatiently. "Really, we're about to sit down at the table."

"Oh, this will only take a moment." The young man set down the vacuum cleaner and its attachments with a metallic crash.

Rapidly, he unrolled a long-illustrated banner, showing the vacuum cleaner in action. "Now, if you'll just hold this while I plug in the cleaner—"

He bustled happily about, unplugging the TV set, plugging in the cleaner, pushing the chairs out of his way.

I'll show you the drape scraper first." He attached a hose and nozzle to the big gleaming tank. "Now, if you'll just sit down, I'll demonstrate each of these easy-to-use attachments." His happy voice rose over the roar of the cleaner. "You'll notice—"

Ed Fletcher sat down on the bed. He groped in his pocket until he found his cigarettes. Shakily he lit one and leaned back against the wall, weak with relief.

He gazed up, a look of gratitude on his face. "Thanks," he said softly. "I think we'll make it after all. Thanks a lot."

# LAST OF THE MASTERS

CONSCIOUSNESS COLLECTED AROUND him. He returned with reluctance. The weight of centuries, an unbearable fatigue, lay over him. The ascent was painful. He would have shrieked if there were anything to shriek with. And anyhow, he was beginning to feel glad.

Eight thousand times he had crept back thus, with ever-increasing difficulty. Someday he wouldn't make it. Someday the black pool would remain. But not this day. He was still alive. Above the aching pain and reluctance came joyful triumph.

"Good morning," a bright voice said. "Isn't it a nice day? I'll pull the curtains, and you can look out."

He could see and hear. But he couldn't move. He lay quietly and allowed the various sensations of the room to pour in on him. Carpets, wallpaper, tables, lamps, pictures. Desk and vidscreen. Gleaming yellow sunlight streamed through the window. Blue sky. Distant hills. Fields, buildings, roads, factories. Workers and machines.

Peter Green was busily straightening things, his young face wreathed with smiles. "Lots to do today. Lots of people to see you. Bills to sign. Decisions to make. This is Saturday. There will be people coming in from the remote sectors. I hope the maintenance crew has done a good job." He added quickly, "They have, of course. I talked to Fowler on my way over here. Everything's fixed up fine."

The youth's pleasant tenor mixed with the bright sunlight. Sounds and sights, but nothing else. He could feel nothing. He tried to move his arm, but nothing happened.

"Don't worry," Green said, catching his terror. "They'll soon be along with the rest. You'll be all right. You *have* to be. How could we survive without you?"

He relaxed. God knew, it had happened often enough before. Anger surged dully. Why couldn't they coordinate? Get it up all at once, not piecemeal. He'd have to change their schedule. Make them organize better.

Past the bright window, a squat metal car chugged to a halt. Uniformed men piled out, gathered up heavy armloads of equipment, and hurried toward the main entrance of the building.

"Here they come," Green exclaimed with relief. "A little late, eh?"

"Another traffic tie-up," Fowler snorted as he entered. "Something wrong with the signal system again. Outside flow got mixed up with the urban stuff, tied up on all sides. I wish you'd change the law."

Now there was motion all around him. The shapes of Fowler and McLean loomed, two giant moons abruptly ascendant. Professional faces that peered down at him anxiously. He was turned over on his side. Muffled conferences. Urgent whispers. The clank of tools.

"Here," Fowler muttered. "Now here. No, that's later. Be careful. Now run it up through here."

The work continued in taut silence. He was aware of their closeness. Dim outlines occasionally cut off his light. He was turned this way and that, thrown around like a sack of meal.

"Okay," Fowler said. "Tape it."

A long silence. He gazed dully at the wall, at the slightly-faded blue and pink wallpaper. An old design that showed a woman in hoopskirts, with a little parasol over her dainty shoulder. A frilly white blouse, tiny tips of shoes. An astoundingly clean puppy at her side.

Then he was turned back, to face upward. Five shapes groaned and strained over him. Their fingers flew, their muscles rippled under their shirts. At last they straightened up and retreated. Fowler wiped sweat from his face. They were all tense and bleary eyed.

"Go ahead," Fowler rasped. "Throw it."

Shock hit him. He gasped. His body arched, then settled slowly down.

*His body.* He could feel. He moved his arms experimentally. He touched his face, his shoulder, the wall. The wall was real and hard. All at once the world had become three-dimensional again.

Relief showed on Fowler's face. "Thank god." He sagged wearily. "How do you feel?"

After a moment he answered, "All right."

Fowler sent the rest of the crew out. Green began dusting again, off in the corner. Fowler sat down on the edge of the bed and lit his pipe. "Now listen to me," he said. "I've got bad news. I'll give it to you the way you always want it, straight from the shoulder."

"What is it?" he demanded. He examined his fingers. He already knew.

There were dark circles under Fowler's eyes. He hadn't shaved. His square-jawed face was drawn and unhealthy. "We were up all night. Working on your motor system. We've got it jury-rigged, but it won't hold. Not more than another few months. The thing's climbing. The basic units can't be replaced. When they wear out, they're gone. We can weld in relays and wiring, but we can't fix the five synapsis-coils. There were only a few men who could make those, and they've been dead two centuries. If the coils burn out—"

"Is there any deterioration in the synapsis-coils?" he interrupted.

"Not yet. Just motor areas. Arms, in particular. What's happening to your legs will happen to your arms and finally all your motor system. You'll be paralyzed by the end of the year.

You'll be able to see, hear, and think. And broadcast. But that's all." He added, "Sorry, Bors. We're doing all we can."

"All right," Bors said. "You're excused. Thanks for telling me straight. I guessed."

"Ready to go down? A lot of people with problems today. They're stuck until you get there."

"Let's go." He focused his mind with an effort and turned his attention to the details of the day. "I want the heavy metals research program speeded. It's lagging, as usual. I may have to pull a number of men from related work and shift them to the generators. The water level will be dropping soon. I want to start feeding power along the lines while there's still power to feed. As soon as I turn my back, everything starts falling apart."

Fowler signaled Green and he came quickly over. The two of them bent over Bors and, grunting, hoisted him up and carried him to the door. Down the corridor and outside.

They deposited him in the squat metal car, the new little service truck. Its polished surface was a startling contrast to his pitted, corroded hull, bent and splotched and eaten away. A dull, patina-covered machine of archaic steel and plastic that hummed faintly, rustily, as the men leaped in the front seat and raced the car out onto the main highway.

***

Edward Tolby perspired, pushed his pack up higher, hunched over, tightened his gun belt, and cursed.

"Daddy," Silvia reproved. "Cut that."

Tolby spat furiously in the grass at the side of the road. He put his arm around his slim daughter. "Sorry, Silv. Nothing personal. The damn heat."

Mid-morning sun shimmered down on the dusty road. Clouds of dust rose and billowed around the three as they pushed slowly along. They were dead tired. Tolby's heavy face was flushed and sullen. An unlit cigarette dangled between his lips. His big, powerfully built body was hunched resentfully forward. His daughter's canvas shirt clung moistly to her arms and breasts. Moons of sweat darkened her back. Under her jeans her thigh muscles rippled wearily.

Robert Penn walked a little behind the two Tolbys, hands deep in his pockets, eyes on the road ahead. His mind was blank. He was half asleep from the double shot of hexobarb he had swallowed at the last League camp. And the heat lulled him. On each side of the road fields stretched out, pastures of grass and weeds, a few trees here and there. A tumbled-down farmhouse. The ancient rusting remains of a bomb shelter, two centuries old. Once, some dirty sheep.

"Sheep," Penn said. "They eat the grass too far down. It won't grow back."

"Now he's a farmer," Tolby said to his daughter.

"Daddy," Silvia snapped. "Stop being nasty."

"It's this heat. This damn heat." Tolby cursed again, loudly and futilely. "It's not worth it. For ten pinks I'd go back and tell them it was a lot of pig swill."

"Maybe it is, at that," Penn said mildly.

"All right, you go back," Tolby grunted. "You go back and tell them it's a lot of pig swill. They'll pin a medal on you. Maybe raise you up a grade."

Penn laughed. "Both of you shut up. There's some kind of town ahead."

Tolby's massive body straightened eagerly. "Where?" He shielded his eyes. "By god, he's right. A village. And it isn't a mirage. You see it, don't you?" His good humor returned, and he rubbed his big hands together. "What say, Penn. A couple of beers, a few games of throw with some of the local peasants. Maybe we can stay overnight." He licked his thick lips with anticipation. "Some of those village wenches, the kind that hang around the grog shops—"

"I know the kind you mean," Penn broke in. "The kind that are tired of doing nothing. Want to see the big commercial centers. Want to meet some guy that'll buy them mecho-stuff and take them places."

At the side of the road a farmer was watching them curiously. He had halted his horse and stood leaning on his crude plow, hat pushed back on his head.

"What's the name of this town?" Tolby yelled.

The farmer was silent a moment. He was an old man, thin and weathered. "This town?" he repeated.

"Yeah, the one ahead."

"That's a nice town." The farmer eyed the three of them. "You been through here before?"

"No, sir," Tolby said. "Never."

"Team break down?"

"No, we're on foot."

"How far you come?"

"About a hundred and fifty miles."

The farmer considered the heavy packs strapped on their backs. Their cleated hiking shoes. Dusty clothing and weary, sweat-streaked faces. Jeans and canvas shirts. Ironite walking staffs. "That's a long way," he said. "How far you going?"

"As far as we feel like it," Tolby answered. "Is there a place ahead we can stay? Hotel? Inn?"

"That town," the farmer said, "is Fairfax. It has a lumber mill, one of the best in the world. A couple of pottery works. A place where you can get clothes put together by machines. Regular mecho-clothing. A gun shop where they pour the best shot this side of the Rockies. And a bakery. Also there's an old doctor living there, and a lawyer. And some people with books to teach the kids. They came with TB. They made a schoolhouse out of an old barn."

"How large a town?" Penn asked.

"Lot of people. More born all the time. Old folks die. Kids die. We had a fever last year. About a hundred kids died. Doctor said it came from the water hole. We shut the water hole down. Kids died anyhow. Doctor said it was the milk. Drove off half the cows. Not mine. I stood out there with my gun, and I shot the first of them came to drive off my cow. Kids stopped dying as soon as fall came. I think it was the heat."

"Sure is hot," Tolby agreed.

"Yes, it gets hot around here. Water's pretty scarce." A crafty look slid across his old face. "You folks want a drink? The young lady looks pretty tired. Got some bottles of water down under the house. In the mud. Nice and cold." He hesitated. "Pink a glass."

Tolby laughed. "No, thanks."

"Two glasses a pink," the farmer said.

"Not interested," Penn said. He thumped his canteen and the three of them started on. "So long."

The farmer's face hardened. "Damn foreigners," he muttered. He turned angrily back to his plowing.

The town baked in silence. Flies buzzed and settled on the backs of stupefied horses, tied up at posts. A few cars were parked here and there. People moved listlessly along the sidewalks. Elderly, lean-bodied men dozed on porches. Dogs and chickens slept in the shade under houses. The houses were small, wooden, chipped and peeling boards, leaning and angular—and old. Warped and split by age and heat. Dust lay **over** everything. A thick blanket of dry dust over the cracking houses and the dull-faced men and animals.

Two lank men approached them from an open doorway. "Who are you? What do you want?"

They stopped and got out their identification. The men examined the sealed-plastic cards. Photographs, fingerprints, data. Finally they handed them back.

"AL," one said. "You really from the Anarchist League?"

"That's right," Tolby said.

"Even the girl?" The men eyed Silvia with languid greed. "Tell you what. Let us have the girl a while, and we'll skip the head tax."

"Don't kid me," Tolby grunted. "Since when does the League pay head tax or any other tax?" He pushed past them impatiently. "Where's the grog shop? I'm dying!"

A two-story white building was on their left. Men lounged on the porch, watching them vacantly. Penn headed toward it and the Tolbys followed. A faded, peeling sign lettered across the front read: *Beer, Wine on Tap.*

"This is it," Penn said. He guided Silvia up the sagging steps, past the men, and inside. Tolby followed. He unstrapped his pack gratefully as he came.

The place was cool and dark. A few men and women were at the bar. The rest sat around tables. Some youths were playing throw in the back. A mechanical tune-maker wheezed and composed in the corner, a shabby, half-ruined machine only partially functioning. Behind the bar a primitive scene-shifter created and destroyed vague phantasmagoria: seascapes, mountain peaks, snowy valleys, great rolling hills, a nude woman that lingered and then dissolved into one vast breast. Dim, uncertain processions that no one noticed or looked at. The bar itself was an incredibly ancient sheet of transparent plastic, stained and chipped and yellow with age. Its n-grav coat had faded from one end. Bricks now propped it up. The drink mixer had long since fallen apart. Only wine and beer were served. No living man knew how to mix the simplest drink.

Tolby moved up to the bar. "Beer," he said. "Three beers." Penn and Silvia sank down at a table and removed their packs as the bartender served Tolby three mugs of thick, dark beer. He showed his card and carried the mugs over to the table.

The youths in the back had stopped playing. They were watching the three as they sipped their beer and unlaced their hiking boots. After a while one of them came slowly over.

"Say," he said, "you're from the League."

"That's right," Tolby murmured sleepily.

Everyone in the place was watching and listening. The youth sat down across from the three. His companions flocked excitedly around and took seats on all sides. The juveniles of the town. Bored, restless, dissatisfied. Their eyes took in the ironite staffs, the guns, the heavy metal-cleated boots. A murmured whisper rustled through them. They were about eighteen. Tanned, rangy.

"How do you get in?" one demanded bluntly.

"The League?" Tolby leaned back in his chair, found a match, and lit his cigarette. He unfastened his belt, belched loudly, and settled back contentedly. "You get in by examination."

"What do you have to know?"

Tolby shrugged. "About everything." He belched again and scratched thoughtfully at his chest, between two buttons. He was conscious of the ring of people around on all sides. A little old man with a beard and horn-rimmed glasses. At another table, a great tub of a man in a red shirt and blue-striped trousers, with a bulging stomach.

Youths. Farmers. A Negro in a dirty white shirt and trousers, a book under his arm. A hard-jawed blonde, hair in a net, red nails and high heels, tight yellow dress. Sitting with a gray-haired businessman in a dark brown suit. A tall young man holding hands with a young black-haired girl, huge eyes, in a soft white blouse and skirt, little slippers kicked under the table. Under the table her bare, tanned feet twisted. Her slim body was bent forward with interest.

"You have to know," Tolby said, "how the League was formed. You have to know how we pulled down the governments that day. Pulled them down and destroyed them. Burned all the buildings. And all the records. Billions of microfilms and papers. Great bonfires that burned for weeks. And the swarms of little white things that poured out when we knocked the buildings over."

"You killed them?" the great tub of a man asked, lips twitching avidly.

"We let them go. They were harmless. They ran and hid. Under rocks." Tolby laughed. "Funny little scurrying things. Insects. Then we went in and gathered up all the records and equipment for making records. By god, we burned everything."

"And the robots," a youth said.

"Yeah, we smashed all the government robots. There weren't many of them. They were used only at high levels. When a lot of facts had to be integrated."

The youth's eyes bulged. "You saw them? You were there when they smashed the robots?"

Penn laughed. "Tolby means the League. That was two hundred years ago."

The youth grinned nervously. "Yeah. Tell us about the marches."

Tolby drained his mug and pushed it away. "I'm out of beer."

The mug was quickly refilled. He grunted his thanks and continued, voice deep and furry, dulled with fatigue. "The marches. That was really something, they say. All over the world, people getting up, throwing down what they were doing—"

"It started in East Germany," the hard-jawed blonde said. "The riots."

"Then it spread to Poland," the Negro put in shyly. "My grandfather used to tell me how everybody sat and listened to the television. His grandfather used to tell him. It spread to Czechoslovakia and then Austria and Roumania and Bulgaria. Then France. And Italy."

"France was first!" the little old man with beard and glasses cried violently. "They were without a government a whole month. The people saw they could live without a government!"

"The marches started it," the black-haired girl corrected. "That was the first time they started pulling down the government buildings. In East Germany and Poland. Big mobs of unorganized workers."

"Russia and America were the last," Tolby said. "When the march on Washington came, there was close to twenty million of us. We were big in those days! They couldn't stop us when we finally moved."

"They shot a lot," the hard-faced blonde said.

"Sure. But the people kept coming. And yelling to the soldiers. 'Hey, Bill! Don't shoot!' 'Hey, Jack! It's me, Joe.' 'Don't shoot—we're your friends!' 'Don't kill us, join us!' And by god, after a while they did. They couldn't keep shooting their own people. They finally threw down their guns and got out of the way."

"And then you found the place," the little black-haired girl said breathlessly.

"Yeah. We found the place. *Six* places. Three in America. One in Britain. Two in Russia. It took us ten years to find the last place—and make sure it was the last place."

"What then?" the youth asked, bug-eyed.

"Then we busted every one of them." Tolby raised himself up, a massive man, beer mug clutched, heavy face flushed dark red. "Every damn A-bomb in the whole world."

There was an uneasy silence.

"Yeah," the youth murmured. "You sure took care of those war people."

"Won't be any more of them," the great tub of a man said. "They're gone for good."

Tolby fingered his ironite staff. "Maybe so. And maybe not. There just might be a few of them left."

"What do you mean?" the tub of a man demanded.

Tolby raised his hard gray eyes. "It's time you people stopped kidding us. You know damn well what I mean. We've heard rumors. Someplace around this area there's a bunch of them. Hiding out."

Shocked disbelief, then anger hummed to a roar. "That's a lie!" the tub of a man shouted.

"Is it?"

The little man with beard and glasses leaped up. "There's nobody here has anything to do with governments! We're all good people!"

"You better watch your step," one of the youths said softly to Tolby. "People around here don't like to be accused."

Tolby got unsteadily to his feet, his ironite staff gripped. Penn got up beside him and they stood together. "If any of you knows something," Tolby said, "you better tell it. Right now."

"Nobody knows anything," the hard-faced blonde said. "You're talking to honest folks."

"That's so," the Negro said, nodding his head. "Nobody here's doing anything wrong."

"You saved our lives," the black-haired girl said. "If you hadn't pulled down the governments, we'd all be dead in the war. Why should we hold back something?"

"That's true," the great tub of a man grumbled. "We wouldn't be alive if it wasn't for the League. You think we'd do anything against the League?"

"Come on," Silvia said to her father. "Let's go." She got to her feet and tossed Penn his pack.

Tolby grunted belligerently. Finally he took his own pack and hoisted it to his shoulder. The room was deathly silent. Everyone stood frozen as the three gathered their things and moved toward the door.

The little dark-haired girl stopped them. "The next town is thirty miles from here," she said.

"The road's blocked," her tall companion explained. "Slides closed it years ago."

"Why don't you stay with us tonight? There's plenty of room at our place. You can rest up and get an early start tomorrow."

"We don't want to impose," Silvia murmured.

Tolby and Penn glanced at each other, then at the girl. "If you're sure you have plenty of room."

The great tub of a man approached them. "Listen. I have ten yellow slips. I want to give them to the League. I sold my farm last year. I don't need any more slips; I'm living with my brother and his family." He pushed the slips at Tolby. "Here."

Tolby pushed them back. "Keep them."

"This way," the tall young man said as they clattered down the sagging steps into a sudden blinding curtain of heat and dust. "We have a car. Over this way. An old gasoline car. My dad fixed it so it burns oil."

"You should have taken the slips," Penn said to Tolby as they got into the ancient, battered car. Flies buzzed around them. They could hardly breathe: the car was a furnace. Silvia fanned herself with a rolled-up paper. The black-haired girl unbuttoned her blouse.

"What do we need money for?" Tolby laughed good-naturedly. "I haven't paid for anything in my life. Neither have you."

The car sputtered and moved slowly forward, onto the road. It began to gain speed. Its motor banged and roared. Soon it was moving surprisingly fast.

"You saw them," Silvia said over the racket. "They'd give us anything they had. We saved their lives." She waved at the fields, the farmers and their crude teams, the withered crops, the sagging old farmhouses. "They'd all be dead if it hadn't been for the League." She smashed a fly peevishly. "They depend on us."

The black-haired girl turned toward them, as the car rushed along the decaying road. Sweat streaked her tanned skin. Her half-covered breasts trembled with the motion of the car. "I'm Laura Davis. Pete and I have an old farmhouse his dad gave us when we got married."

"You can have the whole downstairs," Pete said.

"There's no electricity, but we've got a big fireplace. It gets cold at night. It's hot in the day, but when the sun sets it gets terribly cold."

"We'll be all right," Penn murmured. The vibration of the car made him a little sick.

"Yes," the girl said, her black eyes flashing. Her crimson lips twisted. She leaned toward Penn intently, her small face strangely alight. "Yes, we'll take good care of you."

At that moment the car left the road.

Silvia shrieked. Tolby threw himself down, head between his knees, doubled up in a ball. A sudden curtain of green burst around Penn. Then a sickening emptiness as the car plunged down. It struck with a roaring crash that blotted out everything. A single titanic cataclysm of fury that picked Penn up and flung his remains in every direction.

***

"Put me down," Bors ordered. "On this railing for a moment before I go inside."

The crew lowered him onto the concrete surface and fastened magnetic grapples into place. Men and women hurried up the wide steps, in and out of the massive building that was Bors's main offices.

The sight from these steps pleased him. He liked to stop here and look around at his world. At the civilization he had carefully constructed. Each piece added painstakingly, scrupulously with infinite care, throughout the years.

It wasn't big. The mountains ringed it on all sides. The

valley was a level bowl, surrounded by dark violet hills. Outside, beyond the hills, the regular world began. Parched fields. Blasted, poverty-stricken towns. Decayed roads. The remains of houses, tumbled-down farm buildings. Ruined cars and machinery. Dust-covered people creeping listlessly around in handmade clothing, dull rags and tatters.

He had seen the outside. He knew what it was like. At the mountains the blank faces, the disease, the withered crops, the crude plows and ancient tools all ended here. Here, within the ring of hills, Bors had constructed an accurate and detailed reproduction of a society two centuries gone. The world as it had been in the old days. The time of governments. The time that had been pulled down by the Anarchist League.

Within his five synapsis-coils the plans, knowledge, information, blueprints of a whole world existed. In the two centuries he had carefully recreated that world, had made this miniature society that glittered and hummed on all sides of him. The roads, buildings, houses, industries of a dead world, all a fragment of the past, built with his hands, his own metal fingers and brain.

"Fowler," Bors said.

Fowler came over. He looked haggard. His eyes were red-rimmed and swollen. "What is it? You want to go inside?"

Overhead, the morning patrol thundered past. A string of black dots against the sunny, cloudless sky. Bors watched with satisfaction. "Quite a sight."

"Right on the nose," Fowler agreed, examining his wristwatch. To their right, a column of heavy tanks snaked along a highway between green fields. Their gun-snouts glittered. Behind them a column of foot soldiers marched, faces hidden behind bacteria masks.

"I'm thinking," Bors said, "that it may be unwise to trust Green any longer."

"Why the hell do you say that?"

"Every ten days I'm inactivated. So your crew can see what repairs are needed." Bors twisted restlessly. "For twelve hours I'm completely helpless. Green takes care of me. Sees nothing happens. But—"

"But what?"

"It occurs to me perhaps there'd be more safety in a squad of troops. It's too much of a temptation for one man, alone."

Fowler scowled. "I don't see that. How about me? I have charge of inspecting you. I could switch a few leads around. Send a load through your synapsis-coils. Blow them out."

Bors whirled wildly, then subsided. "True. You could do that." After a moment he demanded, "But what would you gain? You know I'm the only one who can keep all this together. I'm the only one who knows how to maintain a planned society, not a disorderly chaos! If it weren't for me, all this would collapse, and you'd have dust and ruins and weeds. The whole outside would come rushing in to take over!"

"Of course. So why worry about Green?"

Trucks of workers rumbled past. Loads of men in blue-green, sleeves rolled up, armloads of tools. A mining team, heading for the mountains.

"Take me inside," Bors said abruptly.

Fowler called McLean. They hoisted Bors and carried him past the throngs of people, into the building, down the corridor and to his office. Officials and technicians moved respectfully out of the way as the great pitted, corroded tank was carried past.

"All right," Bors said impatiently. "That's all. You can go."

Fowler and McLean left the luxurious office, with its lush carpets, furniture, drapes and rows of books. Bors was already bent over his desk, sorting through heaps of reports and papers.

Fowler shook his head as they walked down the hall. "He won't last much longer."

"The motor system? Can't we reinforce the—"

"I don't mean that. He's breaking up mentally. He can't take the strain any longer."

"None of us can," McLean muttered.

"Running this thing is too much for him. Knowing it's all dependent on him. Knowing as soon as he turns his back or lets down it'll begin to come apart at the seams. A hell of a job, trying to shut out the real world. Keeping his model universe running."

"He's gone on a long time," McLean said.

Fowler brooded. "Sooner or later we're going to have to face the situation." Gloomily, he ran his fingers along the blade of a large screwdriver. "He's wearing out. Sooner or later somebody's going to have to step in. As he continues to decay…" He stuck the screwdriver back in his belt, with his pliers and hammer and soldering iron. "One crossed wire."

"What's that?"

Fowler laughed. "Now he's got me doing it. One crossed wire and—*poof*. But what then? That's the big question."

"Maybe," McLean said softly, "you and I can then get off this rat race. You and I and all the rest of us. And live like human beings."

"*Rat race*," Fowler murmured. "Rats in a maze. Doing tricks. Performing chores thought up by somebody else."

McLean caught Fowler's eye. "By somebody of another species."

***

Tolby struggled vaguely. Silence. A faint dripping close by. A beam pinned his body down. He was caught on all sides by the twisted wreck of the car. He was head down. The car was turned on its side. Off the road in a gully, wedged between two huge trees. Bent struts and smashed metal all around him. And bodies.

He pushed up with all his strength. The beam gave, and he managed to get to a sitting position. A tree branch had burst in the windshield. The black-haired girl, still turned toward the back seat, was impaled on it. The branch had driven through her spine, out her chest, and into the seat. She clutched at it with both hands, head limp, mouth half-open. The man beside her was also dead. His hands were gone; the windshield had burst around him. He lay in a heap among the remains of the dashboard and the bloody shine of his own internal organs.

Penn was dead. Neck snapped like a rotten broom handle. Tolby pushed his corpse aside and examined his daughter. Silvia didn't stir. He put his ear to her shirt and listened. She was alive. Her heart beat faintly. Her bosom rose and fell against his ear.

He wound a handkerchief around her arm, where the flesh was ripped open and oozing blood. She was badly cut and scratched. One leg was doubled under her, obviously broken. Her clothes were ripped, her hair matted with blood. But she was alive. He pushed the twisted door open and stumbled out. A fiery tongue of afternoon sunlight struck him, and he winced. He began to ease her limp body out of the car, past the twisted doorframe.

A sound.

Tolby glanced up, rigid. Something was coming. A whirring insect that rapidly descended. He let go of Silvia, crouched, glanced around, then lumbered awkwardly down the gully. He slid and fell and rolled among the green vines and jagged gray boulders. His gun gripped, he lay gasping in the moist shadows, peering upward.

The insect landed. A small airship, jet-driven. The sight stunned him. He had heard about jets, seen photographs of them. Been briefed and lectured in the history-indoctrination courses at the League Camps. But to *see* a jet!

Men swarmed out. Uniformed men who started from the road, down the side of the gully, bodies crouched warily as they approached the wrecked car. They lugged heavy rifles. They looked grim and experienced as they tore the car doors open and scrambled in.

"One's gone," a voice drifted to him.

"Must be around somewhere."

"Look, this one's alive! This woman. Started to crawl out. The rest all dead."

Furious cursing. "Damn Laura! She should have leaped! The fanatic little fool!"

"Maybe she didn't have time. God's sake, the thing's all the way through her." Horror and shocked dismay. "We won't hardly be able to get her loose."

"Leave her." The officer directing things waved the men back out of the car. "Leave them all."

"How about this wounded one?"

The leader hesitated. "Kill her," he said finally. He snatched a rifle and raised the butt. "The rest of you fan out and try to get the other one. He's probably—"

Tolby fired, and the leader's body broke in half. The lower part sank down slowly, the upper dissolved in ashy fragments. Tolby turned and began to move in a slow circle, firing as he crawled. He got two more of them before the rest retreated in panic to their jet-powered insect and slammed the lock.

He had the element of surprise. Now that was gone. They had strength and numbers. He was doomed. Already, the insect was rising. They'd be able to spot him easily from above. But he had saved Silvia. That was something.

He stumbled down a dried up creek bed. He ran aimlessly; he had no place to go. He didn't know the countryside, and he was on foot. He slipped on a stone and fell headlong. Pain and billowing darkness beat at him as he got unsteadily to his knees. His gun was gone, lost in the shrubbery. He spat broken teeth and blood. He peered wildly up at the blazing afternoon sky.

The insect was leaving. It hummed off toward the distant hills. It dwindled, became a black ball, a flyspeck, then disappeared.

Tolby waited a moment. Then he struggled up the side of the ravine to the wrecked car. They had gone to get help. They'd be back. Now was his only chance. If he could get Silvia out and down the road, into hiding. Maybe to a farmhouse. Back to town.

He reached the car and stood, dazed and stupefied. Three bodies remained, the two in the front seat, Penn in the back. But Silvia was gone.

They had taken her with them. Back where they came from. She had been dragged to the jet-driven insect. A trail of blood led from the car up the side of the gully to the highway.

With a violent shudder Tolby pulled himself together. He climbed into the car and pried loose Penn's gun from his belt. Silvia's ironite staff rested on the seat. He took that too. Then he started off down the road, walking without haste, carefully, slowly.

An ironic thought plucked at his mind. He had found what they were after. The men in uniform. They were organized, responsible to a central authority. In a newly assembled jet.

Beyond the hills was a government.

"Sir," Green said. He smoothed his short blond hair anxiously, his young face twisting.

Technicians and experts and ordinary people in droves were everywhere. The offices buzzed and echoed with the business of the day. Green pushed through the crowd and to the desk where Bors sat, propped up by two magnetic frames.

"Sir," Green said. "Something's happened."

Bors looked up. He pushed a metal-foil slate away and laid down his stylus. His eye cells clicked and flickered. Deep inside his battered trunk motor gears whined. "What is it?"

Green came close. There was something in his face, an expression Bors had never seen before. A look of fear and glassy determination. A glazed, fanatic cast, as if his flesh had hardened to rock. "Sir, scouts contacted a League team moving north. They met the team outside Fairfax. The incident took place directly beyond the first roadblock."

Bors said nothing. On all sides, officials, experts, farmers, workmen, industrial managers, soldiers, people of all kinds buzzed and murmured and pushed forward impatiently. Trying to get to Bors's desk. Loaded down with problems to be solved, situations to be explained. The pressing business of the day. Roads, factories, disease control. Repairs. Construction. Manufacture. Design. Planning. Urgent problems for Bors to consider and deal with. Problems that couldn't wait.

"Was the League team destroyed?" Bors said.

"One was killed. One was wounded and brought here." Green hesitated. "One escaped."

For a long time Bors was silent. Around him the people murmured and shuffled. He ignored them. All at once he pulled the vidscanner to him and snapped the circuit open. "One escaped? I don't like the sound of that."

"He shot three members of our scout unit. Including the leader. The others got frightened. They grabbed the injured girl and returned here."

Bors's massive head lifted. "They made a mistake. They should have located the one who escaped."

"This was the first time the situation—"

"I know," Bors said. "But it was an error. Better not to have touched them at all, than to have taken two and allowed the third to get away." He turned to the vidscanner. "Sound an emergency alert. Close down the factories. Arm the work crews and any male farmers capable of using weapons. Close every road. Remove the women and children to the undersurface shelters. Bring up the heavy guns and supplies. Suspend all non-military production and—" He considered. "Arrest everyone we're not sure of. On the C sheet. Have them shot." He snapped the scanner off.

"What'll happen?" Green demanded, shaken.

"The thing we've prepared for. Total war."

"We have weapons!" Green shouted excitedly. "In an hour there'll be ten thousand men ready to fight. We have jet-driven ships. Heavy artillery. Bombs. Bacteria pellets. What's the League? A lot of people with packs on their backs!"

"Yes," Bors said. "A lot of people with packs on their backs."

"How can they do anything? How can a bunch of anarchists organize? They have no structure, no control, no central power."

"They have the whole world. A billion people."

"*Individuals!* A club, not subject to law. Voluntary membership. We have disciplined organization. Every aspect of our economic life operates at maximum efficiency. We—you—have your thumb on everything. All you have to do is give the order. Set the machine in motion."

Bors nodded slowly. "It's true the anarchist can't coordinate. The League can't organize. It's a paradox. Government by anarchists...anti-government, actually. Instead of governing the world they tramp around to make sure no one else does."

"Dog in the manger."

"As you say, they're actually a voluntary club of totally unorganized individuals. Without law or central authority. They maintain no society—they can't govern. All they can do is interfere with anyone else who tries. Troublemakers. But—"

"But what?"

"It was this way before. Two centuries ago. They were unorganized. Unarmed. Vast mobs without discipline or authority. Yet they pulled down all the governments. All over the world."

"We've got a whole army. All the roads are mined. Heavy guns. Bombs. Pellets. Every one of us is a soldier. We're an armed camp!"

Bors was deep in thought. "You say one of them is here? One of the League agents?"

"A young woman."

Bors signaled the nearby maintenance crew. "Take me to her. I want to talk to her in the time remaining."

Silvia watched silently as the uniformed men pushed and grunted their way into the room. They staggered over to the bed, pulled two chairs together, and carefully laid down their massive armload.

Quickly they snapped protective struts into place, locked the chairs together, threw magnetic grapples into operation, and then warily retreated.

"All right," the robot said. "You can go." The men left. Bors turned to face the woman on the bed.

"A machine," Silvia whispered, white-faced. "You're a machine."

Bors nodded slightly without speaking.

Silvia shifted uneasily on the bed. She was weak. One leg was in a transparent plastic cast. Her face was bandaged, and her right arm ached and throbbed. Outside the window, the late-afternoon sun sprinkled through the drapes. Flowers bloomed. Grass. Hedges. And beyond the hedges, buildings and factories.

For the last hour the sky had been filled with jet-driven ships. Great flocks that raced excitedly across the sky toward distant hills. Along the highway cars hurtled, dragging guns and heavy military equipment. Men were marching in close rank, rows of gray-clad soldiers, guns and helmets and bacteria masks.

Endless lines of figures, identical in their uniforms, stamped from the same matrix.

"There are a lot of them," Bors said, indicating the marching men.

"Yes." Silvia watched a couple of soldiers hurry by the window. Youths with worried expressions on their smooth faces. Helmets bobbing at their waists. Long rifles. Canteens. Counters. Radiation shields. Bacteria masks wound awkwardly around their necks, ready to go into place. They were scared. Hardly more than kids. Others followed. A truck roared into life. The soldiers were swept off to join the others.

"They're going to fight," Bors said, "to defend their homes and factories."

"All this equipment. You manufacture it, don't you?"

"That's right. Our industrial organization is perfect. We're totally productive. Our society here is operated rationally. Scientifically. We're fully prepared to meet this emergency."

Suddenly Silvia realized what the emergency was. "The League! One of us must have got away." She pulled herself up. "Which of them? Penn or my father?"

"I don't know," the robot murmured indifferently.

Horror and disgust choked Silvia. "My god," she said softly. "You have no understanding of us. You run all this, and you're incapable of empathy. You're nothing but a mechanical computer. One of the old government integration robots."

"That's right. Two centuries old."

She was appalled. "And you've been alive all this time. We thought we destroyed all of you!"

"I was missed. I had been damaged. I wasn't in my place. I was in a truck, on my way out of Washington. I saw the mobs and escaped."

"Two hundred years ago. Legendary times. You actually saw the events they tell us about. The old days. The great marches. The day the governments fell."

"Yes. I saw it all. A group of us formed in Virginia. Experts, officials, skilled workmen. Later we came here. It was remote enough, off the beaten path."

"We heard rumors. A fragment—still maintaining itself. But we didn't know where or how."

"I was fortunate," Bors said. "I escaped by a fluke. All the others were destroyed. It's taken a long time to organize what you see here. Fifteen miles from here is a ring of hills. This valley is a bowl—mountains on all sides. We've set up roadblocks in the form of natural slides. Nobody comes here. Even in Fairfax, thirty miles off, they know nothing."

"That girl. Laura."

"Scouts. We keep scout teams in all inhabited regions within a hundred-mile radius. As soon as you entered Fairfax, word was relayed to us. An air unit was dispatched. To avoid questions, we arranged to have you killed in an auto wreck. But one of you escaped."

Silvia shook her head, bewildered. "How?" she demanded. "How do you keep going? Don't the people revolt?" She struggled to a sitting position. "They must know what's happened everywhere else. How do you control them? They're going out now, in their uniforms. But—*will they fight? Can you count on them?*"

Bors answered slowly. "They trust me," he said. "I brought with me a vast amount of knowledge. Information and techniques lost to the rest of the world. Are jet-ships and vidscanners and power cables made anywhere else in the world? I retain all that knowledge. I have memory units, synapsis-coils. Because of me they have these things. Things you know only as dim memories, vague legends."

"What happens when you die?"

"I won't die! I'm eternal!"

"You're wearing out. You have to be carried around. And your right arm. You can hardly move it!" Silvia's voice was harsh, ruthless. "Your whole tank is pitted and rusty."

The robot whirred. For a moment he seemed unable to speak. "My knowledge remains," he grated finally. "I'll always be able to communicate. Fowler has arranged a broadcast system. Even when I talk—" He broke off. "Even then. Everything is under control. I've organized every aspect of the situation. I've maintained this system for two centuries. It's got to be kept going!"

Silvia lashed out. It happened in a split second. The boot of her cast caught the chairs on which the robot rested. She thrust violently with her foot and hands. The chairs teetered, hesitated—

"Fowler!" the robot screamed.

Silvia pushed with all her strength. Blinding agony seared through her leg. She bit her lip and threw her shoulder against the robot's pitted hulk. He waved his arms, whirred wildly, and then the two chairs slowly collapsed. The robot slid quietly from them, over on his back, his arms still waving helplessly.

Silvia dragged herself from the bed. She managed to pull herself to the window. Her broken leg hung uselessly, a dead weight in its transparent plastic cast. The robot lay like some futile bug, arms waving, eye lens clicking, its rusty works whirring in fear and rage.

"Fowler!" it screamed again. "Help me!"

Silvia reached the window. She tugged at the locks; they were sealed. She grabbed up a lamp from the table and threw it against the glass. The glass burst around her, a shower of lethal fragments. She stumbled forward—and then the repair crew was pouring into the room.

Fowler gasped at the sight of the robot on its back. A strange expression crossed his face. "Look at him!"

"Help me!" the robot shrilled. "Help me!"

One of the men grabbed Silvia around the waist and lugged her back to the bed. She kicked and bit, sunk her nails into the man's cheek. He threw her on the bed, face down, and drew his pistol. "Stay there," he gasped.

The others were bent over the robot, getting him to an upright position.

"What happened?" Fowler said. He came over to the bed, his face twisting. "Did he fall?"

Silvia's eyes glowed with hatred and despair. "I pushed him over. I almost got there." Her chest heaved. "The window. But my leg—"

"Get me back to my quarters!" Bors cried.

The crew gathered him up and carried him down the hall to his private office. A few moments later he was sitting shakily at his desk, his mechanism pounding wildly, surrounded by his papers and memoranda.

He forced down his panic and tried to resume his work. He had to keep going. His vidscreen was alive with activity. The whole system was in motion. He blankly watched a subcommander sending up a cloud of black dots, jet bombers that shot up like flies and headed quickly off.

The system had to be preserved. He repeated it again and again. He had to save it. Had to organize the people and make *them* save it. If the people didn't fight, wasn't everything doomed?

Fury and desperation overwhelmed him. The system couldn't preserve itself. It wasn't a thing apart, something that could be separated from the people who lived it. Actually it *was* the people. They were identical. When the people fought to preserve the system, they were fighting to preserve nothing less than themselves.

They existed only as long as the system existed.

He caught sight of a marching column of white-faced troops, moving toward the hills. His ancient synapsis-coils radiated and shuddered uncertainly, then fell back into pattern. He was two centuries old. He had come into existence a long time ago, in a different world. That world had created him; through him that world still lived. As long as he existed, that world existed. In miniature, it still functioned. His model universe, his recreation. His rational, controlled world, in which each aspect was fully organized, fully analyzed and integrated.

He kept a rational, progressive world alive. A humming oasis of productivity on a dusty, parched planet of decay and silence.

Bors spread out his papers and went to work on the most pressing problem. The transformation from a peacetime economy to full military mobilization. Total military organization of every man, woman, child, piece of equipment and dyne of energy under his direction.

***

Edward Tolby emerged cautiously. His clothes were torn and ragged. He had lost his pack, crawling through the brambles and vines. His face and hands were bleeding. He was utterly exhausted.

Below him lay a valley. A vast bowl. Fields, houses, highways. Factories. Equipment. Men.

He had been watching the men three hours. Endless streams of them, pouring from the valley into the hills, along the roads and paths. On foot, in trucks, in cars, armored tanks, weapons carriers. Overhead, in fast little jet-fighters and great lumbering bombers. Gleaming ships that took up positions above the troops and prepared for battle.

Battle in the grand style. The two-centuries-old full-scale war that was supposed to have disappeared. But here it was, a vision from the past. He had seen this in the old tapes and records, used in the camp orientation courses. A ghost army resurrected to fight again. A vast host of men and guns, prepared to fight and die.

***

Tolby climbed down cautiously. At the foot of a slope of boulders a soldier had halted his motorcycle and was setting up a communications antenna and transmitter. Tolby circled, crouched, expertly approached him. A blond-haired youth, fumbling nervously with the wires and relays, licking his lips uneasily, glancing up and grabbing for his rifle at every sound.

Tolby took a deep breath. The youth had turned his back; he was tracing a power circuit. It was now or never. With one stride Tolby stepped out, raised his pistol and fired. The clump of equipment and the soldier's rifle vanished.

"Don't make a sound," Tolby said. He peered around. No one had seen. The main line was half a mile to his right. The sun was setting. Great shadows were falling over the hills. The fields were rapidly fading from brown-green to a deep violet. "Put your hands up over your head, clasp them, and get down on your knees."

The youth tumbled down in a frightened heap. "What are you going to do?" He saw the ironite staff, and the color left his face. "You're a League agent!"

"Shut up," Tolby ordered. "First, outline your system of responsibility. *Who's your superior?*"

The youth stuttered forth what he knew. Tolby listened intently. He was satisfied. The usual monolithic structure. Exactly what he wanted.

"At the top," he broke in. "At the top of the pillar. Who has ultimate responsibility?"

"Bors."

"Bors!" Tolby scowled. "That doesn't sound like a name. Sounds like—" He broke off, staggered. "We should have guessed! An old government robot. Still functioning."

The youth saw his chance. He leaped up and darted frantically away.

Tolby shot him above the left ear. The youth pitched over on his face and lay still. Tolby hurried to him and quickly pulled off his dark gray uniform. It was too small for him of course. But the motorcycle was just right. He'd seen tapes of them. He'd wanted one since he was a child. A fast little motorcycle to propel his weight around. Now he had it.

Half an hour later he was roaring down a smooth, broad highway toward the center of the valley and the buildings that rose against the dark sky. His headlights cut into the blackness. He still wobbled from side to side, but for all practical purposes he had the hang of it. He increased speed. The road shot by, trees and fields, haystacks, stalled farm equipment. All traffic was going against him, troops hurrying to the front.

The front. Lemmings going out into the ocean to drown. A thousand, ten thousand, metal-clad figures, armed and alert. Weighted down with guns and bombs and flame throwers and bacteria pellets.

There was only one hitch. No army opposed them. A mistake had been made. It took two sides to make a war, and only one had been resurrected.

A mile outside the concentration of buildings he pulled his motorcycle off the road and carefully hid it in a haystack. For a moment he considered leaving his ironite staff. Then he shrugged and grabbed it up, along with his pistol. He always carried his staff, it was the League symbol. It represented the walking Anarchists who patrolled the world on foot, the world's protection agency.

He loped through the darkness toward the outline ahead. There were fewer men here. He saw no women or children. Ahead, charged wire was set up. Troops crouched behind it, armed to the teeth. A searchlight moved back and forth across the road. Behind it, radar vanes loomed and behind them an ugly square of concrete. The great offices from which the government was run.

For a time he watched the searchlight. Finally he had its motion plotted. In its glare, the faces of the troops stood out, pale and drawn. Youths. They had never fought. This was their first encounter. They were terrified.

When the light was off him, he stood up and advanced toward the wire. Automatically, a breach was slid back for him. Two guards raised up and awkwardly crossed bayonets ahead of him.

"Show your papers!" one demanded. Young lieutenants. Boys, white-lipped, nervous. Playing soldier.

Pity and contempt made Tolby laugh harshly and push forward. "Get out of my way."

One anxiously flashed a pocket light. "Halt! What's the code-key for this watch?" He blocked Tolby's way with his bayonet, hands twisting convulsively.

Tolby reached in his pocket, pulled out his pistol, and as the searchlight started to swerve back, blasted the two guards. The bayonets clattered down and he dived forward. Yells and shapes rose on all sides. Anguished, terrified shouts. Random firing. The night was lit up, as he dashed and crouched, turned a corner past a supply warehouse, raced up a flight of stairs and into the massive building ahead.

He had to work fast. Gripping his ironite staff, he plunged down a gloomy corridor. His boots echoed. Men poured into the building behind him. Bolts of energy thundered past him. A whole section of the ceiling burst into ash and collapsed behind him.

He reached stairs and climbed rapidly. He came to the next floor and groped for the door handle. Something flickered behind him. He half turned, his gun quickly up—

A stunning blow sent him sprawling. He crashed against the wall; his gun flew from his fingers. A shape bent over him, rifle gripped. "Who are you? What are you doing here?"

Not a soldier. A stubble-chinned man in stained shirt and rumpled trousers. Eyes puffy and red. A belt of tools—hammer, pliers, screwdriver, a soldering iron—around his waist.

Tolby raised himself up painfully. "If you didn't have that rifle—"

Fowler backed warily away. "Who are you? This floor is forbidden to troops of the line. You know this—" Then he saw the ironite staff. "By god," he said softly. "You're the one they didn't get." He laughed shakily. "You're the one who got away."

Tolby's fingers tightened around the staff, but Fowler reacted instantly. The snout of the rifle jerked up, on a line with Tolby's face.

"Be careful," Fowler warned. He turned slightly. Soldiers were hurrying up the stairs, boots drumming, echoing shouts ringing. For a moment he hesitated, then waved his rifle toward the stairs ahead. "Up. Get going."

Toby blinked. "What—"

"Up!" The rifle snout jabbed into Tolby. "Hurry!"

Bewildered, Tolby hurried up the stairs, Fowler close behind him. At the third floor Fowler pushed him roughly through the doorway, the snout of his rifle digging urgently into his back. He found himself in a corridor of doors. Endless offices.

"Keep going," Fowler snarled. "Down the hall. Hurry!"

Tolby hurried, his mind spinning. "What the hell are you—"

"I could never do it," Fowler gasped, close to his ear. "Not in a million years. But it's got to be done."

Tolby halted.

"What is this?"

They faced each other defiantly, faces contorted, eyes blazing. "He's in there," Fowler snapped, indicating a door with his rifle. "You have one chance. Take it."

For a fraction of a second Tolby hesitated. Then he broke away. "Okay. I'll take it."

Fowler followed after him. "Be careful. Watch your step. There's a series of check points. Keep going straight, in all the way. As far as you can go. And for god's sake, hurry!"

His voice faded as Tolby gained speed. He reached the door and tore it open.

Soldiers and officials ballooned. He threw himself against them; they sprawled and scattered. He scrambled on as they struggled up and stupidly fumbled for their guns. Through another door, into an inner office, past a desk where a frightened girl sat, eyes wide, mouth open. Then a third door, into an alcove.

A wild-faced youth leaped up and snatched frantically for his pistol. Tolby was unarmed, trapped in the alcove. Figures already pushed against the door behind him. He gripped his ironite staff and backed away as the blond-haired fanatic fired blindly. The bolt burst a foot away. It flicked him with a tongue of heat.

"You dirty anarchist!" Green screamed. His face distorted, he fired again and again. "You murdering anarchist spy!"

Tolby hurled his ironite staff. He put all his strength in it. The staff leaped through the air in a whistling arc, straight at the youth's head. Green saw it coming and ducked. Agile and quick, he jumped away, grinning humorlessly. The staff crashed against the wall and rolled clanging to the floor.

"Your walking staff!" Green gasped and fired.

The bolt missed him on purpose. Green was playing games with him. Tolby bent down and groped frantically for the staff.

He picked it up. Green watched, face rigid, eyes glittering. "Throw it again!" he snarled.

Tolby leaped. He took the youth by surprise. Green grunted, stumbled back from the impact, then suddenly fought with maniacal fury.

Tolby was heavier. But he was exhausted. He had crawled hours, beat his way through the mountains, walked endlessly. He was at the end of his strength. The car wreck, the days of walking. Green was in perfect shape. His wiry, agile body twisted away. His hands came up. Fingers dug into Tolby's windpipe. He kicked the youth in the groin. Green staggered back, convulsed and bent over with pain.

"All right," Green gasped, face ugly and dark. His hand fumbled with his pistol. The barrel came up.

Half of Green's head dissolved. His hands opened and his gun fell to the floor. His body stood for a moment, then settled down in a heap, like an empty suit of clothes.

Tolby caught a glimpse of a rifle snout pushed past him—and the man with the tool belt. The man waved him on frantically. "Hurry!"

Tolby raced down a carpeted hall, between two great flickering yellow lamps. A crowd of officials and soldiers stumbled uncertainly after him, shouting and firing at random. He tore open a thick oak door and halted.

He was in a luxurious chamber. Drapes, rich wallpaper. Lamps. Bookcases. A glimpse of the finery of the past. The wealth of the old days. Thick carpets. Warm radiant heat. A vidscreen. At the far end, a huge mahogany desk.

At the desk a figure sat. Working on heaps of papers and reports, piled masses of material. The figure contrasted starkly with the lushness of the furnishings. It was a great pitted, corroded tank of metal. Bent and greenish, patched and repaired. An ancient machine.

"Is that you, Fowler?" the robot demanded.

Tolby advanced, his ironite staff gripped.

The robot turned angrily. "Who is it? Get Green and carry me down into the shelter. One of the roadblocks has reported a League agent already—" The robot broke off. Its cold, mechanical eye lens bored up at the man. It clicked and whirred in uneasy astonishment. "I don't know you."

It saw the ironite staff.

"League agent," the robot said. "You're the one who got through." Comprehension came. "*The third one.* You came here. You didn't go back." Its metal fingers fumbled clumsily at the objects on the desk, then in the drawer. It found a gun and raised it awkwardly.

Tolby knocked the gun away. It clattered to the floor.

"Run!" he shouted at the robot. "Start running!"

It remained. Tolby's staff came down. The fragile, complex brain unit of the robot burst apart. Coils, wiring, relay fluid, spattered over his arms and hands. The robot shuddered. Its machinery thrashed. It half-rose from its chair, then swayed and toppled. It crashed full length on the floor, parts and gears rolling in all directions.

"Good god," Tolby said, suddenly seeing it for the first time. Shakily, he bent over its remains. "It was crippled."

Men were all around him. "He's killed Bors!" Shocked, dazed faces. "Bors is dead!"

Fowler came up slowly. "You got him, all right. There's nothing left now."

Tolby stood holding his ironite staff in his hands. "The poor blasted thing," he said softly. "Completely helpless. Sitting there and I came and killed him. He didn't have a chance."

The building was bedlam. Soldiers and officials scurried crazily about, grief-stricken, hysterical. They bumped into each other, gathered in knots, shouted and gave meaningless orders.

Tolby pushed past them. Nobody paid any attention to him. Fowler was gathering up the remains of the robot. Collecting the smashed pieces and bits. Tolby stopped beside him. Like Humpty-Dumpty, pulled down off his wall he'd never be back together, not now.

"Where's the woman?" he asked Fowler. "The League agent they brought in."

Fowler straightened up slowly. "I'll take you." He led Tolby down the packed, surging hall, to the hospital wing of the building.

Silvia sat up apprehensively as the two men entered the room. "What's going on?" She recognized her father. "Dad! Thank god! It was you who got out."

Tolby slammed the door against the chaos of sound hammering up and down the corridor. "How are you? How's your leg?"

"Mending. What happened?"

"I got him. The robot. He's dead."

For a moment the three of them were silent. Outside, in the halls, men ran frantically back and forth. Word had already leaked out. Troops gathered in huddled knots outside the building. Lost men, wandering away from their posts. Uncertain. Aimless.

"It's over," Fowler said.

Tolby nodded. "I know."

"They'll get tired of crouching in their foxholes," Fowler said. "They'll come filtering back. As soon as the news reaches them, they'll desert and throw away their equipment."

"Good," Tolby grunted. "The sooner the better." He touched Fowler's rifle. "You, too, I hope."

Silvia hesitated. "Do you think—"

"Think what?"

"Did we make a mistake?"

Tolby grinned wearily. "Hell of a time to think about that."

"He was doing what he thought was right. They built up their homes and factories. This whole area, they turn out a lot of goods. I've been watching through the window. It's made me think. They've done so much. Made so much."

"Made a lot of guns," Tolby said.

"We have guns too. We kill and destroy. We have all the disadvantages and none of the advantages."

"We don't have war," Tolby answered quietly. "To defend this neat little organization there are ten thousand men up there in those hills. All waiting to fight. Waiting to drop their bombs and bacteria pellets, to keep this place running. But they won't. Pretty soon they'll give up and start to trickle back."

"This whole system will decay rapidly," Fowler said. "He was already losing his control. He couldn't keep the clock back much longer."

"Anyhow, it's done," Silvia murmured. "We did our job." She smiled a little. "Bors did his job, and we did ours. But the times were against him and with us."

"That's right," Tolby agreed. "We did our job. And we'll never be sorry."

Fowler said nothing. He stood with his hands in his pockets, gazing silently out the window. His fingers were touching something. Three undamaged synapsis-coils. Intact memory elements from the dead robot, snatched from the scattered remains.

*Just in case,* he said to himself. *Just in case the times change.*

# ABOUT THE AUTHOR

Philip Kindred Dick was born in Chicago on December 16, 1928, and grew up in the San Francisco Bay Area. He began publishing short stories in 1952, mostly finding homes in popular science fiction magazines, but he had little commercial success until he published *The Man in the High Castle* in 1962. He followed with novels such as *Do Androids Dream of Electric Sheep, Ubik,* and *Flow My Tears, the Policeman Said,* establishing him as a writer of science fiction. Following years of drug abuse and a series of mystical experiences in 1974, Dick's work dealt more explicitly with issues of theology, metaphysics, and the nature of reality. He died in 1982 in Santa Ana, California, at the age of 53, due to complications from a stroke, only months before the movie *Blade Runner* was released.

# FIRST PUBLICATIONS

"Beyond Lies the Wub," *Planet Stories*, July 1952

"The Gun," *Planet Stories*, September 1952

"The Skull," *If*, September 1952

"The Eyes Have It," *Science Fiction Stories*, no. 1, 1953

"Tony and the Beetles," *Orbit*, no. 2, 1953

"Mr. Spaceship," *Imagination*, January 1953

"The Defenders," *Galaxy Science Fiction*, January 1953

"Piper in the Woods," *Imagination*, February 1953

"Second Variety," *Space Science Fiction*, May 1953

"The Variable Man," *Space Science Fiction*, vol. 2 no. 2, July (UK)/
    September (USA) 1953

"The Hanging Stranger," *Science Fiction Adventures*, December
    1953

"The Crystal Crypt," *Planet Stories*, January 1954

"Beyond the Door," *Fantastic Universe*, January 1954

"The Golden Man," *If*, April 1954

"Prominent Author," *If*, May 1954

"Adjustment Team," *Orbit*, no. 4, September-October 1954

"The Last of the Masters," *Orbit*, December 1954

www.ingramcontent.com/pod-product-compliance
Lightning Source LLC
Chambersburg PA
CBHW061502210726
48287CB00007B/2620